THE ASSASSIN TRIALS

THE ASSASSIN TRIALS

Amy Kulp

Preparation

"I'll get the door!" I called as I set the sponge down in the sink. Normally, I would ring it out, but I knew it was probably a neighbor who wanted to repurchase eggs. Most knew by now that they could take as many eggs as needed and then stick the money in the mailbox. It was an honor system that worked well. However, we still had a couple of people who were uncomfortable and didn't want to take the chances that someone thought they were scamming us. We wouldn't mind though. A neighbor always helps a neighbor when in need. I made sure to wet my fingers and slick back any stray hairs that sprung out from my ponytail first. My mom always said to look nice for neighbors. "What can I help you with?" I asked as soon as I opened the door.

My smile quickly faded when I saw two men in forest green standing on my front porch. At their feet were huge black mud boots that went past their knees. As my eyes traveled up, I saw the green onesie until it reached their black gloved hands, and hazmat mask. By the time that my eyes could see the lighted green dots where their eyes should be, my smile was completely gone and I turned back to yell for my mom.

I should have rung that sponge out because I would not be returning to do those dishes.

Before my mom could get to the door, one of the gloved hands reached out and grabbed my arm. I resisted and looked back to see if my mom was coming yet. I had to see her before I left. I braced my feet against the carpet but as I got dragged toward the door, I felt the rug burn beginning to affect the soles of my feet. However, I knew lifting would only make it easier for them to get me in their van.

As soon as my feet hit the porch, I screamed at the top of my lungs for my dad. I was hoping he was somewhere in the barn and not yet in the fields. He would never hear my screams from there. Maybe I could stir up our cows and pigs to get someone's attention.

I just wanted to say goodbye first.

"What is with all of this ruckus?" my dad asked as he came out of the barn. He already had his overalls stained with the oil needed for our equipment but for once, I wasn't embarrassed to see him. He dropped hold of the rag in his hands and ran straight for me. "Darling, I love you so much!"

He knew not to get close enough to the green folk or else he would be zapped with electricity. It came from the rod they held in their hands. However, it didn't harm them. It must have been from where they held it.

"Tell mom I love her too!" I yelled.

"I'm right here, baby!"

I arched my neck to try and take a glimpse of her, but I already heard the van doors open. Once all three of us were in, I was able to see a glimpse of my mom in her pretty blue Sunday dress hugging my dad in his greasy, stained overalls. It was probably the most affection I've seen from both in quite some time.

                                    AMY KULP

All it took was for them to lose their daughter to show it.

#

I stayed quiet as the van doors opened and I had one green suit in front of me and one behind. I stared straight ahead and knew not to look anywhere else. After all, these green suits had their staffs of electricity ready to prod me if I misbehaved, and if I tried to escape, I would certainly be killed. Anyone who defied the government was murdered.

When I was little, I would sneak out of my bed and listen to my parents talk about the hushed news that neighbors were assassinated at night for conspiring against the government. I assumed they were made up until I was older, and the playground bullies would try to scare me with the knowledge of what could happen. When I was finally brave enough to ask my mom, she sat me down and we had that discussion.

You cannot have beliefs different than the government. Who decided these beliefs? Some old guys from millions of years ago. Back when the United States of America was united and Europe and Asia were two different continents. The world was different now and I wondered if it was time for them to form a new council and decide on new beliefs. However, I knew saying that thought out loud might get me on the Assassin's List. Although I wasn't sure how long that list was and how long it would be until it was my turn to be killed.

I guess I would find out soon because I was going to be in the trials that decided if I would become an assassin. Every year, they picked ten elitists and ten inductees to join for the chance to be the class of assassins. It was considered such a high honor to be an assassin.

If you were an elitist anyway. Elitists were able to afford training to prepare for the trials and some even had designated Preparatory Schools to become an elitist. Your family put in a bid and the five highest bids for girls and boys were accepted and they were put into the trials. I thought it was an unfair advantage since they got that extra training.

I was an inductee though. I didn't want to be here but somewhere along the road, a teacher, neighbor, or an enemy flagged my profile to the government. I had good enough grades, decent physical strength, and the capabilities to survive in the trials. However, I had no ambition to kill people.

I just wanted to take care of my chickens.

"Elitist or inductee?" a man with the same green suit on as the other two asked. The only difference with him was he wasn't wearing his mask. I felt a shock in my lower back and glared back at the man who had tapped me with his electricity. "You answer when you are spoken to."

"Inductee," I grumbled. I touched the part of my back that was sore from the electricity and felt how hot my skin was. My mom did tell me that they were going to be extreme if I didn't listen to directions. I have never had to be told to repeat myself in school or at home. I always listened. Now I knew the repercussions of that.

                                        AMY KULP

"Go to your right and change into your new uniform," the man commented. I nodded and accepted the clothes that were thrown in my arms. Despite how much I wanted to stay in my clothes, I knew I didn't have a choice.

The first thing they did when you arrived was strip you of your identity. They were nice enough to send that in the brochure when they sent the letter that I was assigned to be part of one of the upcoming classes. We never knew when I would be chosen, and I secretly wished that they had forgotten. It had been six years since I had gotten that letter. As soon as I saw the green suits standing on my porch, I knew it was my turn.

The green suit that was behind me, followed me into the room and stood with the prodding stick. They didn't speak to me and didn't instruct me to do anything. I took it upon myself to go into the only stall they had to change.

I unclipped one of the straps on my overalls and watched as it swung down to reveal the plain purple shirt I was wearing. I was going to miss wearing whatever color I wanted. While I was here, I would only be wearing lime green. It signified that I was training to become an assassin. If I got to wear forest green, it meant I was already an assassin. I hoped I didn't upgrade. I didn't want to get rid of my purples, pinks, blues, or greys. However, as I undid the other strap and took off my overall shorts, I had to slip on the lime green pants that were given to me. These pants were not flattering. However, they were tight against my hips and along my thighs. They dug in uncomfortably and as I tried to stretch them out, I realized they weren't going anywhere. I let them fall back into my skin and watched as the tightness started giving way at my knees and flared out at the bottom. Wouldn't the flare at the bottom be a safety hazard for an assassin?

Regardless, I stripped off my purple shirt and put on the lime green t-shirt as a replacement. It was unflattering even though it looked the same as the one I previously wore. There was too much green now. I needed a splash of black or another color to offset it. It was too much.

Quickly putting on the lime green socks and black shoes that were provided, I knew that I was ready to go back out there. I balled up my previous outfit in my hands and tried to smile as I got out of the stall.

"Dispose of it." He pointed to the garbage can next to him and I nodded in compliance. I could feel his creepy eyes on me as he held the prodding stick up to me. I already knew he had it but the way he was waving it around made me more nervous. Why was he doing that? I quickly placed my items in the garbage can and before I could turn around, I felt a tug at my hair. Placing my hands on my head to prevent any hair loss or damage, I felt a few of my hairs get snagged as my ponytail scrunchie was being pulled out. "You are only permitted to have lime green items right now." I whipped around and watched as he flung it into the trash. When I opened my mouth to say something, he swung the prodding stick at me threateningly.

I knew not to fight it.

                              AMY KULP

I walked forward and out of the room with him trailing behind me. Every time I slowed down, I could feel the electricity near my back. It reminded me to walk a little faster. Even if I didn't know where I was walking to. I guess that was part of the mystery and power they had over everyone here.

I walked until I was moved toward a closed door. Once facing the door, I let the green man behind me unlock it before I followed him. The hallway was narrow but it was white – just like everything else here. White walls, white floors, white computers, white desks, white changing rooms, white everything except for the green color of everyone's clothes. The white must signify that it is a government building. I have never seen any white buildings: my farmhouse and home were brown, schools were red, preparatory schools had green roofs, every other building was black, and government buildings were white. I have never stepped foot in one before but I didn't think that the inside would be white as well. Just like the inside of my house is not brown.

When the green man stopped, he turned to me and ushered me forward without a word. Just the look at his mask told me to obey everything he did. After all, he did graduate as an assassin. He and all the other workers in this building were probably older. They couldn't be in the field to fight or kill anyone. I have never seen an assassin up close but I'm sure that they had to be quick and quiet. Maybe fight someone too.

I walked down the hall by myself and was looking back at the green man when I saw other people dressed in lime green suits. My steps quickened as soon as I realized this. The green man behind me was now just a memory.

Walking in, the space seemed bigger than my entire house. There were four couches in the middle and one giant screen TV that was mounted on the wall. Of course, these were all white too. There was a billiard table too and a gaming station at the other end of that. The pool table was already in use by two people in lime green suits. Their backs were turned to me but I could see that one was a bigger guy and one had blonde, short curly hair. When my gaze moved over to the couches, I could see two girls sitting there. They didn't seem impressed by anything, and I was weary to go up to them.

As I stepped closer to get into the room, I could see that there was a kitchen coming off of the living space. When I walked in, someone was rummaging through the fridge. Everything in here was white too and it was alarmingly clean. Two long tables could sit ten each. The fridge was big enough so that everybody could fit a meal in there.

I quickly walked out and back into the room. This time, I must have been louder because the two boys at the pool table turned around to glance at me. The chubby one smirked and hit his elbow into the curly-haired guy's stomach. He looked at me too but he didn't smile as he turned back to his game. The two girls on the couch perked up and one of them came up to me excitedly.

"I'm Heather," she said as she introduced herself. I nodded my head to be polite and continued to look around the room. "I think you're one of the

                    AMY KULP

last to arrive. Are you an elitist or inductee?" she wondered. I didn't answer as I heard some people laughing down the hall. How could someone be enjoying their time here? "Go down the middle hallway," she whispered to me. She got closer as she said it and when I looked into her eyes, there was a warning signal to me.

What was she warning me about?

She quickly went back to her seat and continued to look unimpressed with her friend. Her eyes glanced at me again and it forced me to start moving. However, I didn't move fast enough. As I began going down the hall, a billiard ball crashed into the wall. It fell with a thump and left a hole in the wall. The hole cracked and if pushed upon, would send more cracks up, down, sideways, and every which way through the wall. When I turned back, I could see the chubby guy laughing at me. He high-fived the curly blonde and when our eyes met, he just smirked as if it was funny.

I turned back without giving a reaction and continued to walk down the hallway. Once again, it was long and thin so I couldn't see anything until it suddenly opened into a smaller living space. There were no pool tables, couches, TVs, or gaming stations but there were two chairs and a table for conversation and some beanbags with a candle warmer, and a board game for someone to enjoy. This room then split off into two more rooms, but I wasn't going to investigate those yet.

"There's someone else here!" a voice yelled. From one area two girls came running out and one boy came from the other area. I immediately stepped back from their enthusiasm and stared at them. The two girls started giggling while the boy held out his hand for me to shake. I did and quickly put it back to my side as the two girls rushed to hug me.

"I'm Jade!" the one girl said excitedly.

"Nia," the other girl said.

"Toby." I nodded at all of them and Toby stayed there for a moment. "Who are you?" he asked as if it was obvious they were waiting for me to talk. My cheeks blushed as Nia and Jade giggled but I knew it wasn't anything malicious. They just seemed to be those naturally bubbly, popular girls that everybody loved.

"Bridget."

"Oh, I love that name!" Jade squealed. She held onto my wrist and pulled me away from Toby and Nia. "Let's show you our rooms."

I followed behind her but mostly because I didn't have a choice. Her grip on my wrist was tight and despite not willingly wanting to follow her, I knew I would eventually need to know where I was going to sleep. She opened the door and it immediately closed behind us. When I looked back at it, I was surprised to see it was automated. Maybe for our privacy. Maybe for our safety.

"Your bed is right next to mine," she said as she led me to the white-furnished room that had my name plaque over it. She plopped on her bed, and I did the same to mine. It looked comfier than I thought it would be. I looked around at some of the other beds and could see people sleeping, rummaging through their drawers, and talking with other girls. "Did you just get here?" she asked me.

                    AMY KULP

My eyes must have been full of curiosity because she welcomed me regardless of what I was going to say. Although, I do believe that I wasn't going to answer. I was too shocked to be friendly. "I've been here about a week already. Some arrived earlier. I think it depended on how far away you live from this government building."

"Is this where the trials happen?" I asked as I looked around. For once, she didn't seem to have an answer and just shrugged her shoulders. The movement of her hair made me wish that I had my hair tie and I pantomimed putting it up. Her hair was short so that she didn't need one but I felt like I did. My hair was long and went halfway down my back. It knotted easily but I hated feeling the hair stick to my neck when I began to sweat.

"Oh, here," Jade said noticing my reaction. She leaned over her bed to her side table and opened one of the drawers. She held the item in her hand and walked closely over to me. Making direct eye contact, she didn't move until I held my fist out. Putting it in my hand without much spoken between us, she went back to her bed without saying much.

I opened my hand up to see a slightly-off of lime green, scrunchie. I smiled and pulled my hair up with it. I combed my fingers until the knots were gone and felt my mood instantly improve because of this small act of rebellion. When I was done, Jade grabbed my wrist and led me into the bathroom. She looked under the stall doors and when we were all by ourselves, she breathed out.

"We got each other," she said. I nodded my head and when I opened my mouth to speak, a siren blared from inside. "That means everyone has arrived." She led me out of the bathrooms again and I watched as everyone started clearing from our bedroom too. She leaned closer to my ear so that I could hear her. "We have a lot to learn together. I've been listening to some of the elitists' conversations and have been learning so much." She paused before speaking again. "I would stay away from most of them. They hate inductees."

When we got back into the main living space, I could see everyone gathering around the four couches. While there was an empty cushion on one of them, Jade pulled me away from that space and more toward the filled couches. There wasn't a place to sit so we sat on the floor next to the couches and I couldn't help but look at the spare cushion at one of the other couches.

I had to assume those were filled with some of the elitists. The blondie was there along with his chubby friend. They were all laughing about something but the blonde looked more serious. He didn't joke around but he was listening and nodding to show that he was there. His eyes moved to each person who talked and he nodded to show that he was listening even if others may not have been.

Chatter was coming from everywhere. I could hear Jade's voice above everyone else, but she was laughing with Nia again. Toby was on the other couch that was close to us, and he reached out to Nia to tap her on the shoulder. I couldn't hear what he was saying from Jade being so loud, but all three busted out laughing. I felt like this wasn't the appropriate time to do so and the elitists didn't seem

                    AMY KULP

to like that either. Dirty glances were being thrown toward them and when some started to yell back, the room got quiet when a tall figure was introduced in the group.

He was wearing a dark forest green suit and his black boots thudded against the white tile loudly. His back was straight, and he had scars on his face. He looked old but he also looked like he could beat me up if he needed to. He had a small whip in his hands and hit his hands a couple of times. The noise radiated around the room from how quiet everyone had gotten. Was this the leader? Or maybe the director?

"This is a safe space," he said. "I do not care if you do not get along outside of this space. When you are in the kitchen, the bedroom, your own living spaces, you can fight if you want. Spit at each other if you want. While we are in this room, we will behave ourselves. Six of you will be future assassins. Everyone else in this room will die. Either from your own stupid mistakes or from another person in this room. It does not matter." He paused and looked at all twenty faces. When the stare got to me, I couldn't keep the contact and looked down at the floor. "I am Bischoff. Whether that's a first name, middle name, last name, or a made-up name is none of your business. You will address me as Bischoff." I nodded my head and looked around. Everyone else seemed to be captivated by this man too. "Welcome, future assassins." He smiled briefly. "You are here because your family won the bid-" Celebrations came from the elitist's side. "Or you were flagged in our system, and you had exceptional qualities about you." Our side was extremely quiet, but the elitists filled it with boos. "Let me provide you with statistics." The TV screen turned on and a presentation displayed. "We have been holding the Assassin Trials for over one thousand years." Celebrations from the elitists made me wonder if there was any possibility of this ending. "As you can see, your ages range. The oldest in the group is thirty-three, Leah Humphrey."

From our side of the room, a female stood up. She kept her back straight and her hands clasped in front of her. I looked up in admiration at her. The elitists booed her, but she didn't look in their direction. Instead, she kept her gaze on Bischoff. Despite her age, it seemed that hardship must have fallen on her. She had wrinkles where there shouldn't be any and her hair was beginning to salt itself with white specks. She had it cut into a black bob and despite everything, she was smiling. She must have used this program to escape something terrible. When Bischoff nodded at her, she sat back down on the couch and received claps on the backs from the other inductees.

"Our youngest from the group is twelve, Audrey Beck."

Standing up from the elitist group was a young girl. Her hair was a deep brown that looked black if the lighting wasn't good. She stood at attention with her arms by her side and stared at Bischoff. There wasn't a smile on her face and even though she was so young, I could see the worry in the corner of her eyes. She wasn't ready for this competition, but her parents were too cocky and bid too much.

                                      AMY KULP

"In past years, the oldest person to ever graduate from the trials was twenty-three and the youngest was fourteen." Bischoff nodded his head for the girl to sit back down and she listened. Heather gave her a weak smile and shook her hand. When she turned back to her friend, I could see just how scared she was for Audrey. "So, if we have had a thousand classes and six assassins graduate from each class, how many assassins is that?"

My brain raced to do the multiplication but just as I started multiplying by the tens place, someone already stood up and shouted the answer. I looked over toward the elitists and watched as they smirked with smugness. Some of them looked over at us as if to brag but instead of giving in, I stared straight ahead at Bischoff. I would not become petty.

"And what's your name?" Bischoff asked.

"Justin Frazier."

"Very well, Justin." He sat down and the pink that was in his cheeks began to settle down. "Out of six thousand assassins, only about one thousand have been females." I looked around at the smug looks on the males' faces. I think they were smart enough not to celebrate at that. From the elitists' side, the girls were all glaring at the guys. "Only about five hundred assassins have been inductees."

Once again, the elitists were celebrating. I felt Jade tense up next to me but I didn't realize why until the billiard ball landed between us. Whoever was the one throwing these things, definitely had terrible aim. I looked up and could see the pudgy boy from earlier hollering with his friends. The blonde was smiling but he didn't seem to be enjoying the fact that they missed hitting one of us. I grabbed the ball before anyone else could and placed it in my pocket. None of them seemed to notice over on their side except for the blonde. He didn't say anything though and quickly went back to his group.

"Throw it back!" one of the boys from my side said. He grabbed my shoulders and shook me. I'm not sure how that would make things better though. I grabbed his hands to stop him and turned around to stare at him. His face was red, and he gestured over toward the elitists. "We can't just sit here and take it from them!" He leaned down to go into my pocket and I quickly swatted him away. "You can't let them win-"

"I'm following the rules," I said. I looked over at Jade, but she didn't say anything to me. Was I in the wrong? We weren't supposed to fight. What happens if I hit someone and cause damage? What happens if I hurt someone? What would the repercussions be for that?

"So, you're allowing them to taunt us?" he asked. I didn't say anything and he rolled his eyes at me. "Well, at least we know that you won't be making it very far in the trials – you'll be at the top of their assassination list."

I turned around without giving him much more of my time. Everyone around us was busy chattering away and when I stared back up at Bischoff, he was staring at me. He nodded his approval of my choice and clapped to get everyone else's attention back. There was a moment where the hushing was louder than anyone's whispers but it

                    AMY KULP

was quickly dampened when they realized they were too loud now.

"Before we begin with the trials, we need to prepare you for what's to come." He looked over at the elitists. "Many of you already know what is to come but your counterparts - the inductees - have not been prepared. Most of you probably would never have imagined you would be here." He looked over at us and while I could sense that some of them were answering him, I felt like I couldn't. His stare was too magnetic to stop focusing on. "We already started the process of preparing you by taking you from your homes. An assassin cannot have any emotional baggage so if you graduate from here, you will never be allowed back in your home, friends, or family. The life you once knew is now gone."

I stared at him as he continued to ramble on about the importance of having a solid head. An assassin had to be well-rounded - smart, sociable, physically fit, and observant. They couldn't be vulnerable, emotional, or weak in any sense. However, I never imagined that after this program I wouldn't be able to go back home. I didn't know that I would lose my family members. What about my mom? What about my chickens and cows? What about my dad? Would they miss me? Or would they move on?

"So, after you were taken, we had other assassins rid your house of you. Pictures, computers, and personal belongings were taken. Everything was gone until there was no trace of you left in your house." He paused and looked at everyone once again. "Your parents were warned that if they spoke of you at all, they would be assassinated." I felt tears coming up in my eyes. I didn't know that. "Your life is dependent on these Trials."

He stepped away and the TV seemed to protrude more from the wall now. It was the main focus and for a second, there was a black screen until it slowly melted into those grey and white snowflakes. Once the fuzz was gone, there was a green version of black and white. It must have been night vision and standing in the middle of the screen was a guy in a mask who gave a thumbs up. In the background, a huge mansion with no cars, houses, or neighbors near them. It seemed to stretch on and on and for a second, I felt myself to be envious of this mansion.

"Well, I guess we know that it's not an inductee's house," the blondie said as he made the rest of his group cackle.

I rolled my eyes and continued to watch the screen as the men stormed the house. They walked around until they were met with two parents who had a garbage bag full of things. The men in the video scoured through it and nodded before looking at the rest of the house. I wish I knew what they said but it looked like those parents already had everything trashed for them. They were prepared to leave their child behind. I looked over at the group of elitists and wondered whose house that was. Whose parents were so willing to ditch them? Who was prepared so well that they were willing to give up their kids?

As soon as they were done with the house, the screen turned black again and another house was on the screen. This one was a little more conservative

                          AMY KULP

and had neighbors. Maybe it was in the city, I wasn't too sure. One of the elitists made a joke about how this had to be an inductee's house but when I stared at them, I could see the discomfort come from Heather. She shifted in her seat and her laughs weren't as loud as they had been for everything else. Her eyes moved away when she saw the parents on the screen. She didn't want to watch if they were prepared to send their daughter away. After all, it was considered such a high honor.

When the screen went black again, it showed up at an apartment. The next one showed up to the lakehouse. The one after that showed up in a gated community. The one after that showed a group home. Then a rundown house with the roof falling off.

There was another that showed up at a huge mansion. It seemed to have its own zip code. The landscaping was beautiful, and the camera panned all around to make sure that they didn't miss anything that possibly identified them. When they got inside, it was bare. Messes were nonexistent but nothing about the house seemed normal. It didn't seem to be lived in. Everything had its spot, and nothing was out of place. As they scoured the rooms, there didn't seem to be anything that resembled someone who lived there. Once they were descending the stairs, they managed to pick a portrait off the wall. My eyes were glued trying to figure out who it was but when I saw the curly, blonde hair, I knew it was blondie from over in the elitists.

I looked over at him as everyone seemed captivated. His mansion was bigger than everyone else's. It felt fake though. Why weren't there pieces of him in each room? I studied his reactions, but he remained still and focused. Almost as if he was watching a movie. Where were his parents? I looked back at the screen, but they were still going through rooms. However, it didn't seem like parents were living in the house. Turning back, I studied him as he watched them peer through each room. He didn't watch it like his privacy was taken for the enjoyment of others. It seemed he watched it to see what was coming up next. It was a different reaction than I expected, and he was hiding his emotions more than anyone else here. I felt like he would be successful by showing no vulnerability.

"Oh, hell no!" one of the Elitists yelled. They slapped their knees and laughed as everyone else was. Even some of the Inductees were laughing too. "We got ourselves a hick around these parts!"

"Yee-haw!" someone else called out.

I looked over at the screen and saw my barn up there. I blushed red instantly and wanted to bury my hands in my face. However, I couldn't. I continued to watch the screen and listen to more hick jokes as they went around the barn and took things that said my name. I felt a nudge from Jade in my ribs and she quietly whispered if I was okay. Did her house already come up on here? I smiled at her and looked back over to the Elitists who were still making fun of how dirty my house seemed to be. I caught blondie's glance for a second but was too embarrassed to keep looking at them.

They did not need to know it was my house. I turned back to the screen and could hear more people shout out about lassoing cows and how to ride

                    AMY KULP

a horse. When my chickens came on screen, I watched as they kicked one away. The rooster was there to protect the females. I watched as he attacked and attacked until they finally hit it with a bit of electricity to daze him and then stomped on him. I grabbed onto Jade's arm and shoved my face into her sleeve so I couldn't see the problems they were causing. They better not hurt any more of my chickens. After a couple of seconds, I peeked out and saw they were investigating the fields now. Nothing in there but crops that my dad worked hard to grow. I could hear some Inductees making jokes now.

As they left the crops in the fields, they started making their way to my house. The porch was littered with shoes so muddy that my mom probably had to yell at my dad before he tried to step foot in the house. After a busy day with phone calls and setting up meetings at the office, she did not want to clean up the house after an adult male. I helped with the messes at the house when I was out of school but now that I wasn't there, who would remember to feed my chickens and make sure that the mama and baby cow were separated from the males? They couldn't afford to hire anyone new. Maybe mom would join in and get her hands dirty.

I stopped thinking about it as soon as I watched them open the door. They seemed hesitant at first because so far, they have had to break down every door. When you're from a small neighborhood though, you tend to help your neighbors. If someone were to need a place to stay, they were welcome on our couches. There was no point in locking our doors because we were also the poorest on our street. If someone wanted to steal something from us, they had to be pretty desperate and needed it more than us. That didn't stop them from taking key chains with my name, a small picture with my first chicken, and other things that were targeted toward me. They had garbage bags full before they got to my living room. There were blankets with family photos that they were tearing off of the couches, someone stuffed a pillow that my great-gram had knitted for me, and there were videos of our family together. I knew they would eventually explore where all the pictures were framed going up the stairs and when they got there, I held tighter to Jade's arm. They smashed the frames and took out each picture of me.

"No!" I jumped at the random sound that the video played, and all hillbilly jokes stopped. When I popped an eye open, I could see my mom on the screen. She was fighting for the picture that had all of my school pictures on it. It resembled a clock and each year; a new picture was added. We only had my graduation photo left to fill out. My mom yanked the picture from the man in green and he came back with his electricity. "You took my baby from me! Let me have something to remember her!"

"Mary Lou!" my dad yelled. He came into the picture and stood in front of mom when they swung the electricity prodder at them. He yelled in pain and landed right on his back. He was going to be useless now.

"I just want my daughter back!" my mom yelled as someone slapped her wrist. I could hear the shards of glass break and she knelt to try and grab the photo. They wrenched it out of her hand and tore it

                                        AMY KULP

up before she could do anything about it. She cried into her hands and just left her there as they went up the stairs.

Up there was my room. My room was cluttered with cheap trinkets that said my name, collages of my family and friends, and clothes that would not fit my thin, frail mother. They stuffed everything in those garbage bags, and I heard more sniffling and crying to know my mother had followed them up. As they pulled the last thing in my room that resembled me, I could see my mom heaving as she tried not to make noise. It was a stuffed animal that I tried to hide in the corner of my bed so nobody would see it. I wasn't that good at hiding it.

"Please, let me keep it," she said. She stepped forward with her arms snuggled around her. "It doesn't have her name on it and I could say it was a childhood toy." She brought her hand out to take the stuffed animal, but they put it in the bag and then held onto my mom's arm. She tried to get them to let go but she already knew what they were aiming for. I closed my eyes as I could hear her make a noise as it was being cracked by one of their fists. They grabbed the chain that was around her neck and popped open the locket. Our first family photo was in there. "Please don't take my baby!" They tore the tiny picture up and then stomped on the necklace so it shattered underneath them. "No!" she wailed.

I hid my face in Jade's arm and knew that I was crying. Nobody else had cried when their homes were entered and destroyed. However, it seemed my home had the most taken from it. My home was the only one that had audio on it. Probably to torture me.

As I let the tears fall from my eyes, I could hear my dad soothe my mom and tell her that their memories would not fade. They would remember me despite the government not wanting to. That comment led to my dad getting zapped again.

When the TV went dark, nobody joked around about the countryside or that I was crying. I felt a pat on my back and could see Nia and Toby sending me sympathetic looks. I kept my head in the crook of Jade's arm as the next houses played. Some of them had audio - only if their families threw a fit. However, once they were shocked they seemed to shut up. I could feel the mood becoming sadder as people watched. Once the TV went black for the final time, Bischoff came up and smiled at us.

"I think that's enough erasing for today." He smiled as some of the Elitists started to straighten their backs and pay attention. They have been prepared for that their whole lives. As Inductees, we had no way of knowing it would be that intense. I would've preferred that it was done without me knowing. "We will be going to erase you from government records tomorrow morning."

As soon as he left, the lights were brightened and some of the more unaffected Inductees started heading back to our bedrooms. I looked over at some of the Elitists and noticed that they were going back to their bedrooms in droves too. Despite how prepared they seemed to be, it did seem like they were still affected. When I was ready, Jade helped me off the floor and Nia and Toby instantly hugged me. I wiped the tears from my eyes and felt a tap on the back. The rude kid from the Inductees gave me a

AMY KULP

nod before he headed back to his room. Jade, Nia, and Toby all tried to include me in the conversation as we moved to our bedroom, but my mind couldn't process anything right now.

"Hey, ponytail!" My body tensed as Jade slowed us down. She looked up at me and eyed the hair that was in the scrunchie she had given me. Nia and Toby safely made it into the hallway that led to our bedrooms and turned around to stare at us. Neither of their hair was in a ponytail and as I turned to the voice, I looked at everyone else's hair to make sure they were talking to me. Nobody else had ponytails in. "We want our ball back."

I stared at the blonde for a moment before I placed my hand in my pocket. I rolled the ball around in my hand before leaving Jade's side. I kept eye contact as I walked closer to the blonde. He held his hand out and as I walked right next to him, I made sure to get super close to him as I placed the ball on the table. Smirking, I whipped around as the chubby guy placed the ball where it needed to go. Jade's eyes were wide as I made my way back but it wasn't until she squinted and began to flinch that I knew something was being thrown at me. I didn't have the reflexes to turn around completely but I was able to turn around a bit before my side was hit with a foreign object.

At least he had aim.

I bent down quickly to get the object before I could see that their group was turned back around at the table. I gritted my teeth to stop myself from saying anything. Grabbing Jade, we successfully made it to our living space before she yanked me to our bedroom. She didn't give me a chance to protest before taking me to the bathroom. She started one of the showers and looked at me for the longest minute of my life.

"You and your parents were close?" she asked as I watched the steam come up from the water. I nodded my head and watched her shoulders sag for a moment. "They were your parents, weren't they?" I nodded. "Don't let anyone know how much that has affected you, okay?" I just nodded again and looked at her. As she sat on the bench, she looked down as she leaned forward, and I swear I could see tears growing in the corner of her eye. I brought her into a hug and knew that was the right choice. "Take a hot shower, you need it. I'll pick out some clothes for you to wear."

I quickly got into the heated shower. Despite how hot the water was, the room around us was freezing. Hanging on the walls were permanent shampoo, conditioner, body wash, and facial cleanser that dispensed into your hand once you were done. I found it shocking since everyone seemed to vary with their hair and facial needs. A disposable loofa was on the wall too and as I yanked it off, another one sprouted in its place.

"What is it like having a mom?" Jade asked as I let the shampoo fall from my scalp. I opened my mouth to answer back but accidentally inhaled the water that was overhead. When I finished choking, I could see Jade's silhouette sitting next to my shower. "I only had my dad and he was great – but I just never had a mom. I imagine it was like having an older brother."

                                    AMY KULP

I just let Jade talk as I finished up. She didn't need me to acknowledge what she was saying but she did need to tell someone. I still wasn't sure what house was hers, but she seemed lonely. She greeted me when I first arrived, and she has been nice to me ever since. She had been here for weeks before me, and I had to assume that meant she was one of the first people here. How much did she know?

"Okay, didn't think you would have an ass," Jade said when I stepped out in the wardrobe she picked out. I turned red immediately but looked in the mirror to see if she was telling the truth. Maybe these shorts just accentuated it. "We can use that when we distract some of the boys during the trials." I walked closer to the mirror and saw toothbrushes with everyone's names under it. When I took mine from its place, a small dollop of toothpaste was already on it. While brushing, I cocked my eyebrow at Jade. "Some of the boys seemed to already love you." She paused and got up from the bench. "Or, at least, your body." She shrugged and grabbed her toothbrush too. "Although, I do think Garrett and the other Elitists are just like that all of the time."

"Who's Garrett?"

"He's the pervy, chubby one," Jade answered. I nodded my head. He seemed to always be with the blonde and playing pool. I wanted to ask her who the blonde was because I kept seeing him glancing at me every chance he could take. By the time I spit out my toothpaste, Jade was already onto the next subject. "Do you want to work together?" she asked. I looked at her funny and she looked around to make sure that nobody was listening. "The thing with the Elitists is that they all work individually. If we work as a team, we are most likely to survive these trials." She paused and we sat back down on the bench. "Have you ever seen the televised trials?"

"What?" I looked up at her as I tried to put my ponytail in and shook my head. "These are televised?"

"Apparently, the government profits from it."

"Who told you that?" I wondered. "Why would they televise the methods in which they train their Assassins?"

"Stupid, right?" Jade asked. She shook her head. "I may not be an Elitist but that does not mean I'm poor." She lowered her voice. "I got my letter two years ago, so my dad bought the televised version from last year. We studied it and studied it. There's no way of my dad knowing that I'm alive, but he wanted to make sure I survived. Team efforts are what worked best. Instead of it being one versus one, it'd be four versus one."

"Four?"

"Nia and Toby," she said to me. I nodded my head. "Are you in?"

"No."

#

We walked down the white hallway in four single-file lines – one for the Elitists males, one for the Elitists females, one for the Inductee males, and one for the Inductee females. We all followed Bischoff exactly as he ordered and went to part of the

                                   AMY KULP

government building that was roped off. All around us, we could feel the stares from the forest green suits and I felt like a perfect target in the lime green ones. Were we sure that this wasn't a setup or target practice?

I was behind Leah in line so I was thankful that I didn't have to lead. The last girl from our room was behind me and then Jade and Nia were behind her. I already knew what they were discussing and felt like they would be judgmental about it. However, Jade was still friendly toward me this morning. I was thankful for that. At least she was showing that she wasn't just using me to be in her clan.

"You will be seated in a waiting room," Bischoff announced. "Four of you will be called at once where you will be erased from the government's database. This erasing can get very intense. Once you are done with that screening, you will have your fingerprints removed. This is a very painful process, and the smell is not that great either. Good luck future assassins."

Bischoff smiled as he stepped aside. We all went in to prepare ourselves and it looked like a normal doctor's office – except everything was white. I sat down next to Jade and she smiled gently at me as everyone else seemed to partner up together since the chairs were only sat two next to each other.

"Justin Frazier, Tanya Booth, Shane Newfeld, and Cassandra Vise."

Four people stood up and walked toward the government employee who had called their name. I pinpointed who Shane was from yesterday though. It felt good to know who the mean Inductee was. He didn't seem to like playing by the rules, but he had to have done something right to get here instead of on the Assassination List.

"Garrett Arnold, Audrey Beck, Toby Ernst, and Jade Tricase."

I squeezed Jade's hand before she went in and she showed that she appreciated it by smiling at me. However, it wasn't long before she moved next to Toby and they were each other's support systems while they were there.

"Asher Johnston, Jordyn Carr, Daniel Brown, and Nia Williams."

I barely knew anyone in that group except Nia. The only people left in the waiting room that I knew was blondie, the nice Elitist girl Heather, and the oldest possible assassin from our group Leah. A couple of the other people looked familiar as the Elitists I didn't know had all hung out near the pool table. I had to wonder if that was a show or not. Were they really all friends or were they doing it to make us feel inferior?

"Colt Kirkman, Heather Flick, Anthony Denkins, and Leah Humphrey."

Just like that, I felt like I knew nobody in the waiting room. At least now I could pinpoint that blondie was either Colt or Anthony. I watched them all get up to leave and was left with the last of the quads.

"Eddie Marlowe, Jamie Scott, Colin Teft, and Bridget Soloman."

I followed everyone back into another waiting room. Colin and Jamie went in first and Eddie and I were left here. There was some sort of

                                    AMY KULP

delay. I didn't know what that meant though so I just continued to watch Eddie squirm in his chair.

He was an Elitist definitely. I remember him standing near Garrett and blondie. He seemed to enjoy all the jokes that they shared but wasn't very good at pool. He or his team lost every single time. He was extremely skinny though and I was afraid that if he had to do any type of physical activity, he would break. If he was an Elitist though, he had to be good, right?

"Stop staring at me," he grumbled. He crossed his arms across his chest and rolled his eyes. I immediately looked away from him and stared at the floor. He didn't seem like he would be mean and when I looked at him again, I could see that he was eyeing me this time. "You're not bad for an Inductee. It'll be sad when you're assassinated first."

I didn't say anything in response. It seemed to be working in my favor with the less I talked. People were spilling things to me that they normally probably would not have. Plus, I wanted everyone to underestimate me. I didn't want them to see me as a threat. While I didn't want to be in the trials, I knew that I wanted to live. If I were to fail, nobody could tell me it was because I didn't try enough. I was going to use what people were telling me against them. Only if I absolutely needed to though.

"Bridget Soloman."

I stood up as the person in green called my name. I looked back at Eddie and he was just looking at me with interest. When I caught his eyes, he made a disgusted face at me. He didn't say anything though. That motion alone told me that his attitude was an act. Just like I'm sure most people's here were.

"Please sit," the girl instructed. The space that we were in now had absolutely no privacy. I could see Colin ahead of me and Jamie behind me. Up in the corner was blondie but he wasn't accompanied by anyone. He seemed to be staring off until two people came back over him. "I asked what your full name is," she repeated.

"Oh." I shook my head and looked at her. "Bridget Soloman or Solomon. I've seen it spelled both ways." She typed on the computer and when I looked back at blondie, he seemed more stressed than what he just was. The two working on the computer with him were hunched over the computer with intensity. It made me more interested.

"Select which one was your address," the girl said. I looked back over to her and was surprised to see that there was now a small computer screen. I picked the one that had my farmhouse's address, and she nodded her head. "Alright, that was the easy part. You are erased from the government's database. Your name doesn't seem too popular." I tried to smile at her as I knew she was just doing her job but I didn't want to encourage it. I didn't want to encourage what they were doing here. "The harder part is removing your social media accounts and any mentions or pictures of you from your friend's social accounts."

The lady kept smiling as she deleted all my accounts that they found on my computer at home. She continued to delete fake ones and aliases that I have used in the past. Any websites that I went on

                    AMY KULP

were bookmarked and they made sure to remove all the accounts there too. She kept smiling as she edited my friend's photos to crop me out. She kept smiling every time I nodded my head to confirm that was my picture. I nodded my head again when another account was on there and it was my fake one.

They found my fake accounts. I really couldn't take anything.

"Alright, you are all done with being erased. Congratulations, you have never existed!" she said excitedly. "Can you do me a favor and put your thumb on this scanner?"

I nodded and placed my right thumb on the scanner. I watched as it scanned and scanned and felt the metal heat up under my skin. I felt little prickles begin to hit my thumb and with the heat that was on there, I shifted in my seat. After a moment of hesitation and it finally becoming too much, I flinched my thumb off the glass. I looked back at my finger and saw that it was red and bleeding. Wiping the blood on my pants, the girl looked at me with disapproval.

"You need to keep the thumb on until it is done. Let me see." She inspected my thumb and just nodded her head. "Alright, it did damage your skin enough that we won't need to redo it. Can I see your other thumb now?"

"Can you do all of my fingers at once?" I asked. She looked at me in surprise. "That way I only have to go through the pain once."

"If you can handle it. Here's a wipe for the blood and then I'll bandage all your fingers once you are done. It's best if you don't concentrate on it."

I nodded my head and set both of my hands down on the metal scanner. I looked at the room and watched as Jamie walked out of the door and saw that her fingers were now bandaged. Colin kept flinching and groaning as he did each finger individually. He was moving so much that the lady who was helping him had to press his fingers down. Eddie was finally up here too but he still seemed to be removing himself from the database. When my eyes landed on blondie, they had bandaged his entire hand in white gauze and were in the process of holding down his other hand on the metal scanner.

"Alright, you did well. Most of our girls tend to do better with the physical pain than the men." She smiled at me as I focused back on her. "Let me just wipe any blood off..." She did so but was careful when she pressed. I flinched each time and jolted when she got my left hand. "Let me give you some numbing spray. Lay your hands flat out for me." She sprayed and wafted the spray so that it could evaporate into my skin. Once it was dry, she continued to wipe the blood and bandage my fingers. "You can go through that door and wait patiently while everyone is being finished."

I nodded again and got up from the chair. I was already sore, and I knew that I would be for a while. Would this affect how I would do these trials? Were we still expected to do the trials after this? Like a week from today or start it tomorrow?

"Oh, sorry," I whispered as the blondie cut me off. He looked back at me and my eyes lingered on his bandaged hands. He shook his head and started walking toward the door before trying to decide how

                               AMY KULP

best to go through without hurting his hands. "Oh, let me." I shimmied past him to open it and I looked back at him. He didn't want my help. "Why did you get all of your hands burned off?"

He reached out his hand and pushed my shoulder into the door. He pushed me so hard that my back hit the wall so hard that I felt breathless. His hand was so aggressive on my shoulder that I could see the pain on his face. He brought his face very close to mine and I couldn't help but stare at him.

"You need to learn that I am not here to be your friend, ponytail. Mind your business before it gets you in trouble." I stared into his eyes and watched as he brought his other bandaged hand up onto my neck. He grabbed a strand roughly and tucked it behind my ear. "You missed a piece."

"Well," Eddie said he came over to the door. He smiled as he looked between us. "Come on, Colt, don't want to be seen near her for too long. People will think you're giving tips to an Inductee." He slapped his hand onto blondie which startled us both. We broke eye contact, and I looked over at Eddie who was smirking at me. "Although, I don't think anyone would mind if you shared her."

"My standards aren't that low," I said. I smirked at both before I motioned my shoulder to knock blondie's hand off. "Colt, huh?" I asked. I looked him up and down before resting my eyes on his face. "I prefer blondie."

"Let's go," Jade said. I looked at her and saw her standing behind him. She looked between all three of us before I walked with her. She grabbed my hand and made me follow her to the couch. I didn't even realize that they were all in this room. "Cool it," Jade whispered as she plopped down. I could feel stares from everyone but my own was on Colt. "Don't be a traitor to the Inductees."

"You said it yourself," I said. I could see Eddie, Colt, and Garrett all joking with each other before Colt looked over at me. I looked at Jade with a smirk. If I was here, I might as well have fun with it. "I can distract some of the boys while I'm here. He seems to be the ringleader of the boys."

"I think it's a bad idea," Jade stated. I leaned closer to her and felt her fingers wrap around my arm again. "I got to know Colt well when I first arrived. He was the only person to be here before me. He knows a lot about these trials…"

She droned on and on but my mind was too busy focusing on the fact that her fingers weren't wrapped in gauze like everyone else's.

                                    AMY KULP

Trial #1

I groaned when the brush fell out of my weak grip and hit my fingers. It came crashing down onto the tiled floors and I watched as the brush skidded to one of the showers. I leaned my palms onto the sink and just stared at my reflection. Tasks that were so normal and so easy now were challenging. I couldn't grip anything without getting hurt. I couldn't do anything without feeling the little pulses of pain run through my fingers and through my arms. I felt like I couldn't touch anything and even the gauze was hurting me. I was always told to let cuts and anything else breathe overnight by my parents and it would harden. I was hoping that if it was hard, it wouldn't hurt as much. However, that didn't seem to be the case.

After removing the gauze, I placed my hand underneath the lotion dispenser and allowed the cream to soak into my palm. Gently, I began to move my palm over my burned skin and winced as it began to sting. I closed my eyes and put my forehead on the sink's counter to avoid getting dizzy. Any major injuries didn't seem to hurt me but something like this was killer to me. Now that I was healing, I would feel the skin grow back and feel it stretch over each tip until it met with the old skin. I shuddered just thinking about it. "Here," Jade said as she wrapped the towel around her body tighter. She moved the shower curtain back so that the water would drip down it and grabbed my hairbrush from the floor. I looked up at her through my arms and voiced my appreciation. "How are your fingers?" she wondered.

I didn't answer and just showed her my hand. "I'll put some antibacterial cream and more gauze on it." She dropped my hand and I picked my head up to stare at her. "Just let me get dressed first."

She jogged toward her clothes that were on a bench and quickly changed from her towel. She allowed her hair to airdry before coming back over to me. I nodded my head to indicate she could use my brush and watched as she ran it through quickly. Once her knots were detangled, she placed the brush down on my hair first.

"Can I braid it?" she wondered. I handed her the scrunchie she had allowed me to use. "I'm surprised they didn't confiscate this," she stated. "You're the only one who had enough balls to use it."

"Maybe it looks too much like lime green," I stated. I shrugged my shoulders as she braided one side of my head. I held onto it gently with my teeth as she quickly did the other side. "Why are you being so nice to me? I told you no to joining your group."

Shrugging, she answered with, "I want our time here to be as fun as I can possibly make it." She paused as she grabbed all my hair to throw it in a high ponytail. "Listen, I'm going to be frank with you, there is a very slim chance that both of us will make it out as assassins. Did you hear the statistics Bischoff listed? There are not a lot of females who make it but even fewer of them are inductees. I don't want to hate everyone here like the elitists. Honestly, most of them are great when they're by themselves."

"So… why didn't you get your fingerprints burned off?" I asked as she picked up my hand and

                                    AMY KULP

started putting gauze on it. "Are you secretly a bad guy?"

"Like a mole?" Jade asked as she kept helping me. She shrugged her shoulders. "Colt burned my fingers with the burner on the stove." She winced and when she was done patching up my left hand, she showed me her fingers. There weren't any fingerprints there either.

"What an asshole," I said. I shook my head and huffed. I hated this guy. How could he hurt Jade? It seemed plausible too. It made sense as to why his entire palm was then burned off. Can't attack another assassin.

"Oh no, he-"

Jade dropped my hands to cover her ears and I covered mine with my arms. I could see the three flashes that indicated that we were needed and waited impatiently for the alarm to stop sounding. When it stopped blaring, I looked over at Jade who just nodded her head. We needed to get to the living room before all the good seats were taken. She grabbed my wrist and as we exited the bathroom, we could see that some girls were barely awake. Some threw on the nearest shirt they could find while others rushed to brush their hair.

I looked down and realized that I probably should have finished wrapping my fingers.

As soon as we got outside of our bedrooms, we could see that the pillows on the chairs were rearranged. People seemed to be more comfortable with each other but as we made it out into the hallway, we could see that we were separating ourselves into the groups. Jade and I were not going to be the ones to break that cycle.

We managed to score a spot on the couches, and I sat on the edge. Jade was much better at making friends than me and it was evident when people started moving to sit closer to her. She smiled and engaged them in conversation, but I couldn't concentrate on them. I was focusing on Bischoff.

He was staring at everyone. He was surveying the way we behaved and interacted with each other. Some people would stare at him and catch him looking but he never seemed to make eye contact with them. He almost seemed like a robot on the prowl for something. I wouldn't be surprised if he had supersonic hearing or extra cameras in other rooms so that they could always hear what we were discussing. I eyed Jade at the thought and made a mental note not to talk to her so much about the government. We could be killed for some of the commentary we made.

"Thank you all for joining me," Bischoff said as Colin joined our couch. I scooched over so that he could try to sit next to me but he didn't take it and instead, sat on the floor beside me. "And thank you for not making me do the second alarm." He smiled a bit and I heard a couple people let out the breaths they were holding. "I'm sure that we are all sore from yesterday's erasure." He looked around and I saw people nodding their heads. I could see people fidgeting with their fingers while Jade tried to hide that she wasn't hurt. "Today starts your first trial." My eyes grew big as I stared down at my own hands to see that I didn't have gauze around one of them.

"One of the most powerful tools that an assassin needs is… What?" he asked. He looked around the room, but nobody wanted to speak up. "Nobody wants to answer?" he wondered. The room remained silent, and he snapped his fingers once. Green men with their electric prodding sticks came out. One came out of the hallway nearest the inductees, and one came closer to the hallway near the elitists. "Let's try that again. One of the most powerful tools that an assassin needs is... What?"

"A fully loaded gun," Garrett announced. He smiled at his friends around him, but they all were facing forward. The air in the room was different than yesterday. Today, it was dawning on people that not everyone in the room would be coming back.

"With a silencer," Eddie added. He gave Garrett a knowing nod and together, they gave each other a high-five. Obviously, a big mistake, I could see their stupidity cross their faces as they tried to act like that didn't hurt.

"A knife," Shane announced. I looked over Jade to see him nod to himself. He seemed cocky about his answer. "I have much more control over hurting someone."

"But you pose a risk of getting hurt yourself," Leah corrected. Shane immediately glared at her with disgust, and she shrugged her shoulders. "Or having it knocked out of your hands."

"A map," Justin announced. He looked over at the Bischoff who wasn't showing any emotion. "If I had a map, I would be able to know the layout of the nearest exits, entrances, and how the rooms were.

I might know where the target would most likely be too.”

“I’m not sure,” Audrey announced. She looked around at the others and Heather nodded for her to continue with what she was saying. She side glanced towards us but she wouldn’t have been looking at us long enough to see if any of us were encouraging her. I was hoping that she wasn’t falling into the trap of hating the inductees just because we were less fortunate than her. “But having a partner would greatly increase the likelihood of the target being killed.”

“Anybody else have a guess?” Bischoff asked. He looked toward us as if he wasn’t satisfied with what we had been saying. After all, only Shane suggested anything. I could hear the green man with the electricity come closer to us. The electricity sounded sharper and more dangerous than before. When I turned a centimeter, I could see them right behind my couch. Without thinking, I grabbed Jade’s hand, and she squeezed back too. I was surprised to feel that she was sweating and was surprised that my fingers weren’t hurting despite how hard she was grasping them.

“Surveillance?” Cassandra asked. She seemed just as nervous as I was but calmed down when the man stepped back toward the hallway. She made eye contact with Leah and Nia before looking down at the ground. She didn’t want to be wrong or right in this scenario. However, I knew she wasn’t going to offer more for that option. I was too nervous to speak too.

"No," Bischoff said shortly. "What every good assassin needs is to use their brain." I immediately rolled my eyes and lessened my grip on Jade's hand. She still held on though. "Without your brain or knowledge, could you use a gun? Would you know how to attack with a knife? Would you know how to read a map? Would you know what to do with a partner or surveillance?" He shook his head. "We pride ourselves on having some of the smartest masterminds become the highest achieving assassins. Your first trial will be on your knowledge." He paused and smiled as there seemed to be a shuffle in all of us. "This test will have some history that you learned in schools, math, spelling, science, and all of that good stuff." I could see Shane tense up as he sat next to Jade. "However, there will also be scenario questions, strategy questions, and trick questions. You must read all directions and answer all questions." He paused and looked at everyone. "This is a timed test but nobody should need all of the time." He looked at everyone again and started nodding his head again. "Let me show you the room we will be in."

We filed in after everyone else but I made sure to let go of Jade's hand as we started moving. I didn't want to be dragged along as she moved up and I tried to stay as far back as I could. Eventually, the crowd stopped moving and while I wasn't in the room, I could stand on my tiptoes to see inside.

Unsurprisingly, the room was all white. However, the room was so big that it looked like it spanned two football fields. There were white desks and white chairs for everyone to sit at. Stalking the perimeter were men in green uniforms who were pacing back and forth. They had their electricity prods and seemed ready to attack anyone who stepped out of line.

"While the desks are spread far apart, you want to make sure that you keep your eyes on your own desk. Each time you look where you shouldn't be, one of our certified assassins will jolt you with electricity." Bischoff faced everyone now and smiled. "Pick your seats and I will give you more instructions when we're ready."

As I was the backend, I watched as people pushed others to get to the seat they wanted. The first row was picked fast but some people ran for the last spots. I walked to a desk I wanted and just sat down. It didn't matter to me who I was by or where the location was. I just needed to control the anxiety and nerves I felt in my stomach. I was smart, but was I smarter than everyone else here?

"Now, you have paper and pencil," Bischoff said in a microphone. He stalked the front of the room and stood still when everyone started staring at him. "However, all your answers must be submitted on the holographic screen in front of you. Good luck. Your three hours start now."

I watched as he went to sit back at the desk too. His back was straight, and he clasped his hands in front of him. He seemed satisfied with the challenge and for a second, I had no idea what he met by holographic screen. The only thing on my desk was a paper and pencil. As I looked around, I could see some people were already hard at work.

                                    AMY KULP

I felt a small jolt of electricity to my side and looked to the right. The green man smiled nastily at me before continuing to stalk down the aisles. I watched him but when he came back down, I focused on my paper and pencil test.

Picking up the pencil, I was surprised to see my paper enlarge itself and become wrapped around myself and the desk. I couldn't see anybody anyway with how big this thing was. I quickly touched the holograph to see if I could shrink it a bit but instead, I saw an answer was clicked on accident. Instead of allowing me to select a different option, it highlighted red and moved on to the next question. Tears started flowing into my eyes as I panicked and hit the screen again – red showed up again and I was moved to the third question.

I shook my head and forced my hands to hit the desk. I couldn't risk answering any other questions wrong. These people were the smartest of the smart already. I'm not sure about the elitists but the inductees were flagged for their popularity, smarts, physical fitness, and our ability to fit in. I had to admit that there were different types of smart people – brainiacs, street smarts, and manipulation. I had more of a brain for school stuff. While it came easy to me when I was younger, once I hit seventh grade, I had to start studying and working for my grades. I was one of those students who cried if she got below a ninety on a test. I scoffed my head at how silly that seemed now.

Now was the time to focus though. While I couldn't see anyone else because my holographic screen was still surrounding me, I could hear pencils scratching against the paper and desk. I could hear someone tapping their foot from anxiety: this was a life-or-death situation now. I just happened to pick two wrong answers at first too. I shook my head again and ran my fingers through my ponytail. It has always been a bad habit for me and even worse now because of my fingers.

I looked down at the question that was being asked of me and sighed. It was an order of operations question, my sixth-grade teacher would be so proud. As I grabbed the pencil to begin rewriting the expression, I felt my fingertips burn as they touched the white, wooden pencil. Staring down at the hand that wasn't gauzed, I groaned as silently as I could. Of course, the hand that wasn't gauzed was the dominant hand. I grimaced as I held tighter onto the pencil and scratched out the problem on the paper.

Before I could finish writing it down, my brain was already on the next step. I barely had time to write down the answer before I dropped my pencil and clicked on the correct answer. I held my breath as it buffered before it turned green and swooped me onto the next question. Reading it and then rereading it, I knew there was a possibility I would get this question wrong. I was never too good at the history of our land. I could study and study and study but five minutes later, I could get all of the same questions wrong.

What year did we first start to become the land that we are today? I squinched my eyes closed and rubbed my temples in hopes that would help me remember. Looking at the choices, I could immediately eliminate two of them and was left with

 AMY KULP

two more. I closed my eyes so hard together. I had to try and remember what year had the pandemic. I had to remember what year our textbooks started teaching us about their history. They said anything before that was irrelevant. All that information was locked up tight. If you wanted to access anything before that year, you had to get special permissions, go before a judge to make sure you had good intentions, and you had to agree to be watched forever. It always made news when someone wanted to do it. In my lifetime, I believe only one person tried.

They ended up killing themselves from the knowledge that they gained.

I clicked on an option and waited impatiently for the question to go through. Was it going to be red or green? I let out a sigh of relief when it turned green and moved to the next question. It tested multiple areas of my brain, and I knew people were leaving before me. I could feel them brush past my holographic imprisonment. However, I took my time to read the directions and questions. I was getting through them and eventually, was at my final three questions.

Who is most likely to survive the trials? My eyes scanned the two options and while I wanted to put that it would be inductees, I remembered Bischoff's answer. Elitists were more likely to be an assassin. I immediately pressed that and waited for my question to buffer. However, before it switched to the next question, this one didn't ring in as green or red.

Who is most likely to survive the trials? Once again, I scanned the choices of female or male and bit my lip. I wanted to put female because I was one. According to Bischoff's statistics, males tended to become the actual assassins in the end. I clicked that button without a word and watched as it went to the last question on my exam.

Which person is least likely to become an assassin? Below it, the answer choices were all our names. How did they expect me to answer this? I didn't know everybody well. I didn't know what the elitists were capable of, and I barely knew any of the boys from the inductees. I didn't try to communicate and socialize with everyone. When I was able to, I slept in my room and Jade told me more about the trials that she viewed on TV. I hadn't even explored the house yet. I knew where my room, the kitchen, and the living room were. Was there more to the house than I knew of? Probably. However, I couldn't pick someone for this answer.

My eyes viewed the clock that was upfront and noticed I had about forty-five minutes left. Looking back at my questionnaire, I knew that I wasn't going to purposely answer this. I shook my head and looked around at the other people in the room. Before I had a chance to see more than one blank seat, I got shocked with electricity and focused back on my paper. I refused to answer this question though. Did everyone else answer it? Did they just put someone random down? Was this one of those trick questions that Bischoff was talking about?

I silently mulled over the names on the list and kept shaking my head. I still refused to pick one

                                        AMY KULP

though and as time eventually moved on, I knew that I was risking getting a lower score. Who was I supposed to pick? I looked back up and had my brain wandering even more: maybe I should answer this question. If I were to think of Bischoff's statistics, it would probably be Leah. She was older than the average person, she was female, and she was an inductee. I bit my lip and reached out my hand but before I could click on her name, my holographic screen disappeared, and my hand was just hovering in the air.

"Time's up," Bischoff said to me. I looked around at the empty room and stood up to greet him. "Time to join the rest of the group while the scores are being calculated."

He put his hand on my back to guide me toward a doorway we hadn't been in. As soon as I came through, I could see another white room with twenty circles. Nobody was standing in them and they were all sitting or standing near the walls. When I saw that most of us were split into our two groups, I joined mine while Bischoff made his way to the front.

"What took you so long?" Jade asked as I got to her. I shrugged my shoulders and motioned that I would tell her later.

"Welcome back, future assassins," Bischoff started. Any whispering and murmuring that was happening before was now quieting down. "Behind me, you see twenty circles for twenty assassins." He lengthened his arm out to show everyone. "I will call each of you one by one by the assassin who scored the highest." He paused and looked at all of us. "The smartest of the group is Justin Frazier."

He walked to his circle and as he stepped onto it, it turned bright green under his feet. He smiled to himself and then to his friends. He wasn't over-celebrating either. Compared to the other elitists, he seemed calm and assured of his capabilities. He pushed his brown hair out of his eyes before nodding toward Bischoff.

"A surprise second place is Bridget Solomon."

I stayed where I was until I heard a couple of claps from around me. Jade clapped me on the back and Anthony pushed me forward. When I looked back at him, he just smiled and clapped along with everyone else. There weren't as many claps as Justin got and I knew that I looked a little awkward as I passed Bischoff. I made eye contact with none of the elitists but some of them didn't look too happy for me. I avoided trying to look at any of them before I got to my circle. Justin offered me a hand and I missed it at first. When my circle turned green under my feet, I looked back at him and shook his hand. He congratulated me and I nodded my head at him to indicate that I was congratulating him too.

"Colt Kirkman."

Blondie got pats on his back from Eddie and Garrett who continued to hype him up way too much. Some of the girls swooned and yelled for him too and he even bear-hugged Justin. I reached my hand out to congratulate him, but he just shoved his shoulder into me. Losing my balance from the sudden jolt, I grabbed onto Justin instinctively. Both Justin's and

                              AMY KULP

mine feet moved out of our circles, and we saw our green turn to yellow. I sent him an apologetic look before shooting a glare at Colt who had his arms crossed smugly across his chest. His circle remained red though. When Justin and I moved our feet back into our circle, we stayed yellow as Colt's turned that color.

"Heather Flick," Bischoff announced like nothing had just happened.

"You cheated," Colt whispered to me. I looked over at him and raised an eyebrow. How would I have cheated? I shook my head in disbelief and stared forward as Heather came over to us. I gave her a handshake and a friendly nod and she did the same. When Heather got to Colt, he smugly shook her hand appropriately. When her feet were in her circle, hers turned a bright green. Ours still stayed yellow.

"Jade Tricase."

I clapped happily as soon as I heard her name. She smiled as she gave all of the inductees a hug. They all hugged her back and when she made her way over to the elitists group, they seemed hesitant to interact. However, Asher, Audrey, and Jordyn all hugged her. When she got over to Justin, he shook her hand and gave her the same smile that I had received. I hugged her and congratulated her. I was so relieved to hear her name called. When she got to Colt, he happily shook her hand and brought her into a hug. He eyed me as he moved his palms along her back and gave me another smirk before letting go. He leaned into her to whisper something and she shook her head and moved on.

"Leah Humphrey."

"I saw you get zapped twice," he mumbled. I stared straight ahead and gave a hug to Leah. I knew to just ignore him. He didn't like me and I didn't like him. He was going to do anything to get under my skin. He was jealous of me. "Whose paper did you look at to steal those answers from?"

"Tanya Booth."

"You are scum," Colt said to me at last. I could see him exaggerate rolling his eyes until he stood up straight and pretended to listen to the others that were called.

"Asher Johnston."

I could tell that my ignoring his antics was annoying him. His jaw was set in anger, and I could hear him getting more violent as he spit out his next words. He acted like the word inductee was a slur and maybe to him, it was. However, I didn't see it as one. I refused to let it bother me that I wasn't trained for this sort of thing.

"Jordyn Carr."

I could see from the corner of my eye that Colt moved his mouth and made a motion toward the ground. I tried not to think about it until I could feel it hit the top of my shoe. I could see him smirking wildly at me but when I glanced at him, he moved his vision to the next person being called.

"Audrey Beck."

When I shook her hand, I looked down to see his spit on my shoe. When I looked back up, he shrugged his shoulders. He whispered that I was an inductee and scum before turning straight ahead. I

AMY KULP

wanted to shake it off but could feel the anger boiling up in me.

"Anthony Denkins." I shook his head like everyone else and smiled seeing how low Colt's friends were. Maybe they would get out soon. "Eddie Marlowe." I looked at everyone else and felt my skin beginning to grow white as Nia and Toby were still not called. "Jamie Scott." The more people I knew and was comfortable with, the better I would do on these trials. "Garrett Arnold." He high-fived Colt as he walked by and he just eyed my shoe. When he looked down to confirm, he gave him another bear hug.

I looked at the crowds of people left and felt myself slump forward. They were all inductees now. I wanted to prove that not all elitists would make it based on what their parents paid. I had optimism for them but knew that we were not given the same opportunities as the elitists.

"Shane Ernst." He walked with his head held high. He didn't shake anyone's hands and walked right to his circle. Everybody's but Justin's, Colt's, and mine were green. "Cassandra Vise." She seemed relieved to be called and slumped forward to her spot. She seemed too embarrassed to shake anyone's hands. "Nia Williams."

"That's where you should be. At the bottom," Colt whispered. I stared straight ahead as I clapped for her. I just had to remember that if I didn't show it bothered me, he would leave me alone.

"Toby Ernst. Daniel Brown and Colin Teft."

As the last two got into their places, the circles below their feet turned red. I looked back at mine to see if it had changed but was saddened to see that it was still yellow. So was Justin's and Colt's. I wondered what all of these circles meant. All I had to do was look up at Bischoff and have him explain it. He was there for a reason and I knew that there were secret cameras in this room that were televising us to all of the people who could afford to watch it.

"I want everyone to look at the circles around your feet," Bischoff instructed. I did so but as I was looking, I was more focused on the spit that was sitting on my shoe. It made me angry to see it but I was also humiliated that it happened to me. "If you have a green circle that means you will be moving on to the next trial." Fifteen sighs of relief were heard at once. "If you have a yellow circle that means you will be moving on to the next trial, but you will either have a penalty during your next trial or you will have a punishment that you have to face. The choice will be yours in a private meeting." I was glad that we were moving to the next trial, but I wasn't sure how to feel about the penalty. I looked at Justin who seemed to be contemplating his decision before I looked ahead. I didn't care to know what choice Colt was looking forward to. "A red circle means you will not be moving onto the next trial – you are not worthy of becoming an Assassin." Bischoff looked at the two boys. "Daniel, you were second-to-last place so you will be killed first. The person to assassinate Daniel will be Jordyn Carr."

Jordyn and Daniel's lights started to blink. She was given a nod from Bischoff who handed her a blade. She walked from her circle to take the blade and twiddled it in her hand. She looked back at

                              AMY KULP

Bischoff for reassurance, and he just nodded his head at her. I turned back to Daniel to see how he was reacting, but he looked too stunned to say anything. His eyes were big from shock and despite the circle under his feet blinking, he stayed still.

"An assassin's job is to kill with any instrument necessary. This trial's weapon of choice is the knife. There are multiple ways that someone can be killed with a knife and assassins tend to use the most efficient methods they can think of."

Bischoff nodded again at Jordyn, and she looked between Daniel, her blade, and Bischoff before throwing it at him. I jumped from the sudden movement and looked over at Daniel who had a knife in his eye. He began screaming and yelling for help and Jordyn pushed him over quickly. She took the knife from his eye and plunged it into a soft spot in his brain. She twisted the knife as his body fought for an instant but soon, she left his side. She looked over at Bischoff who gave a satisfied nod to her. Returning to her circle, I couldn't keep my eye off the body that was just lying there.

She just killed someone... Like it was nothing. I looked around to see how everyone else was reacting. Some of them were just staring ahead without looking, some were staring at the body in disbelief, some had smiles on their faces, and some had their hands in their faces. When I turned to see how Colt was reacting, he quickly put a mask on to cover any emotions someone might see. However, I could have sworn that I saw a queasy face.

"Killing our last place finisher will be Shane Newfeld."

Shane smiled as his circle began blinking. Without any further instructions, he went over to Daniel's body and grabbed the knife that was still in his head. The blood fell down the blade and onto the white floor. It stained and smeared as he smudged his feet into the splatter but it looked menacing as he walked up to Colin.

Instead of just submitting to his death like Daniel, Colin shook his head and begged for him not to kill him. I couldn't watch as he got down on his knees and started crying. I closed my eyes and turned my head into my shoulder from accidentally seeing anything. When Colin started screaming, I opened my eyes to see that Justin was absolutely horrified. I shut my eyes harder as his screams got louder and more desperate. Eventually, I brought my hands up to my ears and squeezed them shut. I could still hear them though. I could still hear him begging. When it got silent, I opened my eyes and saw the scene down the line.

Colin was beheaded. It looked like it took a lot of hacking to get that way and Shane was covered in blood. Toby and Nia also were covered in blood, and it seemed to be everywhere. Nia was crying into Toby as he brought her closer to him. However, neither of them strayed from their circles. When I looked at some of the other horrified faces, my gaze landed back on Colt. He was ghostly white and was rocking back and forth. Almost as if he was trying to soothe himself. His eyes were glued to the scene in front of him.

Shane dropped the knife in front of Bischoff's feet with a nasty grin on his face. When

                                    AMY KULP

his back was turned, I could see Bischoff motion for somebody so when I turned around and saw a green man with a prodding stick, I was prepared for it. He hit him twice in the back and while it always knocked the breath out of me, Shane only grimaced.

"As an assassin, you want to kill efficiently. Hacking and gnawing at someone's neck to kill them would take unnecessary time and would alert those around them." Bischoff shook his head as he tsked with disgust. "If you have a green circle around your feet, you are free to go. I suggest washing up and fine-tuning your skills for the second trial. Good luck, future assassins."

As soon as everyone's green circle started flashing, they seemed hesitant. I could see Jade carefully watching other people as they moved from their circle first. When she moved, she grabbed onto the nearest person, and together, they walked out of the room. Nia and Toby were wrapped in each other's arms as they tried to get some of the blood off. Audrey looked almost afraid of Jordyn and I could hear Shane gloating to her that he did a better job. Jordyn didn't seem to agree but also wasn't proud to say who did.

"My three yellow circles," Bischoff started when the door closed behind the last person to leave. "Assassins always need to be focused on what they are told to do. You either stepped out of your circle or caused someone else to step out of their circle which meant that you were not focused on listening to who made it through the trials. This is rather alarming since you three were our top pupils of today's trials. You need to do better." He paused as a green man came out from behind him. "Now, I need to know whether you want a punishment or you want a penalty for your next trial."

"What is our next trial?" Justin asked. Bischoff smiled and shook his head. He wouldn't give us that information.

"As elitists, you have a higher chance of surviving the next trial as is. Inductees tend to be out first. You will need to think of your possible choices here. The punishment may affect you in the trial as well from soreness or fatigue but is not guaranteed to." He paused again and the green man started approaching all of us.

My first reaction was to jolt away from him, but I could see that Justin and Colt weren't doing that. I shouldn't either then. I allowed him to put something over my head so that I couldn't see. My breathing became faster but at least I could still hear everything around me. That was calming enough for me.

"I am giving you a moment to ponder over the decisions."

I already knew what I was going to pick. There were very slim chances that a female inductee would be an assassin. I could not chance a penalty that could get me killed. Although he did say that the punishment can also affect our ability in the next task.

"If you would like to take the penalty, I need you to let me know now – silently." I waited a moment for him to say about the punishment. When he followed through, I raised my hand and brought it back down once the sack was taken from my head.

                    AMY KULP

"Okay, if you chose the penalty, that will be given to you at your next trial." Bischoff looked over at Justin and nodded his head. Justin returned the favor and when his green circle started blinking, he exited the room. "You both chose punishment." I tensed at the thought. "Your punishment this time is to clean this room." I looked around at the mess that Shane made and grimaced. "Not today. Not tomorrow. You might never know when. However, we will let you know."

"Is that it?" Colt asked. I looked over at him and felt my eyes going wide. Did he want to make this worse for us? "We just have to clean blood off of a white floor?"

"With the person you hate the most in the trials," Bischoff said. He walked toward Colt with energy that scared me. I could feel myself wanting to shrink as they both started comparing their height and muscles. "We always have eyes on you guys. We see how you interact with people and how you interact with each other." He shook his head and looked down at me. "Although, I guess I can make it more interesting for the both of you." He stepped away and rested his finger on his chin.

I stood there stunned at the two of them. It was like they were facing off with each other and I was just there. Why did I have to be involved? I would have been fine with just cleaning blood off of a white room. That sounded hard enough!

As soon as the circle around me started to blink, I bolted out of the room. I had no idea if Colt was following or if he was still having his stand-off with Bischoff. I didn't care. I just needed to be by someone who wasn't crazy. Why would he want a harder punishment?

When I got back into our rooms, I knew that mostly everyone was in bed for the night, or they were still cleaning the blood off of them. I was fortunate enough to be one of the few people to get nothing on me. While I did want to go to bed and just mull over what had happened with today's trial, I knew that I was hungrier than normal. I hadn't eaten since before we got our fingers burned off. I was probably going to grab a small snack anyway.

I was startled to see someone doing the same thing as me. I flipped the switch to the kitchen on and watched as they peeked behind them once. I felt the color drain from my face when I realized it was Justin, but he didn't act differently. Instead, he grabbed applesauce and grabbed two spoons. He sat at the table and looked at me expectedly.

"Are you going to sit?" he wondered. I hesitantly joined him as he started to dig into his apple sauce. He mushed it around in his cheeks before staring into the container. It wasn't what he wanted. It wasn't what I wanted either but to be polite, I stuck my spoon in there and swirled it around. I would eventually get enough courage to put some in my mouth.

"I'm sorry," I said. Justin looked up at me and stopped scraping the contents in the bowl. I shook my head. "It's my fault that you had to take a punishment or penalty."

"It's Colt's fault," Justin said. He dropped his spoon in the empty apple sauce container and looked up at me. "Your reaction was just that – a reaction."

                                        AMY KULP

"You aren't mad?" I asked.

"I'm upset," Justin answered. "But I know that you couldn't have helped it." He paused before grabbing my sauce that I wasn't eating. "Besides, I did the calculations. I'm smart and any trial they throw at us, we must use our brains. I could probably afford to denounce myself a couple places in this next trial." I nodded my head as I watched him finish my apple sauce. When he was done, he threw it out and sat back down at the table. "I can tell there's something else you want to ask me." I nodded my head and looked around. Nobody was in here but I couldn't hear anyone trying to come in either.

"What did you say for the last question?" I picked at the white tablecloth that was on the table and felt his eyes scanning me. When I looked back up, he smiled.

"Remember how Bischoff said there were trick questions?" I nodded my head, and he leaned in closer. "That was the only one and I know how you tricked the question." I raised my eyebrows up as he got out of his chair and stood next to me. He crouched down and got so close to my face that I was afraid if I flinched, we would kiss. "You let the timer run out. I bet that you would have been one of the first five done." I instantly started shaking my head and he smiled at me. "I picked myself."

"That was risky."

"You haven't been to a preparatory school," Justin said. "While I don't hate the inductees like some of us do, I did have the advantage of learning about these trials. Assassins don't think about things, they just follow rules."

"So, voting for yourself was the correct answer?" I wondered.

"I don't think there was a correct answer." He shrugged as he stood back up. "Although, like you, I am curious about who voted for who. Have you visited the training rooms?" I instantly shook my head and he smiled amusingly at me. "Come on, I'll show you them. It's where brainiacs can test their skills, muscle heads can test their abilities, and anyone else can improve their weaknesses. A lot of the elitists have been up there, but they won't mess with anyone because the injured assassins are in there."

"Who?" I asked. I stood up with him as he started leaving the kitchen. "Who are the injured assassins?"

"They really don't teach you anything in public school, do they?" he asked.

"About the trials? Nothing."

"Any assassin who comes back injured has those electricity sticks." He shook his head as he led me out of the room. "These rooms never close so if you can't sleep one night, you are more than welcome to come to them."

"Do you use them?"

"Sometimes," he answered. "Just follow me."

He led the way out of the kitchen. There seemed to be more people out and about now. On the couches were Audrey, Jordyn, and Heather crowded together. Heather was in the middle of them and she favored Audrey more than Jordyn. They were all deep in thought and didn't seem to want to talk too

AMY KULP

much. I think their minds were still reeling about what Jordyn had to do earlier. How prepared she was for it. I was shocked too. Near the pool table were Colt, Garrett, Eddie, Jamie, and Tanya. They were laughing obnoxiously with each other and as Justin and I passed them, I tensed up. I saw Garrett nudge Colt and they shared a knowing look toward each other.

"Hey, ponytail!"

Justin slowed down and looked back at me once before nodding for me to continue. I did and wasn't planning on talking to them or acknowledging them. I sighed when we got a little further down the hall and I heard something hit the wall. I stopped frozen for a second before hearing Tanya's high-pitched cackle.

"Hey, ponytail, I'm talking to you!"

"Let's go," Justin whispered at me. He eyed me and then looked over my shoulder. He began moving again and while I wanted to, my feet were stuck where they were. When I was done staring at the ball, I followed Justin but felt a force stopping me from moving.

"Don't ignore me when I talk to you." My hair was yanked back from me, and I felt Colt wrap his hand around it. I tried to look at Justin, but he was shaking his head and continued without me. Colt ripped my hair and spun me so that I could see him and tightened his grip on my hair.

"Get off of me," I said as I shoved him away. I felt the stinging of my fingers and tearing in my hair as he lost his grip and his balance. I yanked some of my hair back but saw some of it stay in his palms. I turned around but instantly hit Garrett.

"Don't touch him!"

"You're a cheater!" Tanya yelled as she came closer to me.

I circled myself around until I realized that they were enclosing me. Colt came up to me and yanked on my ponytail again. I felt the scrunchie come off and let my hair fall out of the braids it was in too.

"I bet you thought you looked so nice for all the boys here," Jamie whined. "Well, now look at you!"

"Hey, ponytail," Colt said again. I turned around to face him and felt someone shove me closer to him. Losing my balance, I hit his chest and pushed him to the ground. I could see the anger as I scrambled to get off him. His friends pushed me back down though and I found myself scared to move. "Are you excited to work with me all by yourself?"

"Don't flatter yourself," Tanya said. She crossed her arms and rolled her eyes. I could see Garrett and Eddie push her away and come closer.

"What is wrong with you?" I yelled as I pushed him away from me. He stood up and I immediately kicked at him. "Get off of me!"

"Can the smartest girl not figure a way out of this?" Garrett taunted.

"Smart enough to cheat," Tanya said as she pulled up my shirt. She pushed me back down to the ground and slapped the painful spots on my back. "I see you have two failed attempts."

                    AMY KULP

"Get off of me!" I yelled as I swatted her hands away. They all closed in on me and I suddenly felt claustrophobic. I looked for a small window between any of their bodies and nuzzled myself through that. "Leave me alone!"

I felt another yank on my hair before falling onto my back from the pain of electrocution. Next to me, Colt was lying still too. He managed to let go of my hair and I saw an injured assassin taking down everyone who was involved. When I came to my senses, I could see that Tanya, Garrett, and Jamie had escaped without being electrocuted. I looked up to where the injured assassin came from to see Justin standing in the hall. He gave me a smile and a nod before he went back down the hallway.

"You will receive additional punishments later," Bischoff said. I closed my eyes as I rested my head on the floor. I didn't know he came in. "Assassins do not hurt other assassins unless it is their mission."

"We were sparring," Colt said.

"Sparring is one-on-one," he said. "It's in the practice arena anyway. Not the living room. Unhand her hair and all three of you will be dealt with later." When my hair was let go, I reopened my eyes and stood up. I was still in pain, but I didn't want to be here when Bischoff and the injured assassin were still here. I walked off and instantly ran back to my room. Jade was happy to see me but when she saw that I wasn't smiling, she started asking fifty million questions. However, I sorted through the drawers until I saw what I was looking for and rushed to the bathroom. Holding it up high for her to see, she

yelled out in objection for me to stop. When the razor
hit my skin, she stood stunned for a second before I
turned around.

"Are you okay?"
"Can you help me shave my hair off?"
"How much?"
"All of it."

                                    AMY KULP

Trial #2

"You're like a furball." Instead of greeting me like a normal person or hugging me, Justin took his hands and swooshed them into my hair. I froze out of reaction and glared at him when he was done running his hands through my short hair. "You look better than half of the boys here."

"Are you sexist, Justin?" I wondered out loud. He retracted his hands from me and just stared hard. Almost like he was trying to figure me out. I continued to stare at him too and crossed my arms over my chest. He sighed for a moment and instead of answering, grabbed my arms to lead me to the training rooms.

I made sure to get up extra early to run into Justin. He was an early riser, but I never knew where he had been going once he was done eating. I waited right inside the inductees' living space and checked in on who was in the room. On days that we didn't have trials or were woken from an alarm, I usually woke around ten. If I was on the farm, it would be whenever the rooster crowed. Barely anything else seemed to ever wake me.

"A little," Justin answered when we were far enough down the hall that nobody could hear us. He stopped and turned back to me. "But I'm unlearning it." He smiled softly at me, but I could see the weariness in his eyes. "We all have different circumstances that we grew up in." I nodded my head and he finally let go of my arm. "I have seen so many kickass women in my life but I grew up with a dad who was wronged by one woman." He shook his head. "At least I'm giving everyone a chance."

"Why are you?" I wondered.

"Well," Justin paused. He looked down at me and looked around to make sure we weren't being listened to. However, we both knew that there were cameras probably everywhere. Justin was the smartest one here and he has studied previous trials. "Because you were the second smartest person here." He shrugged his shoulders. "Because you were willing to show compassion toward Colt despite how evident it is that he hates you because you're an inductee. It made me ask myself why I hate you because you're a girl."

"That doesn't make sense," I answered. I leaned against the white wall, and he just shook his head.

"I'm not rich like the other elitists," Justin admitted. "You remember that second house that we saw get ransacked?" I denied it. There were too many houses to remember. "Well, that was my house. It had neighbors and a fence." I stared at him. That little description wasn't going to help me. "Forget it."

He shook his head and turned around. I followed him silently and wished I knew what to say. I felt like he wanted me to help him feel better. I didn't understand though. If he was sexist, why would he help me? Why would I suddenly make him question how he thought and acted? He was the smartest person here. He should have realized that far before now. As he continued to stalk forward, I felt myself slowing down. He was the smartest assassin

AMY KULP

here and suddenly, he felt like he had to change his mind. That didn't sound right to me.

"Are you setting me up?" I questioned. I stopped in my tracks and watched Justin slow down. He seemed confused when he looked back at me. He shook his head when he turned toward me and walked back. He grabbed my wrist to usher me forward and I tried to flick my hand away. "Why are you trying to help me all of a sudden?" I stared at him as he pondered what to say. This seemed suspicious especially since I knew that he had to share a bedroom with Colt, Eddie, and Garrett.

"You're smart," Justin finally answered. "But you don't know anything about the trials." He watched me carefully and stepped closer to me. "There's a reason that a lot of inductees don't become official assassins. You don't know what to expect. You aren't taught about the secret pros of this place." His face softened as he stared at me. "I observe everyone. While you are reserved, you are kind to everyone. If I tell you about the secrets here, you will tell everyone."

"Why do you want that to happen?"

"I want the best assassins to win," Justin finally said. "I don't care if that means I won't make the cut. I want the best people to win. How is it fair that we all know about this stuff and you guys don't?"

"It's not," I answered.

"Exactly. You can choose to come if you want," Justin said as he turned back around. "I underestimated how smart you were, and I think you did too. If you think this is a trap, you aren't as observant as you think you are." He shook his head. "I don't get along with a lot of the elitists."

"Do you get along with Heather?" I asked. Despite feeling uneasy, I still followed Justin down the hallway. I stared at him as we walked and could see a small pink blush spread from his neck up to his cheeks. "Does she know where you live?" He nodded his head, and I sighed out.

I remember Heather acting weird about a house being mediocre. At the time, I assumed it was hers but knowing her and how kind she was, I had to assume she was embarrassed for Justin. I hope that wasn't an act just by his reactions. I hope that meant that they were going to be friends and stay away from that group that I dealt with yesterday.

As soon as we entered the training room, everybody who was in there stopped to turn toward us. Since it was so early in the morning, there didn't seem to be as many people here. There was someone who was working on the treadmills but someone else was working on what looked to be a matching game.

"You can train your physical fitness over there," Justin said. He pointed to the area, and I didn't recognize any of the machines besides the treadmills. When I looked back at him, he was climbing up some stairs and I had to jog to catch up with him. "Here, you can train your brain. There are matching games, trivia, and scenario questions. There are also tutorials and videos on past trials. I felt like that would benefit you the most." He turned around and I looked at the screen. I nodded as I touched it and it started giving the history of the trials. "We're not done yet." He walked backward as

                                    AMY KULP

he led me up more stairs and got to the high point of the area. As soon as I got to where Justin was, I could see down below an arena. "That is for sparring and combat matches."

"What's the difference?" I wondered. I started walking down the stairs to look at the field closer. It reminded me of a hockey rink with how the seats were turned toward the center. It seemed to be dirt and grass. I could see gym mats bunched up in the corner but nothing else.

"Sparring is where we're pitted against each other. It ends when one of you wants to quit," Justin said. He set his arms on the arena's ring and leaned forward. "Combat matches depend. You can choose to use an injured assassin and they'll help you and give you tips. You might get a bit beat up but they're there to help you." He paused. "You can also choose to do it with one of us. It doesn't end until both of you decide to quit." He paused and looked at me awkwardly. "Or until one of you passes out." He eyed me as I nodded my head and looked out there. There seemed to be blood stains on the white floor and while not a lot, it was visible. Maybe they chose not to clean it up. "I'm sorry," he whispered.

I stopped looking around the arena to look back at him. He had a sorrowful look on his face and sat down at one of the benches. However, my nerves were on a high end as I looked around the arena to see injured assassins flooding the place. I had hands on my shoulders and hands pushing me into the arena before I could figure out what was happening. I looked back at Justin, but he refused to meet my gaze as he sat back in his chair and watched the middle of the arena. I turned my gaze back to the arena to see what was interesting to him, but the hands forced me over the ring.

I landed with a plop but once I was in, I didn't have any more hands on me. I dusted my clothes off and tried to stare out to the seats but now that I was in, there seemed to be a haze that I couldn't see through. When I turned back around, Colt and Eddie were now standing at the edges too. When they noticed me, they gave each other a look before walking over to me. I felt the blood drain my face and I ran opposite of them. When I ran into the wall and had no more space to run, I watched as Colt and Eddie got closer to me. However, both of their faces dropped when they saw me.

"What happened to your hair?" Eddie howled. He doubled over with laughter and only stopped when Colt elbowed him. It wasn't until they were right next to me that we saw three other people at the other end of the arena.

"Come one, come all," Bischoff called. "To the punishment of Eddie Marlowe, Colt Kirkman, and Bridget Solomon." He stepped in the middle of the arena and the three other people that were across from them stepped forward. I didn't recognize any of them. When I looked back out of the arena, I could make out blobs of elitists and inductees sitting around the arena. Some were intently watching while others were busy talking to their friends. I pinpointed Jade, Nia, and Toby sitting together with their backs turned away from the action. When I could see Justin, he was sitting with Heather, Audrey, and Jordyn. They were all staring into the arena but didn't

                AMY KULP

seem to be enjoying it. Maybe they were concentrating. "Assassins do not harm others without it being their mission. So, I have brought three of my best." He brought his arm out with a flourish to show off his band of green assassins. "To join you in a combat match."

"I don't want to be part of this!" I said quickly. I put my hands up ready to surrender and could see Eddie and Colt's disgusted faces with me. I looked back at Bischoff to see an amused smile on his face as well.

"That would be a sparring match. This is a combat match where everybody must give up before the match ends," Bischoff noted. When I looked over at Colt and Eddie, they both shook their heads.

"I could take them," Eddie gloated. "Bring it on."

There was a bell from somewhere in the room and instantly, the three assassins at the other end came running toward us. I quickly lost sight of two of them and kept my eyes on the one who slowed his run to a walk. He walked toward me menacingly and I could see the evil smile on his face. Thankfully, he did not have an electricity stick so I knew that it would be at least fair that we were both fighting with just our hands. I ran away from him and to the right. I kept going and when I looked back, I could see that he was still just walking. He wanted this to be torture for me.

While he was walking, I looked around and could see that Eddie was on the floor. He was being tag-teamed by the remaining two assassins. I could see kicks with their legs and punches with their hands. He grunted with every assault that occurred to his body. I wanted to help but with the other assassin after me, I wasn't sure how much time I had.

I wasn't a fighter. I didn't know how to throw a proper punch, nor did I want to hurt anybody. Could I defend myself? I had no idea. I couldn't the other night when the elitists attacked me. That was the entire reason we were in this predicament today. However, I was smart. I could work my way out of this.

I looked behind me once again to see how close or far the other assassin was from me and knew that I had some time. I looked around the arena trying to find something to help me and as soon as I saw the mats again, I ran toward them. I felt a sweat break out from my forehead and when I was as close to them as I could get, I felt something crash into my side. My immediate reaction was that it was the assassin that was trying to get me. However, when I looked up, I could see blondie running away from me.

I couldn't tell if that was intentional or accidental.

"Dude, I already forfeited!" I yelled as the assassin hovered over me. He brought his boot up to stomp on me, but I quickly moved my leg out of the way. I wiggled away from him and regretted not standing up as soon as I could. I was at a disadvantage right now. He reached down and grabbed my leg. With all his might, he pulled me toward him and jumped on top of me. I let out a shriek and looked behind me. I just need a mat to protect myself. I reached my hand out and stretched

                              AMY KULP

but the assassin that was on top of me dug his nails into my arms. "Why are you trying to hurt me? I'm just trying to survive the trials." I crawled away from him and managed to hold onto one of the mats. He grabbed my leg again and pulled me away.

From around the arena, I could see that Colt and Eddie were teaming up together against one of the assassins. Looking around, I couldn't seem to find the other one though. I didn't have much time to look because I could feel hands around my neck and pressing so that I couldn't breathe. My lungs began to burn and he dug my nails into his hands. Slapping me across the face, my cheek stung and he grasped my neck harder. I looked back at Colt and Eddie to see that they had won their tangle with the assassin and were just staring at me. I tried to beg for help, but no noise came out of my throat. I reached my hand out toward them as black dots started dancing around my vision, but they just stared at me. I knew that they weren't going to help so I did the only thing my brain could think of, I stuck a finger right into his eye.

He jolted back and let the pressure on my neck go. I immediately twisted around and gasped for air. I tried to scramble away but he grabbed onto my leg again and slid me toward him. He got on top and held down my arms. I could see movement from the corner of my eye and was hoping that it was Colt and Eddie. However, I knew that they were just watching me struggle with a smile on their face.

The movement I saw was that of the other assassin's boot stomping down on my face which broke my nose and had me pass out. At least then, they left me alone.

#

When I became conscious again, I didn't open my eyes first. I allowed myself to try and figure out where I was. Yet, there was no noise and there wasn't a soft, cushiony bed underneath my body. Instead, it felt hard and firm. Maybe it was the floor or a bench. I allowed myself even longer to sit there and wait to feel anything. My face hurt and I could barely breathe through my nose but that seemed to be it.

"Get up." I didn't move and kept trying to make air move through my nostrils. It felt blocked. "I know you're awake, get up." I heard noise from somewhere else in the room and could hear them walking closer to me. I immediately recoiled away from them and blinked my eyes a couple of times before I could straighten out that blondie was in front of me. He seemed perfectly fine. I wasn't sure that he was hurt at all.

"Where am I?" I asked as I looked around. Everything was white but everything around here was. It was hard for me to pinpoint the differences between some of the different rooms. When I saw the blood in the corner of the room, I nodded my head. "We're onto our second punishment, aren't we?"

"You are a genius," Colt replied coldly. He bent down beside me and handed me a rag. He dipped his rag into a bucket of warm water and started scrubbing. "I'm not going to do all of the work." He didn't look at me again before beginning

                                        AMY KULP

to scrub. There was a second bucket that when I got up and bent down toward, I could smell it was chemicals. Maybe bleach.

"Did we win?" I asked as I kneeled where some of the blood was. He scoffed and kept scrubbing. He didn't seem interested in conversation, so I set the same tone with him. I could do my job without talking to him.

"You really are stupid," he commented. He came back over to the bucket and rung out his bloody rag. "Of course, we didn't win our punishment." He shook his head and dipped the rag in again before moving across the room. "Clearly, you passed out and Eddie was ganged up on from the beginning."

"Why didn't you help me?" I asked. I turned around and stared at him. He pretended not to notice and kept scrubbing away at the blood that was on the walls. I threw the dirty rag at him and waited for him to turn around. Instead, he kept scrubbing. "And why aren't you hurt? There doesn't seem to be a scratch on you!"

"It's because I actually use my brains," he commented. He turned around and I could see the fury in his eyes. He charged toward me and when he got too close, I stepped back. My foot went into the bucket of bleach, and I tried getting my foot out. Falling over the object and bucket, my body landed backward and as I landed, I felt a sharp pain run through my entire body. A yell came out of my mouth and before I could react, I moved away from the pain and rammed my body into Colt's legs for protection. I instinctively reached for one of his hands and held onto it as I tried to think about what just happened.

Neither of us said anything as we stared at the circle of blood. It was Daniel's circle that stung me. When Colt inched forward to peer at it, I did too. I didn't want to but with my body pressed against his legs, I didn't think that I had a choice. He leaned over me and peered into the circle. When I looked too, I could see my handprint mark on there. Looking back at my hand, I could see that it looked like the entire first layer of skin was burnt off.

"Looks like Bischoff did amp it up a little bit," he whispered. He crouched down next to me and gently took my hand away from my body. He opened up my fingers and looked at the discoloration of my hand. "The circle is still red. Maybe we can clean the other ones but not the rings with red around it."

"You stick your hand in there and you can find out," I said as I took my body part away from him. His expression softened a bit as I hid myself away from him.

"Like I said, I'm going to actually use my brains."

He stood up at once and grabbed the bucket that had tripped me. Going to a circle that had green on it, he hesitated and looked back at me. When he realized that he had my interest and that I was staring at him, he threw the bucket into the circle and waited. When nothing happened, I looked back up at him to see him put his foot down in the circle. He hopped in again and again and gave a thumbs up to me.

"So, we know to clean everything but the two red circles," Colt mentioned. I nodded my head and

                                    AMY KULP

tossed the rag at him. He caught it and went right back to scrubbing.

Okay, we weren't talking again. I knelt too and scrubbed carefully around the two red circles. You could barely see what color they were from how much blood had completely soaked through. I could hear Colt moving around the room faster than me, but my hand was killing me. Between that and my nose, I wasn't sure how much more pain I could take. I knew I had to be strong though. Maybe I should start using my brain too. Get him to scrub most of it off the floor. He wasn't injured at all.

"How did you get out uninjured again?" I wondered. He was ringing out his rag over the bucket of water and just smiled at me. I scrubbed at a smear of red on the floor next to me and watched as he moved across the room. He started wiping down the walls, but he was smart enough to keep me in the corner of his eyes.

"I pretended to pass out," he mentioned. He shrugged his shoulders at the thought. That was so smart. I would never have thought of that. "Don't steal my secret."

"Hopefully, I won't be in another combat match," I mentioned. I aimed the rag toward the bucket and made it in with a splash. I could hear some of the water droplets hitting the red circle and found the sizzling to be soothing. "I don't know if my nose can take another hit to it."

"I don't see any more blood anywhere," Colt mentioned. He turned around and threw his rag in too. He looked at me for a second before walking toward me. "I'm sorry about your nose getting broken. It looked brutal." He stared at my face and when he outstretched his arms, I didn't feel the need to revolt away. Instead, I let his hands cradle my chin. He moved his body closer to mine and while staring at my nose, I could see his eyes linger a little lower too.

Hearing the doors open up behind us, I tried to look but felt his fingers gripping my chin harder. He took one hand and quickly pinched the bridge of my nose before I could react. I yelled out in pain but before I could squirm away, I could hear my nose snap again as he pushed it. I whipped away from him and heard some shouts of approval for him. I put my hands into my face and felt more blood falling out of my nostrils. I'm not sure who was beside me, but they ushered me toward the side and aggressively took my hands away.

"Come on, our second trial is starting." Jade pushed me to where we needed to stand and it took me a second to look up. "Is your nose dry?" she wondered. I let my hands fall from my face and she grimaced as she looked at it. "On the bright side, it looks like it's straight, If it was crooked, they might have to realign your nose." She ran a finger gently down the bridge and smiled again. "You were lucky there."

I nodded my head and repeated that word before turning toward Bischoff. I could see Colt on the other side of the room and while he was actively paying attention to what we were being told, I saw his eyes flick toward me for a second. Did he just realign my nose? Or did he do it so that it would hurt me? Could it have been both?

                                    AMY KULP

"Do I have any volunteers to go first?" Bischoff asked as he looked around. I instantly started to panic as I watched hands rise in the air. What did I just miss? I looked over to see Shane and all the elitists raising their hands. Bischoff smiled at everyone's eagerness and quickly scanned the crowd again for his first victim. "Asher Johnston."

The shortest elitist stepped forward and smirked at everyone as he walked up to the door opposite everyone. He got into a stance for running and when a buzzer rang out, he bolted through. The doors quickly closed behind him, and I was only able to peek inside to see pitch-blackness. What was this challenge?

"How'd your punishment go?" Jade asked as her eyes scanned my face. "You really need to stay out of trouble. Try to keep a low profile."

"I am trying to do that," I whispered to her. "What is this trial?" I looked around as everyone started sitting down. They continued to stare at the door and when Jade and I were some of the last people standing, we followed suit and sat down too. Mostly everyone was talking in hushed voices on our side but the Elitists were completely quiet.

"Physical fitness," Jade said.

I looked around at the others and could see some were stretching their limbs. Jade bent down and I copied her movements. I loosely grasped one foot with my bad hand and tried not to wince. I didn't need anybody to know I had a weakness right now. I could feel the tension in the backs of my legs as I leaned forward. I usually never stretched and felt inadequate in my ability to stretch properly.

"Now," Bischoff said getting back to the front. "We have two courses to speed things up a bit." He looked around at everybody and some of the Elitists already started raising their hands. "On this second course, I have decided on someone who didn't volunteer last time and probably isn't prepared." I felt myself beginning to shrink behind Jade. This couldn't have been directed at me, right? "Would Colt Kirkman, Bridget Solomon, and Justin Frazier please step forward?" Jade looked behind herself and made way for me to be the center of attention. On the other side of the room, Colt stood proudly while Justin seemed less confident than before. "These three have chosen whether they wanted a punishment or a penalty for their next challenge." I made sure that my hands weren't facing Bischoff and pressed them into my body. While it stung, I didn't need him to know what had happened. "Justin had chosen the penalty." Justin nodded his head and walked toward the second door that was there. "Your penalty is a ten-second delay. Good luck."

I watched as he got into a stance to begin running and as soon as those doors started to open, he dashed through. I could see further into this one as they were still opening as he ran. It still seemed rather dark, but I could see that it was a straight runway. I'm sure it was going to be harder than it looked though. If they were testing our physical fitness, they wouldn't just have us run.

"Colt, you did volunteer so once someone finishes, you will be next up." Bischoff then turned to me and I felt my nerves getting to me. "Bridget,

                    AMY KULP

you did not volunteer so you will run the course after Colt." I nodded and swiftly looked over at him.

He didn't move from his spot up front and I felt like I had to mimic all his movements. I had no idea what was considered respectful versus rude. I wanted to go talk to Jade and Nia while I waited. I didn't want to just stand here and think about what this course could look like. I wasn't too worried about my fitness since I did live on a farm. It had its advantages – I knew that I was strong enough to move a cow. However, I didn't have endurance. I couldn't run forever, and it took me forever to catch my breath. As my eyes looked back at Colt, I could see that he had muscles on his arms. His calves were like steel, and he had shown me that he could scrub the floors and walls without getting sore. He would be doing well in this trial.

"Colt," Bischoff said. Colt nodded his head and went to the door that started opening. "You may begin."

Off he went and this time, his path was light. I could see that there were materials littered all over the floor. They were too far away for me to tell exactly what they were, but it would have to be something to jump over. As the doors began closing, I could also see a wall. Nothing beyond that grey slab of concrete though. It was there to prevent everyone from seeing exactly what we were up against.

"Bridget." I looked up at him confused but he motioned for me to step to the door. Justin was done already? "You may begin."

I copied Justin's movements and started running before the doors opened all the way. I wasn't the fastest runner, but I tried my hardest. As soon as I heard those doors close behind me, I slowed my pace and looked around. My room was dark just like Justin's and Asher's. As I started catching up to the grey wall, I could see the black circles on the ground. I stopped completely when my shoe hit one and knew the smell – these were tires. I hopped one foot in one and another in a second one. I knew I was supposed to be quick, so I hurried along. I smiled as I got the hang of it and quickly hit one of my hands off the top of my knees. If I kept high knees, I should be fine with this. My body hopped along until my shoe hit the dirty ground. When I was out, I was face to face with the grey wall.

It was ginormous and had to be as tall as my house – maybe even taller! There weren't any holes for me to grab onto and when I put my hands on it to feel it, the coolness helped soothe my burn. However, the wall was greasy and slippery. There was no way I could climb this. I looked up to make sure I wasn't missing anything but there wasn't a rope that I could use to climb up. If there was, I think it would be too painful for me to grip properly.

Maybe this wasn't just a physical fitness test. I looked around at my feet and grabbed two tires. I stacked them on each other and grabbed more. If I made this high enough, maybe I could reach the top. I was the second smartest person here anyway. Were there any rules to these trials? I heaved two more tires on the pile and just scratched my head. This was going to take too long. There had to be some other way.

                              AMY KULP

I jumped on top of my stack of tires and found just how wobbly it was. My balance betrayed me, and I instantly capsized onto my side. Getting the breath knocked out of me, I watched as the tires rolled everywhere. How was I supposed to get up this wall? I picked up any tires that were around me and when I got to the one that was in the farthest corner, I could see that the wall didn't stretch the entire length of the walkway. I threw the tires in my hand back and pressed my body against the wall. I squeezed my way through and didn't breathe until my entire body made it through.

That was easier than expected.

I looked up to see that the wall had nets coming from it now. While the goal was to get up the wall and then grab onto the net, I still wasn't sure how people got up there. Maybe I didn't need to touch the net. The floor seemed fine and as I ran across, I made it to the next obstacle.

There were barbed wires that were very close to the ground. If I tried to run through, my legs and feet would be mauled with scratches and cuts. I might even get my ankle cut off. This would be something I have to crawl through. I lowered my body instantly and ducked my head underneath as I shimmied my body through. I could feel some of the razors cutting my scalp and was so thankful that I cut my hair. Imagine having to tear your hair out if it got caught on one of these? I shook my head and kept it low as another one hit me. I reached my elbow into the ground ahead of me and saw the razors get lower. I couldn't lower my body anymore though. I accepted my fate and let the wire scrape the skin off my lower arm and catch in my pants. As soon as I saw the end, I got up too soon and the spike caught on my clothing. I had to wrangle it free with my hand and to do that, I had to grab hold of the wires and yank it off. My fingers felt almost useless as they dripped blood onto the floor. I pressed it harder into my clothes to stop the bleeding and looked at my next obstacle.

It was a rope swing and it seemed to go on for miles. Falling off didn't seem to be an option as underneath, was black. I didn't know how deep this was but as I kicked off a shoe to listen to it hit the ground, nothing could be heard. I listened for a couple more seconds before shaking my head and looking at the swing again. I could not hold onto rope. My hands were too mutilated for that and the rough strands would probably make me fall off into this black hole. I listened a second longer to see if my boot hit yet but no noise was heard.

I sat down and carefully grabbed the rope with my feet. As it got closer to me, I worked on the end to make a knot. If I did it strong enough, I could possibly step on it and just swing down like that. My left hand was killing me though and I knew that I was wasting time. I wanted to survive though. I needed to survive. I worked through the pain that I was feeling until it knotted itself. When I tugged on it, it seemed to be strong enough. I put the foot that had the boot on the knot and quickly stood on it. I wrapped my arms around the rope and held it so close to my body. I had no idea how to get this to swing to the other end. Maybe a running start? I backed up and ran with all my might. I closed my eyes as I began sliding

                                    AMY KULP

down and waited until I felt the momentum stop. When I opened my eyes, I instantly panicked as I wasn't at the end of the swing yet. Underneath me was all black. I could no longer see if I was closer to the end I started at or the end that I needed to go to. Everything around me was just black.

I closed my eyes again and refused to move. I didn't know how to do this. I knew my balance was off and if I looked, I was going to plummet to the bottomless pit. As I tried not to cry, my belly moved from the intense sobbing I may have done. This motion caused my swing to move forward and I stopped instantly. I jutted out my belly again and felt the motion too. Maybe if I swung like it was a tire swing, I would get somewhere. I continued to do this until I felt land hit my feet. I fell forward and quickly scampered along the floor.

Looking back behind me, I could see the swing retreating to the starting position and could see the lights turn on. I looked down at the ground to see if there was a bottom but before I could look completely, the lights were, once again, turned off.

I shouldn't even be focusing on that right now. I had to get through this obstacle course. I looked straight ahead and could see different ladders all around. While my brain wanted me to avoid them, I could see the glass that was scattered all through. It seemed to shine in the darkness. I quickly climbed the first ladder I saw and as my skin pressed into the first step, I felt the splintered. I cursed under my breath but continued to climb. When I came back down on the other side, I was met with another ladder. Thankfully this time, there were no splinters.

I continued to the other side and jumped to make it to the next step. There was a tiny space where if I wasn't paying attention, I could have fallen through.

What was my next obstacle? I put my hands on my stomach as I had to bend down to catch my breath. I needed to keep going though. There were three long twisty black tubes now. I knew that I was expected to go through them, but it seemed to be stupidly twisting and turning. I didn't have time for this. I climbed on top and as my body moved across them, I kept my foot in the middle of where the two were meeting At least this way, if I fell, I was falling between the two tubes and could easily get my footing back. Another fear was that my body was going to cave in a tube. They didn't seem that steady to begin with.

However, as I made it to the other side in a much shorter time than I would have if I crawled, I knew that I was getting toward the end. While it was dark, this next part I just had to run. So I did. It felt weird to run with one shoe on and one shoe off so halfway through, I kicked it off. I felt my speed improve immensely and despite how much my lungs were burning, I continued to run. I ran and ran. Maybe I ran miles, but I knew that if I got to the finish line, I would need to take a breather. I forced myself to continue though. I didn't stop until I got to another rope.

Once again, this rope was suspended over a black bottomless pit. However, there wasn't anything to cross it with. I carefully placed my foot on it but felt it waver. If I tried to run across this, I would fall off. I didn't have that great of balance to

AMY KULP

begin with. How else was I supposed to do this? I got onto my knees and placed my hand on the rope this time. The scratchiness did not react well with my burnt and splintered hands. Instead, I bent down lower and wrapped my arms in the rope. I inched forward like a worm and the rope brushed roughly against my neck. I moved forward and as I did; my body began to droop, and I tucked the rope between my legs. My body flipped itself, but I continued to move like a worm. If I didn't think about the near possibility of death, I could make it across.

When I finally felt the floor press against my back, I let out my breath and let go of the rope. I lay there for a minute to catch my breath but knew that I couldn't last long. I got up and despite how out of shape I was, I continued. This looked like another long run. I ran as fast as I could but knew that it wasn't lasting. My pace was slowed, and I was tired. My body was all scratched up from the ropes and I wasn't in good shape to begin with.

I didn't get to rest my body in preparation for this trial. I was beaten up in combat, then I had to clean an entire room with someone who hated me, and then I was thrown into this immediately. I knew that the first nap I took after this was going to be the best thing I had ever experienced. I would probably be sleeping for days. No noise would reach my ears and I would wake up refreshed and more youthful than I am.

I just needed to finish this trial.

With the lights completely out, I couldn't see anything anymore. I ran and ran, and I may have only run for five minutes but with the darkness, I couldn't keep track. I stripped off my shirt so that I didn't feel suffocated and continued to run. I could feel the sweat dripping off my body and only when I hit a wall, did I take a breath. Why would they have a wall in a pitch-black section of this?

I barely picked my head up when the wall opened, and I could see a white room. Asher, Justin, Colt, Shane, and Heather were staring at me. I kept my body on the ground and let myself breathe.

"Bridget, your timer is still going on. You must come into the room," Justin said as he looked up. I'm assuming it was because of a timer. I nodded my head and just rolled my body toward everyone. When I finally made it onto the white floor, I allowed myself to stare at the ceiling. I looked up toward the door too, but the timer reset and someone else was now running the track. "You okay?" he wondered.

"Yeah, I just need a nap," I said as I turned to my side.

"How about you move from the door?" Justin asked. I already had my eyes closed and made some sort of noise coming from my mouth. I felt two hands grab my arm and two hands grab my waist before they pushed me closer to them. I was so close to them that I could feel their shoes on my back as I kept my eyes closed. "Forgive me for setting you up for the combat matches?" Justin whispered to me. I heard him and I believe I nodded my head, but I was already so comfortable that I knew I was falling asleep.

Surprisingly, sleeping on the floor was amazing compared to the beds that they provided.

#

"Colt Kirkman."

He smugly made his way up to the front and stood proudly in his circle. His stance was wide as his feet touched both ends. He held his hands behind his back and pointed his chin up toward the ceiling. Probably just another way to show that he was better than everyone else.

"Shane Newfeld."

He gave Colt a nod but other than that, they didn't shake hands. It made me question whether this was really a competition to pit Elitists and Inductees together. Nobody seemed to be working together yet. Although I do believe that Justin and Jade might be the exception. Justin talks to us and Jade talks to them. At least, she did when she was one of the only people here. I have only seen her talk to Nia, myself, and Toby. She was friendly with everyone but did not interact with them anymore. At least, when I was around her. I seemed to be spending more time with the Elitists anymore – whether it was for punishment or to understand them more. I would have to introduce her and Justin together if they didn't already talk.

"Heather Flick."

I mildly clapped along. I was surprised to see a girl so high up in the ranks, but I was proud. She shook Colt's hands and when she went to shake Shane's, he avoided it. There was no pushing or shoving. Instead, she went to her circle with a smile on her face. It was so weird to see how different people reacted to each other.

"Eddie Marlowe."

I turned my attention toward Jade. She seemed to have taken a lot more injuries than me. While her hands were rope burned too, she had a couple scratches on her face and all up and down her body. I'm sure that we would all have to take care of ourselves. Those razor fields seemed to do a lot of us damage. She was clapping along as everyone was called and despite how much it hurt her, she made sure to do it loud. She was like everybody's cheerleader.

"Asher Johnston."

I looked around at everyone to compare how exhausted I was to them. They all seemed to be staring straight forward as if they had a chance to change the outcomes. Maybe it was the proper etiquette that I hadn't learned yet.

"Audrey Beck."

She slunk forward as her name was called. She seemed to be exhausted and I could see her legs jiggle with every step. For as young as she was, I was surprised she did so well on this test. Maybe she was destined to be a good assassin.

"Tanya Booth." Even she didn't have enough energy to snub the Inductees, she quietly shook everyone's hands and walked over to her circle. "Anthony Denkins." He walked forward and took his place. "Justin Frazier."

I tried to look at him as he moved forward but he was determined to get to his circle. With his penalty, I'm surprised that he scored so high. It made me feel worse about myself. I was still here and didn't get called. As I looked around, it seemed that

                    AMY KULP

most of the females scored in the lower half of the physical fitness test. That made me even more determined to do better next time.

"Jamie Scott." There was a slight pause in Bischoff's words as he looked at the Elitists and Inductees. "The next two people came in at the exact same time but are placed based on if they volunteered – Cassandra Vise." She hopped forward and I clapped along with everyone else. I had to support her. "Nia Williams." Next to Jade, Nia skipped toward her circle. Almost as if she wasn't nervous about these outcomes. "Jade Tricase."

I clapped as Jade sent me a smile. However, with her leaving my side, I felt insecure about my abilities again. There were only four other people still sitting here. They all seemed confident that they were going to make it through. I stared back up at Jade so that she would reassure me, but she was too busy chatting about something with Nia. I gulped and looked at the line that was forming and even Justin was busy. He seemed to have a telepathic conversation with Heather. The only person that was looking at me was Colt.

"Garrett Arnold."

When I felt a hand grab mine, I stopped my staring contest with blondie and looked at Toby. He smiled at me sympathetically. I squeezed his hand too. While I hated these trials, I had no desire to die. I hated what I would have to do if I survived, but I didn't want to die. I had so many things I wanted to experience.

"Toby Ernst."

"You are fine," Toby whispered to me as he got to his circle.

I gulped as I looked at the three remaining circles. When I looked around, there were only two of us left. My eyes went back over to the circles and counted again – one, two, three. There were three circles left. Yet when I counted the remaining participants, there were only two – myself and Leah. Where was the third person?

"Bridget Solomon, you beat the bottom two by one second."

My jitters stopped instantly, and I looked back over at Leah. She smiled at me and held out her arms. She wrapped me in them, and I could see the tears beginning to form in her eyes. She nodded her head for me to go and despite how many hateful glares I was getting, I tried to shake everyone's hands. Colt led the reactions of everyone else and while he refused to shake my hand, he didn't spit at me this time. I quickly tried everyone else's and only a couple more refused.

It wasn't until I shook Toby's hand that I stepped into the circle. I felt my feet vibrating and stared down at the circle. Maybe it's because last time I had boots on and couldn't feel it, but the vibrations felt nice against my aching arches. It was concerning though. As I moved my feet around in the circle, it seemed to take a second before it found me again. I finally stopped when he announced Leah's name.

"Finally in last place, Jordyn Carr." I stared at the empty room and I could see others staring at each other. "Unfortunately, Jordyn did not make it

                                   AMY KULP

out of the physical fitness course." He paused and turned toward all of us. "While this was physical fitness, we still wanted you to use your brains. If there is a black hole, it is obviously not going to have a fall. Some of you did great with this – whether you threw a boot or stacked all of the tires up to get over that wall, or simply ran the course as you needed to. Others were hung up on how to go over the wall, some of you didn't know how to get through the barbed wire, and others simply couldn't combine their athletics and their brains." Bischoff turned toward Leah. "Leah, you are, unfortunately, not made out to be an assassin."

"Cut with the anticipation and just tell me who is killing me." She crossed her arms and closed her eyes. "I'm too old for this."

We all looked at our circles and I held my breath in hopes that I wouldn't be picked. I grabbed onto Toby's hand next to me and while I stared at his circle, he stared at mine. When I could hear someone moving out, I let go of Toby's hand and stared toward the front of the circles. Colt was handed a gun and while I would normally assume he would be excited; his face was ghostly white. He had no expression and despite this, he still looked worried.

He didn't say anything as he walked toward Leah. Almost making it more torturous by not just shooting her. She had to listen to him walk toward her. He kept getting closer and closer. He got closer to her and closer to everyone in the circles. He didn't stop moving until his arm was touching my skin. I wanted to step back but knew that I would be out of my circle if I did. Instead, I stood up straighter and pressed my skin into his. He looked at my entire body briefly before holding up his gun right next to Leah's forehead. I knew she could feel the metal.

I kept my gaze on Colt as he blasted the gun. He looked away as he pulled the trigger, and we kept eye contact as her body hit the floor. He was covered in blood, and I could feel it running down my body. I could see it on my left arm and feel it on my face. I could see it running down Colt's as well. I broke our eye contact first to look at the blood running down him. He handed the gun off to Bischoff without saying anything and when people started moving, we both broke our contact to look at Leah's lifeless body.

It was only when Garrett pulled Colt away from me that either of us moved. But I could see it in his face. I could see that he had never killed anyone before. I could see that he had never wanted to kill anyone. I could see just how emotional he was underneath the mask he was wearing.

Maybe there was a little something more to him than I thought.

                    AMY KULP

I winced as soon as Jade put the gel on my hands, but I made sure to stay as quiet as I could. A small groan escaped my lips and I had to take a moment to close my eyes. If I became too overstimulated or too much pain was felt in one place on my body, I was fearful that I would pass out and make a commotion. My goal before the next trial was to heal any existing wounds I had and to stay under the radar. I felt that my best bet was to stick with Jade or Justin. I knew that I couldn't be alone or that the Elitists would gang up on me.

"Can I wrap them now?" Jade asked. She waited until I opened my eyes and nodded my head before unrolling the gauze in her hands. She kept eye contact with me as she began wrapping my right hand and tried to make it as tight as she could without hurting me. I would never admit when she did, but she has learned to read my facial expressions – a slight eye twitch or curling of my lips were two signs that it was going to be too much. She carefully tucked the gauze's end and reached for my second hand. I gave it to her without protest and watched as she delicately redid the same process. When she was done, she set the roll beside me and looked at my face. "There seems to be very little swelling."

"But the bruising," I noted. I turned toward the mirror and could see the dark black bruises on my nose and around my eyes. I wanted to shake my head, but Jade was ready to wipe my face with a cold washrag. She placed her hand under my chin and lifted it until my head was tilted in the correct lighting. I closed my eyes as the pressure rubbed against my nose and she placed it on my eyes for a couple of seconds. When my face was very swollen, it helped to keep some of it down. Now, it just seemed to give me a slight chill. She turned back to the sink and twisted the washcloth out until no more water could be rung from it.

Turning back to me, she had the antibiotic cream ready for some of the nasty cuts that were around my body. I prepared by rolling up my pant legs and moving my shirt for her to get the worst ones. They were blotchy red with pink irritation surrounding them. The cream didn't make a difference to me, but she swore it helped heal it faster. The cuts didn't matter to me as much as the burns on my hands did.

Satisfied with her work, she sat down on the bench beside me. I could see her guard falling as she sat there and stared at herself in the mirror; her back began to hunch, the smile disappeared, and the worry lines appeared on her forehead. I gave it a couple more seconds before I stood up and grabbed the peroxide and a cotton ball.

Now it was my turn to help her. While Jade swore by the antibiotic cream, I swore by peroxide. At least with that, you could see the germs being killed. She closed her eyes as I dunked the brown bottle into the cotton and let the liquid soak into it. I pressed onto her face and watched as the deep red fizzled into white. I could see her skin turning a light pink surrounding it and as I dabbed more on it, the skin kept getting pinker. It was almost like I could see the peroxide spreading through the body.

                                AMY KULP

I repeated this process on her on all the cuts on her body. She confided in me that she was embarrassed to have them. Despite having a better time than me in the last trial, she felt that she made a lot more mistakes. She was one of the only ones who seemed to be more beat up than me. She tripped over the tires, she couldn't grip the rope, and she found it difficult to crawl. However, we were both planning on helping each other today with our weaknesses. I was just hoping that I wouldn't need to do too much with my hands.

"I don't think that Nia is coming," Jade commented. "And I feel uneasy about going with Justin."

I nodded as I put the bottle and cotton ball back. I knew to stay quiet when I disagreed with people so that I didn't start an argument. However here, staying quiet seemed to make people think that I was ignoring them. I didn't want to be rude, but I was still trying to figure people out. I couldn't tell who I was going to be friends with and who was going to hate me. I didn't want to accidentally expose the wrong side to the wrong people. I wasn't sure if any of the Elitists were the right people though – they all wanted to be part of this. The inductees seemed more trustworthy but some of them gave me the creeps – specifically Shane. Why were people getting excited to kill people?

"You okay?" Jade asked. I nodded and turned to face her. She grabbed my arm in comfort and stayed quiet. I finally looked at her to ease the tension. "Are you thinking about the blood?"

I nodded again. I couldn't get Leah's blood out of my head. I swore that I tasted it when I ate sometimes. The metallic taste always smeared into my sandwiches, and I gagged every time. I haven't been able to complete an entire meal yet. There was never any blood in them though so someone would eat what I didn't want. If it wasn't the taste in my mouth, it was the feeling of the drops dripping down my face. The cool liquid felt too realistic to be part of my daydream. By the time I made it to a mirror, all of it was gone but I could still feel it.

"How come you weren't affected by it?" I asked as we left the bathroom. We were careful not to make too much noise as we crossed the bedrooms. Cassandra and Nia were both still sleeping underneath their blankets. We originally invited them, but Cassandra immediately shot us down while Nia wasn't too sure. I wasn't going to force either of them but would've loved it if they had come with us. Cassandra knew that it was too early for her.

She always seemed to be sleeping. The only time she was ever up was to go to the bathroom, get some food, and partake in the trials. I wasn't even sure if she showered and most of the time, it didn't look like it. At least she didn't smell.

"I wasn't right next to it," Jade commented. "Didn't you grow up on a farm?" Jade asked as we stepped foot in the kitchen. I nodded, but I wasn't sure that she could see me as her gaze was already geared toward the boy who was rummaging through the fridge. "Don't you like… kill your cows and chickens for food?"

                    AMY KULP

"My dad does," I stated. Justin turned around and had a half-peeled banana hanging from his mouth. He stopped rummaging and closed the door. He came up to us and smirked as he bit hard into the food. "I never have and have no desire to. Most of them we sell though."

"The blood?" Justin asked. Jade nodded her head and with the confirmation, he gave me a sympathetic look. I hated that look. He side-stepped toward me and held out a hand that I stepped into so that he could give me an attempt at a hug. He was still trying to prove to me that he felt bad about setting me up before the trials. No matter how many times I told him he was forgiven, he grew harder on himself. Almost as if he didn't believe me.

I wasn't sure if I did believe him though. He was probably told he had to do it or face consequences of his own. Anybody in his position would pick to do that.

"Do we plan on sticking together or spreading out?" Justin asked as he threw his peel away. We started walking past the empty living area and down the hall. Jade and I both slowed down together as Justin took charge.

"She is helping me with using my brain strategically and I am helping her with her physical fitness,' Jade commented coldly. Justin looked back at both of us and nodded his head. He was smart and he could hear the coldness in Jade's tone. She was actively excluding him, and it made me ponder why. Did something happen between them that she wasn't telling me?

"And since you're the smartest out of all of us," I said as I grabbed his arm. He was trying to speed up to avoid his embarrassment. When my hands linked around his arm, he slowed to our pace and looked at me. "You can help me, help her." He nodded his head, but he was less enthusiastic about it now. "And I'm sure you have a weakness too?" I looked at him and then at Jade. "Maybe we can help with that?" Jade was about to speak but when she turned to face me, she faltered. I must have had a very convincing look to include him.

"I'm not telling you my weaknesses," Justin said. He slipped his arm away from my grasp and shook his head. "People are sneaky here." His eyes looked over at Jade, but I didn't turn to see her reaction. "You never know who you can trust. Everyone wants to be in that graduating class of assassins." He shook his head. "Some people are ruthless."

"Maybe the Elitists do," Jade responded. I could hear the anger as she spoke and every word, she said was cut off sharply. She was trying to make a point. "I got pulled away from my dad. We were perfectly fine without me being here. Now I'll never get to see him again."

Justin eyed her but didn't make another comment. For someone so smart, he knew how to say stupid things. Almost none of the Inductees wanted to be here. I still doubted that all the Elitists did too. Why would someone want to kill people? I knew it was looked at as one of the highest jobs you could get, but I didn't understand the hype. It sounded like the Elitists and their families had something severely wrong with them. Or were they convinced that it was the right thing to do?

There were so many ways to get onto the Assassin's list. They didn't care if you were old or young. If you said it jokingly as a child, your name would still be on the list. Any demeaning talk about the leaders of the world added you onto the list. We didn't know who the leaders were though. Was there one? Were there ten? Was it a woman or a man? Why didn't we know who led us? We just had a bunch of rules we needed to follow: don't wear green, you have to believe in the leader – not a God or multiple gods, you can't plan to leave – assassins are lining the borders, you can't talk about the news, you can't talk about politics, you had to shun those that did or your name could also be added to the list. So many rules that everyone had to follow. I was told at a young age that it was probably best if I kept quiet so I wouldn't break the rules. That advice is probably what got me through elementary, middle, and partially through high school with being well-liked. At least, until I came here.

Now silence is seen as a bad thing here.

"Maybe I'll catch you guys later," he said once we got in the area. There were still some places in here that I did not know but as Jade entwined her arms into the crook of my elbow, I could only wave to Justin as she pulled me into a different direction than him. Probably on purpose.

"Can you believe him?" she asked. She shook her head in disgust before pulling me to a machine that I wasn't familiar with. "Let's start with your speed. If you run faster than everyone, they can't catch you to kill you." She shook her head and started the machine up for me. I walked in place and looked over at her. This was too easy. "We also need to build up your stamina. You can't have the lead and then let your body give out." She hopped onto the machine next to me and started it at a faster pace. "Let's try walking for ten minutes today. Maybe a faster pace tomorrow for 15 minutes and keep going like that."

I nodded. Who knew if we had that long for this to be effective for me? I wanted instant results now. Even though I was thinking about it, I knew that would never be the case. I would have to work toward building my stamina. I would have to work harder than Jade would with her smarts. Maybe Justin could give me pointers too. My head whipped around the room to try and locate him, but he was nowhere where I could see him. He could have been upstairs too, in the arena, or in a section I haven't seen yet.

"Okay, press the red button," Jade said as she slowed down her machine. Her face was beet red and she had sweat dripping down her forehead with little beads near her hairline. When I stopped mine and turned to her, I could see that she had dark circles on her shirt and patches of sweat in various places. I wanted to look at my reflection, but I already knew that I wasn't sweating as much. "You did pretty good. Maybe you are a bit more athletic than you think."

"Before you show me anything else, maybe we can switch on and off on who is training who?" I asked. "Come on, let me show you a specific machine I wanted to try." This time it was my turn to

                                    AMY KULP

grab her wrist – or as much as I could. She followed closely behind and as we went up the stairs to the second floor, I could see Justin at one of the familiar machines.

"I'm having trouble believing you now," Jade said under her breath. I rolled my eyes and didn't say anything. She wouldn't take my silence as being offensive. At least, I hoped she wouldn't. I would have to push my questioning on why she didn't like Justin. That wouldn't be something she told me willingly. Especially if she knew I liked him. "What are these machines?"

Justin looked over briefly before a small smirk formed on his mouth. He was too focused on the machine to answer her. I sat down in the one next to him and Jade sat next to me. She stared at his screen for a moment before turning to me.

"It depends on what you want to do," I said. I sat back in the chair and started my machine up. I pressed the button on hers too and she copied my exact movements. "You can choose to learn the history of the Trials, history of our land, or trivia. I think those would be the least likely to help though." I shrugged my shoulders. I peered back over to Justin and could see him closing his eyes to try and remember an answer. "There is also information on the specific things they tested for each trial and I'm curious to if there is a pattern to what trial would be next. I'm going to watch and read about that one." I looked over at her. "There are stats on each graduated Assassin and what they are known as – genius, athletic, stealthy, and more."

"So, you can figure out the odds of you surviving?" Justin asked. He looked over at me and I nodded my head. "You don't have very good odds as is."

"Why is that?" Jade asked through gritted teeth.

"We're Inductees," I mentioned.

"No, what does *he* have to say?" Jade asked. I looked over at him and he shrugged his shoulders.

"You are Inductees but you're also female-"

"Are you seriously being sexist right now?" Jade asked. She stood up from her chair and I knew she was angry. Instead of yelling at him like I thought she was going to do, she turned to me and started pointing her finger. "How can you be friends with him? I tried to give him a chance and he is over here spouting speeches about how superior men are."

"Don't yell at her," Justin said calmly. "You were there when Bischoff said the statistics about female Assassins. This isn't me being sexist, this is me spouting facts that you don't want to hear." Jade opened her mouth to say something, but Justin shook his head to deny her comeback. "I am sexist, Jade." She shut right up. "I'm not proud of it but it was how I grew up." He shook his head. "I'm not used to being around girls especially opinionated ones like yourself. I want you to call me out when I am being sexist but right now, wasn't one of those times."

"What?" Jade asked. She looked over at me quickly before looking back at Justin. He ran his hands through his hair for a moment out of frustration and licked his lips out of nervousness.

"I'm sorry for what I said when we first met." He looked at me and I could see a blush creeping up from his shirt and up to his neck that went all over his cheeks. "I wanted to impress the other Elitists." They kept eye contact for a solid minute before he broke and looked back at his screen. "I'm still learning not to underestimate." He jutted his chin toward me. "She was the reason I realized that girls were almost equal..." He stopped talking immediately and closed his eyes. Before I could stop her, Jade reached out and backhanded him right in the face. "I deserved that." He got out of his seat and looked at both of us. "I know you said you wanted to train your brains more, but can I show you something I just recently found? I don't think anybody really knows about this room."

I looked back at Jade to see how she was reacting but instead of the disgust, she seemed curious. Justin got up and started walking and that's when Jade looked back at me and after careful consideration, nodded her head for us to follow. We stayed a bit back to watch from a short distance to see if he was going to pull anything. After all, the last time I followed him, he tricked me into going into a combative battle for my punishment.

"What did he say to you that was so bad?" I whispered to her as we started descending the stairs to reach the first level. Jade shook her head and remained quiet for once. Maybe she was taking a page from my book.

"Do you think he's actually trying to change?" Jade wondered. I watched as he kept looking behind him to make sure we were still following me. I didn't sense any hesitation that would signify he was guilty of something right now.

"Yes," I blurted. We had to get closer to Justin now because at every other turn we seemed lost. "Although it's probably hard if you were conditioned to believe it." I looked at her. "And you are surrounded by Elitists who believe the same things."

"Colt would never doubt a girl," Jade mentioned.

"I never said Colt's name." We picked up our speed to catch up to Justin. He walked further and further to the back of the room, and I felt like we've been walking forever. He found a hall that was labeled for bathrooms and as we started going down it, we saw one for the men and the women. However, we kept walking until we saw a dead end. Justin kept walking though, so we kept following. As he almost hit into the wall, he took a sharp right turn to enter another doorway. I would have never known it was down here. "What is this?"

"It's target practice," Justin said. He smiled broadly and I could see the different weapons that were arranged in a row – knives, daggers, guns, swords, arrows, throwing stars, bats, and others that I wasn't familiar with. "These are the different weapons of an assassin. They expect us all to know how to use them."

"I don't know what half of these are," Jade admitted. She walked up to the gun and picked it up. There was a metal chain attached to it. "Do you know how to use these?"

                    AMY KULP

"Not all of them, but we can try to figure it out together."

"And get better with our aim," I mentioned. I walked closer to the weapons and picked up the bat. I swung it a couple of times before looking at Jade and Justin. Justin was parked at the knife. He was holding it carefully before throwing it at the target practice dummy. It landed with a loud clatter on the ground and as I peered at the sheet, it didn't seem to have made any cut into it. The walk to retrieve his weapons seemed to be humiliating and he was sheepish as he returned. "When you throw it, twist your wrists."

"I've never held a gun," Jade said as she looked over the body of it. Her hands grazed it and she looked up with a twinkle in her eye. She didn't seem to know how to hold it. At least with the bat, it had a very specific handle. Same with the knives and daggers. "I've only seen Colt use one." Jade immediately looked at me and I shuddered at the thought. "Sorry." She walked to try and comfort me, but the gun reached the limit of the metal chain. At least with the knives, their chain was longer. The gun fell from her hands and without a second to think, I heard the gunshot go off and closed my eyes out of reaction.

Just closing my eyes. Not jumping down or hiding. I could feel the blood on my face when Colt shot Leah. I could feel it drip down and the taste of it in my mouth. The cool metallic dripped down my throat and I couldn't get rid of it until I opened my eyes.

I was okay. I wasn't hurt and there was no blood in the room. That was relieving. My eyes went over to Jade who had her eyes shut, body low to the ground, and had her hands over her ears. Justin was lying flat on the floor and almost seemed to be protecting her. Although I'm sure neither of them would admit that. Before that gun dropped though, they were not that close together.

I opened my mouth to speak and was quickly interrupted.

"Already?" Jade wondered. Both of their eyes popped open, and they both got up from the ground. "I haven't had a chance to heal yet!" She looked down at my hands. "We're going to have to take the bandages off before we start this next trial."

"Maybe they'll be useful to her though," Justin said.

Just like that, they seemed to be back to their disagreements.

#

Having only three days to recover from the last Trial, I could sense that the people in the room were no longer thrilled for the next challenge. Everyone was broken off into two groups and as the groups formed, I could see micro-groups between the Elitists and Inductees. There was Jade, Nia, Toby, and I. Although I was the outcast in this scenario. Cassandra and Anthony huddled near each other but from the way they were interacting, I knew that they weren't close. It could have been that Leah's death had forced them to be together. Cassandra was a loner anyway and I found it hard to get her to participate with us. After all, I did invite her to workout with us this morning, but she denied it instantly. Over on the Elitists' side were four groups of friends: the first was Heather, Justin, and Audrey, Asher was the loner, the third group was Tanya and Jamie, although they were trying to impress the fourth group, Eddie, Garrett, Colt, and… I had to do a double-take to make sure I was seeing correctly. I looked back over at our group and counted the heads.

"What's Shane doing over there?" I whispered to Jade. She looked skeptical before her eyes rummaged through the crowds of people by us. She uncrossed her arms when she was done searching our crowd and stared blankly at Shane.

"Are you really surprised?" Nia asked. Jade turned back around and we both stared at her. She shrugged her shoulders and Toby interjected instead. Almost as if she was allowing him to continue the gossip she only heard.

"He had so much fun killing in the first round." He shook his head. "He has always wanted to be here. He just didn't have the money to be an Elitist." He looked down at the ground and back over to him. "He has said some pretty messed up stuff in our bedroom. I don't think he's ever felt welcomed by anyone." His eyes scanned back over to Anthony but he was busy chatting his nerves away with Cassandra. "I feel like he's a traitor to the Inductees."

"Almost like someone else we know," Nia interjected. Before I looked at her, I was going to question her statement but by that point, I could see her eyes were narrowed at me. Toby instantly grabbed her by the arm and turned her to Bischoff and Jade grabbed me by the arm and turned me toward the front too.

"Ignore her," Jade whispered next to me. She kept her hand on my arm and pushed me forward so that we could hear. Or maybe it was to get away from Nia. "She's still upset that you didn't want to join an alliance with us."

I nodded my head but stayed quiet. It wasn't a wild concept that she would see me as a traitor. I had to look at Jade too, but she was too focused up front. Was I a traitor to her? I wouldn't think so. She seems to have a thing for Colt. I looked over toward them and could see that they were all still chitchatting. As my eyes glanced toward Justin, I could see just how happy he was to talk to Heather. I suspected that she was the real reason his mind was changing about females. Or did he just see her as a thing? Maybe I should lay off talking to him so much. Maybe don't interact with him. I didn't want anyone to think I was a traitor to anyone. I especially didn't want anyone to think that I was enjoying these Trials; I would much rather be cleaning out the chicken coop right now.

"As an Assassin, it is important that you aren't seen before your assassination. Sometimes, you aren't seen at all," Bischoff began. I looked up at him and shut off all my other thoughts. Last time I didn't listen, I screwed myself over. I still had to ask everyone how they got over that wall. Did they tell them while I was worrying about my broken nose? "Behind that door, we have replicated a city. You will have fifteen minutes to find a place to

                              AMY KULP

camouflage yourselves. Your goal is to be the last one standing. Last year's graduating class of assassins is coming back and if they find you, they will point a laser at you." He paused and through one door, six people came through – no girls.

They wore their forest green suits with pride. Some of them had smiles on their faces while others looked stern. They carried a small machine with them but once they all came in, they stared intently at us. Some seemed to be studying us and some of them were looking at all the females with interest. I shrunk under their gaze, but I could see a blush creep up on Jade's cheeks.

"In the fashion of the Trials, this laser pointer is not just a normal laser pointer," Bischoff started.

One of the assassins moved from his position and pointed the laser quickly at us. Everyone flinched back as soon as he held the weapon up. I wasn't sure which group he was shooting for, but I knew he was probably an Elitist. He could probably tell which group was the Inductees just by how many people we had standing here. I heard a soft disgruntled noise coming from the other group and turned my head to see the red beam landing on Asher's arm.

He tried not to make it look like it bothered him but as the laser stayed on, I could see smoke beginning to form from the beam. At last, he broke away and the beam continued to shine bright past him. He rubbed at the injury for a second before showing it to those around him. I craned my neck out of interest but that seemed to make me the next target.

I already had enough wrong with me. My fingers were wrapped from their recent burning and my nose was still swollen from being broken. Could they concentrate on someone else? I tried to stare at the assassin who was pointing their laser at me, but I could not pinpoint who it was. It seemed that most of us had the red dot pointed at us.

Standing there, I knew I wasn't supposed to make a big deal out of it. I could see from everyone else's reactions that I was just supposed to take it. Similar to a competition you had when you were younger regarding who could stomach the hottest food. I could feel the heat now. I could feel the skin burning away in a perfect circle. To me, it felt itchy. I wanted to itch at the spot but instead, I closed my eyes and calmed my breathing. This wouldn't be the worst pain I felt in the world. Although it did test my patience. At least when my nose was broken, I passed right out. When my palms were burned, it was instant. This laser had me feeling every layer of skin that was burning off. I felt the heat that was turning to boiling and when I finally opened my eyes to move, I could see all the Inductees staring at me.

All the Elitists were staring at Colt. He was the last survivor of the laser pointers. When I looked over at Jade, she shrugged her shoulders. She didn't get a laser pointed at her and I had to suspect it had something to do with the assassin up front. When my gaze went back to him, he was still staring at Jade with a small smile on his face. When he noticed my look, his face went back to normal. Did they know each other?

                              AMY KULP

"Once you are found, you are out," Bischoff stated. "You will come back to the base and wait until everybody is found. Be careful what you do or say because there will be a microscopic camera following you around for our paying audience."

"What?" Cassandra asked. I looked over at her and saw her immediate reaction was to hide beside Anthony. However, he didn't let her. He nodded at her, and she cleared her throat. "There are people who pay and want to see people die?" I could see some of the Elitists tense. "Isn't the entire point of the Assassin Trials so that people don't know who we are? Why take us away from our families if people can just pay to view it?" she wondered. I thought she was going to stop but I could see her face getting red – she was getting mad and out of breath. It seemed that her mind was reeling, and it seemed that her mouth couldn't get the words out fast enough. "They can figure out that we are an assassin and then hide from us if they see us. They could put us on their list if they had one. They can—"

She was quickly cut off with electricity to the back. She fell to her knees and just continued to stare at the ground. No more comments were made and I could tell that knocked the air out of her lungs. After a couple of moments, Anthony helped her up. She stayed glued to his side and refused to make eye contact. Her gaze was on the ground.

I have never heard her say so much. She was always quiet and seemed to be shy. I never knew where she was or what she was doing because she kept to herself. I always looked over her because I didn't know her but I could see the spunk. Right then and there, she was more willing to voice it than me. That took a lot of guts and I knew now, she would have a bullseye on her back from the Elitists.

I stared over at them but a lot of them stared straight ahead. I could see Justin and Heather holding hands and their gazes were down casted toward the floor like Cassandra's was. When I turned to Eddie, Garrett, Shane, and Colt, the first three were snickering and whispering toward each other. Almost as if it was a joke to them. Even if Shane wasn't an Elitist, I could see him paying to watch the trials. He seemed like someone who would enjoy that stuff. Although he had to know that Garrett and Eddie did not see him as an equal. After all, Shane was an inductee at the end of the day. It was Colt's reaction that struck me as awkward. He was staring over at someone in our group, and they were having a silent conversation. I could see him mouthing words and when I looked back at our group, it was Jade who he was conversing with. After a moment of nothing between them, he finally nodded his head and Jade broke away.

"What was that about?" I whispered toward her. She shook her head and stared straight at Bischoff. Almost ignoring me but not quite. I looked back up at Colt and this time, he was staring at me. Almost like he was threatening me.

"You are never alone," Bischoff started. "Our cameras have been with you for all of the previous trials, since your arrival, and with you everywhere."

"Everywhere?" Anthony asked. Cassandra tensed up next to him and I could see her knuckles turning white from gripping him so hard. She didn't

                              AMY KULP

want him to speak up like she just did. She didn't want him to get hurt. "Even the bathroom?"

Bischoff laughed at that and shook his head. That was a relief. I showered in those bathrooms, and I also had some extreme conversations with Jade in those bathrooms. At least I knew those were a safe space now.

"Let the Trials begin."

The doors opened and everyone ran through them at once. Anthony grabbed Cassandra and together, they ran off. Jade, Nia, and Toby all stayed together, and I broke apart from them. We were more likely to get caught if we stayed in a group. When I looked at the Elitists, they were all scampering away from each other too. Some went in the same general direction as each other while others split apart immediately.

I needed to stop worrying about the others though. I needed to do my own thing and hoped that it would work out.

I was the last one to walk through the doors and they closed loudly behind me. Staring in front of me, I couldn't see anything but the outline of the city. There were buildings all lined up in a row next to each other and some houses. There was even dirt on the ground and uneven sidewalks that I could trip on if I wasn't careful. As I moved around, there were abandoned cars along the street and various convenience stores. Where to hide though?

I opened a car door immediately and listened to the alarm start wailing to go off. I cursed under my breath and saw Tanya and Jamie come out from their hiding spot nearby. They cursed at me and showed me the bird before running in a different direction. That was probably the best bet too. Get away from the place that was making all the noise. I ran opposite of them before stopping.

That's what they would expect, right? They wouldn't expect anyone to be near the noise. After all, we are assassins. We are supposed to be quiet. We are supposed to stay away from the noise. If they thought we knew all of that, they wouldn't search that area. I turned back around and ran toward the car. Maybe there was somewhere I could hide. Getting into the driver's side, I looked for keys that could help me pop open the trunk or allow me to shut off the alarm. However, I didn't want to waste too much time here so after several seconds of searching, I opened the car door and ran toward the convenience store.

It was illuminated with those bright fluorescent overhead lights. I had to squint when I entered and listened to the doorbell ring. I stopped and hit the door open again. The doorbell rang again. If I hid here, I would be alerted if someone were to come in. Walking through the aisles, I could see the various snacks and food they had catered to. It seemed like a huge sponsorship was going on here. Would I be able to hide in here though?

I ran behind the counter and looked for a spot that I could squeeze into. I tried various ones but knew that I wouldn't be able to escape if I were found in there. I would either make too much noise or be too slow at it. This was a stupid idea. I ran to the back to see if there were any spots there but before I could

AMY KULP

squeeze my body into one of the cardboard boxes that was lying around, I could hear the doorbell ring.

I knew that it wasn't time for the assassins to search for us yet, so it had to be somebody with the same idea as me. If two of us had the same idea, then this meant the trained assassins might too. I couldn't risk staying here so once I found a back exit, I pushed open the door and ran right into Shane.

"Aw look at who we have here," he said as he refused to move out of our way. "Colt saw you come in here and we all wanted to have a little fun with you." He smiled wickedly at me as I stood there confused. "With the other trials, you just had to be better than everyone else. Here, you must be skilled and on good terms with everyone."

"You're going to waste your fifteen minutes by taunting me?" I asked. I crossed my arms and rolled my eyes at him. "They don't care about you, Shane. You're an inductee."

"I finally found people who know that they want to be here. They have always wanted to be an assassin," Shane said. He took a step toward me and I'm sure he assumed I would be terrified of him, but for once, I felt pity. He probably wasn't well-liked at school and if he was, it was because he bullied those around him into liking him. They only liked him out of fear. "We just want to have a little fun with you while we can." He paused and rammed his body into mine. I fell back into the brick building, but he held my body up by my arms. "After all, the chances that a female inductee makes it to the graduating class is very unlikely."

"I know the odds," I mentioned. "I'm still going to try."

"Why should you be in the graduating class?" Shane asked as he spit on me. I wasn't sure if it was on purpose or not or because he was so nervous. I could see his breath turning in and out as he continued to deep breathe. He had to either just be running or he was nervous. About what though?

"Why should you be able to decide if I'm in the graduating class?" I asked. I could hear yelling from inside the store and I bet that it was them taunting me. Trying to find me. I didn't know what they wanted to do with me but if it was this group, I could assume they were going to hurt me. "You grew up wanting to be in these trials. Let the best assassin win."

"If you were the best assassin, you could easily get out of this situation," Shane taunted. He gripped my arms harder and braced myself against the wall. He got closer to me and pressed his entire body against me. "Unless you don't want to."

"I'm sorry," I whispered. He looked at me confused as if he didn't know why I was apologizing. He may have had the will, the drive, and the physical strength but he was not that smart. I lifted my leg high and hard right between his legs and he dropped like a fly. "I'm sorry," I said again as I ran away.

There were dumpsters nearby and I hid behind them. I could see Shane clutching at himself as the door opened. Out popped Eddie and Colt. I had to assume that Garrett was upfront. Both bent down and checked to see if Shane was okay. I couldn't hear them but I had to assume that Shane was explaining to them what happened.

"Can't rely on an Inductee," Eddie said loud enough for me to hear.

I watched as Colt and Eddie went back up to the front. They came back around with Garrett and all of them helped him up. Limping away, they shook their heads and started to run. Shane was the weak link now, but he managed to catch up to them. He had to know of known now that what I said was true. They would never accept him fully into their group. He would never fit in there. Somehow, I knew that Shane was used to that feeling back at home.

When the coast was clear, I ran back to the other side of the store. I had to find somewhere to hide and that wasted my time. I don't know how much, but I had to assume that the assassins were going to be hunting soon. I ran like my life depended on it. I didn't know where these assassins would be looking. If it was Bischoff, I could probably figure his pattern out. Since it was people I never met before, I knew that I wasn't going to be able to escape them. I just had to hide well or run well.

Knowing that my physical fitness was not up to par, I knew the decision was simple: I needed to find a good hiding spot fast. I stopped in the middle of the street and surveyed around me. They would probably look in every building but would they look at the roof of the buildings? Could I even get up onto a roof? I looked up high until I saw a window that if I broke and got up to, I could hoist my body to the roof. I would have to use every ounce of strength I had to do that.

Running into the house, I looked for the stairs immediately. Going up them, I could feel my heart beginning to race as I found the window I wanted. I didn't know if any of this stuff was someone's that they stole or if they were just nobody's that were just using as decoration. I didn't want to destroy anything, but I didn't know how to open windows and I didn't have time to try and figure it out. Instead, I found a heavy chair and threw it at the glass. It ricocheted off it and I flinched when I listened to the shards hit the ground. Carefully stepping around the pieces of glass, I planted my legs onto the windowsill and could feel the little pieces embedding themselves into my skin. I would feel the pain later while cleaning it out but right now, I knew I had to get to the top.

I thought I had more time when I heard the door bust open, but I would just have to stick with this hiding spot now.

While sitting on the ledge, I reached my arms up and felt the roof. It was flat so when I managed to get my wrists on it, I flattened my hand over the roof. I still had some wrapping on my skin, so it felt like a glove as I shoved all my weight on it. I tried to grip with my nails and fingertips, but the wrapping prevented me from doing that. I would have to get up faster though. I didn't have time to waste. With all my might, I kicked my feet out from me and managed to hoist most of my body up. Getting both of my elbows and my chin up on the roof, I kicked the wall to help me keep my grip. I knew that my breath was leaving me and I could feel my arms beginning to shake. I had to get up here though. I pulled and felt my hands brushing against the roof. I was losing my traction. I cursed under my breath but refused to let go. They would have to shoot the laser pointer at me first.

Finally kicking my left leg high enough that it caught on the roof, I kicked the rest of my body up. I landed with a splat on the roof and stayed as low as I could. I continued to lay on my back as I heaved in and out. I felt like my chest could explode and my body was aching from the pain now too. I continued to stare up at the sky and watched as it flashed red for a second.

I touched my face out of reaction and tried to find where my head was bleeding. The only wet parts of my forehead were sweat. I kept checking to see if my bandages would turn a deep red, but it was just becoming damper and damper from the sweat. Realizing that it was not my head, I flung my body back onto the roof and lay there. They couldn't see me from down on the streets. Maybe if they were above me, they could see me. How would they get above me? I looked around but already knew that I picked the tallest building to climb on top of.

I saw another flash of red and groaned. I didn't know what that was, but I was clued in that it couldn't have been good. I crawled on my knees toward the edge and peeked over it. Nobody was around me but with another red flash, I, at least, knew I wasn't crazy. The lights were turning red for an instant. Why? I had no idea but I kept my guard up as I peered out over everything. I was hoping it wouldn't be too noticeable.

Movement from the ground caught my eye. I turned to stare at Colt, Shane, Eddie, and Garrett as they roamed the streets. I wanted to warn them that the assassins were hunting but shouldn't they know? Did they not hear the doors open? I shrunk down low but made sure I could still see them as they walked in between the buildings. They all paused for a second before looking up at the roof.

Instantly reacting, I lay flat on my back and hoped they didn't see me. However, I could hear the laughter. I could hear them pounding through the building until they got to the window that was broken. My chest was heaving from the anxiety that they may have seen me. Or maybe they thought about the idea of being on the roof too.

"Assassins!" Eddie yelled.

A flash of red was seen again and I could hear them scamper from the window. Where were the assassins? Did one of them get hit? Is that what that flash of red meant? I waited and listened to the quiet air around me. Despite knowing the assassins were in the building or around the building, none of those boys were quiet as they ran out of the house.

"Alright, you can go back to the base. Just show your mark to any assassin who tries to get you again."

Someone did get caught. I wanted to look below but knew that my odds were not good. There was that assassin but what if there were more? Did they often solo or team up? They eventually would have to team up to find the stragglers. I couldn't stay here forever though. They would eventually be thinking about checking the roofs. They should probably do a sweep right now. I would if I were an assassin: clear the area and then move on.

Once again, I crawled to the ledge of the building and peered over. I could see some of the boys separating from each other as they ran. The assassins didn't seem worried about them though because nobody followed them out. I didn't see any of the assassins. Were they still in the house?

I scratched at the back of my neck as I felt my sweat prickling the skin. I was out of shape if I still couldn't recover from climbing up onto the roof from that window. I shook my head but as I continued to wipe the sweat off, I realized that it was too warm. I had been cooled down already and now that I had taken my bandaged hands off my neck, I could feel how warm it was.

Without thinking, I instantly bailed over the building. I had no plan, and I had no coordination. However, I was able to reach the other building's rooftop as I fell. I didn't have much time to adjust my body before landing on my back. While I was out of breath, I knew that I had to escape the assassin who was trying to mark me. I clumsily ran until I got to a stairwell at the top of the building.

Thank goodness!

Running down the stairs, I slammed the door shut behind me. My lungs were beginning to burn, and I knew that I couldn't keep running for much longer. I needed to find somewhere to hide but the building that I was in made it almost impossible for me to blend in. My eyes scanned the area, and it was just a blank building. There were no decorations and nothing to disguise me. Making a random turn, I could hear the assassin walking through the halls. It angered me that he wasn't challenged enough to run after me. I was worth running after.

I quickly ran to the end of the hall and felt relieved to see an elevator. If I could open and close it fast enough, I could make it down faster than he could run down those stairs. I clicked the button and pressed it numerous times while I waited. When the burning sensation appeared on my neck again, I pressed harder until I was in the elevator. I immediately pressed the button to close the doors and was able to watch as the assassin kept his pointer on and walked closer to me. Still, he would not run. How irritating!

I pressed the ground floor button and allowed myself to lean against the side while I took the trip down. What if he did make it to the bottom floor before me? I bit my lip and quickly pressed the second-floor option. He wouldn't expect me to stay in the building, right? He wouldn't be able to hear the dings from the stairwell anyway.

As soon as the doors opened, I ran out of them. I waited until they closed for me to stop moving. Would I survive a jump from the second floor to the ground? I wasn't sure but I knew that busting the window would cause a lot of noise. Would that attract him to me? Would that attract more of them to me? I bit my lip as I contemplated my choices. I just couldn't wait too long to think about what I was going to do.

I found a blank room that had a huge window. Opening it up, I was relieved to see that I would be able to shimmy my body through if I needed to. That

AMY KULP

wouldn't make much noise. However, before I started squeezing my body in, I watched as Cassandra and Anthony were walking back. When they passed an assassin, they just showed him their marks. He didn't seem to even look at them.

I could see another flash of red from the outside and licked my lips. Time to see how smart I was. Could I hide in plain sight?

I jumped down from the window and landed flat on my back. While causing a little commotion, it didn't make as much as I thought it would. I picked my body up and freely walked the way that Anthony and Cassandra were walking. However, I knew that I could never make it to the doors. I had to stay in this zone for me to win.

I moved my shirt just off my shoulder so that anyone passing by could see the laser point I had gotten from before the trials. I wanted to make it noticeable. How would they know the difference between the first one and the one I was supposed to get?

When another flash of red went off, I assumed it was me. I felt my body up to see if I was burned somewhere but couldn't find a spot. It wasn't me. This seemed to work.

"You need to go back to base if you were shot!"

I turned around and showed my hands and then my mark. He nodded and pointed me to where I needed to go. I nodded my head and walked quietly toward where he was going. Was he supposed to give away his position like that?

"What are you doing?" I heard from around me. I looked and could see Jade hiding in an alleyway. She looked so scared that she gave herself away and looked all around her. However, I wasn't being followed. They already thought that I was out. "Hide…"

I kicked a stone on the ground toward the alleyway and made my way over. I crouched to the ground to pick up my fake rock and stared at her. When I grabbed it, I then tied my shoe. This concerned her as she grabbed me and forced me into the alleyway with her.

"I'm playing," I said. "I'm thinking like an assassin. They are just letting anyone who got hit walk through there toward the gate. I have walked past two assassins already." I pulled my shirt down to show her my shoulder. "They think I've gotten hit." I paused and looked at her. "Come on." She flinched at the red flash. "Just pretend you got hit." It took her a second, but she eventually nodded yes.

"I got separated from Nia and Toby," Jade commented. "I literally hid so far in that alleyway that three people ran past me."

"Why'd you come out?" I asked.

"To save your stupid ass," Jade mentioned. She shook her head at the thought. "Now I'm the stupid ass. I hope this works."

I shrugged my shoulders and moved my shirt over to help show off the wound. As we walked slowly toward the gate, we saw three more flashes of red. It wasn't until we saw the doors that we were finally stopped. He stood menacingly and when I showed him my wound, he nodded before looking at Jade.

"Show him your wound," I demanded. She shrunk beside me and shook her head. "Jade, it's fine. Show him it."

"I never got one," she whispered to me.

I barely understood what she was saying before another red flash went across my eyes and a loud alarm went off. When I looked at Jade, she had a quick laser mark embedded into her cheek. I could see the smoke coming off it and saw the tears in her eyes. I can't imagine getting the laser in the face.

"Congrats on winning this round," the assassin said to me.

I nodded my head awkwardly as we headed back to the doors. He smiled at me. That was so unusual and strange to think about. When he looked at Jade, he nodded his head and she nodded hers. I felt like they knew each other. I did a double take of his face and remembered him as the assassin who wouldn't stop looking at her before.

"Looks like someone has a crush on you," I whispered. I nudged Jade and she instantly turned pink from embarrassment. I shook my head as she yanked me through the doors and saw everybody already standing in their circles.

"Congratulations," Bischoff said. He nodded at both of us and when I looked back, I could see that our circles were yellow as they awaited us. I looked down the line at Eddie, Nia, Heather, Shane, Tanya, Justin, Anthony, Cassandra, Asher, Garrett, Toby, and Colt standing there with little marks on their bodies somewhere. Jamie and Audrey were holding back tears as Jade, and I joined our circles. I kept her hand in mine and waited patiently for him to reveal who would be doing the killings. "Cassandra and Anthony."

Both stepped forward as they were given a small scalpel. Cassandra turned to Anthony and they both then turned to Audrey and Jamie. Anthony stepped forward to take the first cut and surprisingly, both Audrey and Jamie stayed still. Before Cassandra started anything, she looked over at Jade and she nodded her head. With that reassurance, Cassandra stepped forward and quickly, inserted the scalpel into Audrey's temple. Taking it out, she was unconscious immediately and stepped back.

There was no reaction from her or Anthony. Anthony followed in her footsteps and did the same thing – ending the small torture he was giving to Jamie. It took a couple of seconds before our circles started blinking and I know nobody wanted to move.

At least this time I didn't have blood all over me. Granted, I felt like Anthony and Cassandra both had to have a lot more control and precision with that kill. If it was Shane, he would have just sliced his victims up until they were dead. At least Cassandra had the decency to end it early for them. At least someone was still a little human.

Especially considering they only picked Cassandra and Anthony because they talked back to Bischoff.

"That was weird, right?" I asked Jade as she started walking.

"I'll talk to you later!" Jade said as she rushed through everyone.

                    AMY KULP

That was weird, right? My mind told me to follow Jade but instead, I turned my body to see Audrey and Jamie's bodies. Standing next to them in his blinking circle was still Colt. He stared at them with a blank expression and when I opened my mouth to try and console him, he flinched. His eyes stared hard at me, and I knew that I wasn't welcome.

I turned myself around and walked out. I found myself going to the kitchen where I knew that I would find Justin with his applesauce. He was downing two and when I sat across from him, he barely glanced up at me. He did pretty poor but I'm sure he didn't want to talk about that right now.

"I don't give you enough credit," Justin said. He swallowed the last bit of his applesauce before smiling. "However, I want to survive so that means that I am going to need to train a lot more." He got up and smiled at me. "May the best assassin win."

After a couple of minutes, I got up too. There was no point in me doing anything right now. I wasn't Justin who could study all day and every day. I wasn't Jade who could run as much as I wanted and find it relaxing. I was me.

The trials ruined me. I was exhausted mentally and physically each time. I was grossed out by the new way they were killed. I was learning new things about myself that I didn't want to know. I always took a three-hour shower to help contemplate what I was doing. Was it worth it for me? Even though I wasn't affected by Jamie and Audrey's death, it was still hard to watch. It was hard to see everyone getting used to it. Death was just so frequent anymore.

As I walked into our little living space, I was surprised to bump into Colt. His eyes were still hard, and he glared at me as he left. I wasn't aware that we could go into each other's living spaces, but I couldn't ask him. I was trying to avoid him. I was trying to lay low so that I could heal up these wounds. Asking him would be like lighting a stick of dynamite.

So even though I found him suspicious, I didn't talk about it with anyone because when I walked further in, I could see Jade hugging Cassandra. As soon as I came in and noticed them both, they broke apart. Cassandra walked into the bedroom without a word, and I could see Jade's blush forming again.

"You know me, I'm always consoling everyone after the Trials."

While that was true, it was not true that Colt helped.

Trial #4

As soon as my eyes fluttered open, I stretched out to see if Jade was in her bed. Before the third trial, we were constantly waiting for each other to get up and help with our wounds. However, it seemed she was disappearing now. I looked around to see that Nia's bed was neatly made and she was gone too. It usually wasn't weird that Nia was out of her bed and gone. She always disappeared but I never knew where. I didn't care. However, when I turned and limped toward the bathroom, I saw that Cassandra was out of her bed too. That was unusual. Cassandra was a late sleeper and often slept until noon if she was allowed to. Her bedsheets and blankets were usually all over the ground but as I continued to stand and stare there, I could see the military corners and how there was no wrinkle in sight. I didn't know that was possible.

Instead of making a big deal, I shook my head and walked into the bathroom. At least I knew I had my privacy.

Looking in the mirror, I could already see that the burn on my shoulder was becoming a circular scar. I wondered if everybody's burn was turning into that. Most of them had two. Everybody had at least one. I shook my head and applied lotion directly to the spot. It didn't hurt anymore – nothing on me did. My nose was no longer swelling, and my bruised eyes looked more like lack of sleep. As I unwrapped my hands, even they looked mostly healed. I dispensed the lotion from the machine and worked it into my hands. I had a new layer of skin, but it was still so sensitive. I had kept them in the wrappings longer than necessary, but I was certain I could keep them off today. I just needed to test them out.

So, when I gripped my toothbrush to get ready to brush my teeth, it felt like I was cracking the skin as I bent my fingers. I haven't done that in a while. The bandages were usually so tight that they barely allowed me to bend my hands or fingers. As I continued to scrub the plaque away on my teeth, I knew it was going to be hard to get my skin back to the toughness that it previously was. I used to work on a farm – my hands would constantly be bleeding. The skin would just rip away if I were to go back.

Once done in the bathroom, I shuffled back into the bedrooms. Maybe it was just a coincidence that Cassandra, Jade, and Nia were not here. It could have been that they were not together. There was so much space that I never explored yet. The only reason I have ventured out was because of Justin's kindness. Jade could have been there too. As far as I knew, Nia and Cassandra didn't know about it. I should probably go there. I needed to work on my fitness. From the last trial, I understood that I needed to improve my arm strength and my endurance. I had none of it. While Jade offered to help, I wasn't too sure if I would find her so that she could help me.

Walking out of the bedrooms, I listened for chatter or laughter outside. That usually indicated if I could come out safely or if I needed to be on guard. Although listening now, there didn't seem to be any noise. It had been quiet since Audrey and Jamie were taken. Despite how young Audrey was, she took her defeat like a champ. I still didn't understand why her

                    AMY KULP

family offered so much money when she was young. Shouldn't they have waited a little bit?

I looked over at the pool table and couches, but they were all abandoned. That was weird. They were usually always full of Elitists. I shook my head though and turned toward the kitchen. I usually could find Justin there if he weren't already training.

"I'm sorry," I said as I smashed into someone. I stepped back to look and before I could say anything, Colt glared at me and ripped away from me. I just shook my head out of frustration. There was nothing that I could do to get him to be nice to me. I had to take Jade's advice and stay away from him.

Walking further in, all the chatter that was in the room stopped as soon as I stepped foot in there. I looked around at the table to see Nia, Jade, Cassandra, and Toby all sitting there silently. After a moment, one of them began to eat the food that was on their plate again. A few seconds later, the rest joined them. I greeted them all with a morning but none of them responded to me.

"I'm gonna get going. Not usually a morning riser," Cassandra said. She clanked her spoon down in her bowl and waved bye to everyone else. She waved to them as she left and I listened as everyone responded to her.

"What were you guys talking about?" I asked as I sat down with a bowl of cereal. I started chomping down on my spoon to remove the awkwardness from the air. However, nobody answered me and instead, Toby finished quickly and excused himself. "Okay…" I turned to Jade. "Do you want to head to the training area with me? I could really use some help on my endurance and arm strength."

"I'm actually…" She looked at Nia and cleared her throat. "I'm busy."

"Oh, okay," I said. I nodded my head and put another spoonful in my mouth. "Maybe tomorrow or later in the week?" I watched as she glanced at Nia and looked back down at her food.

"I'm probably going to be busy then too." I nodded my head again. "I'm going to show Nia and Toby the training area."

"Oh, can I come? I could really use—"

"Just Nia and Toby," Jade corrected.

"Oh."

"But you can have your buddy, Justin, help you, right?" Nia asked as she got up. I made accidental eye contact with her as she got up to put her dishes in the sink. She didn't seem angry with me though. I couldn't pinpoint what she was feeling. I didn't know Nia that well. Jealousy, maybe?

"Maybe some other time," Jade said as she got up. She patted my arm gently and removed herself from the table too.

I couldn't help but watch after her as they both walked out. That was weird. I knew that was weird. Jade, Nia, and Toby weren't usually like that. They were inviting toward me. Now that Cassandra was with them, they didn't want to include me. They didn't need to either. Not all of us were going to make it to the graduating class. I suspected most of us wouldn't and it would mostly be filled with Elitists and males.

                          AMY KULP

Thinking of Elitists and males, was Colt part of this meet too? He was just in this room and he didn't have Eddie or Garrett with him. I knew that Jade and him were… friendly toward each other too. I still had to ask her about that but it seemed like I wouldn't be getting a lot out of her today.

"Hey, surprised to see you in here," Justin said as he walked in. He smiled at me and quickly went to the fridge to grab his applesauce. He did a doubletake before smiling and sitting down across from me. "You don't have the bandages on your hands." He slurped up some sauce on his spoon and dug it in again. He always ate everything so fast that I wasn't sure he was breathing between chomps. At least he noticed I didn't have the bandages. Jade didn't talk to me about it, and I thought she would have noticed. "Are you okay?" He scraped the inside of his apple sauce container before taking all his and my trash and throwing it away for me. When he returned to the table, he remained standing and motioned toward the door. "You want to train with me?"

I nodded and got up with him. As we left the room and entered the living space, I could see there were now people at the pool tables. Taking a closer look, I could see that it was Colt, Garrett, Eddie, Shane, and Tanya. I passed quietly but continued to stare at the lot of them. Only Colt paid attention to Justin and I as we passed. However, he didn't say anything to me. Instead, his eyes seemed to be giving me a warning that he would never verbally say.

Maybe I was imagining it.

"Do you think something is going on that we don't know about?" I wondered. Justin remained quiet as he led the way to the training area. I knew he heard me though. "I think Jade is avoiding me."

"Why do you think that?" he wondered as he opened the door to the training area. He started moving without me and didn't seem to care if I was following him. Maybe I was predictable or maybe he could sense that I was desperate. Either way, I followed him up the stairs and to the brain games. He sat at one station, and I sat down next to him. He didn't look like he was going to start his machine. He was waiting for my response.

"She didn't want to come to the training area to help me." I watched Justin's face to see his facial reactions, but he didn't seem impressed. He egged me on to continue as if the first reason wasn't enough. "Okay." I turned toward him completely instead of facing my screen. "I also think there's something suspicious going on with Colt."

Justin started up his machine and selected to practice his memorization skills. He glanced at me as he continued selecting matching sets. Almost as if our time together was being wasted. I started my machine up too and worked on scenario questions. I read through it and sighed when I selected an answer.

"They always seem to be with each other but break apart as soon as I come into the room." I selected another answer to a question and watched as it lit up green. "I feel like they're hiding something."

"So?" He shrugged his shoulders and paused his game. "Maybe Jade and Colt have a thing for

                    AMY KULP

each other." I sat there and felt the disgust creep on my face. "What? What is that face for?"

"She told me to stay away from him and that he was bad news."

"She probably felt threatened."

"About you?"

"About you," Justin said. He shrugged his shoulders and continued the game. "You are attractive, Bridget even with your bald head." He rolled his eyes as if I should have known that. "Besides, she might be sneaking around so you don't get upset that she is hanging out with Colt." I opened my mouth to talk but he shook his head. "Kind of like how she doesn't like us hanging out."

"It's different."

"How?"

I sat there pondering for a second. How was my situation with Justin different than Colt and Jade's? We were both different genders and from opposite teams. However, Jade and Colt never seemed to interact with other people. At least when I get a chance, I talk to Justin. Although even he has someone else to talk to. Was I the only person who didn't have someone to talk to?

"I'm just alone," I admitted.

"So am I," Justin remarked. "Why do you think I'm always willing to come to the training center with you?" He shook his head. "I do not get along with the other Elitists."

"What about Heather?"

"Well, yeah," Justin said. "But I like her for other reasons." He paused and stared at me for a minute. "Listen, we are all trying to survive and be assassins. Maybe Jade is smarter than what you are giving her credit for. Out of three trials, she has scored lower than you in two. She's probably trying to manipulate you into doing poorer."

"Why would she do that?"

"We are here to be Assassins. We don't need to be friends." Getting up, I followed Justin as he led us back down the stairs. "Target practice?" he wondered. I nodded and followed him down the weird aisles with twists and turns. About when we were in there, I ran my body right into his back.

"Anthony?" I questioned. He turned around slowly as if we were going to hurt him. When he realized that it was me and Justin, he closed his eyes and sighed. "What are you doing in here?"

"The same thing you are. I'm practicing using each of these." He showed me the gun in his hand and when I looked at his target practice, he seemed to be a good shot.

"Where's Cassandra?" I wondered as I looked around. I stepped forward as if to see her practicing with a different instrument where I couldn't see her before. However, it was only us three in here. When I looked back at Anthony, he seemed uncomfortable. "I thought you guys were inseparable."

"We were." He turned around and pointed the gun at a new target. "Until the last trial." He shot another round and watched as it was off-center. Correcting himself, he got the target right in the head. "I waited for her for two hours before coming in here. We never stepped foot but since you invited her, she was curious." He shrugged as if he could pretend that didn't hurt. "We're both shy and don't like huge hordes of people." He eyed Justin but thankfully, he couldn't see him doing that. Justin was focusing on what he had come to do. I envied him for being able to do that. "Especially Elitists."

"Oh, he's—"

"I don't care." He shrugged again. "If Cassandra doesn't want to be around me, I understand. However, I am a force to be reckoned with." He shot at the target again and smiled as he finally put the gun down. "Do you guys want help?"

"I could use help with my stamina," I said. "Also arm strength." I flexed a bit and saw a small smile appear on his lips.

"I'll leave you guys to it, then."

My eyebrows fell down my face and I watched as he exited the room. It wasn't until his footsteps were no longer echoing down the hall that Justin turned to me. He seemed annoyed but I wasn't sure at what. I carefully picked up the gun that Anthony had just been holding and wished that I paid more attention. I should probably learn how to use one of these things. The best I could do was throw things since I was constantly throwing stuff at my chickens when they were where they shouldn't be.

"We shouldn't hang out with him," Justin commented. I didn't say anything as I looked at the gun in front of me. Justin carefully watched me and grabbed it out of my hands. He showed me how to hold it correctly and then handed it to me. "There's a huge recoil on that."

I didn't know what that meant but I wouldn't admit that to him. I closed one of my eyes as I peered at my target and felt my finger squeeze the trigger. Without much warning, the gun flew back out of my grasp and hit me straight in the face.

"I warned you."

I could hear the snarkiness in his voice. I didn't want to remove my hands from my face to see him. He would probably be smirking at me. Gloating perhaps.

"Anthony doesn't seem to want to hang out with us anyway," I mentioned. Removing my hands from my face slowly, the pressure lessened, and I could twitch my nose again. Okay, that wasn't rebroken at least. That hurt though.

"There are things you just don't understand," Justin said. He shook his head and went over to the throwing stars. "There are ways to play these Trials." He threw all of them at once and then looked back at me. I walked toward his window and saw that most of them hit a vital spot on his target. When I looked back, he already had something else picked up. "You are not playing them correctly."

"How do I play correctly then?"

"Yeah, how does she play correctly, Justin?" I looked at the entrance and watched as Garrett, Eddie, Colt, Shane, and Tanya filtered into the room. When I looked back at Justin, he seemed to be pondering what to say. "We aren't helping the inductee, right?" My eyes glanced at Shane, and I could see him suck his cheeks in.

"It is rare that an Inductee makes it to the graduating class," Tanya sneered.

"Even rarer for girls," Shane said. It was Tanya's turn to suck her cheeks in to avoid saying

                               AMY KULP

anything that would get her kicked from the group. Garrett stepped up and pointed at Justin.

"You're not helping her, right?" he wondered. I looked over at Justin and saw him swallow whatever lump was in his throat. His eyes darted back to me and back to Garrett. He was threateningly bigger and taller than Justin. "Whose side are you on?" His voice grew as Justin stayed silent and while all the attention was on him, I knew this was my chance to leave quietly.

Eddie was so enthralled with what was happening to Justin and Garrett that he didn't feel me squeeze by him. If he had, I was sure that he would stop me. Maybe torment and laugh at me that I wouldn't last much longer. I didn't want to hear that right now. I was doing good with staying low and staying out of trouble. Now that I'm insecure about something, they came and knew how to pick on me. Did they do this with everybody or just me? What did I do to these people that they hate me so much? I wasn't the only female Inductee here.

I passed both Shane and Tanya without either of them saying anything. Maybe it was the loyalty of me being a female to Tanya and being an Inductee to Shane. I wasn't sure but they let me pass without saying anything to anybody. I knew they noticed me leaving but averted their eyes away from me. They didn't want anyone to say there was proof of that.

As I was walking away, I could see Garrett and Eddie continue to taunt Justin. I didn't want to know what they were going to do but I knew that Justin had a weapon in his hands still. Would he use that? Or would he allow them to continue taunting?

Did he care? He just told me he was an outcast. Did he hate it though? Or did he think it made him stronger? Was I going to leave him here with them?

I felt a hand land on my shoulder, and I looked up to see Colt blending in next to the door. I was hoping he would ignore me but as he stepped closer to me and his fingers dug into my skin, I tried not to show weakness. Yes, this hurt but he didn't need to know that. He curled his upper lip at me and showed me his teeth as he sneered. He pressed harder into my shoulder and came closer to me. I would not back down to him though. He lowered his head to my ear and I waited for him to say something. Instead, his hand let go of my shoulder and when I looked back up at him, his face was masked with pain. He brought up his other hand and I flinched out of response. However, he took the dart that landed in his hand and dropped it to the floor. He was bleeding but it only seemed to break the top layer of skin – no real damage was done.

"Don't touch her," Justin warned. He pushed through Garrett, Eddie, and Shane to get to us. Tanya immediately sidestepped as he walked through and watched from the side. I could still see that his hand had some more darts in it as he grabbed my shoulder. He pushed me lightly away from Colt and straightened his back. "You can be friends with whoever you want but just because we are all Elitists or are male does not mean we are guaranteed to be assassins." He pushed me closer to the exit and turned around to face everyone. Nobody moved but instead, they listened. "You have seen how well Bridget does in trials – she was second in smarts—"

                                   AMY KULP

"Third last in strength," Colt corrected.

"But you remembered that," Justin noted. He looked around and all of Elitists nodded their heads. When I looked at Shane, his expression remained cold. Mine probably did too. I didn't know what that meant. "In the last trial, she got first place again. That is better than everybody here." He shook his head. "She has been here every day—"

"We get it, Justin," Eddie finally said. He smirked and grabbed the nearest weapon. He played with the bat in his hands and looked up with a twinkle in his eye. "You're kissing ass so she—"

I didn't get to hear what Eddie said because Justin ended up throwing three darts directly at him. It was the quickest thing I have ever seen. He threw one then one then the last one so fast that I thought it was all in one motion. Eddie stopped talking as immediately when one landed in his leg pants. It probably felt like a little bee sting. The second one hit his bare arm and the third one hit in a more sensitive spot on his hand. He dropped the bat he was holding, and Garrett ran by his side to help remove the shots.

"Just shut up and let the next trials determine how good of a player everyone is," Justin said. He pointed at everyone and dropped the last darts to the ground. Pushing me harder so that I would leave, he traveled right behind me. When we left the exit, I tried to turn around, but he pushed me harder until both hands were on my arms and I was losing my balance from the speed. Trying to head out the normal way, I felt Justin's hand tense up on my arms before pushing me in a way I didn't want to go. My feet tripped over themselves, but he had enough grip to steer me into the bathroom. "Shut up," he warned. He looked around and let go of me once the door closed. He pushed me against the wall.

For some reason, I didn't feel threatened. He checked under all the stalls and when he came back, he pushed his body against mine again. I didn't move at all and just watched as he nervously licked his lips, checked the mirrors, and then faced me again. He pressed his body against mine and I could feel the goosebumps rising along my skin. His body heat was causing mine to warm up and soon the goosebumps started to sweat.

"This is the only place we will have complete privacy." He looked around again and put his hand against the wall to stabilize himself. I nodded my head and watched as he looked around. "Bridget, there is so much Inductees don't know about these Trials."

"So, tell me," I said. He immediately looked at me as if I was too loud and I closed my eyes. "Justin, just tell me."

"These trials…" I could hear the crack in his voice, and he wouldn't look at me. It was like he was choosing his words carefully. "They're not tailored for inductees to win." He removed his hand from the wall and lessened the pressure on my body. "They're tailored to see who the best robots could be." He stepped away from me and looked me up and down. "People who follow orders without thinking about them." He kept eye contact, and I could see his face getting sadder. Maybe a little colder too. "People who don't question anyone."

                                    AMY KULP

"So, Cassandra?" I asked. He shook his head and closed his eyes.

"I guarantee that she and Anthony will be eliminated next round."

"Why not the last trial when they spoke out?"

"It was memorable," Justin stated. He looked at me for a second before going over to the sinks. I stayed at the wall. "You are memorable, Bridget." He looked in the mirror and just stared at himself. "Am I memorable?" I didn't think he was asking me. He continued to stare at himself and finally sighed. "The Elitists have been watching and studying the trials from previous years. Every year some people speak out. Every year those people are killed."

"Why?" I asked. Justin turned to me and angrily came close to me. I let my body melt into the wall again as he came closer to me again. He shook his head before stepping away from me. "Justin?" He shook his head again and sighed.

"Protests."

"What does that mean?" I asked. I shook my head and watched as he eyed me. He shook his head and started walking back toward the hall. "What does that mean, Justin?" He continued to walk out and when I heard the bathroom door open, I ran after him. As soon as I got in the hall, I shouted Justin's name and felt my cheeks blush red as I looked to my left.

Tanya was watching me.

"Justin?" I caught up to him and grabbed him by the arm. He fought me off by shaking his arm and walking to the machines. I followed him to the brain activities and when I stared at him, he continued doing what he needed to do. "Justin, are you serious?

I don't know what that means." His face was hardened and as I sat there staring at him, I watched what he had chosen.

Assassin Class #5

My eyes stared at his screen briefly before a video began to play. I watched when someone spoke up about the trials being stupid and watched when they were eliminated next round. We watched another class and another class. Each time, someone spoke out and then they were eliminated. When Justin clicked on another one, I looked at him and sat in my chair without saying a word.

"These people cause protests," Justin whispered. I didn't know what that was but before I could ask, I saw Tanya moving from the doorway straight toward us.

Even I knew to drop the subject if Tanya would be around and when I looked back at Justin's screen, he was already on a matching game. As if this entire conversation didn't happen.

#

I hesitated while opening the door and could hear the chatter in the bedroom. After listening more, I opened the door wider and walked in. As soon as they heard me, the conversation went dead, and they acted like they weren't just talking and laughing. It was so rare to hear anyone laughing anymore that the noise was a foreign sound to me. At least they weren't just staring at me. Jade was walking away into the bathroom, Nia was snuggling into her bed, and Cassandra was folding her clothes. I waited to see if they were going to greet me but when they continued to pretend that I wasn't there, I sighed and walked forward. I stopped right near Cassandra and waited until she looked up at me. She only momentarily stopped her folding to stare at me.

"Anthony is in the living space. He said he has been waiting for you." I watched a mix of emotions span her face within two seconds. She nodded and put the last of her clothes away before standing up. She raced out of the room without a second chance. "Nia?" I wondered. I looked back to see if her body stirred and when it didn't, I marched toward the bathrooms.

Jade was looking for whiteheads on her face. The only reason I knew that was because she was sitting on the sink with her forehead almost pressed against the mirror. I saw it when she accidentally touched her forehead against the glass, and it left a greasy residue on it. However, she only started picking at her face if she was nervous about something. I wanted to be the one to help her through it like I had previously but with how she has been acting, I was surprised she didn't run away as soon as I stepped foot in here.

"Did I do something wrong?" I wondered. I stepped over to the benches that were nearby her and sat down. She didn't move from her position at the sinks and continued to try and get one near her nose. I could see the skin around it turning red as she irritated and prodded it for longer periods.

"No," Jade responded when she popped the hard one. She twitched her nose from the pain and looked at the bleeding dot. She wiped at it and then wiped at the pus that sprayed onto the mirror. She moved on to the next one and I could see exactly how many she had already prodded at. With her pale skin, anything showed up on her face. "I'm just busier now."

I nodded my head to try and show her that I understood. I didn't though and I'm not sure I ever would. It felt like I had done something to her for her not to want to hang out with me. She has always been friends with Nia and Toby and still made time for me. It had something to do with Cassandra, but I didn't know what.

"Are you sure you don't want to train with me?" I asked. "I have a lot of new information for us."

"I'm busy," Jade said again. She shook her head and got off the sink. She washed her hands quickly and when she turned around, she looked straight at me before rushing out.

Even though she was no longer in the bathroom, I nodded as if she could see me. I wanted to accept the behavior change and Jade's decision, but I didn't understand them. I wanted to understand but she wasn't willing to talk to me. If it were something I said or did that made her uncomfortable, then I would take it back and move forward. However, if she couldn't, I would completely understand that. I have never fought with a friend before. If this is considered a fight, I'm not sure. My friends back at home – my ex-friends, I guess – we never fought. We were friendly in school and then I would tend to my farm. I was so busy with that after school that I never spent much time with them other

                    AMY KULP

than in school. Jade felt like someone I had gotten so close to in such a short time.

Getting up, I walked back into the bedroom and saw that Jade wasn't in her bed like I thought she would be. Nia was still in hers though and at this time, it seemed like she was in a deep sleep. I tiptoed passed her and quietly walked into the living space to see Anthony and Cassandra both crying. She was holding his hand as he stared off with his leg shaking. I made eye contact with Anthony, but he didn't out me or acknowledge that I was there.

"It was fun while it lasted," she whispered. I could hear her choking on sobs that she didn't want to let out. At that moment, she seemed genuine and honest with her emotions. "To progress to become an assassin, I must work with a group of people. We are more likely to win with alliances."

"I just don't understand why I can't be part of that alliance," he said. He let go of her hand and she reached for it again. He didn't let her take it this time and his leg started bouncing faster. This seemed like the most teenage thing to happen here. A breakup happening here in the trials? I didn't know people could trust others enough to form a relationship.

"You wouldn't understand," Cassandra whined.

"Try me," Anthony said. "Tell me before you count me out."

Cassandra closed her eyes for a second and formed three wrinkles on her forehead as she tried to figure out what to say. When she opened them, she looked at Anthony and something I did must have caught her attention because she looked over at me and the emotion that was on her face, disappeared. She shook her head and got up from the seat.

"It's over, Anthony."

I didn't move until I heard the door slam shut. When I did, I joined Anthony in the seat that Cassandra was just sitting in. I just stared off and waited until his leg shaking seized. I looked over at him and could see tears in the corner of his eyes and tears that were stained on his cheeks.

"She would've told you if she didn't see me," I whispered. He nodded and reached over to pat my knee gently. Almost as if to tell me that it was okay. What was okay? I wasn't sure but he didn't seem upset with me. "Did you guys know each other before the trials?" I wondered.

"No," he answered. He shook his head and stared at the ground. "Most of our group got eliminated pretty quickly—Daniel, Colin, Leah, and Audrey."

It surprised me to hear their names brought up again. It seemed that nobody talked about the dead anymore. It also surprised me to think about how they all were a group. I always assumed that most of them were loners. Then again, I didn't pay attention to anyone when I first got here. I was trying to figure it all out.

"Audrey?" I wondered. She was the youngest person here, but she was an Elitist. I didn't think that she hung out with Inductees.

"Surprising?" he asked. Anthony shook his head for a second. "She was like a double agent. Trying to pull the friends she made from the Elitists side over to us." He shrugged his shoulders. "She

                    AMY KULP

was friends with Leah mostly. Too scared to talk to all of us but clung by Leah's side. I think because they were the oldest and the youngest, they formed that bond of being outcasts together." He looked at me and sighed. "Leah always knew she wouldn't make it far."

"Why?" Anthony stared at me for a second before opening his mouth and closing it immediately. He shook his head and then stared at me again. I wasn't sure if he was trying to read me or waiting for me to think about the answer. He shook his head a final time and crossed his legs in the chair before he began picking at an invisible thread on his jeans.

"We got closer," he started. "When our group started getting smaller, we realized how much we hated being here." He eyed me but I just nodded my head. I didn't think anyone liked to be here. He paused and sighed. "We thought that spending time with each other would lessen how much we hated this place and it worked. We liked each other and we got together." He smiled briefly. "It's why she got so flustered about there being cameras everywhere." I stared at him, and he smiled. "Because…" He motioned for me to fill in the blanks, so I nodded my head. No need for him to think I was stupider than I seemed. "I guess I'll just do this thing by myself."

"I can always—"

"No," Anthony said. He stood up and stretched his legs before walking toward his bedroom. He turned around back around and stared at me. "You are trouble." I opened my mouth to protest but he held up a hand. "You attract trouble. The elitists don't like you and you need to figure out why. Why specifically you? Why not any other inductee?" He paused. "Find out why Colt doesn't like you."

"Do you know?" I wondered.

"No," he answered dryly. "I just think them hating you is killing your chances of winning." He looked at me and I could see the sadness grow in his eyes. "Now, I just got broken up with so if you don't mind."

I nodded again and watched him go. So now Cassandra was avoiding Anthony because of her alliance with Jade, Nia, and Toby. I knew that Jade was good with her people skills, but I didn't understand how she was convincing people not to talk to others and why it had to be so exclusive. On one side, I was glad I didn't accept the alliance but what was Cassandra being promised to give up Anthony? Was Anthony not worth it? Was this her way of getting out of the relationship with him?

I shook my head and got up from my spot on the chair. Walking out of there and into the kitchen, I suspected that nobody would be in there to annoy me at this hour. My eyes were stinging from how tired I was, but I knew my mind would keep racing about this. I might as well get some food to fuel the thoughts that were coming. Seeing the lights were on, I was already prepared that people were in there. I was prepared to have to face the small talk and I was prepared to be annoyed with them since I didn't have my sleep. However, I was in there to enjoy my snack and think my thoughts. I'm assuming anyone who was up at this time had the same mindset.

                     AMY KULP

I groaned to myself when I heard hooting and hollering from the table. My anxiety levels were now going through the roof and as I opened the fridge to figure out what I wanted, I tried hard not to let their comments get to me. I stared at the contents blankly and listened to what they were saying about me. I wondered what they were talking about before I came into the room. Did they have a plan? My stomach growled loud enough to knock me out of eavesdropping and looking back to see what was in here. It seemed that there was almost nothing that would satisfy me now. So, as I reached in and grabbed one of Justin's applesauces I knew I wouldn't enjoy my snack. It always tasted like baby food to me.

"Stealing your boyfriend's food?" Eddie asked as he laughed into his fork. I barely glanced to tell what he was eating.

"Oh, she's not talking to us," Garrett agreed.

"Probably going to run off to the bedroom since she no longer has friends," Colt whined. I glanced over at him and arched my eyebrow. He hadn't been taunting me as much lately but since his friends were here, I guess it was different. I took the lid off and plopped my spoon in before I walked over to the table and sat directly across from Colt. I chomped down hard on my spoon and intently watched all of them.

None of them spoke and none of them continued to eat. Instead, they all sat there and stared at me. I could see that they were glancing at each other and maybe communicating telepathically but nothing was said aloud. It continued like that until I finished. I perked my head up and stared at all of them. When I got up to throw the container away, I could hear someone getting up and walking out. However, when I turned back, I knew Colt was still in the room. So, I grabbed another applesauce from the fridge and sat back down. He remained silent as he watched me slurp the gunk off the spoon and he didn't move from his seat when I grabbed another one to eat too.

"I have an empty stomach and Justin has an infinite number of applesauce," I said as I tore the lid off another one. "We could do this all night." I got up to throw the lid away and when I got back, Colt had my spoon in his mouth and the apple sauce container in his hand. I arched my eyebrow and grabbed another one from the fridge. I made sure to keep eye contact as I scooped the food into my mouth. Colt made horrendous noises as he swallowed it and for a brief second, I could see the disgust on his face. That made for two of us. I wasn't sure how Justin liked this stuff. As soon as we both scraped the sides of the containers, Colt got up and grabbed two more for us. He sat down and arched his eyebrows as I shuddered for a moment. I wasn't going to back down though. I dipped my spoon in there and watched as Colt slurped it straight from the container with no reaction.

"Call it a draw?" Colt asked. He continued to slurp the rest of the applesauce and his whole body shuddered. Maybe it was a reaction to the nasty substance, or maybe Colt had already eaten. His face was becoming paler, and his fingers were jittering. "I have somewhere to be."

"With Jade?" I questioned. I remembered that she wasn't in the room when I left. It made sense that she would be seeing him. However, his face didn't betray a thing to me. "I don't back down from challenges, I win them."

"An applesauce challenge?" he questioned.

"Not everything has to be a challenge."

"With you it does," I spoke. "Why are you so awful to me around your friends?" I wondered. Colt's face didn't change as he grabbed two more containers for us. "What did I ever do to you?"

"This is a competition for killers," Colt said. "If you don't like it, just lose the next challenge and kill yourself." He paused as he slurped the rest of the container. "We didn't think you'd last the second challenge—"

"You are one to talk," I whispered. Screw this staying under the radar thing. I tried it and it's not working. "You were so close to getting out last round. Maybe you don't have what it takes to be an assassin." I stood up and slurped the rest of the applesauce just like he did. His face hardened as he searched my face to see if I meant what I said. "You're not so tough without your goons around."

I searched his eyes as he walked closer to me but instead of hurting me, he crushed the container in his hands and dropped it on the ground. When my eyes followed the trash, he pushed his chest against me until I was leaning backward on the table. His hands caressed the back of my hair as it hit the hard surface and he grabbed my hands for the container.

"You win this round."

He crushed the container and his eyes looked at my lips for one second before he straightened himself back up. He threw both containers away and walked out of the room. I sat right back in my seat and grabbed another container of apple sauce for my spoon to splatter in. I laid my upper body down on the table and allowed my head to fall on my arm. I played with the spoon in the sauce for a moment and felt my eyes beginning to close.

I wanted to sleep but I found my body too lazy to go back into the bedroom. While my eyes and brain were tired for the day, my stomach was digging into the waistband of my pants. I overate and knew what I was doing as I was doing it. However, I wanted to win against Colt. Even if it was something so small. I wasn't competitive but he didn't respect me and maybe, this small little win would gain more respect than when I was winning the Trials.

They were changing me. The Trials were changing me. I felt like it wasn't for the better either. I came in here so confused and scared. I wanted to make friends, but I knew that I shouldn't trust anyone here. I didn't want to kill anybody, and I didn't want anybody to get hurt. Now I was challenging boys who didn't like me in hopes that they would respect me. If my mom were ever able to find out what was happening, she would kill me. I didn't need anybody's respect but my own. If I had that, I would be set. She also didn't raise me to enjoy people's suffering. The scary part of this was that I was used to it now. If I was injured, it wasn't too bad, but I was also used to hearing other people yell out. I wanted to help them but now, I tended to hide if we were in the Trials. What happens if they were using that against me? Try to lure me out so they could kill me or taunt me.

I closed my eyes tight as I let my head roll on my arm. Would they make us kill for fun? How would they determine when to stop? What if they didn't have enough people for a graduating class? What happens—

"Are you okay?" I felt a prod to my arm and groaned. I didn't lift my head, nor did I say anything out loud to them. I was too tired. I felt another poke and when I was unresponsible again, I could hear them reach for the container of applesauce. What they were going to do with it, I didn't care. "Let's get you back to our room." I groaned again but felt their arms wrap underneath my armpits. They tried to hold onto me, but I started slipping. They pinched the skin as I slid down and listened to them huff. "It would help if you would try to walk back to the room." I groaned again and kept my eyes closed. When she finally had a good enough grasp on me, my body hit off hers until she put me down in the living space. "Get up. We don't want them to think we're weak."

"So, tell me..." I slapped my lips together and opened my eyes. I could see a blurry Cassandra standing right in front of me. "Why did you think Anthony was weak?" She rolled her eyes at me and sat down next to me. "What is going on with you?" I wondered.

"Are you drunk?" Cassandra asked.

"Avoiding the question," I noted. I blinked a couple more times and my vision became clearer at each blink. "I'm tired."

"I-I can't tell you." Cassandra looked around and stood in front of me. She crouched down to my eye level and placed her hands on my kneecaps. She stared at me, and I could feel the uneasiness as I refused to make eye contact. I just wanted my lids to stay closed. I was tired and the light was bothering my sight. "I'm sworn to secrecy." She looked at me and I nodded my head. "I'll tell you after this Trial, okay?" I nodded my head again. "Besides, I'm surprised you aren't included in it."

"Me too," I whispered.

"Come on, let's go to bed."

Cassandra hiked me up and I could feel her annoyance. I limped lazily along before we both stopped when we heard a shriek from the kitchen. A shrill voice yelled at the top of their lungs and as I listened to what was being said, I looked at the first alarm clock I could find before seeing what time it was. Early in the morning for some of the brightest people to be getting up while others lazed around.

"Who ate all of my apple sauce?"

#

I knew everyone around me could see the steam coming from my ears. Anyone standing next to me had moved a smidge away and I was receiving minor glances from everyone who wasn't actively talking. Missing from that generalization was Jade. Her back remained to me as I put one foot in front of the other. Of course, I would be picked as the demonstration. I wasn't even told what, but I knew I was mad. Colt smiled smugly as I stood by him, and I felt

                    AMY KULP

claustrophobic. Almost as if I was too close to him despite still being a circle's distance apart.

"When you see these two, I'm sure most of you are feeling uneasy," Bischoff announced. He clapped his hands together, but I refused to look at him anymore. I would continue to stare at my feet which were now surrounded by a red circle. It was taunting me as if I was being challenged to leave it. "That's the goal for today's trial," he commanded. "Today's trial is the Vulnerability Trial." I wanted to stare at him and ask a question, but I watched my feet. No toe was going to get out of line for this. I was going to win. "You are paired up with someone we don't think you get along with." He paused and looked back at us. I felt my cheeks burning red but refused to acknowledge it. "As Assassins, you need to lay your cards on the table. Fairly, your opponent will rate you based on how badly they think your stories affect you being a good assassin. Do you have a baby sister and therefore, freeze up when you see a little girl?" He paused and looked through us. "Are you such a wild card that they think you would ruin a mission by assassinating someone you weren't supposed to?" He paused again. "Assassins need to lie, manipulate, and tell the truth from time to time. We have done extensive research into your family's, background, and culture, if you are caught lying, you will be zapped." He looked back at the injured assassins coming inside. "Now, as the Trials progress we are assuming you are adjusting to the pain tolerance of their sticks." He paused and I could hear the whirring of electricity coming from them. I looked up at once and stared at the injured assassin.

"The amount of volts running through each electricity stick has significantly increased."

I looked over at the two groups in front of me and watched as they stepped back out of fear. My eyes grew huge at the insinuation, and I watched as the injured assassin turned toward Colt and me. As he stepped forward menacingly, I looked down at my feet to see that the circle was still bordered with a deep red. It wasn't blinking and it wasn't ready for me to move. My eyes darted toward the assassin and then at Colt. However, Colt kept staring ahead. He didn't seem scared and while initially I didn't understand why, I knew it was because the injured assassin wasn't coming for him. He was coming directly at me.

I cringed to the back of my circle and as far to the rim as I could go before, I felt a burning sensation run from my foot to the muscles in my leg. I stepped forward and closed my eyes as I knew the pain would be coming. I felt the movement and fell to my knees as the pain radiated through my body. My knees must have fallen outside the circle because burning went through my knees. I grabbed onto the nearest object and balled my fists into the material. I wanted to scream but as a noise pierced my ears, I was satisfied that the noise didn't come from my mouth.

Opening my eyes, I kept Colt's shirt balled into my fists and tried to get my head away from his chest. However, his fingers that kept the pressure on my neck made it hard for me to get away. When a couple of seconds of peace fled our bodies, he opened his eyes and made eye contact with me. We both untangled ourselves from each other and stood back in place in our circles. He stood in the center of his and I stood as far away from him as possible. Just staring at the ground, I could see exactly where my knees had hit, and I could smell the burning flesh. Or was that from the electricity?

"As you progress through the Trials, higher voltage will be used," Bischoff announced. "As you just saw, it can change you as a person. We just had two enemies in each other's arms." I blushed red and my gaze looked over toward Jade. She seemed concerned but it wasn't directed toward me. Her look was staring at Colt who wasn't staring back. Maybe he was embarrassed for himself or maybe, he was embarrassed that the electricity that went through my body, had gone into him the second I touched him. "Garrett Arnold and Nia Williams will be our next couple." I looked down at my feet but was disappointed to see my circle was still red. "Eddie Marlow and Cassandra Vise." Both swaggered up to their spots, although I could sense hesitation from Cassandra. "Justin Frazier and Jade Tricase." Jade stepped forward without hesitation and I could see Justin trying to look at me. I stared straight ahead though. Justin couldn't help me now. "Heather Flick and Tanya Booth." My eyebrows arched as two Elitists stood side-by-side with each other. I guess everything wasn't okay in paradise. "Asher Johnston and Anthony Denkins." I looked at the last two and once again, was surprised that it was two from the same team. "Toby Ernst and Shane Newfeld." Although I knew why Shane was paired up with him. "You each have a door and a table to walk through.

You will not be released until we believe you have shared enough information. Good luck, assassins."

The door in front of me and Colt opened. Instead of the hallway we had come from, the room opened with two chairs and a table. Once the circles started blinking, we walked in, and I surveyed the room. I wish I could have stared longer but there wasn't much to take note of when it was all white. As soon as I was done, I sat down and listened to the door close. What happens if I was killed in here?

"Do you want to start?" Colt asked. It sounded like it was supposed to be a whisper, but it echoed and bounced off all the walls. I stared at him until his voice disappeared from the room. Even then, I wanted to shrink away from his eyes. They were judging me. They traveled down my upper body and slowly traveled back up to my face. When his eyes finally made contact with mine, he smirked at me and leaned back in his chair. He continued to study me with that smirk on his face and it irritated me more than anything he could be doing now. "You have to talk to me, farm girl."

"Farm girl?" I questioned. "I thought I was ponytail?"

"You see," he started. He leaned his arm against the back of the chair and propped his leg up. "That didn't make much sense once you cut your hair." His eyes flew to my head and suddenly, I felt self-conscious.

"I didn't want you to be able to use it against me again," I responded. His eyebrows arched at the comment and his lips formed into a smile.

                    AMY KULP

"Now, that shows you were thinking like an assassin." The compliment fell flat to me and after a couple of awkward seconds of staring at each other, he faced the table and drummed his knuckles on the metal. "Would you like electricity to flow through your body?" he asked. I shook my head no and before he could talk, I leaned forward.

"I am not telling you a thing."

"Well, then, it was nice knowing you," Colt said. He stood up and smiled politely at me. "I hope I'm the one to kill you. I'll make it nice and slow just so you can feel what it's like. How happy I'll be without you competing. How—"

"Shut up," I answered. I rolled my eyes.

Despite his threats, I didn't believe them. I didn't believe him. I've seen him in the previous killings, and he didn't look any better than I. He always seemed like a mess and that it affected him. Despite his rough exterior, I knew that there was something about him that was vulnerable. I didn't know what and I didn't know how to get to it. He could lie and I would never know. Would the injured assassin know? Would Colt be willing to take that chance? He knew what it was like to get that electricity through him. He knew how it felt. We both got knocked down from it. Would he risk a lie for the electricity? Or would they let him go because he's an Elitist?

"You know, talking like that won't make you a lot of friends." Colt sat back down and stared at his knuckles as he brushed his fingers over them. "I heard you were… lonely."

"I don't want my problems aired on TV for people to laugh at me." I crossed my arms and pursed my lips. The only person who had known I was feeling that way was Justin. He was the only person willing to talk to me. I couldn't figure out if I was mad, betrayed, or annoyed with him. Right now, I had to survive. I shrugged my shoulders. "I'll take the electricity."

Colt moved out of his seat and toward me without saying anything. He rushed so fast to me that I didn't react when he put his lips up to my ear. At the same time, the door busted open and there stood an injured assassin with his electricity stick. I stared at him and felt Colt tense as he whispered hurriedly to me.

"After Cassandra's comments, they pulled the airings off the TV." We both straightened up as the assassin walked to us. His heavy boots clunked against the ground, and I could hear his footsteps slow down the closer he got to us. "Just say, you will talk." He backed away from me when the assassin came too close to me. I could hear the electricity on the end of his stick and as he pointed it toward me, I closed my eyes.

I gritted my teeth as it made physical contact with my skin. It felt even worse this time. The skin was hot from where he touched, and it pulsed through my body. I slammed my head down on the table and waited for the pain to subside. My teeth were clenched so hard that I thought that they might break from the pressure. If I had my eyes open, I was sure there would be black splotches running through my vision. If I was standing up, I would be knocked down again. I felt nauseous and thought that I might pass out. However, the pain started going away and as I picked up my head, the tears were rolling down my face and the snot was wiped away.

"Alright," I agreed through gritted teeth. I looked at the injured assassin and he backed out of the room. When the doors closed behind him, I stared Colt down. His eyes were wide, and he didn't seem to understand. "How do you know?" I questioned.

"We have the station they broadcast it," Colt said. "I also managed to watch a little bit of the news and they're saying they pulled it because they thought it was too similar to the Purge or the Hunger Games."

"What are those?" I wondered. I shook my head as I tried to normalize my breathing patterns. When Colt didn't answer right away, I looked up and could see he was thinking. "Blondie, what are those?"

"I-I'm sorry. I forgot those were banned from the public." His cheeks' redness deepened as he stared at me. "I grew up learning about them and having to recite the consequences of taking after them."

"Wait," I said. "So, Elitists get the advantage to see material that Inductees don't?" I shook my head and scoffed out loud. "You guys get another advantage and yet everyone wonders why Elitists win more. That is ridiculous, it's—"

"They don't teach you to fight or anything," Colt mentioned. "It's banned because of the—"

"I don't care," I said while shaking my head. "It is not fair that the Inductees are at such a disadvantage." Colt opened his mouth to say something but instinctively closed it and nodded in agreement.

"They're still recording it but it's for future Assassins to study."

"Future Elitists," I remarked. "How do I know you won't lie to me?" Colt immediately turned around and pointed to the injured assassin in the room. I made eye contact with him and immediately scoffed at the idea of him being here. It didn't mean that he wouldn't lie to Colt.

"Do you…" Colt asked. I looked up at him and he arched his eyebrows. "Feel lonely?"

My eyes darted toward the injured assassin, and I sighed. I just wanted to get out of this as fast as I could. There was no way for me to tell if Colt was telling the truth. There was no way for him to know if I was telling the truth. Did I want to risk it though? I looked at the injured assassin again and he held his stick tightly as he noticed my staring. I sighed once more and began nodding my head.

"Yeah, I do."

"Why?"

I looked up at him and started picking at the corners of my nails. I wasn't sure that I wanted to tell him. How do I express that he stole my best friend? Were they friends? Were they more than friends? I didn't want to seem like a jealous person or anything. I opened my mouth but quickly shut it instead. I was contemplating what I wanted to say and how I wanted to say it.

"Who do you think my best friend is?" I wondered. I looked up at him and he seemed to ponder for a second.

"Justin." I shook my head and watched as he thought more about it. When he looked up, he didn't have to say anything before I started nodding.

"And now Jade is not talking to me. Instead, she's talking to you." I looked up at him and studied his reactions. However, he was guarded. "I cannot figure out why she is talking to you though. You have been nothing but awful to me and yet, she is still talking to you. She is avoiding me and I'm sure it's something you said."

"You're friends with Justin and Jade doesn't like that." He shrugged his shoulders as if that was the fairest point. I nodded my head to agree and looked off to the side. I had no idea how to express that Jade and I had bonded. While we may not be true friends and may have never become friends if it wasn't for the Trials, she was someone that I was close to. She was someone who helped me with challenges and increasing my athletic abilities. "I'm sorry." I nodded and felt myself flinch when I started pulling the hangnail on my finger. He looked back at the injured assassin and he shook his head no. "Okay, we need to share more about each other. What about your home life?"

"It's the last thing I have," I mentioned. I shook my head and continued playing with the skin around my fingers. "I don't want you to ruin the memory of my family." I looked up at him and placed my hands in my lap. "You hate me. You have made it clear from day one that you don't like me. I don't know what I did to you but that's not the point. I don't trust that you won't just say that my backstory is so messed up that I wouldn't be a good assassin."

"I wouldn't do that," Colt dismissed. "I'm just doing what I grew up to do." He looked at me and for a second, I could see his mask break. I couldn't tell what emotion flooded it because he switched it to a blank stare. "I might not like you and I might not have a reason about why I don't like you – I just don't. However, I wouldn't risk a good assassin to be thrown away because of my feelings. I think that would show a lot of insecurity from me."

"How do I know you're telling the truth?"

"You don't. Just like I don't know what you'll put about me. Just start talking so we can leave and never talk to each other again." He paused and watched me. I just nodded my head. I don't see why I had to go first.

"Well, I grew up on a farm—"

"Yeah, I was there when everyone was being removed from their family's lives."

"Okay." I looked at the table instead of at Colt. I didn't want to see his reaction as I told him my sob story of a life. I knew that mine wasn't bad. However, it was still my life. I didn't want his pity and I didn't want him to know about it. Maybe if I left a few details out, I wouldn't be electrocuted.

"You're lucky they were so willing to fight for you," Colt added. He tapped his knuckles on the table, and I just stared at him. I think that was a compliment. I didn't want to make a big deal out of it though. That was not the type of person Colt was. He didn't compliment you just to get you

                                    AMY KULP

somewhere. It was genuine. Then again… I didn't know Colt. Maybe he was hiding stuff as well. Maybe this was a ploy to get me to trust him. Maybe he was going to strike against me and… "That was awkward. Please continue."

"Okay," I whispered. I took a deep breath in and let it out. I still didn't want to look at him. "I guess I'll start with my dad." I briefly made eye contact with him and could see him nodding his head. "Um, my dad is a farmer – it's his passion. He loves the animals, although, that's not why he does it. He loves being in the field and harvesting food for us. We sell it," I mentioned. "That's where we got a lot of money from. From such a young age, my dad took me out and taught me how to care for the animals – feeding them, which ones to avoid, and cleaning up their pens. The assassins killed my rooster and I'm sure my dad had to pay a fortune to buy another one." I looked at Colt. "He's cheap." I smiled. "But, we were the only farm in our area and the neighboring areas. When people came around, they bought from us – eggs, meat, and the crops." I looked up at him and studied Colt for a second. He was nodding, but he wasn't looking at me. "I live in a poor neighborhood so some people can't afford to buy it." A wrinkle appeared on Colt's face. "We were cheaper than a store though so sometimes, people would just take it and pay us later. We never asked for it back though. If they—"

"Why not?" Colt asked. He continued to stare off to the side of my head. He didn't seem to make the connection. "Why wouldn't you make them pay?

You could've alerted the assassins and they would be added to the list."

"Everybody struggles." I shrugged my shoulders. "They're our neighbors. We can't just watch them starve. We all grew up together."

"That's why you're an Inductee."

"My parents don't believe in violence." There was a harsh tone to my words. Colt didn't have a right to say anything to me about it. "Even if we had the money, they wouldn't send me to the Preparatory schools. I grew up learning that we take care of each other because the government—"

"You can continue," Colt warned. I watched him for a second and this time, he made eye contact with me. His back was straighter, and he seemed to be on high alert. He darted his eyes to the side of him and when I looked, I could see the injured assassin had moved forward. Oh right, I forgot that I can't say anything about the government. I swallowed the words I was going to say and sighed.

"Anyway, sometimes the farm didn't do so good. It could have been that that food had risen in price, the weather was too hot, or that we had a sickness spreading through our animals—"

"Or that you gave away free food."

"Do not interrupt me when I'm talking." I shook my head aggressively and huffed. "The weeks that did bad, my dad would be in the fields all day. Sometimes, I wouldn't see him before I went to bed. I resented him a bit for that." I nodded my head and licked my lips. Little tears started to form in my eyes, but I quickly blinked them away. It felt weird to say that you didn't like your dad because he was trying

　　　　　　　　　　　　AMY KULP

to provide for you. It felt selfish to say it out loud. I wish I didn't say it. "My mom made more of an effort to be in my life – she showed up to school events, helped me with my homework, and asked me about my day. She didn't work on the farm. In fact, she didn't know anything about it. Often, I wondered how they ended up with each other. I'm not exactly sure what she does but a lot of her money helped to support the farm." I looked at Colt and shrugged my shoulders. That was my life.

"How did you score so high on the academic trial if you went to public school?" He paused for a moment and then continued. "I'm assuming you went to public school."

"You assumed correctly." I said it with a bitter taste in my mouth. "I studied like crazy." I shrugged my shoulders at the simple answer. "It was instilled into my brain that my mom and dad wanted me to succeed in life which meant that I would go to college. We can't afford college though. I would need a scholarship—"

"Those are only for Elitists," Colt interrupted.

"Not if I'm smart enough. I can get those scholarships away from them."

"That's never happened."

"We were going to be the first to try," I said. I shook my head. "I didn't do that hot on the athleticism trial because I don't have endurance. I have strength though. I'm so used to moving bails of hay and moving stubborn cows." I flexed my arm muscles for a second and smiled. "As for the last trial we did, I figured that hiding in the most obvious places is the best. I can't tell you how many times my dad would be shouting for me and I'd just be laying with the cows." I smiled and looked at Colt. I was finished. I didn't have a tragedy happen to me. My dad didn't spend as much time with me as I would have liked.

"I have a similar story," Colt responded. "My dad was often away too so I was always left with a nanny." He shrugged his shoulders. "He worked like crazy to afford the Preparatory school and bids."

"I still don't think those are fair for Inductees?" I shook my head in frustration and watched as he remained still.

"You seem to be doing well for yourself, farm girl."

#

"Garrett Arnold."

He marched forward to his circle with a smug look on his face. I wish I knew what his story was. I wanted to know what everybody's story. Even though Colt told me his, there were a lot of questions I had for him. I specifically wanted to know about his mom. I felt idiotic that I didn't ask him about his mom.

"Eddie Marlowe."

He gave his friends a high-five and darted toward his circle now. I felt the sweat on my hands beginning to form and I wasn't sure if I was nervous that they were good killing machines or that I was at the bottom. I looked over to the Elitist group and

                               AMY KULP

most of them looked forward. I just wanted Colt's attention though.

"Colt Kirkman."

He walked forward and celebrated with his friends. He jumped into his circle, and I felt myself close my eyes. I should have asked about his mom. His vulnerability score probably would have gone down a little more. Clearly, he avoided the topic with her so that had to mean it meant something for him.

"Justin Frazier."

He looked back at him and let go of Heather's hands as he moved forward. He took his time and unlike the other three, he didn't seem to celebrate as much. His face looked pained. Did having to talk about his past hurt him? I would have to ask although I was mad at him right now. How dare he tell Colt about my feelings of loneliness! He was the only one that knew about it and he told me that he wasn't friends with those guys anyway. Why would he tell him about it?

"Heather Flick."

There was so much relief on her face that when she let go of Tanya's hands, I didn't notice how nervous Tanya had gotten. I didn't realize they were friends. Tanya usually hung out with Garrett, Eddie, Colt, and Shane. I have never seen her hang out with Heather and Justin. As Heather hurried her step to get in her circle, she smiled brightly. This expression matched with Justin's as he grabbed her hand to hold. I felt myself smiling too but remembered that I had not been called yet.

"Asher Johnston."

My expression began getting cold as I watched him go up. There was only one Elitist left and the rest were Inductees. That meant their training had prepared them to guard their feelings and backstories. I scoffed to myself and shook my head. This was unbelievable.

"Tanya Booth."

Of course. I should've seen that coming. As she walked forward, Shane looked at all of us and rejoined our group. He smiled softly at us and stood between Jade's group and the other outcasts – Anthony and me. I crossed my arms and arched my eyebrows. This didn't seem fair and I was a little mad about it.

"Shane Newfeld."

That made sense. He seemed to not be in tune with his feelings. I felt my nerves get the best of me though. Only six of us were left; only four of us were safe. I peeked around and hoped that I wasn't too emotional. I started crying at one point but I blinked them away quickly. Did Colt see that?

"Toby Ernst."

I tapped my foot along the floor. Colt watched me until he was pulled away by something Eddie had said. Did he lie? Would he lie about letting the best assassins in? Even if I was an Inductee? Even if I was a girl?

"Jade Tricase."

My stomach was feeling pain in it as Jade walked up to her circle. I already knew I was losing the color in my face and had to hold my stomach in. Was I going to puke? I looked at the color on my arms and the redness that was previously there was vanishing into a pale color. I wasn't sure I could take this.

"Bridget Solomon."

I sighed in relief and while my stomach was still hurting, I trudged forward. I walked past Garrett, Eddie, and Colt without a glance. When I got to Justin, he glared at me and then glared back at the group that was left. I high fived him before moving on to the small hug that Heather gave me. Tanya smiled at me and nodded her head – unusual for her. She usually didn't give me the time of day or if she did, she sneered at me. Everyone else ignored me. When I got into my circle, I looked at the remaining people.

Nia, Cassandra, and Anthony. I looked back at Justin, and he nodded his head. Would he be right? Would Anthony and Cassandra be eliminated? Maybe they truly deserved it. Maybe they were vulnerable and wouldn't be good assassins. Nevertheless, I bit my lip and watched Bischoff looked down at the envelope in his hands.

"Nia Williams."

She immediately slumped and walked toward the circles. I was left to watch Anthony and Cassandra and while he wanted to hug her, she remained still.

"Anthony Denkins."

Without getting a reaction from Cassandra, he walked forward. Cassandra moved forward without her name called and closed her eyes as she stood in her circle. Anthony turned to her, but she wouldn't open her eyes.

"Garrett and Nia," Bischoff announced. Both stepped forward and received a bat to kill each of them. He stood back and crossed his arms. Garrett didn't waste any time before destroying Anthony.
I closed my eyes as I heard the whacking of the bat. I listened and listened to the whines, the crying, the bat hitting against something hard, and the pleading for help. When all the noises stopped, I opened my eyes to see Anthony and Cassandra on the ground. Blood was everywhere and while Garrett handed his bat back to Bischoff without a second glance, Nia held onto hers. I wasn't sure she hit either of them until she rotated the bat in her hands so I could see the blood on it. It was also dented. How hard did they hit?

"Come on," Justin whispered to me. I looked at him as he held out his arm to me. On the other side was Heather. Tanya was following closely behind and all I could do was dart my eyes between them. "I know how you get, Bridget. Come on." I looked at all of them again and Heather smiled at me. She placed her head on Justin's shoulder for comfort and he accepted it. "Did you watch it?" I shook my head and could see the relief on his face. "Good, that was brutal."

I walked into his open arm and felt him squeeze tightly to my arm. He moved all of us to the kitchen and we all sat down. Nobody was talking from the shock, but he brought out cups of mixed fruit. When he sat down between Heather and Tanya, he watched everybody remain frozen.

"It would've been applesauce, but *somebody* ate all of them."

AMY KULP

I got up instantly and his face changed from playful to serious. Tanya moved to open her cup and I just shook my head. I couldn't eat right now. I felt disgusted and my stomach hurt still. I left the kitchen and stopped short as soon as I saw Colt and Jade on the couch together.

They both looked at me and then back to each other. I just rolled my eyes. I rushed past the living space, the bedrooms, and a crying Nia to the toilets. My gut wretched everything I ate the past couple of days until I was able to spit into the toilet. I reached blindly for the toilet paper and felt it being placed in my hand. I wiped my nose and mouth before flushing everything down the toilet. When I got up and turned around, I was surprised to see Nia.

"I've been doing it too," she said. Her eyes were swollen red and she sniffed any snot back up. "I killed someone." I nodded my head. I didn't know how to comfort people. "I really killed someone." She looked at me and I could see the distress in her eyes. "I closed my eyes and just swung. I killed someone."

"Cassandra," I mentioned. "Don't forget her," I said.

"I killed Cassandra," Nia said. She gagged and then pushed me so that she could squat in front of the toilet. I handed her some toilet paper like she did with me, and her body slumped against the toilet. "I killed Cassandra."

Her sobs started to get loud as she groaned about Cassandra. After a couple seconds of repetition, I backed up and left the bathroom. I wanted to sleep but I could hear Nia crying. Her sobs got louder and I knew that I couldn't just sit here and listen to that. Eating clearly wasn't the right choice either. I only had the choice to train.

Leaving the bedrooms and the living space, Jade called after me for a second before I could leave her entirely. I paused and watched as she got off the couch to chase me.

"Um… do you want to train tomorrow?" she asked. I looked at her and continued to stare. "Together?"

"Y-yeah." I nodded my head and watched her smile.

"Great. I'm just going to check on Nia." She smiled again and nodded her head.

As she left toward the living space, my eyebrows fell down my face and I just stood there. It wasn't until Colt stood up and we accidentally made eye contact, that I could tell it was him. I nodded my head, and he nodded his back.

"Thank you.

"She's been distant," Jade commented as I continued to run on the treadmill. I could feel the sweat dripping down my back as she increased the speed. She leaned against the machine and looked elsewhere. I was breathing so deeply that I could probably fog up every window in the room. I wanted to respond but I couldn't with how hard it was for me to get any air in my lungs. Jade shook her head and as the stopwatch beeped, she turned off the treadmill. I slowed down and eventually was able to put my hands on my knees and take hard gasps. My face was probably red too. "Your endurance is getting better," she noted.

"Yeah," I agreed. I straightened up when she handed me a water bottle. I felt like I couldn't drink from it though. I was already gasping for air, and I wouldn't have enough time to drink the liquid before I started coughing. This was the hardest that Jade had worked me out, but it made sense why I was reacting so badly – I hadn't practiced when we weren't talking. After a couple of seconds and one sip of water, I looked at her. She had been watching me and probably noting how I was reacting to her exercising. Was she able to do that? "She just killed someone. I think she deserves some space right now."

"I know that but—"

"We don't know what it's like to kill someone," I said. I followed Jade as she moved to a different machine. "I can barely watch as they kill someone. I don't know how I would react when it's my turn." I shook my head and couldn't imagine it.

Especially with a bat. You would have to be angry and keep hitting them. Maybe one swing to the head would silence them. The noises they made were haunting. How Cassandra begged to be killed faster and how Anthony begged Cassandra to stop crying. How Anthony was trying to comfort her as he was dying. Without watching them, I knew that Garrett was brutal compared to Nia. He probably hit nonfatal places to get him to suffer. I felt queasy just thinking about it.

"You're getting pale again," Jade mentioned. I nodded and stepped up on the new machine. I could already feel the pain in my stomach again. I was thinking too much about it and now I was nauseous. "I can't work you if you're going to puke. Go to the bathroom," she instructed.

I nodded and followed her instructions. I ran to the only bathroom I knew we had here and found myself peeking into the target practice room. I could already hear laughter and chatter before I saw anyone in there. Justin had his back to me, but I could see that Tanya had noticed my movement near the doorway. Maybe she was the lookout.

I rushed away and into the bathroom. Sliding onto my knees, I crashed into one of the toilets and felt my stomach beginning to get pressure built up. I groaned in response and waited the few minutes it took for my stomach to obey what my mind was doing. As soon as I was done, I didn't wipe my mouth or nose and instead, flushed the toilet. I got up and spit in it a couple times before turning around.

"Still?" Justin asked.

I nodded my head and brushed past him to wash my face off. I hated vomiting but it seemed to be the newest reaction to the Trials. I wanted to stop but I didn't know how not to send myself into this panic. Once I think about it, I was going to puke. If I felt the pressure building, my worrying forced me to puke. It seemed weird and unnatural since I didn't see the beating occur. I heard it though.

"If you're going to be an assassin, you need to control that," Justin said. He rubbed my back and I leaned into him as he continued. It felt nice but it didn't soothe anything. My stomach was still growling at me that something was wrong. "That probably wasn't helpful."

"Not at all."

"Why are you suddenly impacted by the killings?" he asked. I shrugged and walked to the farthest wall. As I slid down, I could see my reflection in the mirrors: a bald girl with bright red-rimmed eyes who was a sick green color. Justin joined me but kept some space between us as he stared at me. "You know why and you're just not saying it." I looked at him and just nodded my head. There was no point in me lying to him. "What is it?"

"You were right," I whined through my sobs and vomit. I could feel it bubbling up and I placed my hands directly onto my stomach. Maybe if I physically pushed it down, it would stay down. Maybe not thinking about it would help. I looked at Justin and could see his smirk appearing on his face.

"When am I not right?" he gloated.

"You're spending way too much time with those Elitists," I said. I shook my head. "So much time that you're willing to gossip about me to Colt."

"Wow, if I didn't know better, I would have assumed you were an Elitist with how full of yourself you are," he retorted. I stared at him and when he realized that I wasn't joking, he stopped smiling. His joking demeanor was gone. "I can't just ignore them, Bridget. We're on the same team and I sleep in the same room as them." He shrugged his shoulders. "If they want to talk to me about you, then that's what I will do."

"What about me?" I wondered. Justin shook his head out of irritation. Despite how we were very similar, he didn't want me to act like him. He didn't want me to ask questions about myself, but it was okay if he did it. Sometimes, I just liked to hear what gossip was going around about me. Would that be a double standard to him if I asked?

"Let's get back to me," Justin said. He smiled as I frowned and seemed to take joy in my misery. For a split second, I wasn't sure that he was joking.

Justin had come far though. After all, he had three girl best friends – me, Heather, and now Tanya seemed to enjoy his company. While Justin was attracted to Heather, I knew his bad reputation had put her off. I could see it in her body language. She didn't want to have to teach him to be a decent human being to girls. He probably said something stupid that turned her completely off from him at first. Compared to the other boys, though, Justin is a perfect angel. She had to realize that as soon as the other ones came along. All the Elitists seemed to be

                    AMY KULP

sexist and classists. I wondered what they were warping their brains to be in those Preparatory schools.

How could a girl grow up thinking that girls were inferior to boys? How could a girl not want to prove herself to everyone? That's what is pushing me along. None of the boys think a female Inductee could make it. The odds are stacked against me, but I know I can do it if pushed hard enough. I love doing things despite people.

"Why was I right?" Justin asked.

"About Cassandra and Anthony," I noted. "These Trials are rigged." I shook my head and felt my stomach beginning to bubble. "If they don't like what I do or what I say, then I could just be killed." I shook my head. "My skills might not be enough."

"So don't piss anyone off."

"Do you not know me?" I wondered. I threw my hands up in the air to overemphasize my idea. While that was playful, the next second my mood had completely changed. I felt tears running down my face and as I clutched onto my stomach harder, I knew that it was coming up.

I raced toward the toilets and felt myself wretch up what I had eaten last. I didn't think there was more in there. As I did so, I cried out in pain because I was scared. I was so good at making people not like me. I was so good at saying the wrong thing. Even as a little child, I wanted to ask stupid questions that would get me sent home from school with rope burns on my wrists and knees. The torture of having to be strapped down aggressively as they forced me to watch speeches of our leaders and then the consequences of talking bad about them – being added to the Assassin's List and then multiple shot of people being killed. Now that I was going through these trials, I knew that those were probably from different trials.

"Calm down," Justin said. He was right behind me, and he lowered himself down to rub my back as my stomach pumped up more bile. I'm sure he was grimacing, but he didn't seem to care as he sat next to me.

I was so tired of this. This was hurting. My stomach and back were sore from how much extra I was doing. I never worked out those muscles but now, they were stinging. Not to mention that my teeth felt like they needed to be brushed every time afterward. That was so unrealistic. Maybe I needed to carry mouthwash with me. The toothpaste didn't help though – it was the nasty taste in the back of my throat that lingered.

"Maybe, I was wrong," Justin soothed. I rested my arms against the seat and knew that if I were thinking about this, I would be disgusted with myself. I was so tired though. Physically and mentally. "There's a chance."

"How do we know?" I asked. I blinked extra hard to remove any lingering tears in my eyes. They slid down my face and dripped into the water below. With no reaction from my stomach, I flushed the toilet and barely turned to Justin. He seemed comfortable cramped in the stall with me. His body was against the stall door, and he had his legs laid out in front of him. "How do we know that you're wrong?"

                          AMY KULP

"I don't think we can," Justin said. He thought for a moment and when his face lit up, I smiled at him. He would tell me regardless of if I asked. He was just that type of person that had to make sure everyone knew they had come up with an idea. "Unless we find out their vulnerability scores."

"How are we going to do that?"

"We can ask their partners what they were scored," Justin suggested.

"Who were their partners?"

Justin had to think for a second. It wasn't like him to have to think about a minor detail. He crunched his eyes hard to think about who it could have been.

"Asher was Anthony," I answered.

"I think Eddie or Garrett was Cassandra's," Justin added.

"I will take Asher and you find out from Eddie or Garrett."

"Who said that I was helping you?"

"Me," I answered. "Do it because you love me." Justin rolled his eyes as he looked at me. "This could mean I'll stop puking." I got close to his face and smiled at him. Without warning, I breathed out deeply and watched as his face contorted from the rank smell. "Listen, it'll cause a lot of suspicion for me to suddenly get along with Eddie or Garrett. I don't want to raise other people's suspicions."

"Can I tell Heather?"

"Yeah?" I questioned. I shrugged my shoulders. "Tell Tanya too. Maybe she can help you. I've noticed that you guys have been hanging out more."

"Yeah, she wanted to have better friends," Justin said. "Apparently, they have said a lot of horrible things to her." He shook his head. "I wouldn't put her through that again."

"Aw, look at you, caring about someone besides your ego." I rolled my eyes as I stood up. I needed to wash out my mouth.

"Are you jealous of Tanya and I's friendship?" Justin asked. I bent down and cupped some water into my mouth. I gargled and turned around to look at Justin with wide eyes. "Don't worry, nobody will replace you." I quickly turned back around and spit the water back in the sink.

"Really?"

"Well, maybe Heather."

#

"Are you busy today?" Jade asked as she popped her head into the bathroom. I looked up from brushing my teeth and gave her a thumbs up. "Does that mean you aren't busy or you are?" She walked over to me and on the bench as she watched me scrub. I spit it out quickly and wiped my mouth before answering her. "Why are you all of a sudden busy?"

"Hang out with Nia," I said. I instantly looked toward the bedrooms and stepped closer to Jade. Nia was still in her bed. "You know she needs someone right now." Jade pouted in the next second and my eyebrows shot up my face. "Jade, you just went about two weeks without talking to me and now you can't live without me?" I turned to face her but her eyes wouldn't look at me. "What gives?"

                    AMY KULP

"I can't tell you," Jade said. She looked up at me and I could see something in them. "Believe me, I want to tell you, but can't."

I stayed silent. I didn't know how to respond to that. If I am quiet, she would spill something. As I stood there waiting, it didn't seem like she would cave. It must have been a huge secret to her.

"Is this the secret that Cassandra was going to tell me?" I questioned. I watched Jade's reactions, and she allowed her emotions to get through. Unlike everyone else here, she didn't try to mask them either. I turned around and grabbed the mouthwash.

If she didn't want to tell me, that was none of my business. However, I wanted to know what this secret was. I was assuming that Nia, Toby, and Colt also knew it. Why could they all know but I couldn't? Was there something untrustworthy about me? Did they not like me? Maybe Nia, Toby, and Jade were still upset that I denied their alliance. I was just asked too soon and didn't know if I could trust them. If I had the choice, I would make my alliance now: myself, Justin, Heather, Jade, and Anthony. It was just too late for that. It was clear to see who had become fast friends and who was giving each other tips and tricks to survive.

"Hang out with your boyfriend, then," I suggested. I didn't want her to know that I was upset and with neither of us talking, it would end up with one of us exploding our emotions. When I looked back at Jade, she seemed taken aback.

"Who is my boyfriend?" she wondered. At first, I thought she was joking. I smiled at her and rolled my eyes but when I looked at her, she seemed serious. Jade usually wasn't one who was great at lying. Although, I could be wrong.

"Colt?"

"You think Colt is my boyfriend?" she questioned. I nodded my head and watched her smile broadly. "Colt is my friend but he is not my boyfriend. I can't flirt and date people here. Who knows if they'll survive past the trials?" I continued to stare at her. I wasn't sure I believed it. She spent a lot of time with him. "We just… have similar interests. He's nice but has too much baggage."

"What do you mean?" I asked. "I was with him for his vulnerability test and he didn't seem to have that much baggage."

"Because you're not good at pushing people to open up," Jade said. "You just let me get away with telling you I had a secret without asking me more about it."

"I'm respecting you."

"Which I love but sometimes, you need to push. If you asked the questions that pushed Colt to open up, he probably would have been in the bottom three." She stared at me. "Although, I do believe that you would not have been as harsh as me."

"Why do you say that?"

"No reason," Jade said. She got up from the bench and grabbed the brush on the counter. She started brushing her hair and busying herself. "I don't think that boy has the capacity for love in his body." She shook her head and when she was done brushing, she looked at me. "What are you doing today that you can't include me?"

                                    AMY KULP

I shook my head and smiled. "I have my secrets too."

"But see, the thing is…" Jade drawled on. She set the brush down on the counter and looked at me through the mirror. I hated when she did that, but knew I also had the bad habit of doing the same thing. It was like she was speaking to my reflection rather than to me. "I am a pusher." She turned her head farther so that instead of the mirrored reflection, she was now staring at me. I pulled my eyes away from the mirror to stare back at her. "Is it because you don't like me anymore that you're not telling me?" I let my eyebrows fall down my face before I shook my head. She couldn't think I was that dumb to believe her right now, right? "Then just tell me. You know you're eventually going to tell me anyway. You always do." She smiled at me and I could feel my exterior breaking down.

I couldn't tell her that quickly though. She was only ignoring me until I admitted to Colt that I was lonely. It took having him say something for her to listen to me. That left me with so many questions. Were they doing this to tease me? Maybe to test me? If she and Colt could have their secrets, then Justin and I could have ours.

"I can't," I said. I shook my head and closed my eyes. I didn't want to see her face when I told her that. "I don't want you to get in trouble."

"Trouble?" Without seeing it, I could hear the excitement in her voice. "You're doing something that could get you in trouble?"

"Yeah," I said. I nodded my head and looked at her funny. "You told me I needed to lie low because I was too much trouble the one week, remember?" I opened my eyes and watched as her smile faded from her lips. It took her a moment before her face fell solemn and she did remember that. Why was she excited that I was going to get in trouble though? "It's best that you don't know and never find out."

"Come on, just tell me!" Jade pleaded. I shook my head and started walking back to the bedrooms. She followed closely behind and a little too close for comfort. "Who are you trying to piss off?" I kept walking without saying a word to her. She wasn't getting the hint. "Is it Colt? I won't be mad if it is. I know you don't like him." She studied my face as I sat on the fluffy cushion and pulled out my outfit for the day. "Eddie or Garrett? Nobody will really care. Those guys are assholes." I didn't care that I changed until she made a gasping noise. All my insecurities flew to me and I put my clothes on at lightning speed. It wasn't about me though. "It's an Inductee, isn't it?" As soon as I was done changing, I barged out of there and raced toward the kitchen. "Toby?"

"Shut up," I barked. I whirled around and looked at the surroundings. Thankfully, nobody seemed to be around right now. "I just… I don't think the Inductees are losing on our own." I eyed her to try and let her know that this was serious. I really couldn't tell her though. I just couldn't. She would blab to everyone and then it would come back to me.

Jade's expression changed though. Her playful smile was gone and she studied me. Her eyes surveyed my face and body language before she

                              AMY KULP

nodded. She backed up and after a minute, walked back into our living space.

I didn't have time to think about it as I shook my head and entered the kitchen. It was barren like I predicted and as I waited, I sat down and grabbed the newspaper and pencil on the desk. It was no doubt a prop for future Assassins to see. Maybe it was a prop to scare us about what was happening outside of these trials. I didn't know but I was using it as my prop now. I knew not to try and read it though – I didn't want to be upset, scared, or angry about anything.

And then I waited.

And I waited.

And I waited.

And I waited there for four hours. Four hours of people coming in and then looking at me. Nobody tried to talk as they passed but some whispered to their friends. A span of an hour and twelve minutes that nobody tried to speak to me: it was great. Trying not to read this paper was not easy though. As I sat there and my eyes wandered, I caught a few words that would normally keep my attention. Purposely throwing my eyes in a different direction or turning the page, helped me to tune out what I was reading. When I am in bed later, I would try to piece together the puzzle.

"Everyone said you were camped out in here," Justin said. I nodded my head and held the newspaper in front of me. I raised it so that Justin couldn't see my face. "Oh, you're starting today?" I didn't answer him, and he seemed to get his answer quickly. He left the table in a hurry, and I was certain that he was going to get Heather to complete his tasks. He probably forgot.

It wasn't until I heard a munching noise about ten minutes later that I realized the person I wanted was sitting in front of me. I lowered the newspaper down as I pretended to finish the story. Once it laid flat against the table counter, I picked up my pen and underlined a random line. Maybe he would be intrigued by what I circle and write.

"I want your help," I whispered. The first words cracked as my throat warmed and I needed to clear it. I continued circling and underlining random newspaper articles until I heard a grumble back from him. At first, I wasn't sure he heard me.

"No." I looked up at him and was surprised about his decision. "I have nothing to offer you." He flattened his palms on my newspaper which startled me to look up. I knew how to get his attention and now that I had it, he knew how to get mine. "You are already training with the smartest person here." He shrugged his shoulders. "I have also seen you train with Jade and she is more athletic than me." He shrugged his shoulders. "You don't want me to help you with that. Now what do you actually want?"

I paused for a moment and had to contemplate where to go from here. He could already see through my plan so what is it that made him see that? I tried not to make it obvious that I had been tracking him the past couple days. I hung out here and figured out around what time he came around. I never talked to him about anything but what I was eating too. So, I know that I didn't tip him off. Did Justin?

    AMY KULP

"Cut to the chase or I'm leaving," Asher threatened. I cleared my throat and nodded my head to buy myself more time. He rolled his eyes though. "Listen, I'm not going to join your alliance or whatever. Is that what this is about?" I shook my head and he continued to watch me.

"I… Straight to the point?" I asked. He nodded his head. "What was Anthony's vulnerability score?" His body instantly relaxed and he looked up at me.

"Why is everyone suddenly so interested in that?" I could see the sharpness in his eyes and tone as he spoke. He shrugged his shoulders as if it wasn't a big deal. "He scored pretty high so I was surprised he had made it to the bottom two." He paused and I felt my skin beginning to pale. My stomach was already in knots and as I held onto it, I could see Asher's lips moving. "Why do you want to know?"

"Uh," I said. I fidgeted in my chair for a moment as I stared at him. "I just…" I looked around and knew that the only thing that was a blind spot to me was the entrance to the kitchen. "Don't you think it's suspicious that he scored so high and was in the bottom two?"

"What are you saying?" Asher asked. He sat up and stared at me.

I suddenly felt unsafe. I should not have been honest with him. He was an Elitist after all. I didn't know him. I hoped that he would have been a good guy like Justin. Maybe he was lonely because he was the guy right in the middle. He wasn't Colt, Eddie, or Garrett regarding personality, but also wasn't as good as Justin, Heather, and Tanya. He still valued the government and the Trials but he didn't find it necessary to gloat about the killings. Would he tattle on me? Would he rat me out?

I moved from the kitchen to the trash in an instant. My head hit into the trash's lid as I vomited up what I had eaten earlier in the day. When I looked back, Asher was already out the door and out of sight. My body relaxed for a moment before another ping of pain exploded in my stomach.

It's what was going to keep happening as I realized that these Trials were rigged and I was going to have to be the best Inductee I could be. No more talking back to Bischoff or the Elitists. No more talking openly about my defiance. Those were all bathroom talks now.

I couldn't risk it. I did not want to die and if that meant I had to kill other people, then that is what that meant.

#

"I'm going to die," I admitted as soon as I heard the bathroom door close behind me. I didn't have to check twice to know that it was Justin. He always uncertainly opened the door before walking in. He was never sure if someone besides me was in here. I was sure that there had to be a reason for of it. "The Inductees and I are going to die." I could hear him beginning to say something but before I could hear the middle or ending, my head was back in the toilet. When I was handed a toilet paper patch, I wiped my chin off and immediately looked back – Justin never helped me.

Facing me was Tanya and Heather. While Tanya seemed more disgusted about the situation, she was still kneeling as Heather handed me more paper. I looked between the two before looking up at Justin. He shrugged his shoulders as everybody got up and allowed me to wash my face off at the sink.

"We're assuming that since you are puking, you got your answer about Anthony," Tanya started. She gave me a sympathetic smile and then looked back at the other two. "There's nothing we can do to stop it." She shook her head. "Unless you want to be the next Cassandra and Anthony."

"That probably didn't help, Tanya." Heather came toward me and started rubbing my back. "Coming into here, I knew that there probably wouldn't be a good chance of myself surviving either. However, I need to believe in myself."

"And I brought them here," Justin said. "Because they can help you train what to say and what not to say."

"It's about having a presence," Tanya said. I looked up at her skeptically and then eyed Heather.

I wasn't sure if I trusted Tanya. She was mean when Jamie or Jordyn were here – I honestly couldn't remember who was who anymore. I never got to know either of them. Did that make me as bad as them? Tanya was one of those who helped Colt to hurt me because I didn't answer him. She hung out with that group until she saw Justin and I together. Why did she suddenly switch? Was there a motive that I didn't know about? Justin and Heather seemed to trust her and seemed to be friendly toward her.

However, Heather was naïve. Just from how Justin talked about her, I knew she tried to see the best in everybody. It was sweet to see an Elitist who was raised with different views. However, Heather was still an Elitist. She could be kind, but her family knew what they were doing when they bought her way into these trials. I still didn't understand how those people lived. They could choose to spend that money on something else. Instead, they spent it on trying to impress those around them.

"The girls have been taught this since we were five," Heather said. She squatted down to meet my eyes and smiled at me. Tanya joined her soon afterward and Justin begrudgedly sat down with us. "You're a little rough around the edges, Bridget." I ripped my hand away from her as if she spit on it. "I'm sorry."

"Bridget, don't," Justin whined. "They're just trying to help."

"Help?" I asked. I looked between the two girls and while I could feel Heather was backing off, Tanya didn't seem to catch the memo. "Why would I want help from you guys?"

"Bridget, we want you to survive as long as possible," Heather mentioned. She looked back at Justin, and I could see her eyes getting big. They shared a small moment of silence and I felt a pain of jealousy ring inside me. He was supposed to be my best friend here and he still had to communicate verbally with me. "I feel like we're overstepping."

"But if we don't, you're going to be the next person eliminated," Tanya spoke. I looked at her and could see her face was masked. It irritated me that I

　　　　　　　　　　　　　　　AMY KULP

couldn't tell what anyone was thinking unless they wanted me to see it. It was so annoying.

"No," I said. I shook my head and stood up. I felt their hands get off my lap and shook my head aggressively. "I don't want your help. I don't want to fake who I am." I looked at them before snubbing my nose in the air and walking away. I could hear rustling and movement behind me, but I didn't think about the implications when I went through the bathroom door.

I immediately walked to the target practice room and was thankful that it was bare. I looked at everything in my path and tried to figure out what was new. Every week, they added something new to the weapons. I never really touched anything while we were here but today, my anger had me feeling up random balls that were on the table. I twiddled my thumbs over them when Justin came out yelling.

"Are you kidding me?" he asked. He stormed toward me as I kept feeling the balls in my hands. I looked around toward the open practice room and turned away from him. "What is wrong with you? They're just trying to help you survive." As he got closer, his voice got smaller as if that would stop the microscopic cameras from recording our conversation. "Bridget, if you don't take what they say, you can possibly die." He looked around. "And they would make me kill you." I felt his hands on my arms, but I kept twiddling with the balls in my hands. I didn't know what they were. "I don't want to kill you." I could hear the desperation in his voice but as soon as I looked up, I felt my finger press into the little ball. I looked down at my hands and without saying anything, Justin looked down too.

I was holding bombs. I immediately threw the one that I pressed into the target room and while my arm was busy throwing that as far away as I could, Justin was worried about protecting both of us. His body crashed into mine and as we lay on the floor across from the room, I only felt a small blast of heat and my ears rang for a second. I looked up to see that the room was barely damaged.

"What about the other one?" Justin asked as he lifted his head to look down at me. "Where did you throw the other one?"

I looked up at him as I clutched harder onto the other small bomb that was still in my hands. I shook my head and watched as his eyes grew wide. He looked at me and kept staring until he heard Tanya and Heather's voices. He looked at me again and before I could do anything, he yelled at the top of his lungs.

"Don't come in here!" He looked at me again and as I watched him get off me in slow motion, he shook his head. "I'm sorry." He got up and backed away from me. I felt tears forming in my eyes as I clutched harder onto the bomb. "Heather, Tanya, run. Bridget has an unstable bomb."

"Is she okay?" Heather asked.

"An actual bomb?" Tanya wondered. I could see her peek her head around the corner to try and get a better look.

"We're not looking, we're leaving," Justin warned.

"We can't just leave her," Heather argued.

                                    AMY KULP

"Do you want to die?" he wondered. "I'm sorry, Bridget." I closed my eyes as I held onto the bomb. Couldn't I throw this one like I threw the last one? "Guys, let's go."

I waited about ten seconds before I knew they left. All three left me here to die. Why would they put two bombs on the table there? I slowly brought my fist in front of me. I wanted to see what it looked like. I sat myself up and while I could still hear the little fires from the other bomb, I knew it wouldn't reach into this other room. These rooms were built to see the worst that we could do.

"Don't lift the pressure." I looked over at the injured assassin who was overviewing this area. I couldn't get a good glimpse of them but as they walked forward, their face looked familiar. "The bomb will detonate as soon as you lift anything. We'll both be dead." I didn't say anything as I looked over at the other room. I couldn't think about that. When I looked back at the assassin, my mind froze. "I got hurt since you last saw me."

I stared at him. This was the assassin that was really into Jade. He didn't want to hurt her before the Trial and then had to get her burned before knocking her out. He wasn't injured at the time but as he limped toward me, I could tell that there was something wrong with his left leg. Maybe he got shot there?

He lowered his body next to mine and placed his stick beside me. I was tempted to grab it but was more concerned about the bomb in my hand. I didn't want to die, and I didn't want to kill anybody despite what Justin, Heather, and Tanya might have thought.

I didn't want to throw it at them. I just wanted to play with the new weapon. My stupid fault for never seeing an actual bomb before. I thought they would be bigger.

"What happened?" I asked. He brought his gloved hands up and began holding his fist around mine. I tried to make mine as small as possible. I wasn't sure what he was doing. He shook his head to show me he wasn't answering and focusing on his job. "I need to talk, or I'm going to cry and release the pressure."

"We'll both die."

"Doesn't help," I said. I didn't want to think about this. I didn't want to die like this. If anything, I wanted to die from not being good enough. I didn't want to die from that though. I didn't want to die at all. I had to survive these Trials. I didn't want to be an Assassin either, but I was hoping I would get injured fast. "What's your name?"

"Jude," he answered simply. My eyes flicked up at his and he only nodded his head. "I don't plan to be injured for long." I shook my head and he slowly let go of my hand. "Keep the pressure on there, okay?" I nodded my head again and watched as he got up. He went over to a closet and quickly took out a foam outfit. He started putting it on until he looked at me. Maybe the guilt ate at him because then he started putting the foam around me.

"Jude?" I asked. He kept building the wall around me, but he acknowledged me with a small noise from his throat. "Jade?" I wondered. I didn't hear a response as he pressed the foam into my back.

He remained quiet and I felt little tears forming in my corners.

I wasn't going to die. I was meant to be here longer. Who was going to annoy Colt? Who was constantly going to challenge him? What about being a thorn in everyone's side? I wasn't going to die so I wasn't sure why I was getting emotional.

Justin was leaving me to die. He chose Heather and Tanya over me. I know it was my fault that he did. He protected me from the first bomb. As soon as he realized I had the second, I saw the worry flash in his eyes. He tried not to show it, but it was there. Just like Jude was trying to show me that he wasn't worried. He was though. He was distressed. I wasn't sure what he was doing, and I wasn't sure what he thought he was doing. Did he think this foam would work?

"Keep talking," I reminded him.

"Right," he replied.

"Jude?" I asked as he put more foam around me. After a moment, he sat down and looked at me as if to answer me. "Jade?" He stared at me as he moved closer to me and when he was too close, he looked at me again. "Am I going to die?"

"This," he said as he patted the foam, "will save you. What you're going to do is you're going to throw that bomb as far as you can. This foam is a secret weapon, it can last explosions and bombs." He smiled up at me. "It's great."

"Jude?" I wondered. Despite him smiling, he stopped when he looked at me. "Jade?" He just shook his head instead.

"I need to get close. I'm the seal to stop the flames from coming back in. So, if you die, I also die." He shrugged his shoulder. "So, get close." He scooted closer to me and as he did so, I couldn't help but look at him.

He had freckles spreading over his cheeks – Jade didn't have that, she had clear skin. His skin wasn't brightening with pink as he moved closer. He wrapped himself around me and pushed his hands into my back and hips before molding it into the foam. However, he wasn't blushing pink like Jade did. His hair was a blonde color though and it was the same shade as Jade's.

"Jade?" I asked.

"Don't know her," he said as he kept eye contact with me. His eyes were the same color as hers too. He smiled as he leaned back a little. "You ready to throw it?"

"Jade?"

"On the count of three: one, two… three."

My arm barely moved as he forced all his energy into the throw. His strength was what propelled it. As soon as we let go, he bellyflopped on me, and I watched as he closed his eyes. He didn't think he would live either. However, after a few seconds of nothing, he opened them and stared at me.

"Jade?"

"I'm Jude," he mentioned. He started getting up from me and looked around. The foam barrier between us fell from us and as he surveyed the room, he sighed. "It must have been a dud." He looked back at me and smiled. The same smile that Jade had – one of her teeth also always got snagged on her lip. "If it

                                    AMY KULP

goes off, it'll be contained in there. Just knock someone off their feet if they're not expecting it." He turned back to me like that was relieving. He instantly removed the foam from him and then started around me. "I'm an assassin, I do not have any family."

"You don't have any *family*?" I asked. I looked at him and he nodded.

"I don't have any *family*."

#

"Why would you not tell me?" I whispered as I pulled Jade into the bathroom. "We're alone. Remember, they can't record in the bathrooms."

"I remember," Jade whispered. She looked back toward the entrance and sighed. "Nia could still hear us." I looked back too but I knew she wouldn't hear us. She hasn't been herself. She has only been sleeping and puking. She was still affected by having to kill someone. I knew I would be the same way after I killed too. I just hoped it wouldn't be anytime soon. "What are you talking about?"

"You didn't tell me," I said. I stood with my hands on my hips and waited for her to think about everything she didn't tell me. I leaned in closer to her and when she took too long of a pause, I finally whispered, "About Jude." When I leaned away and looked at her, she seemed to freeze in place.

I couldn't read the emotions that she was feeling but I could tell that she was thinking; about how to proceed with this conversation. She paused too long for her to act like she didn't know what I was talking about. Was she going to cry? Was she going to explain it to me? I knew something was up when I first saw them see each other. However, I just thought it was because he found her attractive. Now that I knew the truth, it was probably like seeing a ghost.

Jade had to forget him. She was forced to. I didn't know what their relationship was like but if she was close, that must have been hard on her. Even now, she probably couldn't talk about him openly. We were supposed to forget them forever. I wasn't sure if the rules did or didn't apply once we became assassins. Now that I'm thinking about it, I don't think there is a rule. It wasn't common for two Inductees to be picked from the same family.

It was impossible. So many people were randomly chosen over the years and only one percent of them were selected to try and be an assassin. The only time I could see this working was if a rich billionaire had enough money to enter both of his children in, so his bids were kept. I looked up at Jade though. She was still frozen trying to think of a reaction. What did I know about her? I knew that she had a dad and she lived in a lake house. That showed that she had money, at least. Was it possible that Jade has fooled everyone into believing that she was an Inductee?

I looked back up at her, but her hand already swung back to slap me across the face. The sound echoed off the walls and exploded into my ears, but I wasn't worried about the noise. I was concerned about my face. I could see from the corner of my eyes

                              AMY KULP

that there was a red mark on my cheek, and it was turning into a deep red. Would this bruise?

"Don't talk about that traitor to me."

When I finally made eye contact with her, I could see the anger in them. They soon softened and showed some sadness. At least she didn't leave the room after she hit me. That would make me think she wasn't thinking when she did it. She meant to hurt me. She was mad at him, and I wanted to figure out why. However, I could see that she didn't want to talk about it. She shook her hand and looked down at her fingers before showing me how pink her fingers were.

I opened my mouth to talk but instead, an alarm sounded. I groaned and looked at the mirror before we both exited for the bedroom. My cheek was almost purple from how hard of a slap she had landed. I wanted to touch it but was worried it might begin to throb and I might start to feel the pain there. Right now, I was still too shocked to feel anything.

"Come on, Nia," Jade said as she bent down to her. I stopped and watched as Jade struggled to get Nia to roll out of bed. "We have to go. The next Trial is starting." She got onto the bed and pushed her from one side to the other. As she rolled, I bent down to soften the blow of her falling on the hard floor. She didn't make a noise as we lifted her to her feet.

Her eyes were glassy as she walked toward the door with us supporting her. She almost seemed like a zombie and wasn't thinking. Her legs carried her, but her mind was somewhere else. Somewhere distant. It's been there since her last trial. It's been there since she killed someone.

Once we left the bedrooms, Toby got up and embraced Nia. This was probably the first he had seen her since the Trial. I cannot remember a time when she wasn't in her bedroom. As he hugged harder, his hand moved to her hair, and I watched as the little pieces twisted around his fingers and he was caught up in them. When he tried to remove his hand, her head followed, and he apologized profusely.

She didn't react though.

I watched a little longer as Toby attempted to remove his fingers but just as I was about to help, Jade started walking away. I guess she thought it was his problem now. He was too focused to notice so when I slipped out too, I didn't feel so bad. I tried to stay up with Jade and as we walked into the meeting room, I made my presence known to her. She wasn't getting out of this conversation as easily as she wanted. She was the one to say that I didn't push people enough, here was the proof that I was trying to.

"If you want to talk about it, I'm here," I whispered. She eyed me and just nodded. Her mouth stayed closed, and her jaw remained clenched. There was no easing the tension between her and the emotions right now. Jade didn't like to show them.

Nobody liked to show their emotions here. They hid their feelings because they believed it made them a better assassin. I thought the opposite. If they couldn't be true to themselves and learn to fight for what they wanted, what was the point? They weren't robots. They were going to explode if they kept all their feelings in. The explosion was what was going to ruin their chances. Jade's explosion was slapping me across the like face but that wasn't big enough. Which meant she was telling someone else how they felt.

And as he walked in, I couldn't help but glare at him. Colt sat where he always did, and he had his goons right beside him. They were all laughing about something probably stupid. How could they find joy in this dull, dark place? How were they so okay with everything happening? How was Colt okay while Jade was sitting here not able to speak? Did he know? Could he sense it? He hasn't looked over here yet. Was he trying to be sly? It was obvious to me that they were hanging out but was it obvious to everyone else? To Eddie, Shane, and Garrett? Did anybody care anymore? Shane was an Inductee who was friends with the Elitists. I was friends with Justin, and he was an Elitist. For the most part, we were all still separated into our two groups. The only person who ever dared to cross that line was Shane.

I probably would never cross that line. As I sat away from the Elitists, my eye wandered from Colt and onto the trio who was now walking in: Justin, Heather, and Tanya. Tanya and Heather were chatting excitedly while Heather was casually bumping into Justin. He seemed annoyed but didn't move his body away from her. As they sat down, he nudged her body to make room for himself to sit next to them. Heather didn't pay much attention to him as her conversation with Tanya seemed more important.

"What happened?" Jade asked me. I looked over at her and saw her eyes watching Justin. "Between you and Justin?" She looked back at me and then back toward them. I was afraid that she would make it obvious, but I knew if she didn't, Justin would still look over at me. He was smart. He would sense that I was mad. He would realize that I was upset with him. He would know that I felt betrayed by him.

"I'll only tell you if you tell me," I whispered. When I looked back at the group, Justin stared at me just like I thought he would. I immediately looked away and stared at Bischoff who was waiting for our final two to enter the room.

Justin left me to die when he realized that I had the second bomb. He really, actually, and truly left me to die. He didn't come back to look for me. He never scoured the living spaces and asked for me or what happened. I wasn't sure if anybody besides him, Heather, and Tanya knew. While Tanya was a gossip, now that it was just her and Heather, she seemed to keep to herself. Was Justin, Tanya's friend? Or was he just there because he liked Heather? I continued to watch them and after a bit, he engaged in their conversation. He talked with them and kept eye contact with them. Either he was playing this role well or he genuinely liked Tanya too.

Maybe Justin was playing the game. After all, he was an Elitist male. I knew that the big group of them didn't like me. He thought he could get to know me and pretend to be friends, but he outed himself by not helping me. I imagined he was afraid when he realized I had the bomb and he helped me with the first one, but what about the second one? He looked at me, apologized, and left with Heather and Tanya. I saw the worry on his face. I saw how scared he was.

　　　　　　　　　　AMY KULP

But he was going to leave me to die. He was going to leave me to die alone. I thought we were friends. Could I not trust anyone here?

My face glanced at Jade at the thought. Could I trust Jade? She has always been so welcoming and sweet to me. Ever since I first came here, she was like that. She was almost like a mother figure helping me know everything. She told me who to avoid and who was good. However, I knew nothing about her. She has this secret about her family member being an assassin and I'm supposed to believe she was an Inductee? She's admitted she's watched the Trials. I've only watched little tidbits of them. Maybe she was playing the Trials well too. It would explain the hot and cold toward me. She was cold to me because she found value in someone else – Cassandra. Cassandra was more valuable to her than me. That last trial didn't need an alliance though. So why did she replace me with Cassandra? What did I do to her?

What was Cassandra going to tell me if she had made it through that Trial?

"Thank you for joining us," Bischoff announced as Toby and Nia entered the room.

Toby nodded, and I could tell that he was mostly supporting her body for walking. However, her eyes weren't glassy anymore. They were moving and she was taking in the scene around her. While slow, they both plopped down on the couch beside us and paid attention to Bischoff. Toby always kept his arms on Nia and while she was listening, it seemed she didn't have enough energy to stay up. She looked like she was still going to throw up.

"We have officially weeded out most of the Assassins that we believe would not have what it takes to assassinate someone," Bischoff announced. I could feel people's eyes gravitate toward Nia and I felt embarrassed for her. However, as the eyes started to fall back on Bischoff as he spoke, I felt two pairs still stuck on me: Colt was openly staring at the purple blotch on my cheek while Justin was staring at me. When I turned to look at Colt, he immediately turned away out of embarrassment. On the other hand, when I turned to look at Justin, he kept staring at me. He had no expression to tell me what he was feeling. "This is where you will start combining your mind, athleticism, camouflage, and hiding your vulnerabilities. For today's trial, two of you will never see this room again." I stopped glaring at Justin to pay attention to Bischoff. "Two of you will be assassinated by any means by your fellow members." I looked around and instantly gulped at that. I knew that I had a huge target on my head. "This may take days or weeks to complete. While inside, you will have approximately four hours to hide as you wish and get as far away from each other as needed. Once you hear an alarm, that is your cue you may begin killing." He looked around. "The two of you that assassinate the person, will receive first and second place. Afterward, you will be ranked according to how well you played. Were you close to killing someone? Were you a good hider?" Bischoff asked us. "I do want to say that if you have an alliance, I hope you trust those that you're in an alliance with. Hopefully, there are no…" He paused for a moment and thought about his word choice. "Betrayals."

                                AMY KULP

This was the first time I could see emotions on Bischoff's face. He has always remained stoic, fearless, and unexpressive. I assumed he was a robot here to narrate the Trials and give directions. I have never seen him talk to anybody besides to prompt us into the next Trial. He always seemed like a machine – just practicing his lines and giving us formal directions. I never imagined he was human. As he surveyed the room, though, I couldn't help but see the glint of excitement in his eyes.

He was excited that some of us were going to die. While previously he had assigned the killers, he had never shown that he liked to watch. Like I said, I thought he was a robot. The glint in his eyes was met with a broad smile. It seemed to grow as he thought about what could happen in this Trial. He was truly going to see everyone's colors and I was seeing his for the first time.

Of course, Bischoff would be an Elitist. I never thought about it, but it made sense. I wasn't sure if he was an assassin previously but with his knowledge, I wouldn't be surprised if he was. I wouldn't be surprised if he somehow weaseled his way into these Trials so that he could watch them in person. It must have been a disappointment when he realized that he was never in the actual Trials. He could only see what the cameras picked up. He wanted to watch us hurt each other. He wanted us to kill each other and betray our friends. He wanted us to cry when our friends died. He wanted to see the bloodshed. He wanted to see the devastation on all of us. He would be better if he were a robot.

"Many of you will be separated to start. I hope you find each other before the time runs out and the assassinations start," Bischoff said. I stared into his cold eyes and turned away when he started calling people. "Justin, Jade, Eddie, and Asher." They all got up from their seats and went to the front line. "This is where you will start. Everybody else, follow me."

We all got up and followed closely behind Bischoff. As we started moving toward the training area, I looked back to see Toby and Nia falling behind and felt uneasy that they wouldn't be able to catch up. I knew how much of a maze it could be like in here. I stopped myself and watched as he limped with Nia's full weight. He wouldn't be able to keep that up for long. I went back and grabbed Nia's free arm. I swung it over my shoulder and helped lift her. I wasn't strong so I knew that Toby had most of the weight on him.

"We're fine," Toby said. To prove his point, he limped faster with her on his side. I said nothing as we caught up to the group. I'm sure he was just saying that so they wouldn't be picked on when it was time to kill.

I let go as soon as we met up with the group and stood at the arena. I haven't been here since my punishment and wondered how many people used it. Whether it was to spar or for combat. It didn't seem useful since we usually had weapons to kill people. One stab at those and then the person we were fighting would be dead. How could you fight that?

"Heather, Toby, Garrett, Bridget."

I jumped over the arena's edge and landed on the dirt underneath me. As I got in and only counted two others, I watched Toby fight his decision on whether to leave Nia. He seemed to be whispering to her and while she was physically here, she didn't seem to have the cognition functions. He let go of her to hop in the arena and her body wavered a bit. I was worried that with a big gust of wind, she would fall over.

"This arena leads into the bigger playing field. A force field will be put up so that you cannot escape in the meantime," Bischoff announced. "Everyone else, follow me."

The final four followed behind Bischoff and I was surprised to see Nia walking without assistance. Did she fake everything she did? While she didn't want to be there and seemed to be dreading every step, she was walking by herself. No assistance was needed there. She was even in front of people this time. I glanced at Toby to see his reaction, but his head was down, and he was staring at his feet.

This arena was spacious for the four of us. Maybe I would spend my entire time here. It didn't seem easy to find since the tunnel appeared to get smaller the more you walked through it. I peered in to see if I could see any light from the other side, but there didn't seem to be any. Garrett was doing the same thing and shook his head at the thought.

"I'm coming for you," Garrett warned. I looked up to see who he was talking about but wasn't surprised to see him staring at me. Could he be any more predictable? "When I get you, I'm going to twist your head off like a little toy." He made a popping noise with his mouth, and I just rolled my eyes.

It was better to stay away from him than feed into his twisted fantasies. I wanted to stay away from all of them though. They purposely kept me away from Jade and I knew that was for a reason. They wanted us to be alone and scared. They wanted us to be worried when the alarm went off and we weren't with the team we imagined we would be with. It made sense and was smart. When we're on the field as actual assassins, we won't be able to huddle with our groups. All we are going to do is complete our mission.

I was hoping to complete this mission by hiding the entire time.

"Did the blast from the bomb do that to you?" Heather asked. She walked closer to me with her arms crossed. When she got close enough, she pointed to my cheek and was so close to touching it. Common sense must have taken over for her and she stopped short of touching it. "It looks like it hurts. You always seem to have some sort of bruise or cut on you." She paused as I stared at her. "Justin has been eating himself over the decision he made." She bit her lip and stared at me as if that would make me want to talk to her. "He wanted to come back once Tanya and I were safe." She paused again. "I wouldn't let him." She looked up at Garrett as he started acting like a fool in front of Toby. I wasn't sure what happened, but they seemed to be sparring or wrestling. "He cares about you. You're his best friend."

I was hoping that I had learned to mask my own emotions on my face because despite how mad I was at them, that made me want to smile. I looked

  AMY KULP

at her to see if she was lying, but she was staring at me. She was trying to see what emotions I was feeling. I just nodded as if that was enough reason. While it felt great to hear Heather say it, I wanted Justin to tell me. He hasn't tried. Sending Heather over to me to talk about it wasn't what I wanted.

"Don't forgive him right away," she commented. I had to do a double take and I knew my face gave away what I was feeling now. "I understand why he did what he did, but he doesn't understand why you're upset about it." She looked at me. "Justin still has a lot of unlearning to do about girls. Forgive him in your own time, but don't blame me and Tanya." I opened my mouth to say something but shut it. Instead, I gave a small smile. "Thank you."

She didn't let me get another word in before walking to Toby and Garrett. They seemed to be good-natured about everything and as soon as she came over, Garrett smiled at her. After all, she was an Elitist. Toby was a male. They both had at least, one thing that Garrett liked about them. Nia, myself, and Jade had nothing. He didn't like us because we weren't Elitists and because we weren't males. It was like I was gifted with a double-edged sword. I wanted to join in with them before the Trial started but I knew that I wouldn't be welcomed by Garrett. Heather and Toby might.

They were only doing this to ease their minds from what was to come. Despite what the government said, I didn't trust everyone wanted this job. I didn't believe that Elitists wanted to be here more than the Inductees. They did it because their parents and families wanted them to. What other way could the Elitists get their parents' approval? It seemed that most of them were working all the time and didn't have time to stop by to check on their children. There were the few rare like Heather's parents that didn't need to try to be rich – they just were. That seemed to give her a little more time with her parents so that she was taught what was right and wrong. Out of all the Elitists, she appeared to be the only one with a hint of compassion.

I am petrified of hearing those alarms go off. As I stood back and watched the three fight and argue with each other, I couldn't tell that they may have been nervous. Were they nervous? They were laughing and smiling at each other. Right now, it didn't seem to matter to anyone if you were an Elitist, Inductee, male, or female. None of that seemed to matter as Heather let out a high-pitched giggle as she leaned toward Toby with a slap to his wrist. Instead of flinching away, he laughed loudly and jabbed at Garrett. I wasn't sure what they were doing but I was jealous. They could fit in so easily with each other. I wanted to be able to do that. I wanted to be able to make friends like that. I wanted to be able to switch something in me to stop holding a grudge against everyone.

I couldn't though. It made me uncomfortable to want to laugh and smile in a place where two of us were going to be killed by the others. In such a serious moment, it would make me look ill if I started playing around. She would be disappointed to know that I wanted to make friends with people who were okay with doing this. My mom would be disgusted if she knew that I was thinking any of this. She wouldn't want me as her daughter. She wouldn't want me to be a follower.

Yet, I found myself walking toward the group anyway. My mom would understand that I was tired of always being alone. My mom would acknowledge that I wanted more friends. My mom would accept that I wanted to fit in with everyone here despite how bad of people we might be. My mom would see how scared I was that I was being singled out. That I only had one friend. That they started hating me from the moment I walked in. My mom would know that I go into the bathroom to cry. My mom would know I must hide that because who would want to be friends with a girl who still cries for home?

Who would want to be friends with a girl who lives on a farm? Who would want to be friends with a girl whose best friend was her pet chicken? Who would want to be friends with farmgirl? Who would want to be friends with ponytail? Who would want to be friends with a girl who cut her hair off because a boy called her a mean name? Who would want to be friends with me? Why would anyone want to be my friend?

I uncrossed my arms when Garrett's face recognized that I was walking over to him. Despite how nervous I was, my legs kept walking closer. At this point, Heather and Toby both turned in their unnatural poses and looked at me. Heather's face had a small smile on it while Toby was watching me curiously. Garrett's face was the only one that remained concentrated on what they were doing. He quickly jabbed them as their bodies were turned and sent out a round of gasps. Heather and Toby stepped back and made room for me as I infiltrated their triangle. I stood unsure of what to do and watched as Toby and Heather posed in unnatural ways. Feeling ridiculous, I followed them. I kept my eyes locked with Garrett until he nodded for me to join.

On the inside, I was screaming out of happiness.

My eyes carefully scanned Garrett's body as he thought about what move to make. He reached his hands out toward me and as the alarms blasted the arena, he pushed me toward the ground. I could hear all of them running toward the tunnel.

I couldn't be mad at them though. I was just accepted into whatever pity party that was. While it may seem stupid to want that with all these people, it made me feel accepted. Now that the Trials were underway, I knew to avoid Garrett. I knew that I could probably sly away from Heather. I knew not to underestimate her though. Toby would be too preoccupied with saving Nia for him to hunt. If I planned on killing anyone, I would aim for Toby and Nia.

But I wasn't. I planned was to hide from everyone. After all, I was one of the best hiders. I had to use that to my advantage. So, I didn't start moving until all three of them disappeared into the darkness. My body started moving slowly and once my body was engulfed in the darkness, I closed my eyes and crept forward.

I didn't want to see something in the dark. I didn't want to freak out by thinking there was a shape in the wall when there wasn't. I didn't want to see something that wasn't there. Closing my eyes and moving along the edge was my best bet. I didn't want to freak myself out.

As I moved along, goosebumps started to form along my arm and my hair started to stand up on my neck. Reactively, my body began to shiver, and my fingers stopped touching the cool wall. My eyes stayed closed though. They wouldn't open until I felt something on my face. Until I was aware that I would be out of the dark.

After all, the dark is where assassins were and if this was where I was going to die, I didn't want to see it coming.

The coldness made me want to stay where I was though. It took every ounce of courage and strength for me to shovel my feet forward. It may have only been an inch each time, but it was better. I preferred to shuffle rather than walk. When the light hit my eyelids, I stopped walking and opened them.

It looked like a life-size maze. All the walls towered over anything I could see. All I could see were the walls. They were walls made of ice. I looked down to the floor and felt the grip of my shoes had lessened. Thankfully, it wasn't too icy on the ground. I looked forward and everyone else had stopped to look at our surroundings too.

If we didn't kill each other fast, a lot of us were going to get hypothermia.

"Hey, so," Garrett started saying. I looked over at him and watched as he came closer to me. He stepped oddly with the ice and almost lost his balance before gripping my wrist hard. "Nothing personal but I did promise that you would be killed."

"You can't kill me yet," I said. I tried to swing my wrist out of his grip, but he held on tightly. "The alarms didn't go off yet."

"Yet," Garrett said. He looked up and around. I wasn't sure if he was trying to see the scenery or if he was trying to find the microscopic cameras. "They will eventually ring though and when they do, you will be killed in a millisecond."

"Don't want to make me suffer even a little bit?" I asked as he started pulling me. I rolled my eyes and followed as he kept his other hand on my elbow. "I always knew you liked me." Without warning, I heard something in my arm snap and a flame run through my arm. My knees buckled but Garrett pulled me along the ice. Unfortunately, with my body heat, I seemed to glide along with him.

"Don't fight it," he finally said. "Just don't fight it. You know that you're going to lose in the end."

"I don't know that," I retorted back to him. "I have been near the top of almost every Trial so far. You're telling me that it is just a coincidence?"

"But you don't have friends," Garrett said. I stopped fighting and allowed him to drag me. "I have friends – Shane, Eddie, Colt, Asher, and Tanya." I didn't say anything as he whispered the last two names. I guess people could be friends without always being with each other. If I were on speaking terms with Tanya, I would let her know that Garrett still thinks that they are friends. "Friends are what's going to get you through these trials." He paused. "Do you think it's easy to watch people you grew up with die?" He stopped and looked back at me. "I

                    AMY KULP

grew up with these Elitists – we were in first grade and moved up together." He lessened his grip on my wrist and while I wanted to run, he turned to me. "I was trained to kill people without emotions. I grew up seeing documentaries and videos on how to distance yourself from your emotions." He paused again and shook his head. He repositioned his hand on my wrist tighter this time. "So, when I see little Audrey – do you remember her?" he asked. I nodded my head. I only remember that she was Heather's friend and the youngest one. "I never interacted with little Audrey. However, I started the preparatory school with her in my class. She was four and I was ten; she died at the age of twelve and I'm still living at the age of eighteen. When I see some inexperienced pricks overseeing little Audrey's death, it's a lot to handle." He paused. "They didn't pick Cassandra and Anthony for no reason. They did it because we knew how to kill little Audrey efficiently – that's what we're taught in our third year at the school. Little Audrey was used as a pawn." I could hear his voice crack and he squeezed tighter onto my wrist. He started moving again and shook his head. "Friends are all you have here."

"Until they're gone."

"And you make new ones."

I remained quiet. I knew that with how he was acting and thinking that I could not get through to him. After all, he was raised to believe these things. He was raised to believe that his friends would get him through this. Maybe that's who he relied on when he was in school. I didn't understand it. I didn't understand the schooling system they had. How was

Audrey in the same year that Garrett was? That didn't make sense to me.

After a minute longer of contemplating, I felt Garrett release my wrist. I stopped sliding with him and just looked up at him. He didn't turn around to acknowledge me, but I could see him turn his head just a bit. He continued to walk and only slowed down for a second. When other bodies came crashing through to him, they were out of breath. Out of reaction, I scampered onto my feet and hid behind one of the little walls they had.

"Where is she?" Eddie asked already exhausted. He was panting so hard that I could see his breath as he exhaled. He quickly put his hands on his knees and looked up at Garrett expectedly. "I thought you would have had enough common sense to grab her."

"I want this to be fair," Garrett said. He turned his attention fully to Eddie. He stepped closer and while I couldn't hear what he was saying, I could see Eddie's reaction.

He stopped breathing so hard so that he could hear what Garrett was saying. Maybe, he was whispering nonsense or maybe he was threatening Eddie. Either way, he nodded his head and they both scampered away. When they were so far away that they were only the sizes of ants, I let my breath go and stared at the ice underneath my knees.

I was freezing. Maybe it was my cold heart or maybe I was just cruel, but I didn't want to thank Garrett for giving me a fair chance. I would have somehow survived without his help. If I were to win this Trial, he would tell others it was because he let me go. I wanted the acknowledgment that I could win without his help. He was trying to be good-natured, but it felt calculated.

I couldn't trust him. I couldn't trust any of them.

"Oh, farm girl!"

My head shot up instantly as I listened to the coos of my nickname. I looked around to see if I could find Colt, but his voice seemed separated from his body. It was getting closer and as that happened, I forced myself off my knees and began running. Most likely, he was not in the maze of icicle walls. Despite my trepidations, I ran into the maze and found myself slipping more than on the plain floor.

Thudding into the first wall, I heard my nickname again and forced myself up. Colt would take me back to Garrett and Eddie. I wasn't sure how they were grouped, and if this was their tactic or if they were all targeting me separately.

I curved around the second wall and found myself getting the hang of gliding around things. As I sped up, I heard the voice getting closer to me. I wanted to look back to see his reflection, but I was more concerned about getting lost. Eventually, it would come to a dead end. If that happened, I would be a goner.

I forced myself to stop when I got to my first choice of where I wanted to walk. I allowed myself to look back and was finally able to see his reflection. He was strolling and had a smirk on his face. His calmness was scarier to me than any evil grin or gaze he could shoot my way. When I knew he was turning the corner, I looked around at the walls to see if I could find a way to escape by going up.

A small crack in the wall was a perfect footholder. I slid my way to the crack and tried to jump to reach it. Instead, I kicked the wall and listened to the ice chunks fall out. The crack traveled down the wall, and I could put my arms on the corner and push myself up. I guess training with Jade was helping me. Once my foot was steady in the crack, I kicked my other foot off the floor and was able to cling my body onto top of the ice. I gripped hard with my fingernails and found that it was too cold for me to hang onto. My grip was slipping and as I looked down below, I could see Colt debating whether to go straight toward me or to the turn. It didn't take a genius to know that he didn't see me yet.

I had to stay as quiet as I could but as I hung there, my arms and legs started to shake from the stress of holding my weight up. My fingernails struck hard into the ice to try and keep me from slipping, but they were beginning to hurt from the cold. My skin was starting to redden, and I was slipping. My muscles were giving up. I tried to fight it, but my body began falling back on the ice and I knew my foot was not going to stay in the small corner that it was standing on. I still fought though because Colt wasn't moving yet.

I wished that he made up his mind already.

When I started sliding more, I closed my eyes and braced for something to hit the ground. Instead, my body stopped moving and I was pulled up to the top. As soon as I realized, I opened my eyes and saw that Jade was helping me up. She was motioning for me to stay quiet and when my body was on top of the ice maze, she exhaled. She sat beside me and despite wanting to sit next to her, I was too cold to do anything.

"You're more of a target if you stand," Jade whispered. She looked down below and watched as Colt ran our way. I held my breath and instantly hit the ground so he wouldn't be able to see me. Silently, we watched as he turned around as soon as he hit the dead end. Oblivious to the ice chunks that had fallen from me getting up here. When he finally disappeared, she exhaled. "I won't kill you."

"Same," I finally said. I let my breath out and continued to breathe heavily onto the ice. Now that I was flattened onto it, it felt more comforting than cold.

"I'm sorry about your face," Jade whispered. She laid down on her stomach beside me and stared at me. Finally looking at her, I could see the sadness in her eyes. "I just get very emotional every time I hear his name or see him."

"Why?" I wondered. I propped my chin on my arms and stared as she watched the scenery around us. It didn't seem that we were very good at sharing our emotions. Although Jade seemed to be better at it than me. "I would love to get another chance to see my mom again."

"Your mom isn't the reason you're here," Jade snarled. She took a second to think about what she said and shook her head again. "I'm sorry." She closed her eyes and we lay there.

It was peaceful. I could still hear the taunting from Colt, but it seemed to be in the far away distance. I could see some people's heads and silhouettes from above them. They were frantically trying to find a way out. I wanted to help them but hoped they could figure it out. I was safe up here. I just hoped that Jade wouldn't hurt me. Just by rolling off this, I could injure myself. Maybe kill myself on purpose. I didn't want to fight her. Everybody loved her; everybody hated me.

"Jude and I are very different," Jade started. I looked back at her and nodded my head. I knew not to talk as that would interrupt her telling me about him. I was curious and this might be the only alone time we get. "My dad is rich, and my brother has always had a fascination with being an assassin." She sighed. "My brother and I are completely different, but my dad tried to show us that we were both important to him. So, when Jude wanted to enroll in a preparatory school, my dad let him. My dad placed a bid for him to join and it won." I could see that she was playing with her fingernails now. Almost massaging them but it looked to be irritating her skin. Maybe that was the ice we were lying on though. "As soon as we were told, my brother told me if he won, he would flag me. He wanted me to join in on what he loved to do. He wanted me to stop telling him how useless it was." Jade closed her eyes. "He did end up winning and I watched the Trials. I watched how he murdered people and I watched how he sacrificed those that he guaranteed his loyalty to. I watched him betray and upset everyone. I watched him graduate as an Assassin." She shook her head. "And I watched my dad get the news that I was flagged. My dad who wanted both of us." She bit her lip at the thought and

                                    AMY KULP

ended up shaking her head. "We prepared my fingers by erasing them ourselves. I promised my dad that I wouldn't be anything like my brother. He only made me make one promise."

"What was that?"

"'Be Jade'." She closed her eyes again and I knew that the sharing was over.

Despite what I thought, it did help me understand her. This was important because it explains why Jade didn't have to get her fingerprints lasered off. It made sense as to why she was helping everyone and why she was rich but wasn't an Elitist. It made me understand that Jade was trying to be friends with everyone. Jade wouldn't betray me on purpose, but I knew there was something she was still hiding. Maybe from shame? Maybe because we weren't close enough yet?

"At least you know who flagged you," I commented. She opened her eyes and stared at me. "I've been trying to figure out who I wronged when I was ten."

"You were flagged when you were ten?" Jade asked. I nodded my head. "I don't even know your age," she admitted.

"Sixteen," I said.

"Eighteen," Jade responded to a question I didn't ask. "Were you an outstanding ten-year-old or were you annoying?" As she held her breath, I could tell she wanted to say something else. However, the longer I didn't talk, it seemed like she wouldn't say what was on her mind.

I tried to think about how I was as a child. In school, I already knew that I needed to do good. My mom and dad both wanted what was best for me and they knew, they probably couldn't afford it. I was told to practice hard and study constantly. Even when things came easy to me, my dad would be at the table hounding away at flashcards. As soon as my mom came home from her long day, my dad would hand her the set and she would quiz me – I remember reciting the alphabet using those flashcards and learning to count as my dad taught me how to take care of the animals. I remember one day, I was counting and recounted and had to recount again until I gave up because I was counting one less chicken. My dad found that it wandered and was killed by the pigs. I always knew to stay away from the pigs until I was older. Even today, they scared me. They would eat anything – I could fall in and they would kill me. They didn't care – I was just their meal. But I don't think I was annoying. I was obedient and quiet. Wasn't that the perfect child?

I shut my eyes as soon as I heard the alarms sound. Two of us were about to die.

"Let's get out of here," Jade whispered. She sat up and waited for me to follow her. "We'll have a better chance if we don't get lost."

"And right now, we can see the entire maze." I started to stand up but felt my shoe beginning to slip out from underneath me. Splattering onto the ground, I heard more of the wall crack and fall. I stayed on my stomach until I was sure that the cracking had stopped. When I sat up again, I could see it right underneath my belly. It was threatening to take me down too.

                              AMY KULP

"Don't become a target. Standing up is too risky." Jade went back on her stomach and slithered over to me. "Lead the way out. I have no sense of direction. The first week I was here, I couldn't figure out our room from the Elitist's room."

"How'd that turn out?"

Jade didn't answer and instead, pointed to me to continue. I began copying Jade's movements until I started sliding with ease. It was icy cold, but I was getting so used to it, that my temperature was becoming one with the ice. It was either that or I was getting hypothermia. I believe that.

"There's a little archway over there that will help us cross to the other side," I whispered. I looked back at Jade, and she nodded for me to continue. After a moment, I began propelling my arms back to launch me forward. It was less action I had to do with my legs and feet. Looking ahead, I instantly tried to stop myself and felt Jade crash into me before she could reject her movements too. She grabbed my leg as I slid a little too much and held onto the ledge. My upper body was too forward, and I hit the side too hard.

"What is it?" she asked. I didn't say anything as I began retracting my body b back with Jade. She held on tightly but as I moved, we both heard the cracking sounds form beneath us. She swiveled closer to me and peeked over at what I was looking at. She groaned and closed her eyes as we listened to ice fall right in front of my own worst enemy.

As soon as the ice fell above his head, he stopped walking. It took him a moment before looking up to see me. We made brief eye contact before he lowered his head and kept moving forward. I didn't exhale until his body turned the corner and as soon as I did, Jade opened her eyes back up.

"What happened? Did he not see you?"

"I guess not," I lied. I looked back at Jade and then down at the fallen ice. It wasn't just little shavings; it was three big chunks. There was no way he didn't see me. We made direct eye contact.

"Come on, then," Jade said. "I don't want to be stuck on this unstable maze forever." She paused as I started going across. "I'll wait. I don't think that'll hold both of us at once."

I gave her a thumbs-up as I went over. It was much thinner than the rest of it and I wasn't sure that I would be able to slide on my stomach. I forced myself up and put a lot of pressure on my knees before I put one in front of the other. Despite the numbness in my hands, I clutched onto it as I began forcing my way over. About halfway through, I heard the cracking sound and didn't hesitate to slide myself quickly over. As soon as I made it, I wanted to flatten my body and kiss the ice. I knew that I had to be there for Jade though.

"The exit is so close," I whispered. "I could see it."

Jade smiled at me as she repositioned herself in the exact way that I was. She put a lot of pressure on her knees, and I could see her pants were getting soaked from holding onto the ice. She must have been sweatier and more nervous than me. She took her time as she went across and with her speed, came the horrible sound of the ice cracking more. With eery crack that sounded, I tried to distract her by

                    AMY KULP

encouraging her to move faster. She would nod her head and crawl a centimeter farther. It wasn't until I heard a huge crack that I stopped celebrating and looked behind her. I could see the entire arch beginning to slide downward. Panicked, Jade looked at me and instead of moving faster, she froze and kept her body clutched to the piece that was falling.

I felt useless as she crashed to the floor, and I was only able to watch. I crouched down and tried to offer my hand to her, but she was so busy making sure she was okay that she didn't notice my assistance. She dusted off her pants and her shirt before realizing that her skin was stinging because of how cold she was. She lifted her shirt just enough for me to see her belly was raspberry red. Any injuries would hurt a lot worse with how stiff we were.

"I'm okay," she finally said. She looked up at me and gave a thumbs-up. "You can see the exit, just tell me how to get there." I nodded my head and looked ahead of me but down below.

I could see the exit but being able to look down on everyone, I could also see about three other heads in the maze. Colt was one and was going the opposite direction that we needed to go so I wasn't worried about him. There was someone else, but I couldn't see who it was. Only the top of them which concerned me since a lot of boys had brown hair here.

"Alright, you're going to go straight and then left at the first intersection." She started moving so I tried to walk with her. It was getting slippier up here and I was losing my balance quickly.

"We need you to stay up there so you can help me find the exit," Jade said. She looked over at me and smiled. "Give me directions and I'll meet you out there."

I nodded and tried my best. The other head in the maze seemed to be leading themselves near Colt so I was losing interest in them. As soon as Jade got closer to the exit, I slithered on my belly to the exit. As soon as I neared it, I heard a scary, familiar voice and froze. Looking below, I could see Garrett guarding the exit. He paced back and forth until he smiled at the sound of someone coming. Looking back, I had no room to warn Jade about the ongoing threat.

She was met at the exit with a punch to her jaw. Garrett didn't seem worried about who it was and when she slid against the ice, he followed her. She kicked at him multiple times but none of them seemed to land into him enough for him to back away. He got on top of her and to my horror, started choking her. I knew that it would be safer for me to stay on top of this and be unnoticed, but I could not stay here and watch Jade get choked to death. I could not be the reason she died.

So, despite my fear of falling and the risk of getting hurt, I shakily stood up on my legs and launched myself onto Garrett's back. I crashed on top of him and felt his arms and legs give out and crash on the floor. Losing my balance, I smashed my head into the wall. I was so dizzy, but I couldn't understand how dizzy I was until I felt Jade pulling me away from him. I started slipping as we ran but Jade held onto me tightly. As I fell into one wall and

AMY KULP

my feet landed into the ice barrier, Jade pulled me so we wouldn't have to stop. Garrett would not give up that easily.

As soon as we passed all of ice maze entrances and exits, we stopped and leaned down to catch our breaths. We knew the risk of doing it but with my head spinning and her mouth aching, we had to collect ourselves before running again. I inhaled and exhaled so deeply that I was worried I would fracture my lungs and chest. However, hearing Jade's breathing get louder, I knew that she was doing the exact same thing as me.

"You ready?" I asked.

"We have to be," she mentioned.

I nodded and we both bolted. I was finally getting my footing back and my body was warming up. I knew the clothes would still be cold but at least I could move them now. I didn't know how far we were planning to run until we felt safe from Garrett but when Jade held out her arm to stop me, I ran full-force into and knocked her down. Losing her grip, she continued to slide. I looked ahead as to what she was sliding into and immediately ran after her. I grabbed onto her arm and pulled her toward me so that she wouldn't have to try to stay up from the huge hole.

It looked like a cliff at the end. There was no other ice or land in sight. I looked as far as I could but the only thing, I could see was the black gap. The last time there was this big of a gap, Jordyn never came back from it. I didn't know her, but I remember our second Trial. I stared out, I realized just how scary it was to see in the light. I really couldn't see the bottom. I peered over at it and could feel Jade getting up to look too. It was mesmerizing but it would hurt to fall in.

"No chance of surviving that," Jade said. She stepped away and I followed her actions. I didn't want to slip and fall in. With my dizziness, it was a real possibility for me. Knowing me, I would grab anything around me, and then Jade and I would both fall to our deaths. "Let's go before Garrett catches up to us."

"Too late," Garrett said. We turned around to look at him and rolled our eyes. He was so annoying, blocking one of the ways out of here. There were only two options but as he walked in the middle of them, I knew that Jade and I would be going through hell to survive this. Instead, he took a step forward and we both inched our way back.

"Don't do this, Garrett," I said. I got in front of Jade and held out my arms protectively. Almost as if shielding her from his sight would protect her. "You want to kill me and not Jade." He took another step closer to us and I could feel Jade shrink back. I moved until I felt her body again. "If you let her go, we can fight one-on-one. Just like you want, right?"

"Shut up," Garrett said. "I want to kill both of you."

"You'll get first place if you kill one of us. They said nothing about both of us," I mentioned. I would have to remember how to talk to people. My voice was quivering, and my body was shaking but I couldn't let Garrett know how scared I was. "Let us go." He took another step and I swear he was doing it to torture us. The evil grin on his face showed me

　　　　　　　　　　AMY KULP

and I looked back at Jade. She was scared too but her lips were glued shut. "Please."

"Bridget—"

"I want you dead!" Garrett said. "I gave you your chance and you hid in that stupid maze!" He took more steps forward and I inched back again.

"Stop moving, we're—"

"You're not that bright because I could have just killed Jade and never would have known you were on top. *That* was a smart place, but it was such a stupid move. You know everyone here has a bounty on your head."

"Let us go!" I pleaded.

"We're close to—"

"She is my friend!" I finally said. "Unlike you, I don't like to replace my friends with new ones."

"Bridget, please stop backing up!" Jade pleaded. I felt her arms clutch onto me and I could feel her shaking.

As Garrett reached out for my shirt, I jolted backward and felt Jade's body resist as much as she could. Garrett latched onto the collar of my shirt and as he pulled me away from Jade, I felt her body's heat leaving mine. I tried to writher from his hands but as I kicked my legs and leaned toward her, I found nothing against mine. Hearing an alarm go off before I could register what had happened, Garrett threw me against the ice maze and turned to face me.

All I could do was stare at where Jade was supposed to be standing.

"Your death isn't going to be that easy!" Garrett yelled.

As soon as my back hit the wall, I began crawling toward one of the clearings I could escape through. However, Garrett wasn't walking now. He ran to me and grabbed my leg. Although his hand was icy and my legs were cold, I could feel his nails dig into my skin and he threw me back to the wall like I was a ragdoll. My back took another hit as I smashed into it, and I felt the breath leave my body. I couldn't sit here though. I had to move quickly and as Garrett stood over me, I kicked my leg up between his as hard as I could.

Falling, he landed on top of me, but I was able to squeeze out from under him. I could hear his groans and protests, but I knew not to care if he was okay. He wanted to kill me and make me suffer for it. I crawled away into the clearing that I wanted as I struggled to get to my feet, I watched three figures run past me.

"Justin!" I yelled. I felt like a baby deer trying to walk as I tried to stand on both legs. There was more damage to it than I would like to admit. "Please, help me!" I yelled.

He continued to run but I could see his speed slowing down. Heather and Tanya followed his directions and slowed down as well. They all turned to me and despite, me running to him with my hand outstretched, he turned back around and ran away from me.

"Come on," Heather said as she ran back to me. Tanya followed her and they both grabbed my arms. Helping me away, we tried to follow Justin's path, but he was too far along the trail for us to find him. Maybe he found a place to hide for everyone.

                                    AMY KULP

"No man left behind," Tanya said. She smiled at me and repositioned my arm so that she had a better grip on me. I felt pain shoot up from earlier before when Garrett dislocated it, but as I moved it again, it seemed she may have knocked it right back into place. "Come on, try to keep up."

I nodded and watched as she struggled to help me along with them. She was sweating despite how freezing it was here and I had to wonder how long they were running for. When I turned back to Heather to see her reaction, she was busy wiping off the blood that was running down her face with her free hand. Her other one was busy making sure she wouldn't accidentally drop me.

They were running from something.

Looking back, I was surprised to see they had Shane behind them. He was running and as soon as we made eye contact, he slowed down.

"Get out of here Bridget. I won't hurt an Inductee."

I shook my head and let my arms fall from Tanya and Heather. Adrenaline would propel me forward despite how much I was already limping. As we picked up speed and the pain stopped hurting, I could run as fast as Tanya and Heather. I could hear Shane's footsteps behind us. They were heavy but his strides weren't long enough to catch up. When I turned back again, Eddie was helping Garrett walk and when he realized I was in the group too, he let him go and started running with Shane. Garrett limped toward us, and we were getting far from him.

"Faster," Tanya whispered to me. I nodded my head and forced my legs to go faster. Tanya pointed for us to turn and as soon as we did, Heather ushered us to make another turn. "They could see us if we're in a straight line, but it'll be more difficult if we keep making turns."

I nodded my head and followed their lead. It wasn't until I saw a little gap in the wall that I finally made a command for us to follow. I slid in with Heather behind me and Tanya filled the last spot. We all crouched down and as we were cramped in here, I felt my leg beginning to burn. Was I ripping my muscles apart? Was it already ripped apart?

"We need a minute to catch our breaths," I said.

"As long as we don't hide in here forever," Heather said. "They're smart, they'll find us."

"Are you guys hurt?" I asked. Heather didn't need to nod her head as I could already see the blood running down her face.

"Hold something to it," Tanya directed. "Take your shirt off."

Heather did it without further instruction. Her elbows hit the wall as she lifted her shirt, but she quieted down as soon as she started applying the pressure to her cut. She grimaced as she applied more pressure and as she loosened it, I forced my hand onto hers. She opened her eyes, and I could see that she was getting tired. Her eyes blinked slower and each time, I wasn't sure she would open them again.

"Your leg," she finally whispered. I looked down at it and could see the bruising. It was swelling and the nail marks had drawn blood. There was nothing I could do about it right now. "Take me to Justin. He'll protect me."

"Justin left all of us to face them," Tanya interjected. "Not just Bridget." She held onto Heather's shoulder and gave her a sympathetic face. "I'm sorry but he won't protect you. He'll sacrifice you. Only one more person needs to die before this Trial ends."

"Peek a boo." Eddie's face appeared in the hole and before anybody could throw a punch, he grabbed Tanya's hair and pulled her out of the ledge.

Heather instantly tried to grab onto her, but her reactions were too slow. The yells that we were hearing were unbearable but as Heather squirmed to get out, I had no choice but to hold the shirt harder on her head. She looked at me with a look of betrayal before swatting my hand from the shirt. I only dropped it once we heard the other alarm.

We both stopped what we were doing for one second. After, Heather rushed out of the hole, and I took my time. I didn't want to see what was happening but as I poked my head out, all I could see was Heather, Shane, Eddie, and Garrett standing over Tanya. When I stood up and made my way to the open space, I could see Tanya's disfigured face and her broken body. I could see blood pooling around her body and as I looked at all of them, I could see blood on all their fists. It was dripping more from some of their knuckles than others. Almost like rain.

"Why are you shirtless?" Shane asked. I looked over at Heather, but she didn't answer him. Her gaze was only at the floor and only at Tanya.

"Why aren't you shirtless?" Eddie wondered. I looked up at him, but my eyes went back to

Heather. She was holding in all of her emotions, but I could see her eyes tearing up.

"Don't touch me," I warned as I saw Garrett move.

My warning didn't mean anything though because he and Eddie came near me. It was like a flurry of motion, one of them held me still while the other tore my shirt off. As soon as it was off, I was cold, but it was different than when I was wearing my shirt. I wasn't being saturated with the wetness. I felt lighter but humiliated. Garrett looked me up and down before shoving me to the ground.

"Not bad, not bad," Eddie commented. Garrett whistled beside him, and they started laughing.

When I looked at Shane, he didn't say anything and began walking back with Eddie and Garrett. Despite how much I had thought he was terrible, he refused to touch me. He warned me he wouldn't touch me. Now, he didn't. He didn't look at my body like Eddie or Garrett and instead, he kept contact with my face. That was weird coming from someone who was hanging out with Elitists.

"Get away," Heather said. "You ruin everything." She shook her head. "I have tried to be nice to you. I have tried to be your friend, but you are insufferable." Finally, she looked up at me. Her voice was cracking each sentence she said, and the tears were starting to fall. "I lost my boyfriend," she said. "Because of you and now I lost my best friend." She looked back down at Tanya. "If you didn't stop me, I could have protected her."

"Or gotten yourself killed," I whispered.

"Leave, Bridget."

I nodded my head and left. I wasn't wanted and I didn't know Tanya that well. I walked to the entrance and remained silent. As I made it back in, I felt stares at my upper body but I refused to acknowledge anyone. I stood by myself and waited for Heather. That's what everyone was doing. We were waiting for Heather.

She wasn't the only one who lost a best friend though. I lost Jade Tricase. I truly felt like we were getting closer to each other and that the last trial was just a fluke. There was something she wasn't telling me, but it wouldn't have mattered because she just told me a lot. She told me about Jude. She told me about her dad. She told me so much that there was no way I couldn't trust her now. However, she told me I was pushing her too much. She warned me to stop backing up but I was so in my head that I was too centered on Garrett. I was too focused to comprehend that she was slipping off the edge. I was too busy for her. I killed my best friend.

As soon as Heather walked in, the doors behind her closed. She was still distraught and the blood on her head seemed to be gushing more now. I wondered if she was picking at it. As she sauntered, she seemed like a zombie. However, she joined the pair of arms that were held out for her, and Justin wrapped her up.

I also lost Justin. He didn't care about me. He didn't care whether I died or not. He has been educating me on the Trials but that didn't mean he would help me in the field. He ran when I had a bomb in my hand. He ran when I begged him for help. He was not my friend. He never was. He was surviving the Trials the best he could.

"Welcome back future Assassins," Bischoff said proudly. He put his hands behind his back and stood with his posture perfect. He looked around at us and for a second, I watched his robotic expression break. "Anybody who needs to see medical attention may do so after your rankings. There will be doctors waiting for you."

I looked around at everyone and knew I would need to see them. With my adrenaline wearing down, I was able to feel the intensity of my leg's wound. When I looked down, it was a deep purple and looked to be twice the size of my other leg. I couldn't see the fingernail marks anymore despite them being the reason I was bleeding in the first place. Did I land on my leg weird to make it hurt like this? I turned to see that Nia and Toby were almost perfect though. Toby had a scratch on his face, but Nia had nothing wrong with her. If anything, he would want that cleaned. The only other inductee was Shane but the only injury I could see on him were bright red patches on his arms – maybe from the ice. Asher was holding his elbow in place, and I was too afraid to see it if he were to let go of it. I knew that Garrett was kicked by Jade and then kicked by me, but I wasn't sure if he would need any medical attention because of that. Justin had busted knuckles and would probably need them wrapped while Heather would need stitches in her head. Looking over to Eddie, I could see the bruised eye and his refusal to smile. I wonder if Tanya was the result of that. Lastly, I stared at Colt who was barely

                              AMY KULP

engaged with anyone. He didn't seem to have anything wrong with him except for the multiple patches of black along his arms. I couldn't tell if they were bruises of hypothermia though.

"Our first-place finisher is the one who assassinated someone first." Bischoff straightened his back and widened his stance. "Killing Jade Tricase is…" I closed my eyes as I could see Nia, Toby, and Colt all flinch and look around as soon as her name was called. "Bridget Solomon." I took a step forward but I wasn't able to make it to my circle before yelling and protests started.

"Are you kidding me?" Nia yelled. She stepped toward me threateningly and while normally I would be satisfied to see her not in her zombie state, I was saddened to see this was how she was reacting. "Jade was one of us! How could you turn your back on her? You were her best friend!"

"What is your problem? She just wanted to help you!" Toby yelled too.

I stared straight ahead at the Bischoff but when I tried to move, Nia and Toby blocked me. I couldn't understand what either of them were saying anymore. Their voices were clashing together and their volume was rising. Nia's instinct was to push her hands into me and when she did, I allowed her to. Her face was getting red from the volume and she was soon running out of breath. She continued though. She continued to push her hands into me and yell at me. Toby stood directly behind her and yelled too, but he wouldn't to touch me.

"That's enough," Bischoff sternly yelled. That wasn't enough for Nia and Toby though. They were both stabbed in the back with the injured assassin's rod. I was afraid to look at the injured assassin but when I did, I was glad to know it wasn't Jude. "Please, take your spot."

I nodded my head and obediently followed the directions. Nobody talked as I made my way there. I refused to make eye contact with anyone as I entered the first place circle. I was sure they had thoughts but I didn't want to know what anyone was thinking about me – Heather, Justin, Garrett, Nia, and Toby have all made their case with me. They have all made it known how they felt about me.

"In second place, assassinating Tanya Booth is Shane Newfeld."

Nobody screamed at him for assassinating her. For beating her up. All I did was accidentally push Jade off a ledge. Shane tortured Tanya. Yet, nobody yelled at him as he stood in the circle next to me. Nobody screamed that he was a traitor at him even though he was always with the Elitists. They didn't hate Shane. They only hated me.

"For assisting in Tanya's murder, Eddie Marlow is third place."

"It's despicable what you did," Shane whispered to me. I turned to him but he wouldn't look at me. He was staring straight ahead as if I wasn't good enough to look at. "You are a traitor to the Inductees. You never turn on your own – even if everyone already thinks you did." I could see his jaw harden but I didn't say anything.

I wanted to, but I didn't. Instead, I watched as everyone else was called: Garrett, Heather, Asher, Justin, Nia, Toby, Colt. I watched as they all walked to the circle. I didn't know what happened with all of them and I didn't care. I wanted to go to my bed and cry. I wanted to fix my leg and cry. What I wanted to do most was go to either of my two friends and talk to them. I wanted to tell them about what went down and I wanted to listen to what happened with them too.

One of them was dead and the other wanted me dead though.

"This is a reminder that if you need medical attention, you may go now."

I waited until our circles started blinking to move. I rushed out of the room and once in the main living space, I saw the doctors ready to work on people. They brought me into a nice room with dividers on it. They cut my leg to drain the excess fluid and then they talked to me like I understood what they were saying. I nodded my head in agreement so they would shut up faster.

"Heather Flick, it looks like you'll need stitches. Follow me."

I closed my eyes as I watched her pass my curtain. Good to know that we can still hear everything around us. I watched the doctor as they paraded around my room with different instruments. They injected something into me and I laid back into the bed. It was beginning to feel numb, but I guess that was better than the pain.

"You can go when you're ready."

I nodded my head and once the medicine fully numbed my leg, I sat up. I didn't want to leave this space though. I wanted to chill here where I knew I would be safe. Instead, I sat up and stretched my toes. I could still feel my toes at least. Just not my leg.

"Colt, what happened?" Eddie asked. I rolled my eyes at the thought that they were all here. It made me shiver and I felt creeped out that I wanted to hide in my skin. I just had to make it back to my room to grab a shirt.

"We saw you tracking her," Garrett mentioned.

"You should have found her before Garrett did. Why were you last place?" Eddie asked again.

I didn't want to hear this. I held my breath and walked out. All three of them stared at me and when Garrett was called back, I tried not to make eye contact. It was terrible though and when I looked up at Colt, he was staring at me.

His eyes gave so much away. It forced me to stop in my tracks and I could see the different looks and emotions in them. I could see that he was shocked at me. I could see that he was surprised and angry with me. I could see the sadness for the loss of Jade. However, the emotion that I saw for a split millisecond was the one that I knew everyone felt toward me.

Betrayal.

"Don't touch the bombs," Jude said as I stared at the table. They added two more bombs and one additional weapon. I wasn't sure what it was but it seemed impractical—almost like a barbarian weapon used in the dark ages. I didn't stop though, I continued to stare at the bombs and how little but impactful they were.

How destructive they could be. I knew Jude was watching me as I stared at the tiny balls. As I contemplated putting my hand around one and activating it. As I wondered what it would feel like to let go of the latch and feel the destruction it could cause. I wondered if I would feel any pain at all. Would the blast just kill me instantly or would I feel the fire burn me alive? Would my ears suffer and ring like before, or would my hearing be lost instantly? Would my body be flung backward into something, or would it just disintegrate? Would my adrenaline make me feel nothing?

I walked past the table with all the weapons and stared into each little target room they had. They were labeled now: bomb, gun, knives, throwing stars, bat, darts, bow and arrow, flamethrower. I stared at them as I wondered which weapon would hurt the worst. Did the Assassin decide which weapon they used on their victims? Or were they assigned them? Would someone have to assassinate me before the trials ended? I knew I didn't get to pick out that weapon. I hoped that whoever would do it to me would hurt me. Keep me alive long enough to hurt me. Keep me alive long enough for me to realize that I'm dying.

Just like Jade did. Just like Jade knew she was falling off that ledge. Just like she yelled out for me to stop moving and when I didn't, she realized that I was going to kill her. Just like when she slipped off the ledge and had to figure out that she would be dying. She probably had the realization for a couple of seconds before she hit the ground. I didn't hear the end, but would it hurt? Or would she die instantly? I hope she didn't suffer.

"Do you know?" I asked as I stared at the guns' silhouette human target. I leaned against the window for the gun and stared at it. I should stand there and let people aim at me. They would probably be more accurate with me than the other target. I looked back at Jude, but he was still staring at the weapon table. "Do you know what happened?"

"In your last trial?" he asked. I nodded to confirm and turned toward him. He was carefully watching me. Maybe studying me. "No, I'm assigned to watch the target room." He held out his arms as if he was showing it off. I could feel him walk closer to me. "What happened?" I shook my head and stared at the target practice. "There's nothing you can't tell me. I experienced it all, remember?" His face got so close that I couldn't look away from him.

"How did you get hurt?" I asked. I looked down at his body to attempt to find an injury. Some of them had limps or were curling in on themselves. I assumed some of them were too old to continue so they called them injured. Looking at Jude, though, I couldn't find something wrong with him.

"Not everybody's injuries are physical," he narrated.

Stepping away from the window, I went back to the table that had the weapons and he looked down at them too. I could see him eyeing different ones and while I wanted to see his reaction, I only knew what I was thinking. I didn't want to stay too close to him. I didn't want to be kind to him and be there for him. We weren't supposed to interact until I became an actual assassin. We weren't supposed to get to know each other. Especially since I had to tell him the news that I killed his sister.

"Jade is dead," I finally whispered. I said it so softly that when I looked back and saw no reaction, I assumed he didn't hear me.

I was not good at giving out bad information. Clearly, I knew I should not have just blurted it out. I knew that but I still did it. He would need time to process what he heard anyway. However, I looked back up and hoped that he heard me. I didn't want to repeat it. It felt wrong to say. Jade shouldn't be dead. Jade should be alive. It wasn't right for Jade to be gone.

Suddenly moving, I watched as he grabbed one of the weapons on the table. He launched it in one of the target spaces and while I was distracted with seeing the impact and what weapon he chose; he was able to grab me by the neck and push me to the wall. His grip tightened around my neck, and I moved my arms out to try and get him away from me. My arms weren't long enough, and I tried to punch and hurt his arms, but nothing was working. Slowly, black blotches were growing in the corners of my eyes, and I felt my body stop fighting. I couldn't breathe and the pain in my lungs was only being matched by the pain around my neck. I could feel each individual finger tighten as hard as it could around my windpipe. Some of my skin was being pinched by his fingers and I could feel his short nails making their way into the skin there. I was making horrid noises as I tried to gasp for air but each time I did, he was able to tighten his grip.

At the last second, my body crashed to the floor and my body fell to the side. I opened my eyes to watch him, but I was too dizzy to understand what he was doing. He was far away from me now. He moved so fast. I turned to my back so that I could heave my chest in and out to try and get the oxygen moving. Gasping for air, this was worse than any exercise I have ever done. I tried to move my arms up, but my brain wouldn't signal them to move. I was too tired and exhausted. I wanted to feel my neck. I knew it was throbbing but was it broken? Were the doctors still out there helping future assassins?

"What did you say?" Jude asked. I eyed him before changing my view back to the ceiling. He was grabbing a weapon, and I could see that. I didn't want to know how he was going to torture me though. I didn't want to know. I closed my eyes and continued breathing heavily as he walked toward me. His boots squeaked against the floor, and they were intimidating. I felt goosebumps growing up my arms as his shoes stopped right next to my body. I felt his presence get closer, but I didn't want to open my eyes. I didn't want to see what he had pointed at my head or if he was staring down at me. "Did you kill her?"

I kept my eyes closed as I tried to listen to him. I couldn't tell where he was nor what part of my body he was going to grab. I was still too out of breath for me to hear him. He was being quiet on purpose. He was too calm for my liking. I would not have held back if my sister had been killed by this person.

"Did you kill her?"

Grabbing the straps to my bra, he roughly threw my body against the wall again. He put his knees between my legs to keep me from falling and when he finally squeezed my cheeks, I popped open my eyes. He was scared. I could see the desperation in them.

"Yes," I squeaked. I kept my eyes locked on his until he turned away from me. Letting go of my body, he threw me down on the floor. I landed with a clunk and hoped I didn't injure my elbows. I tried to hide my face from seeing his, but I already saw the look on them. I already saw what the others were seeing in me. "It was an accident."

"Yeah?" Jude asked. He turned around and walked closer to me. I hadn't realized he had been pacing. When he came to me, he crouched down to my level and forced my head up to look at him. "An accident, you say?" I nodded my head, but he just shook his disapprovingly. "You want to know why I don't believe you?" I watched as he circled the weapons table again. He no longer had whatever he originally picked up. I wonder if he threw it or put it back. "There are so many assassins like you.

Everybody trusts you. Everybody wants to be your friend, but you betray them at the last second. Every year, there seems to be one of you." I couldn't keep my eye contact with him. "Claiming it's a mistake is just wrong. Own up to what you did. Right now, you are just feeling guilty. You should. Let that guilt eat you up. You don't deserve to be happy about it. Telling me that you killed my little sister is not going to help you feel better." He shook his head. "You can deny how you're feeling but that's how I felt when I competed in my Trials." He looked back at the weapons table again and grabbed one of the bombs. He rolled his thumb over it before clicking it and throwing it into the room. I shielded my face in case he aimed it at me. "You're pathetic but don't worry, you'll get through. People will start to doubt Jade and try to trust you again. You'll betray again and again until you win. Remember, once you graduate, you are going to be in a group with all the other assassins. I will, personally, make your life a living hell." He shook his head and grabbed the flamethrower. He pointed it at me but aimed it at one of the target rooms instead at the last second. "I won't kill you now and I won't kill you once you graduate. What I will do is watch you suffer. Nothing is lonelier than having no friends in these Trials." He shook his head and looked at me. "You're going to be your own worst enemy and I'm sorry that this is how you found out about it."

"I'm sorry," I said. I sat myself up and watched the weapons table myself. I stared at all of what was remaining on there and when he continued to pace with his back to the table, I forced my body

                                    AMY KULP

up and ran to grab something I could use. My hands landed on the knife and when Jude tried to wrestle it out of my hands, I watched his face twist in agony as his fingers sliced. "I'm sorry." I raised it up against my own skin before keeping it still.

"You don't have the guts," Jude said. He watched me as I struggled to scrape the knife against my arm. I wanted to. I didn't want to be by myself. I didn't want to be hated. I wanted to have friends. Jade was my friend. "Don't take the easy way out." He wrapped his fingers against the knife and gently took it away. "Get out of here. Prepare yourself for the next Trial."

"We just got back."

"Get out of here before I—"

"Before you?" I whipped my head around to see Bischoff was at the door. He marched forward with his hands on his hips and looked between us. "Jude, if you keep acting like this, you will never pass the psych evaluation again. You won't be able to defend Jade's honor." I watched his face crumble at the mention, but I didn't have time to look at it as he turned to me. "You must deal with the consequences of your actions. I just came because I heard the noise. Who started this fight?"

"She did," Jude said.

Bischoff looked at me for a second before nodding his head at Jude. He walked to one of the closets in the room and brought out his electricity stick. I stuck out my arm hoping that he would stick me there but as soon as he smiled, I knew he wouldn't. He tapped me right on my stomach and I bent over in undeniable pain. They definitely hiked up the voltage.

"Get back to your bedroom," Bischoff instructed. I nodded my head and started moving out. "The target room will be shut down. Jude…" Bischoff looked at him for a second and while I wanted to stay around and listen, I knew they wouldn't say anything important while I was there.

I walked down the halls until I heard them shouting. It was unintelligible with each of them yelling over each other and trying to get the other to listen. I kept moving though. I refused to get caught trying to eavesdrop. Who knows what else would be done to me? I had a temporary bum leg, probably a bruise around my neck, finger marks in my throat, scraped elbows, and probably damage to my lungs. There was no way I was going to heal completely before the next trial.

There was a moment of silence from behind me before I felt a wave of heat hit my back. It was so powerful that I collapsed forward and felt the floor move from underneath me. I closed my eyes tightly to avoid seeing anything else, but my body was rolling and being pushed out of the way by an invisible force field. I covered my ears to protect them from the loud noise of destruction and when I finally stopped moving, I opened my eyes to see the warpath behind me.

Almost like a bomb had just gone off.

#

 AMY KULP

"Did you see it?" Heather asked as more people filed into the room. From the corner of my eye, I could see her look up excitedly toward Justin, but he shook his head. He wrapped his arms around her and held onto her tighter. They filed in and sat on the opposite couch next to me. I could see her continue to excitedly chatter away. "I know we're supposed to stay away, but you're not known for following rules."

"How are we supposed to train now?" Colt asked as he walked in with Eddie and Garrett. They all moved to the billiard table and huddled around it. Despite how annoyed he seemed, his friends seemed excited about the news.

"Is it true?" Nia asked as soon as she got in the room. I could still see some food in the corner of her mouth. She had been out of her slump since hearing about the news on Jade. I was glad because Jade would have wanted to see her progress. However, now I knew that she was only ignoring me. She walked closer to the group of boys as they nodded yes. "Someone actually set a bomb off?" They nodded, and she turned around with the biggest grin on her face. Her chest was heaving in and out and she seemed almost incapable of accepting this news. "So, who did it?"

"Hopefully Bridget," Shane said as he came into the room. He sucked down on the straw to his drink and gulped it down. He stood by Nia's side as she looked around the room. "Never mind." He jutted his chin out toward me.

I curled my knees to my chest and tightly wrapped my arms around them. They didn't need to know that I saw it. They didn't need to know that I was near where it happened. As soon as the blast was heard, seen, and felt, hundreds of injured assassins came around to investigate.

"Where's Toby?" Nia asked. She immediately clutched onto Shane as she looked around the room for him. He looked around too but didn't offer any words of wisdom or advice to her to calm her down.

"Just relax, I'm sure he'll show up," Heather said. She got off the couch and away from Justin to gently calm her down. Guiding her away from Shane, they sat on the floor with each other. I could see her smiling and when Nia finally looked up, she was smiling too.

With Nia away from Shane, he joined his friends near the billiard table. He refused to even look at me as he passed. Almost as if I was nothing. When I looked at Justin, he didn't meet my gaze either. However, when he looked up and smiled, I assumed it was at me. I perked my body up and smiled too but it was dashed as soon as Asher walked in and sat by him.

"Oh my god," Nia yelled. "It was Toby. He's the only one not here!" She slapped her hands to her face and instantly tears streamed. "What did you do?" She got up and came closer to me as she yelled. Everyone else shut up and watched as she wrapped her hands into my shirt. "What did you do to him?" I shook my head to try and tell her I didn't do it but she was so delusional right now that her tears were blocking her eyes. She probably couldn't see

                        AMY KULP

anything. "First you kill Jade and now you kill Toby?"

"I'm right here," Toby whispered. Nia instantly let go of me as she saw him in the doorway and ran into his arms for a hug. "I was just sleeping." As he hugged her, I could see him glance toward me. He was lying but I didn't know how I knew that.

"So, then who set off the bomb?" Eddie asked. He walked away from the billiard table and back to everyone else. It was so weird to see everyone in their own groups but all of them talking to each other. Garrett and Shane turned around too and when I looked at Colt, he was curious, but he was already facing everyone else. "If we're all safe and here, who threw the bomb?"

"I'm sure you all have many questions," Bischoff said. I turned my head around to see him walking toward the living room. "I have no answers for you at this time." I looked at his body up and down but no scratch was on him. He was in that bomb explosion. He was where the fire and flames were. Yet as he walked toward us, he didn't limp and didn't seem like he was hurt. How was he not hurt? I felt the heat that the bomb had caused. How was he alive. "Because of the extent of the fire damage, we have decided to advance the Trials."

I looked around to see how everyone else was reacting and was surprised to see everyone was masking their faces still. However, we were all injured. We all just went to the medical tent to see how we could heal. Were they freaking out as much as I was freaking out?

As soon as the doors opened for us to be debriefed on the new trial, everybody calmly walked in. I watched as they all walked slowly and softly toward the doors. Some sped up to meet up with their friends while others slowed down for them. I just walked at a normal speed. Everyone I once considered my friends has proven to me that I cannot trust them and everyone who had been friendly toward me was not offput by Jade's demise.

I was alone.

Being the last person to step foot in the room, the doors shut instantly behind me. I looked to my sides to see everyone huddled together. Unusual for everyone but it made sense. Shane spent more time with the inductees to show his loyalty to them. However, he was still friends with Garrett, Eddie, and Colt. All the boys liked Asher and Justin. So Heather was brought along with Justin. However, as I scanned, I was surprised to see her latched onto Nia. She had her arm around her shoulder and was whispering in her ear. Toby and Justin were by each of their sides, but they seemed awkward as they just stood there.

I inserted myself in the middle of the group and felt the tension ripple around me. Whispers had now stopped between friends, and I could see people turning their heads to look at each other. If it was Jade and I, we would be sharing a glance too. I knew I shouldn't have inserted myself, but I wanted someone to talk to. They have all been giving me the cold shoulder. They had to know deep down that I would not hurt Jade, right?

As I looked around me though, I knew the answer was no. I could see Heather and Nia staring at each other – their eyebrows were raised, and they were eyeing me up. Nia knew about the tiff between Jade and me. After all, Jade probably went to her about it the most. When my head turned to see Shane and Toby, they were making a similar face. Although Shane's jaw was set very firmly. I could tell that he was still too pissed to be near me. When I glanced toward Justin, he was watching what Bischoff was doing. He didn't pay attention to Heather or me. Eddie and Colt were in front of me, but I could see in their posture that they were uncomfortable. Asher was next to them and while he seemed distant, that is how he had always been to me. The only one who seemed content with my presence was Garrett. After all, he was the only one besides me who knew the truth.

"Thank you for being so willing to start the next trial," Bischoff said. He stood up straight and kept his hands behind his back as he watched everyone. His eyes scanned the room and when I looked around too, I saw the subtle change everyone did: they took a step away from me. I was causing them to cluster into little groups. "For your next trial, we believe you are ready to go out in the real world." He paused and watched all our faces. If I knew them though, they were all masked still. "Your next trial will focus on how many casualties and injuries you can cause to the general public without getting caught." There was instant noise coming from around, but I couldn't tell if it was approval or disgust. I tried looking around but was instantly squished between bodies as they all tried to ask simultaneous questions to Bischoff. "You have a month to complete this task." He paused and remained calm as he spoke. As if he wasn't being bombarded with questions left and right. "We thought that some of you might want to get started as soon as possible and with the damage that the fire has caused, we want to try and get the smoke damage out of the building. There are two vans out back that are waiting for your arrival. Good luck assassins."

The only reason my legs started to move was because I would be squashed onto the floor. The doors behind Bischoff opened and I was carried along with the crowd. There was no use fighting it. I could hear the cheerful jitter from everyone around me – they were excited to shop. They were excited that they weren't cooped up in their bedrooms anymore. We were going to see people we didn't know. We were going to be humans and civilians again.

"This van is full!" Nia said as I tried to step in. I looked over at her and looked at Justin, Heather, Toby, and Asher as they were already buckled in. Nia grabbed the van's door and before I could protest that there were other seats, she slammed the sliding door in my face.

Taken back, I continued to stare at the van until I heard hooting and hollering coming from the other one. I slowly turned around to see Shane, Garrett, Eddie, and Colt leaning against the other van. They were having a conversation but as I groaned and walked near them, I could see smiles growing on Garrett and Eddie's face. When I glanced

　　　　　　　　　　　　　　　　　AMY KULP

at Colt, he remained stoic while Shane showed disgust. I was the one to open the door and as soon as I did, Eddie pushed past me. Too slow to react to that, I felt hands on my back and hips and was pushed forward into the van too. Being grabbed by my belt loops on my pants, I was firmly forced to sit down in between Eddie and Garrett.

Glancing up at Garrett, he kept his smiling weirdly and pushed my body closer to Eddie's. Having both of my legs squished into theirs, I felt claustrophobic. I needed to focus on Colt and Shane right now. What were they talking about?

"Do you think we can shop?' Shane asked. "I miss shopping." He paused as Colt mumbled something to him. I wish I could hear what had been said. "I'm excited about it though."

"Especially the arcade," Eddie said.

"No, what we need to do is focus on our casualties and injuries," Garrett announced. I could hear a mutual agreement between them before Garret suddenly bumped closer to me.

"Move over," I whispered as knocked my body into Eddie. His body didn't sway when I hit him. Instead, he remained perfectly straight almost as if he was expecting to get hit.

"Gladly," Eddie said as he squished me closer. I could see the smile on his face as he forced my body closer to both.

I closed my eyes as we hit a bump in the road and Garrett jumped up. He situated his lower body on half of mine while I struggled to remove him from me. They didn't care that I was uncomfortable though. They wanted me to feel uncomfortable in this van. As soon as I felt hands touch my skin on my stomach, I revolted toward Garrett who just pressed his face into my cheek. The hands kept wandering up and down and goosebumps started to form on my stomach. I didn't want his bony fingers touching me.

"We all appreciate you not putting your shirt back on," Garrett whispered. I crossed my arms over my upper body, but their hands just moved down to my legs. I grabbed onto my skin like I was grabbing onto a t-shirt and started to pull at it. I didn't want Eddie touching me. At least Garrett was only squishing me. The touching was a lot worse. The whispering against my neck and ear was uncomfortable too. Like he was trying to seduce me. "Nobody realized how much of a bod you have."

I closed my eyes as he continued whispering in my ear. I had to bite my lip to stop myself from protesting Eddie's hands and yelling at Garrett's whispers. It would make it so much worse for me. I was in a van full of people who didn't like me. They wouldn't care if I was crying. They wouldn't care if I was screaming. They would laugh and make it worse. It was almost like it was fun for them. I had to imagine it was. They found killing people to be fun too.

As soon as the van stopped, I couldn't take any chances. I pushed Eddie and Garrett off me with all my strength and was able to weasel my body from theirs. I opened the doors and pounded onto the sidewalk. Without hearing the conversation that was taking place inside the van, I held onto my stomach to shield myself and began storming toward the mall. I could hear chatter and laughter coming from the

                               AMY KULP

other van, but I rushed past them before they could see me crying. They couldn't know that I was affected by that.

"Bridget, wait!"

I stormed through the mall doors, and as soon as I saw a sign for the restroom, I went in there. Closing a stall behind me, I silently let my body shake and tears emerge. I couldn't make a noise, though. Nobody could know that I hated that. I was repulsed. I couldn't show emotion because they would then continue to do it to me. They hated me— all of them. They all hated me.

"Bridget?" I popped a hand over my mouth to silence any noises I might be making and watched as two pairs of shoes stopped before my stall. "Bridget, we know you're in there." I shook my head as if they could see me. I didn't want them here. I didn't want them to hear me. They didn't even know what happened – they wouldn't understand.

"We are the only girls in these trials," Nia started. She paused but I could hear her moving closer to the stall door. "The boys are plotting to get rid of us." I allowed my hand to drop from my mouth. "Starting with you."

"We think Asher was planted in our van so that you would have to go with the others," Heather commented. "I don't really know him that much."

"Justin wouldn't want to get rid of you," I said. I took a deep breath and immediately allowed my fingers to wipe the wetness from my face. As soon as that was done, I put them over my stomach again. "Toby wouldn't want to get rid of you, Nia. I have nobody to protect me."

"Are you kidding?" Nia asked. She shuffled her feet and there was a silent pause. Maybe an awkward pause. "Everybody sees how Colt looks at you."

I shook my head at the thought. Colt didn't like me. He didn't try to protect me in that van either. He allowed them to touch me and whisper inappropriate things in my ears. He just watched it happen. Maybe Colt liked my body and my looks like the other boys did, but he didn't like me at all. He was an arrogant Elitist.

"Besides, you have us," Heather commented. "I'm sorry that I blamed you for Tanya's death." I listened intently and while I wanted to lean against the door, I knew I shouldn't. "It took me a moment, but I realize now that you were just trying to protect me from getting too hurt."

"Do you... do you still think I killed Jade on purpose?"

"We don't know," Nia said. "But that's what these Trials are for. Most likely, we will have to kill one of our friends again. We're animals, we're—"

"In public," Heather added. "Will you come out, please? We might not trust you, but I don't think anybody should trust anybody fully. That's what these Trials are for. Kill or be killed."

Kill or be killed.

"Plus, this might be the only time we can shop," Nia said. "Everybody loves to shop. If anything, we can get food from the court."

"And get you a shirt."

I immediately unlocked the door and opened the stall. Looking at them, I watched as their faces

AMY KULP

started to fall when they realized I was crying. I refused to let that bother me though. I sauntered over to the sink and instantly rinsed the tear streaks and blotchiness from my face. When I was done, I looked up and Heather was right there to lend me a paper towel. I blotted my face until I felt most of the moisture coming off. Throwing the towel away, I led us out of there until we were jammed in by a group of girls coming in.

"Green?" one of the girls commented.

"Move away from them, they're assassins."

Without warning, they all ran away from us. I looked back at Heather and Nia, but they ushered me forward. Heather seemed okay with the comment, but Nia seemed taken aback. We couldn't interact with the public like we used to. I wasn't even sure that we could interact with them at all without getting punished. What were the rules?

"Let's go in here, first," Nia said. I followed along with them, and my nose was instantly hit with a massive array of different scented fumes. "What's your scent?" Nia asked as she turned around to face me.

"What?"

"What's your signature scent?" Nia asked. "Like, what shampoo, conditioner, body wash, perfume do you wear? It should be one scent." I stared at her for a second. "What do you use? I haven't looked in the showers in forever."

"Oh my… You use the stuff they give us?" Heather asked. I nodded my head very slowly. "You didn't bring anything?"

"I wasn't aware we could. I was dragged out of my home," I managed.

"Did you put up a fight?" Nia asked. I didn't move as I stared at her, but she started nodding as if that answered her question. "Well, of course, they wouldn't let you take something with you. They were probably afraid you would bolt."

"You didn't fight?"

"My family wanted me in these Trials," Heather reminded me. "I couldn't say no without them being disappointed in me." She shook her head. "I would do anything for my family."

"I have known since last year that I was flagged and would eventually be put in the Trials," Nia started. She looked at some offered scents and opened them up so I could smell them. "I've come to terms with it the best I can." They both turned to me as I shook my head from the scent she was offering me. "Do you really want to die so you won't have to kill people?"

"No," I admitted. "I don't want to die but I did not kill Jade on purpose."

"It's okay if you did," Heather said. She gave a small smile and turned back to the scents. "Try this one." I sniffed it and Heather must have seen something in my reaction because she smiled. "Strawberry it is."

"I don't have any money," I said as they walked to the counter.

"Watch her work her magic," Nia whispered to me. I nodded and Nia stopped both of us from going any further. She picked at a stand and pretended to be interested, but her gaze focused on Heather and the sales associate.

"Welcome, did you find everything…" The sales associate's voice dropped as she looked up from putting the previous customer's money in the drawer. She looked Heather up and down and I could see her body shrinking. "Green?" Heather nodded her head as she put the stuff on the counter. "What do I do?" she asked her coworker who had shrunk back against the wall. It seemed everyone in line had frozen.

"Give it to her unless you want to be put on her list," she announced.

With a nod of the head, Heather asked for a bag, and I watched as the lady's hands started shaking as she tried to open it. Once it was, Heather scooped up the supplies and dropped them into the bag. Then, everybody in line seemed to recoil away from her when she turned around with a smile on her face. She said her thank you's and excuse me's as she left and with a flick of the hair, walked out.

Nia and I followed behind her, but I couldn't help but feel upset about the situation. They were afraid of us. We weren't assassins yet, but they were afraid of us. They feared the trainees. Like we had some magical spell that allowed us to dictate who was put on the list. Did we? I didn't want to put people on my list.

"Loosen up, Bridget," Heather said. "Now you will smell good, and the boys will flock to you even more than they have been." She handed the bag off to me, but I couldn't muster up a fake smile. "You're going to need to impress them if you want a wedding." I looked over at her and arched my eyebrows. "Assassins only marry assassins."

"What?"

I stopped walking and just stared at her. I didn't want to cause any more attention to be centered on us than what was already there, but I wasn't sure I understood what she was saying. It made sense but I assumed I could marry who I wanted to. I didn't see it happening soon, but I wanted to marry eventually. However, I didn't want to marry an assassin. I didn't consider myself one yet. What if they were one of the people who purposely assassinated others? What if they were going to assassinate me?

"Bridget, how did you not know?" Nia asked. "Don't get me wrong, we'll be able to choose from anybody not just our class."

"Shut up," I said. I shook my head. "Please, shut up. I don't want to marry an assassin. I don't want to dress like an assassin. I don't want to be friends with assassins, and I don't even want to be an assassin."

"So, who do you think they'll have kill you, then?" Heather asked.

"Colt," Nia replied.

"Maybe, Justin," Heather replied. They continued to talk as they walked into a shop, and I had to close my eyes before going in with them.

I didn't want to think about this.

"This is cute," Heather said as she pulled out a bodycon dress. She looked at it for a second before showing it to herself in the mirror. "It's a bit too big for me though. Bridget, what do you think?" She held it up for me and I had to crinkle my nose. "Try it on?"

"I need a shirt," I whispered as I crossed my arms tighter against my skin.

"Come on," Nia egged. "We'll all try on ridiculous clothes. Find one for me." She stared at me before pushing me forward to find something through the racks.

As I stepped forward, I couldn't help but notice that the people who were in the store before us were all lined up against the wall. They were eyeing me as I looked at fancy dresses. Whenever I looked up, they went back to scouring through the clothing sizes they were in. Almost as if they were worried, I would kill them. When I turned back toward the entrance, I could see people walking in but realized that I was wearing green and hurriedly walked out. When I made eye contact with one lady trying to leave, she shuddered and sighed. I already saw her face and I might put her life in danger.

I had that much power.

"Come on, I want to try it on," I lied. Heather looked up at me as I nudged into her, and she smiled. She grabbed some clothes and excitedly went over to Nia. When Nia was ready, she seemed disappointed when I didn't pick anything out for her, but we went anyway.

"Can we have a changing room for three?" Heather asked politely. The sales associate nodded their head and without saying a word, handed us the set of keys that were on their pant loops. Heather looked back at Nia, and they shared a glance of being impressed before walking in. "I can get used to this."

Nia agreed while Heather attempted to find the keys to each fitting room. I rushed in first and slammed the door behind me. I couldn't take all that staring. I couldn't take the judgmental looks. The same look my school friends would give when someone would play a fake game in the schoolyard. Before I lost all my friends when they found out I was flagged and would eventually be chosen to partake in the real Trials. I remember the stares I was given as I passed people in the halls. I remember I sat alone at lunch and as a child, that was so hard to understand why. I remember how much I hated going to school because I was lonely. Because I was afraid people were whispering about me. They stared at me like I was a unique zoo animal they had never seen before.

I remember asking my mom to switch schools, but she had to explain that this would always follow me around now. Every school I would go to would know. So, I stuck it out at that school. Nobody bullied me because they were too afraid that I would add them to my list. At that age, I didn't know about the lists. I still barely understand them. I don't know how someone's name gets added to the list.

Despite being flagged, it didn't affect my parents or the farm. Adults were nicer to me and tried to avoid questions about the future. If I did bring it up and how I wanted to go to college, I could see the look of pity in their eyes. I probably wouldn't get to live out that fantasy. They were right too. Here I was in the mall, hiding in a changing room to avoid the stares that people were giving me. I don't know if they were judgmental or scared.

                                   AMY KULP

It reminded me that I have always been alone as I got older. Even now, I could hear Heather and Nia giggling with each other over the clothes they picked. I was by myself. Nobody trusts me anymore. It's just like elementary school.

I really wish I knew who flagged me.

"Open up and let us see!" Heather giggled as they knocked on my changing room's door.

"One minute."

I had to shake my head to get my body moving. I felt like a robot as I removed my shoes and my pants. I struggled to get the tight dress on, and it took me a couple breaths to get the strap up on my shoulder. Every inch was constricting me, and I kept breathing heavier and heavier to loosen the fabric.

I didn't look terrible. It just wasn't something I would ever wear. My rear was almost hanging out and it pushed my breasts together so much that they felt like they were going to fall out of the top. It wasn't me though. I preferred pants and a shirt especially around those boys.

"You're hot!" Nia yelled as soon as I opened the door.

"So uncomfortable though," Heather said as she readjusted one of the straps on me. "Go change, clearly you hate this." Before I could close the door, Heather jammed it and looked me up and down. "In the nicest way possible, stay away from Justin."

I shook my head and opened my mouth but before I could say anything, all I heard were screams. I glanced between Heather and Nia before a bunch of people started running through the dressing room. I instantly followed them and felt hands crushing into

my back and knew to stay upright. If I fell, I would
be trampled.

"There's an exit down this hall!" someone
yelled. That seemed to increase everybody's hope
because the hands on my back pushed me harder than
before. I had to quicken my pace with everyone else.
I couldn't even see where Heather or Nia were
anymore. What was going on?

As soon as we made it outside, everybody
started running in different directions: in front of
cars, toward their car, toward traffic, or out in the
open. I stopped moving and while some people hit
me in the back on accident, I was able to find the van
that I came into. I could see Nia and Heather running
toward the van they were in and as the cold air
brushed against my bare skin, I ran to get into the
heat.

Immediately when I opened the van door, I
was shocked to see that the driver and Shane were
already there. He raised his eyebrows as he eyed
what I was wearing but it wasn't until I heard the van
start that I knew to get in. I picked the backseat and
sat all the way in the corner. There was no escaping
Eddie and Garrett but, at least only one of them could
sit next to me.

"Don't worry about the door," the driver
shouted.

I buckled up as I watched him floor the gas
and pull up to the mall's main entrance. Why weren't
we leaving? What happened in there? Why was there
so much yelling? My mind was frozen, and I knew I
was scared as I held onto the seatbelt in anticipation
for the worst. It wasn't until I saw Colt, Eddie, and

                                    AMY KULP

Garrett walk out calmly that I realized that it had to be something involving those three.

As soon as they spotted me, all their mouths dropped open. I yanked at the end of the dress hoping that it would cover more of me, but it put up a resistant fight. I closed my eyes and turned toward the window when I heard the whistling and comments starting. I just needed to block it out.

"You should come back in the middle," Eddie teased. "We would love to share you right now."

"Who knew you had legs like that?" Garrett asked.

I just closed my eyes tighter as I felt the liquid forming in them. I could not cry in front of these boys. It wasn't until a pair of hands grabbed my hips to try and move me that I let out a small cry. I instantly regretted it, but the hands were removed. My body wanted to untense, and I wanted to be able to relax but as I felt body heat plop next to me, I inched closer to the window to give myself some space from them.

When the van started moving, I forced my hands around the seatbelt. This was my protection no matter how little it was. It took about a minute before I realized that there was no additional commentary on my body and my skin wasn't being touched. I waited a little longer before opening my eyes and looking at the person sitting next to me.

Colt.

He continued to face forward as I stared at him. His face was blank, but he seemed mad. His arms were crossed on his chest and he didn't try to look in my direction. It seemed like he was a brick wall that Eddie or Garrett would have to get through. I continued to stare at him but made sure my body was turned away from him. I didn't want him to think that he could touch me now, but I did feel comfortable enough to take my eyes off him.

"So," Shane said from the front seat. While staring out the window, I allowed myself to listen to them. Nobody was touching me right now and once I got my anxiety calmed down, I might be able to add something to the conversation. I wasn't sure if I wanted to engage though. "Who ended up causing the scene?" There was a shuffle behind me, but I wasn't sure who was the cause of the problem. "How many?"

"Three dead," Eddie proudly exclaimed.

"Two injured," Garrett added.

"But he was caught," Colt snidely remarked. I peeked over at him, and he still seemed to have his tough mask on. We made brief eye contact before I stared back out at the window. "I wish I would have known about it."

"Opportunity just struck."

"You'll have to give me a rundown later," Shane said.

Once the van stopped, I listened to the various seatbelts being unbuckled, shoes shuffling against the floor, and doors opening. However, I still felt Colt sitting next to me. He wasn't moving. I kept my forehead pressed against the window and waited until I felt his warmth leave my closest leg. When it did, I gave it a couple before I felt hands on my skin. My body immediately tensed up and it stayed that

                          AMY KULP

way until I heard the seatbelt unbuckle next to me. Immediately after that, the hands were removed, and I felt his heat leave my body.

I allowed my body to slowly unveil itself. Before getting up and scooting across the seats, I tugged the edge of my dress and felt the fabric begin to stretch just a tiny bit. With that reassurance, I got out of the van and crossed my arms back over my chest while my back curled into itself. I didn't want to give anyone anything to look at.

While our group mixed and mingled with each other while waiting for the other van to arrive, I made sure to stay near Colt. I didn't want to engage with any of them and hoped that the second van would come soon. I yearned to change my clothing as soon as I could. I could still feel stares in the back of my head.

While trying not to look behind me, my eyes wandered onto Colt. He was clearly putting his back to me, but it felt more like he was shielding me from being seen by Shane. It felt protective but as he continued to talk and wave his hands, I couldn't help but see the red that was smeared his knuckles and fists.

Looking at everyone else, I could see the blood stain on Garrett's. When he noticed me staring, he made an obscene gesture and rolled his eyes. He took a step closer to me and I revolted by stepping in front of Colt. Accidentally, bumping into him, I instantly removed myself and made slight eye contact with him. I still couldn't read what they were saying in them.

He punched Garrett. Or at least roughed him up enough that he bled. It could have been one knock or multiple to get him to back off. Why didn't I hear that in the van? I knew what skin against skin sounded like. Why didn't anyone comment on it? Were they still friends? Why did he punch him? Was it because he was grabbing me? Was Garrett even the one who touched me? I had many questions, but they got cut off when the other van came in. It made me remember what Nia and Heather had said about Colt.

"Before you come in," Bischoff announced as the second van pulled up. They all piled out too and I could see the unpleasant expressions on Asher and Justin's faces as they came out first. Next was Heather and Nia as they continued to laugh and chatter with each other. Their smiles were radiant and when they stepped out, I knew the outfits they were wearing were something they were comfortable in. Closing the door behind him, Toby quietly came out too. He removed himself from anyone and just stared blankly at Bischoff. "Due to the fire and smoke damage in the rooms, we will be switching to a different part of the building. Your stuff is packed, and you may only stay in the living spaces. Once you all are changed into appropriate uniforms, I will escort you into the new section."

I tried to see other people's reactions to this news, but I wasn't able to see Heather or Nia. I tried looking around Colt but by the time I did, people were already going through the door. Passing Bischoff and the drivers, I was the last person to enter.

Bischoff didn't lie – there were ten suitcases in the living space. The room was now taped off so nobody could walk to the kitchen, hallway to the main building, living spaces for the inductees and elitists, bedrooms, and the training area. All we could do was be in this room together. Colt, Garrett, Eddie, and Shane immediately went over to the billiard table and started talking with each other. Justin and Asher took a couch as they talked while Toby went to look through the suitcases for his bag. Once he found it, he wheeled it over to the second couch. I followed Nia and Heather to their suitcases as well.

"Do you want to change first?" Heather asked as she unzipped one of the suitcases. I followed her suit and looked through one. "They're staring at you." I turned to see Shane, Eddie, Garrett, and Colt all leaning forward on the pool table to look. Colt had a small smirk on his face. I instantly blushed red and pulled my dress down even more. I heard a slight stretch sound and dug through a new suitcase to find it. "I'm going to kill that boy." I looked up at Heather and then over to where Justin was. Asher and he were also staring.

"It could be at you," I mentioned.

"No," Heather said with a sigh. "It's at you." She shook her head and dug through the suitcase faster.

"How do we do this without leaving the room?" I asked.

Heather and Nia both shared a glance before shrugging their shoulders. Like something had overtaken them, they both stripped their shirts and dresses off. It was like nothing I have ever seen before. I immediately turned around to see that Justin had gotten up from his seat, Asher's eyes grew wide, Garrett and Eddie had both walked forward, and Colt seemed more interested in them than before.

"I can't do that," I said as they both shimmied their pants up and put their shirts on. I shook my head and felt my nerves starting to act up. What if they tried to hurt me? Or tried to touch me again? Heather and Nia couldn't protect me. "I can't have them staring at me. I can't do it. I can't change in front of them. In that van—"

"Calm down," Heather said. She nodded her head and looked at me. "We'll protect you." She stared at me for a second and I didn't care if she blamed me for Tanya's death at this moment. I didn't care that neither of them could trust me. I didn't care about anything because, at that moment, I felt like I could trust Heather and Nia.

"Enjoy the show boys?" Nia asked as she turned around. She smiled at them, and I watched as some grew more excited. Justin sat back down, and Nia cocked an eyebrow. "Because we have one more surprise for you – a grand finale of sorts."

I closed my eyes as soon as I started hearing the whistles. I felt a hand on my wrist and looked at Heather as she and Nia both grabbed a cloth that was in one of the suitcases. She nodded, and I watched as they pulled up a blanket. Boos were all I heard but I changed so fast. I shimmied my pants up and forced a shirt over my dress before I unzipped it and took the straps off. When I tugged on the blankets, they let go and I stared at them.

They were still booing when I raised two of my hands and instantly flipped them the bird.

#

My eyes scoured everyone passing us as we rolled our suitcases to our new living space. Some of them would glance our way but most of them chose to stare straight away. I noticed the varying colors of forest green as the sounds of our wheels echoed through the barren hallway. When everyone else began to stop, I rolled mine slower and made sure to be on the outskirts of the group. I didn't want to get pushed and thrown to the ground so everyone could march in the room.

"Once you find a bed, place your stuff on the blankets. I think you will like the new arrangements," Bischoff said. Once he moved from the door, Shane was the first to march through it.

As we shuffled in, I silently thanked Toby for letting me in before him. I pushed forward and while some people stood there flabbergasted, I tried to get as close to the front as possible. However, I had to stop and look around too.

All our beds were on the far-left side of the room. Some of them were grouped together while there were a couple that were by themselves. Each bed had a little dresser for the clothes we had but as I counted all ten beds, I realized we were all expected to sleep near each other. On the right side of the room was a little dip in the floor. In that dip were two couches side by side and ten TVs mounted on the walls. All the screens were black and just from looking around, it didn't seem that there was a remote to turn them on. Next to the TVs was a scoreboard with eight slots.

At the top was Eddie Marlowe with three dead and two injured.

It wasn't until I saw movement from the corner of my eyes that I saw Nia and Heather rushing toward the beds they wanted. There was a third near where they were sleeping and as I moved closer, I watched Garrett and Eddie stand before me.

"Colt already put his stuff down so he can't protect you now," Eddie remarked. "Seeing your body in that tight dress and without a shirt, we want to sleep next to you." I wanted to gag but I knew not to do it. My eyes went back over to Nia and Heather, but they were already busy chatting away with each other. I could see their smiles grow bigger each moment.

"I won't be intimidated by you," I said. I looked back over at Heather and Nia but knew they wouldn't come to my rescue. They were too busy being involved with themselves to notice that I was being hounded by Garrett and Eddie. "You guys have practiced your entire lives to be part of the graduating assassin class," I stated. They nodded their heads, and I watched as they started to flex their muscles. I wondered if that worked with anybody because it wasn't working with me. "I'm still here in these Trials. I have never trained for this a day in my life, and you might get beat by me. We're on the same level. Imagine how much better I would be if I was trained."

                                    AMY KULP

Garrett immediately chest bumped me and as I lost my balance, Eddie grabbed my suitcase from my hands. I tried to get up but by the time I saw which bed he had chosen; I already knew it was between the two. I rolled my eyes as I went over, and they stayed close by my side. I just wanted to be left alone.

"Colt won't always be here to protect you, y'know," Garrett said. I rolled my eyes.

"I don't need Colt to save me," I said. I crossed my arms and looked between the two of them. I hated their smirks and grins. Like they were better than me. I was in clothes I was comfortable in now. They couldn't take the confidence I had. I could take them and as I lifted my leg to kick him between his, I was interrupted by a shriek coming from Nia.

"Mom?" My eyes watched her as she ran toward the TV screens near our beds. She got so close to the top left screen that I was sure she was delusional.

However, as I watched closer, someone was playing on the screen. They were moving around a small house and as Nia stayed captivated by her screen, another one popped on. Garrett walked away from me and instantly leaned against the back of the couch. The camera kept flipping between rooms as he stared on. The next TV that turned on just showed static. I was confused by it for a second until my TV turned on.

My mom was at the kitchen table. She seemed to be pouring over some legal papers she always looked at. She had a blue pen in her hand and tapped it gently against her chin. She seemed old though. Her bright skin was now ghostly white. I wondered if she was eating because of how skinny her arms were. All the loose skin seemed to be hanging from her. I moved closer to the screen and knew that others were turning on too, but I wasn't watching theirs. I was focused on my mom.

She was still alive. That means she didn't tell anyone that I was in the Trials. My mom could at least do that. She kept her word. Now I got to watch her. I got to see her. It was the next best thing to being able to hold her. At least I knew she was safe. I wish my dad was in the house more. He was probably in the field right now. If he was feeling anything, he wasn't telling my mom about it. He worked through his emotions.

I continued staring at my screen. Even as people left to do other things, I sat on the couch and stared at my screen. I watched my mom kill herself over the paper she was reading. She must have spent so much time looking at the page. I stayed watching as others made their own food. I stayed watching as Heather screamed about us sharing a unisex bathroom. I continued to watch as one of the boys made an inappropriate comment. The only time I got up from watching the screen was when my eyes started to fall due to exhaustion.

I tiptoed over to my bed and watched Garrett snore excessively as he slept on his back. When I looked over to Eddie, he was curled into his blanket and was sound asleep. I wondered how Garrett's snoring wasn't bothering anybody else. I looked around and noticed just how many people were sleeping soundly. Only two beds were empty – mine and someone else's. In the dark light, I couldn't see who anyone was. Everybody could sleep through Garrett's horrendous snoring. Time to see if I could.

I rolled onto my bed and curled under the top blanket to warm my body. I snuggled down into it and while it was scratchy, it felt like the most protected I had been all day. Almost as if this wall of warmth could protect me forever from the boys. As if it would stop them from ogling my body all day. I hated their stares. I hated seeing their evil grins when they saw me catching them. I hated not being able to stand up for myself about it. I was too wimpy.

That's what Jade was for. Jade stood up for me and showed me how to do it herself. Not intentionally but I was taking after her. However, Jade would never kill someone she was friends with. She was too good for that. She would hear someone yelling for her to stop stepping backward. She wouldn't continue pushing them. She would stop and fight Garrett. She wasn't a coward and she had combat skills. She had integrity and was distinguished. She was daring.

As soon as the tears started streaming down my face, I knew I couldn't hold in the noises that I needed to make. Jade was my best friend and I killed her. I couldn't just get over that in the day. I rushed to the bathroom and locked myself in one of the stalls. Sitting down, I allowed myself to break down. Anybody could come in here, but I felt protected with this door. It definitely wasn't soundproof, but everybody was sleeping right now.

I was responsible for someone's life ending. Up until now, I wasn't assigned to assassinate anyone. All our trials were about who was the best and none of us needed to have a defense. The first chance we get, and my best friend ends up dying. I'll never be able to learn more about her. I'll never get to know what her favorite color is. I'll never know those small details about her. Eventually, her image would start leaving my brain too.

I flushed the toilet as I started gagging on my cries. Those horrible ones that usually only kids cry. The one where you are gasping for air but you're too busy having an anxiety or panic attack to calm down. While you are choking, you start wailing harder. Sometimes, snot comes out and you are gagging trying to clean yourself up. The ugly crying. The crying you have when someone important to you leaves you. Sometimes it's overreactions and you feel like you're going to die but in a couple of months, you're fine. This wasn't an overreaction though. Jade was never coming back, and it was all because of me.

"Are you okay?" They knocked their knuckle against the stall door gently and I instantly slapped my palm over my mouth. Almost as if that would help mute the noise. However, I struggled with it and forced my eyes closed. I couldn't stand someone heard me acting like this. I hope they didn't think I was weak. After counting in my head and I was able to calm down, I wiped my eyes with toilet paper and unlocked the door.

My fear that they were still here was a reality. I walked past him when I went to the sink and tried to act normal. I washed my hands slowly and kept my gaze at the running water. It was so calming to

　　　　　　　　　　AMY KULP

look at. It was something familiar. Something from the outside world that was allowed in here.

"It's hard," Toby said. He nodded his head and slowly got off the bench to stand next to me. He reached over me to gently turn the knobs off. "I wish I could help you but I'm so tired." I looked up at him and could see the red rims of his eyes. He had been crying too. "Everything I'm doing is wrong to Nia." He paused. "Everything I'm doing is wrong to me." He looked at me and smiled softly. "Everything about this is wrong but since Nia has started hanging out with Heather – that Elitist – she doesn't see what's wrong with it anymore." He shook his head again before looking back up at him. "Try to get some sleep."

I nodded my head in agreement before feeling his hands shove me. They didn't feel threatening to me. They didn't feel sinister to me. He wasn't trying to sexualize me. He was trying to get me to go to bed. I felt comfortable with that and allowed myself to go back to my bed.

I could hear that Garrett was no longer snoring. I slunk into my bed and gathered all the blankets on top of one another to warm myself up. Maybe if I was warm, it would feel like home. I brought my hands up and nuzzled my face into the cloth. Slowly, my eyes started feeling heavy and I could feel myself falling into the peaceful slumber.

Until I felt hands on me again.

My eyes opened instantly and while I struggled to get them off me, I had too many blankets that helped immobilize me. I looked up at my assailant and rolled my eyes when I saw Garrett. It made sense that he wasn't snoring. He was actually awake and waiting for me. As soon as he lifted my covers, I aimed my hand to slap him in the face. I was slow though. He grabbed my wrist without effort and crawled in anyway.

"Just let me sleep," he said. He rolled his eyes as if I was inconveniencing him. I forced myself to stare away from him and felt his clammy hands lift my shirt. He pressed his body against mine and I felt him beginning to spoon me here. "Go to sleep."

I didn't say anything as I heard his breathing deepen and his hand stop wandering. It went limp on top of me and with the deadweight, he was holding me in this position. I wanted to move and fidget to make him uncomfortable, but I was tired. I was exhausted. I just used all my energy to cry in the bathroom. Despite how sweaty Garrett was getting, I was trying to force myself to think that this was comforting. Maybe if I did it enough, I would fully convince myself of it. After all, if I complied, it wasn't as bad for me.

I forced my eyes closed and listened to his breathing. No snoring right now. I hoped it would stay that way since he was no longer sleeping on his back. Maybe I could fall asleep if he didn't move. I was okay with his arm being across my hips but if he were to put his hands there, it would make me nervous. Right now, I was as separated from him as I could be. I didn't want his face to come any closer because I would feel his breath on my neck.

I didn't want to do this, but I wanted to sleep. I couldn't continue these Trials without sleep. Maybe that was their tactic with this. They wanted to wear me down to the point that I would lose the next one. Maybe I wouldn't remember to do it at all. Or maybe it was because they were alone. Heather and Nia were both claimed, and I wasn't. I was the lone bird, so it was easier to attack me than the other two. I was the outsider, and I was the one who was damaged because of my attack against Jade. They knew I was vulnerable, and they were taking advantage of it.

Despite how much I hated it, I had to admit that they were being smart about it.

#

My jitters weren't stopping as I tried to fall asleep for the second night. I could hear Garrett snoring as he laid on his back. Was everyone else used to this? I shook my head and felt my heart continue to beat quickly. The thumps were so loud and so fast that I was worried I might have an attack. I couldn't keep doing this. I couldn't sleep now after a day of being squandered in these quarters with everyone. I had to watch from the corner of my eye where Garrett or Eddie was for fear that they would taunt or touch me. Nobody stood up to them although I knew a couple of people saw. They knew I hated it. It made me isolate myself. I didn't want to be distracted and have them catch me off guard. I was already isolated from everyone thinking about me betraying Jade. Now if someone came toward me, I went the other way and just stared. Even thinking about it now, I felt my heart begin to race faster. I didn't realize that was possible.

There was no way I was sleeping though. I was too nervous. Plus, Garrett made it almost impossible. I swear the noise echoed around the room bouncing off the walls and radiating in my ear. I couldn't do it. I didn't want anyone to spoon me or hold me or touch me. I wasn't an object for them to do this to, but I was so tired and exhausted. I wanted to sleep. I yearned to close my eyes and get rest. I could feel my eyes stinging to stay open, but I knew if I closed them, I still wouldn't be able to sleep.

Grabbing the throw blanket, I wrapped it around myself as a barrier of protection. Just in case I woke either of them up. I tiptoed across the cold floor and walked toward the couches across the way.

As soon as I sat down, I stared at the scoreboard with Eddie's name on it. He was the only one to try something that first day. I didn't remember that we had the Trial. I kept forgetting that we were in the middle of a Trial. Maybe that's why they had the scoreboard there. To remind us and to think about ideas to use. Who knew when we were supposed to go back out into the real world? I'm sure they wouldn't want us to try and hurt each other.

I didn't want to think about that though. Right now, I needed to calm myself down. I needed to listen to everything around me and couldn't let Garrett and Eddie near me. I just needed to calm down first. I breathed heavily through my nostrils and stared at the TV screens in front of me. I didn't care about other people's. I just wanted to see my mom and my dad.

They were sleeping. They were facing opposite ways on the bed, and I wondered if they

                                        AMY KULP

were fighting. Whether it was with each other or for me. I wanted my mom. She would never believe the things that I have seen. She would hold me and cry with me. She would let me cry as long as I needed to. She would believe that I didn't kill Jade on purpose. Even if I didn't, she would always believe that I would never hurt someone on purpose.

My dad would make me work through the pain I was feeling. He would tell me to talk to the animals – the goats always had feedback for you. It was therapeutic too. I used to clean their pens and talk for hours about something that would bother me. They weren't interested and I bet that they couldn't understand me, but it helped. Sometimes, I helped my dad in the field but that only temporarily allowed me to forget my problems. We were always too far away, or our machines were too loud for him to listen if I talked. I already knew it was useless to try with him. He loved me though. He just wasn't sure how to talk about his feelings.

I wondered how he felt now that I was gone. While usually relaxed in bed, his body was stiff, and his arms were crossed in his sleep. He looked mad but when my eyes scoured to my mom, she seemed elegant and graceful. She always was. As I looked closer though, I could see that she wasn't in pajamas though. She seemed to be in her day clothes. Was she putting in extra hours at her job? I continued to watch them to see if she would wake up so I could see if I was right. I knew her sleeping clothes though. I knew what her pajamas looked like. That wasn't it.

While my heart had calmed down, it picked right back up when I heard a noise come next to me.

My head turned immediately, and it wasn't until I registered that Toby was sitting next to me that my heart began to slow. I watched to verify he wouldn't touch me, and he acknowledged that with a nod to me. He leaned back on the couch and looked up at his TV screen. I wasn't exactly sure which one was his, but I turned my eyes back to my family.

My mom was out of bed and my dad was now taking up the entire space.

"You're wearing more layers," he noted. I nodded as I pulled on the long sleeves of my shirt and rolled down my pant leg, so no skin was covered. I pulled the blanket tighter around me too. Toby kept staring at me as I fidgeted under his gaze. It made my skin crawl to know anyone could watch me. "I miss home." I agreed and continued to stare at my dad sleeping like that. I wondered if he snored while on his back. Does everyone? Or is that just a Garrett thing? "How... how did they find you?"

"I was flagged," I whispered.

"But why?" I looked over at him and just watched him. He kept darting his eyes between his screen and me. "We might not know who flags us, but they tell us why."

"Manhunt," I whispered. I closed my eyes for a second and relaxed against the sofa. "I was playing manhunt. I have no idea if it was at my house or in the school playground." I shook my head. "I never played alone, so I don't know why I was singled out." Toby just stared at me. "I lied; I know why. It was a game where you ran, hid, and got chased. I was never caught. I was good." I shook my head and looked up

                              AMY KULP

at the screens. "It was so stupid to play. I can't imagine how insensitive I was."

"You were a child," Toby said.

"A stupid one." I wrapped the blanket tight around me in hopes that it would cut off some circulation somewhere. Maybe it would let me sleep for a little bit. "Whenever we did the physical fitness test at school, I was always at the top. My grades were always good too. The manhunt took it over the top – I had all the qualities they were looking for in an Assassin." I shook my head again. Saying it out loud, it sounded unreal. Having your fate chosen when you were young. "What about you?" I asked.

"I asked for someone to flag me," Toby said. He looked over at me and shrugged his shoulders. I could see some regret flash across his face as he turned back toward the TVs. "At the time, I didn't want to go to school or work afterward. I was just a young, stupid boy afraid of his future." Biting his lip, I could see that he wasn't sure what exactly he could tell me. I wasn't sure either. Could I be trusted with this? He chose to be here just like the Elitists. He was no better than them. "I forgot about the part where I would have to kill people. I thought of it more as protecting people."

"When did you decide?"

"Last year, when I was eighteen and just graduated high school." His gaze moved down from his screen and onto the scoreboard now. "Everyone was moving on without me. My friends were getting accepted into colleges and my girlfriend got pregnant." I tried to keep my face from showing what I was thinking, but I knew it was. If he looked at me, he would see how horrified I was to hear that. "I didn't want to think about any of that and I was lazy. I thought when I survived these Trials that it would give me an automatic job and be surrounded by people with the same minds." He turned to me, and I watched as he registered my face. "Clearly, we are all on different pages here."

I nodded but didn't say anything. I didn't feel like I needed to. He didn't need to hear my judgments when he was looking for reassurance. Besides, this was the only interaction I have had all day and it felt normal. Maybe like I was in a dorm room.

Something that Toby didn't want to experience.

"Why do you think Colt's TV screen isn't showing a picture?" Toby asked.

"No idea," I answered.

#

"As Assassins, you all need to work on hiding in crowds. While some of you were brave enough to try, you were caught. Points off for that," Bischoff announced. I opened my eyes at the noise and pulled the blanket tighter around my body. I was still sitting on the couch from last night and was surprised to see that I was untouched. Nobody was sitting on the couches with me, but they were all piled on the next one. "Today, we will be playing a game of hide and seek."

"Like the children's game?" Eddie asked while laughing.

                                    AMY KULP

"Exactly like the children's game," Bischoff mentioned. "This is also the time for you to continue trying to get the most casualties. One of you is the seeker but I will not disclose who that is. Once you are found, you return to the van. If you do not return to the van, just remember that we still have our microscopic cameras on you. We will find you and you will have a public assassination."

"What do we get if we win the hide and seek?" Asher asked.

"Satisfaction," Bischoff said. He smiled creepily at all of us. Almost as if he was trying to see who would run. "Some of you have also been appointed as drivers for your vans. Unfortunately, the preparatory schools did not prepare Elitists with a driver's license. Thankfully, we have two inductees who can. Shane will drive the one van and Nia will drive the other one. You are expected to stay in your own van currently. You are expected to try." There was a pause, and I knew people were uncertain about playing the game. However, if I could escape these guys for just a few hours, it would be worth it to me. "We are going into the city. In each of the vans is a GPS that must be followed. When both vans find parking, you have fifteen minutes before you can be sought after." I nodded my head as if he was only speaking to me. I think this was my favorite activity we could have done. "You may proceed to your vans."

All at once, we got up. Looking around, I wasn't exactly sure where our van would be. In our old room, we went through the back doors that opened for us. Now, we were in a room with only one door in and out. It didn't lead to outside though. It led to the internal routes in the building instead. I followed everyone out of the room and for a second, nobody dared to move while we were in the hallway. Eventually, Heather took charge and made a right. While nobody was in our hallway, we could hear chatter coming up as we walked longer and longer.

The more we walked, the more people we saw. There were desks now and people dressed in green at various desks. The people in green were too serious. They had wrinkles on their foreheads and some of them didn't look to be any older than me. Up near the doors were metal detectors with more green men standing there. Looking back, I saw them throwing out whatever was in the one woman's purse. She could see it too, but her face remained calm as the injured assassin next to her held the electricity stick closer to her.

I had to keep walking forward though. My eyes couldn't get off them though. Running into Justin and Asher, I immediately apologized and backed up. I tried to crane my neck up ahead to see what was going on, but instead, Justin turned around and hissed at me.

"Watch where you are going!"

I wanted to retort back but instead; my mind became preoccupied with the sight before my eyes. About four green Assassins were surrounding one person who was bleeding out. They were yelling obscenities all around and trying to get out of the grasp of the assassins that were surrounding them. Their face was completely covered so I couldn't see who it was. Howls of pain were being yelled

                                    AMY KULP

throughout the air and when I looked around, everyone else was staring at the distraction too.

"Let's keep moving," Shane said. He grabbed my arm roughly and squeezed it so he wouldn't lose me. I kept staring at the show that was in front of me and watched as the person started crying for help from the people around them. I heard Heather's name and watched her stare back at them. I heard Justin's name, Garrett's, Nia's, Toby's, Asher's, Justin's, Shane's, Eddie's, Colt's, and finally mine. I was being dragged by the arm with Shane leading the way. Each shove was met with a shake of the head and the group following behind us.

Once in the van, Shane got onto one side while I got on the passenger side. We waited for Eddie, Garrett, and Colt to get on before he started the van and drove. It wasn't until a second later that Shane turned the GPS and we listened to the calming voice telling us to make a certain turn.

"What was that freakshow?" Eddie asked.

"Why were assassins bringing someone in? Don't we just assassinate them?" Garrett asked.

"How did they know our names?" I wondered.

"They probably were someone who watched the Trials when they first aired," Shane answered. He made a right turn, but I could see him nervously drumming his fingers along the wheel.

"It was someone who defied our government," Colt answered. I looked back at him, but he was in the far back row and was looking out the window. He shook his head while making brief eye contact with me. "Probably a leader. Someone they can make an example of."

"Torture," Shane added.

"Stop the van," I said, clutching my stomach. Shane instantly squealed on the breaks before it came to a complete stop. I opened the door and allowed myself to vomit. I groaned as I did it and made sure that I could feel the bile running up my front. They were going to torture that person. I just walked right by them. I was so used to seeing blood anymore that I didn't think anything of them being shot. How they were probably hurting.

"Get it all out," Colt said as he closed the door behind him. He stood next to me and looked out at the city. After a couple of moments, I could feel his hand on my back and despite not wanting to be touched, I didn't shiver away from him. "When you get back into that van, you pretend as if this didn't happen."

"What?" I asked as I put my hands on my knees. I started panting and just shook my head. This was too much. They were going to torture them. What did that mean? "How can you be so okay with this?" I wondered. I felt another wave shoot through my stomach and instantly bent over and opened my mouth. It was coming out without any push. "What is wrong with you? You shouldn't be used to this."

"We are going to be assassins," Colt said. He said it was a sharp tone in his voice that I didn't like. Almost like he thought I would back down if he raised it. "We need to get used to it. That is going to be our new normal."

"Four of us still are going to die," I spit out. I spit any strands of puke away from my face and closed my eyes. He removed his hand from my back and without his touch, I crumbled onto the ground. I allowed myself to kneel there as I watched people continue to walk past me. Almost like I didn't exist. It was dehumanizing but it was the right thing to do. I wouldn't want to talk to an Assassin Wannabe either. "Four of us… are not going to make it out of here."

"Yeah," Colt agreed. "But you can't show those guys in that van that this bothers you because if you do… they will make you a target. They will know you are weak. They will know how to hurt you. If you keep this up, you will be one of the four to die." He stopped talking and waited to see how I would react. I kept my hands on my knees, and while my stomach was still in knots, I didn't feel the need to throw up. "This is your future, farmgirl. You get to decide whether you're going to be a victim or you're going to be an assassin."

I rolled my eyes when I heard him get back in the van. Clearly, he was trying to make a dramatic talk. I didn't want to get used to stuff like that, though. I didn't want to get used to seeing people die. I didn't want to get used to killing people. While I understood that I would need to be an assassin if I wanted to survive, I didn't have to enjoy it. I'm sure there would be other people who felt the same way. I wanted to live, but I definitely did not want to kill people.

"The other van is waiting for us!" Shane called as he rolled the window down. He honked the horn at me, and I straightened myself up. Taking a huge breath, I rolled my eyes and stood up like I wasn't in the mix of crying and throwing up. My stomach still felt disgusting. "Let's go."

I'm sure my face showed that I was pissed because as soon as I yanked on the door handle and sat myself, nobody said anything. Shane sped off while cutting off the oncoming cars and put all his pressure on the gas pedal. I quickly buckled myself up and leaned against the window. It was cool against my forehead, and it allowed me to calm down. Closing my eyes, I tugged the end of my sleeves down my arms and over my fingers. I didn't want any skin showing on me. I just wanted to have a restful nap while Shane drove.

"Fifteen minutes start now," Shane said as he slammed on the brakes. I heard everyone get out of the van and listened as doors were whacked shut. I watched as Shane sped one way and Eddie went another. I could see Heather and Nia sneaking off one way. Only when I saw Colt looking lost did I unbuckle and get myself out.

"We're going to be partners," Garrett said as he grabbed hold of my wrist. I grimaced as his fingers wedged themselves between my sleeve and skin. I tried to pull away, but his grip squished my skin and made me ache. "You won't get out of this. We're partners." He paused as I stayed still. "You're good at hiding."

"And you aren't," I noted. I looked up at him as he smiled. I tried to squirm again, but he kept the tight hold.

Colt was right. They saw that I was weak in that van and Garrett would ensure that I was out before him in the game of hide and seek. How did I know that Garrett wasn't the seeker, though? Could the seeker even partner up with someone?

"Hide in plain sight," I said. I motioned for the crowd of people at the crosswalks. Garrett took charge and I remained behind him so that he could use up all his energy. "That's the first rule of thumb when trying to hide." When we made our way into the center of the crowd, I knew that we would stick out anyway. I heard the murmurs about us wearing green and it was obvious compared to what everyone else was wearing. "You need to tell people I didn't kill Jade on purpose."

"I'm not doing that," Garrett said as he stared straight ahead. We started moving with the crowd as we walked across the busy street. He held onto me like we were dating and it felt normal. When he had to tug me back and hurt my wrist, I knew I had to get away though. Stopping at the next interaction and waiting for our walking man to appear on the sign, Garrett sighed and looked at me. "Was it on purpose?" he wondered. I opened my mouth to talk, but he interrupted me. "We both heard her pleading for you to stop. I watched your face – that's something you need to control. Everyone always knows what you are feeling. You heard her yell to stop pushing, but you kept going. You kept pushing her closer and closer to that edge. So, really, tell me, did you kill Jade on purpose?" I looked up at him and crinkled my eyebrows. After a second though, I brought them back up and flattened my face. "Better."

"I didn't—"

"Shut up," Garrett said as we began walking again. "Just try to look pretty for me."

I didn't kill Jade on purpose. I was so tired of people thinking I killed Jade on purpose. I knew it wasn't true. Yes, I heard Jade screaming at me, but I wasn't processing what she was saying. I thought she was yelling at Garrett. Even in my nightmares, I can still hear her screams, but I cannot understand what they're saying to me. Had she been pleading for me to stop? I bowed my head to look at my feet and crossed with everyone else, but I was trying to hear what she had been saying. Every time I closed my eyes, I saw her face. Garrett didn't understand that I wasn't trained to be an assassin like him and the Elitists. I was an ordinary girl who was thrown into these trials because I played a game of manhunt, and someone thought I was good at it.

Feeling a push in the back, I toppled forward and felt my chin land against the hard concrete. Garrett looked back at me and smartly let go of my wrist. He continued to walk forward with the rest of the crowd as I had to prop myself up and try to stick with them. I couldn't be sticking out like a sore thumb.

That push was intentional. Whoever it was had a lot of nerve to be able to do that to someone they thought was an assassin. I could have whipped around and immediately assassinated them. I wanted to, but I had no idea who it was. So, instead, I grabbed the back of the neck of the person in front of me and I steered them off path.

"Swap clothes with me," I whispered as they turned around to see who I was.

"I-I can't wear green," this person said. "They'll kill me." Their eyes showed fear as they looked over me. I felt my face fall as I stared at them and soon heard their sobs beginning to form.

"Give me your coat," I said, defeated. They quickly took it off and threw it at my feet. I wrapped it around myself to see how much green it covered and sighed. You could still see a lot on me. "Here." I started scuffing up my shoes on the pavement, dirt, and rocks and waited until they were covered in a yucky brown before taking them off and swapping. "Give me your shoes." They nodded their head rapidly as they hurriedly took their shoes off. "Thank you." I began lacing up their boots and listened to them run away from me.

They were afraid of me.

I would have to get used to that. Would I get used to that? I didn't want people to be afraid of me. I wanted them to like me. I didn't even want to kill people, but it was better than having to die. I would have to force myself to get used to it.

As I walked back into civilization, I slowed my stroll and looked around. We were in the middle of a city and the least I could do was try to be as normal as possible. If I kept walking around in circles, whoever was the seeker was going to find me in no time. They would see the flashes of green on my pants and notice it from a mile away. I needed someplace dark where you can't really notice the green pants. Somewhere where you wouldn't be able to see the colors right away.

My eyes brightened and widened with anticipation as I saw one of the buildings had a massive sign on its roof that implied it was a movie theater. Walking in, a blast of fresh air hit me, and I looked up to see the fans pointed down at my head. If my hair was longer, it would be a wreck right now.

I walked up the escalators, looked around, and was stopped at the top when a man demanded for my ticket. I stared at him while he held his hand out for me. I didn't have money, and I didn't have the tickets. I wasn't sure where you bought the tickets either. I grinned politely at the man and moved my coat to reveal the green pants. When he didn't seem to catch what I was showing him, I unbuttoned the coat and revealed my shirt was green, too. I could see him getting pale as he pondered what to do, but when he looked unsure, I plowed through him and looked around me. In the middle were the concession stands while at the two ends were different movie theater sections. I looked up top to see what names of movies were out but realized I didn't know any of them.

I took a wild guess and just went to one and sat down by myself. I leaned my head back into the rest and let my breathing begin to slow and get rhythmic. Trailers began flashing on while the lights began to dim. I let my breath catch in my chest when latecomers sat near me and were whispering loudly despite people's glares at them. As long as they were quiet when the movie started, I wouldn't have a problem with it.

                                    AMY KULP

My eyes glossed over the screen, and it took in every detail. Even before the trials, I have never been to a movie theater. I had to wait until they were available in the dollar stores, which usually took five or more years. TV just wasn't something that we prioritized in my house. It was exciting to see a new movie. As I looked around quickly, most of the seats were filled. A latecomer even sat beside me to fill the gap between the loud family and myself. I tried not to get distracted while I watched the movie though.

This made me feel normal.

So, when the credits started rolling, and everyone got up to leave, I stayed behind and watched the names scroll up the screen. They weren't interesting to me, but they kept my mind occupied instead of thinking about this stupid game of hide and seek. It was probably just another chance for everyone to cause damage, kills, and injuries to civilians. To regular people. I used to be a regular person.

"You've been found, farmgirl." I looked at the person sitting to my left and nodded my head. Despite what was said, neither Colt nor I got up. Instead, we watched the end of the credits together and waited for the lights to come up. Still, I didn't move from my spot, and it didn't look like Colt was going to initiate it either.

I just wanted to be normal again, but as I looked at Colt and studied his face, I could see the cleaners from the corner of my eyes. They were patiently waiting for us to leave and I'm sure they had seen his green clothes. They probably thought I was about to be assassinated since my green wasn't that visible. I didn't want to hold up their jobs, but I didn't want to go back. However, they were reminding me that I was an assassin.

"Why does your TV screen not show your family?" I asked.

His face went through tons of emotions. While before, it was calm, loose, and tension-free, his jaw was set in a hard line, his cheeks were now sucked in, his lips disappeared as he sucked them in, the corners of his eyes became pointed, and he refused to look at me. I looked down to see that his fist was clenching and unclenching and found myself looking at his arms – getting a little distracted as I stared at the muscles and veins. When I looked back up, all emotion was gone on his face, and he startled me by grabbing my arm.

"Ow," I said as Colt began moving. I traveled behind him and tried to wither away from the pain that was shooting through my arm. He gripped harder the more I moved, and I felt him poke his nails into my arm. This felt like déjà vu. Why did they always grab my arm? "Stop, you're hurting me!"

Immediately, he let go, but we were already outside and at the van. He opened the door without looking at me, and he got in. I opened the passenger side door and stepped up in there. Eddie, Garrett, and Shane were all already in there. When I looked at the other van, it seemed they were full too. Rubbing my arm, I smiled at the thought that I was the last to be found. Maybe I was really good at hiding.

Around me, they all talked about nonsense things – hot girls they saw and that they can't wait to see the new scoreboard change. I cursed myself, though. I keep forgetting that we had to do that. I didn't even start thinking about what I was going to do. I think we only had one more week to figure it out too. While others have probably been plotting, I've been in my bed with my eyes closed, listening to everyone talk around me. I haven't been focusing on the trial at hand. I've been worried about having my skin showing or someone touching me. I needed to focus if I didn't want to die.

I didn't want to kill anyone.

As we got out of the van, I tried staying away from Colt, Eddie, and Garrett as much as possible. I mixed my way with the other van's assassins but still didn't talk to anyone. I had to get my head in the game for these trials.

As we got back in, I made my way to the couch and sat there. I watched as Bischoff came into the room and stood at attention. Thankfully, I was already sitting down, and everyone else filed in. Some sat on the other couch while Toby sat next to me. He didn't make eye contact and didn't acknowledge me either.

"With that game, it was clear that Bridget is our best hider," Bischoff said. I didn't smile even though I was given a compliment. How Bischoff said it made me feel like it wasn't a compliment. "Some of you have also taken this opportunity to complete this trial. Let's look at the new standings." He motioned for the scoreboard, and I watched as he moved Eddie's down. "In first place with twenty deaths was Colt Kirkman." My eyes got wide at the thought that he just killed twenty people while we were all playing hide and seek.

Looking over at him, his face remained cold, but he still had tension in his jaw. I wanted to ask so badly what he did, but I just stared at him instead. I would never have enough guts to ask him because I didn't want to think anybody could do such a tragic thing. He leaned against the wall as people congratulated him but he and I knew that they were forced. Nobody wanted him to be on the top of the leaderboard – they wanted to be on the leaderboard. As he scanned the room, his eyes fell on me briefly, and he fidgeted against the wall until he looked away. I looked away, too, and back toward Bischoff.

"In second place, we have Heather Fleck with ten deaths and five injuries."

My eyes grew wide as Eddie's board fell to third place. When I looked over at her, she blushed red, but thankfully, she didn't seem proud. Nia patted on her the back and whispered something that made her smile. This wasn't the Heather I knew. She was an avoider. She didn't kill. What happened out there? How did she manage to kill someone?

I looked next to me as Toby shifted in his seat. He bounced his cushion up and down until I had to straighten my body out to prevent him from moving me, too. His movements were intentional because he pointed to my arm as soon as I turned to look at him. I had been massaging it since we returned because of how sore it was. I must have moved the sleeve up too much because my arm was a deep red with black and blue splotches. I brought my shirt sleeve down in shame and continued to rub over the shirt. It stung, but I continued to do it regardless.

"In third place remains Eddie Marlowe with an additional fourth place being Garrett Arnold with one death and five injuries." I knew that Garrett was smiling, but I didn't want to turn to look over at him. He probably did that right after he left me. "Just a reminder that you will only have two more opportunities to take part in the challenge. Justin, Asher, Nia, Toby, Shane, and Bridget, you still need to attempt something." Bischoff nodded his head and immediately left the room. It took five seconds before everyone started moving.

Toby and I stayed on the couch, but he didn't talk until everyone was doing something else. My mind was somewhere else, but my eyes watched Colt's screen. It was still not showing anything, and I was curious about it. He seemed mad and upset when I asked though. Did something happen to his family? Was there something I wasn't aware about?

"What happened to your arm?" Toby finally asked. I looked over at him and could see Colt eating something from the corner of my eye. When Toby saw my glance, he turned around to look at him. That was enough movement for him to notice, and he looked at us both. His face stayed blank, but Toby turned around anyway. I pulled my sleeve down even more to try and cover it. I didn't need anyone's opinions. "Do you have anything planned for the trial?" I stared at Toby before shrugging my shoulders and turning my body to face the TVs again. I couldn't bring myself to look at mine. I only looked at Colt's. "I don't think I want to do one," he admitted. "I'm okay with dying." I let out my breath and carefully brought my knees to my chest.

Wrapping my arms around them, I placed my cheek on my knees and looked at Toby. He seemed so vulnerable right now. He had already made up his mind, but he needed someone to tell. Clearly, he and Nia weren't speaking.

"I don't want to die," I admitted to him. I closed my eyes for a second and let my breathing catch up with his. "If I have to kill people, I will. I don't care about being in the top spot but I want to survive." When I opened them, Toby was nodding his head. He seemed to understand my perspective.

"Well, let's try figuring out a plan for you. Maybe we don't need to kill people, but we need to injure. Sound like a plan?"

"Thank you," I whispered.

#

Getting out of the van, I pulled down my sleeves so nobody could see how bad my arm had started to bruise. It looked like I had a huge blotchy tan with how dark it had become, and it had swelled before I went to bed. I constantly pushed ice cubes along it to get it to go down, and when I woke up, it was back to its normalcy. I didn't want to cause attention to it, though, because, like Colt had said the other day, I didn't want people thinking I was weak. Including him.

"You may have noticed where we are today. Can anyone take a guess?" Bischoff asked.

"It looks like a butcher shop," Asher noted. He looked around, and his face changed to enjoyment once he noticed the signs in the windows

                    AMY KULP

and the requirement to be a certain age to purchase. "A shooting range?"

There were sounds of excitement as soon as he said that. I looked around and saw how happy that made some people: Garrett and Eddie. When I looked over at Justin and Asher, they both seemed to congratulate each other with a nod, and I avoided eye contact that I accidentally made with them. They were planning something, which meant they would begin their trail here. It made me not want to come in.

"Since the target room had been destroyed," Bischoff continued, "I had thought you might be aching to get some practice in. After all, when some of you become assassins, you must choose what type of assassin you are." I arched my eyebrows in confusion. Type of assassin? Aren't they all just… assassins? "Please remember that you may not harm another assassin candidate."

Bischoff led the way, and I felt myself beginning to linger. I was never enthusiastic about this stuff, and I hope I never will be. I didn't know anything about guns or shooting them. I can wrestle, though, if that ever came up. I could fight. I had some wicked mean chickens that would chase you every chance.

"Come on," Toby said as he egged me to go forward. He grabbed at my arm, and I flinched back without thinking about it. Toby stared briefly before grabbing my arm and pulling up my sleeve. He grimaced and pushed it back down before grabbing me by the other wrist. "I think this is mandatory."

"They're just going to fire at people. There's no guarantee that they won't accidentally hit me with a bullet," I begged, "Please, let me stay out here until I'm ready to go in." I stared at him before he started shaking his head.

He had already given up, but I hadn't. Despite not wanting to go in there, I knew I had to. If I didn't, they could possibly just say I didn't kill or injure a lot of people and have me gone in the blink of an eye. I couldn't go in right now.

I didn't want to die on purpose or on accident. I was tired of getting hurt. I have had more bruises and cuts than I ever have before. I can't remember if I broke my arm, or my leg had been broken or fractured, or I just hurt them badly, and they wrapped them. I can't keep track of the injuries and who has given them to me. For all I know, everybody has hurt me at least once. I probably hurt everyone at least once. It seemed that the longer I spent here, the easier it was for me to get hurt. Colt had put a lot of pressure on my arm, but it should not be swelling and as dark as it was. It should not be as blotchy with brown, black, blue, and purple shades.

What was wrong with me?

"Get up."

I looked at the angry voice when I heard the door go off. I didn't realize I had sat down, so I found it mysterious when Colt boomed over and towered over me. He seemed mad and hot-tempered, but I didn't understand why. Colt waited a few seconds with his fists by his sides before reaching down and grabbing my arm. He lifted me up with barely any thought and only let go when he saw the grimace on my face. Immediately, his face softened.

He watched my face for a second longer before reaching for my bad arm again. I tried to pull back, but he grabbed my shoulder and straightened my arm. Lifting it up, he seemed stunned at the bruised arm as well. Not wanting to see it, he pushed my sleeve down and looked away.

"It'll go away in a couple of days," Colt mumbled. I could see his hands moving on his shirt, so I watched as he started rubbing his fingers on them. I stared hard at them until Colt did all ten digits and then looked back at me. "There's this gel," he stated. "That Garrett stole from a store when we went to the mall. It's supposed to make everything feel a lot worse when you wear it." He scratched his back. "I put it under my fingernails in case someone tries to attack me. So do they." He paused for a moment and looked at me again. "Hide your emotions, farmgirl." He tried to touch me, but I cringed back from him.

I wasn't sad or mad or happy that he told me this. I was confused as to why. What was the purpose? So, I know to avoid him and his friends? I have been trying to avoid them since the very first day. Did he do it so I would trust him? I don't think I can trust him. I couldn't trust Eddie or Garrett. No trust toward Shane, although he still seemed loyal to the inductees. Did that change because he thought that I killed Jade? Nia and Heather seemed to turn against the people they liked because of something they'd heard. Where did they hear that from? Justin doesn't seem to mind as he always chooses himself over everybody. Toby was the only one who seemed to care. Now, he was planning on committing suicide via another assassin.

"What did I say about showing you're weak?" he asked. I looked at him and could feel emotions running through my head. "Hide your emotions." He gripped my shoulders hard, but this time, as soon as I showed that it hurt, he let go. "We need to get in there so we don't get in trouble."

"I don't want to," I said.

"Why not?"

I shook my head and sat back down. Colt huffed and followed suit with me. He crossed his legs and leaned his face onto his hand. He stared at the ground for a minute, and I could feel him playing with the edges of my sleeve. Maybe he was looking at the bruise. I couldn't read his mind.

"I can't just hide my emotions like everyone else here," I said. He looked up at me, and I pulled away from his fingers. "I'm not a robot who can just turn off what I feel. I have always been expressive with my facial muscles."

"Do you want to die?" Colt asked. His voice got loud as he spoke. "Because that's what will happen when you become an assassin and can't hide your emotions. You'll be out in the world, and someone will see your sadness, and they'll know. You're going to kill someone. A lot of places, they'll try to kill you first." He watched me for a second before shaking his head and continuing. "You're on Eddie and Garrett's hitlist because you won't sleep with them and think they're disgusting. Want to know how they know that? Because your face shows

                                    AMY KULP

disgust every time they come around. Shane wants you gone for betraying Jade.”

“I didn’t—”

“I don’t really care what you did,” Colt retorted. “Whatever happens when we are in our trials does not matter. You are thinking like an assassin, and that’s what you are doing. You are surviving just like the rest of us. None of us want to die. We do what we must do to survive.”

“If I go in there,” I started. I refused to look at him as I talked. “And Justin and Asher shoot up the place; there is no guarantee that I will survive.”

“Yes, there is.”

“No, there isn’t.” I shook my head and closed my eyes. Almost as if I was blocking out what he was saying. “A stray bullet could lodge itself into me, and I would die because I don’t have anybody anymore. Everybody has someone. You have your friends, Asher and Justin are friends. Heather and Nia are inseparable, and Toby will always have Nia. I have nobody.”

“You have me,” Colt said. I closed my lips and reopened my eyes to stare at him. “I will protect you from any bullets that come your way. If one hits you before I can react, I will get it out, so you don’t die. Plus, you’ll have a cool scar.” I wish he wasn’t so good at talking and hiding his emotions. I wanted to know what he was feeling. Was he playing a trick on me right now? Was this his plan with Eddie and Garrett?

“Why?” I asked. Colt looked at me quizzingly and I sighed. “Why do you want to protect me all of a sudden?”

"Well…" He thought, and I saw the exact moment he knew what he wanted to say to me. I didn't believe that it was the real reason. If he had a real reason, he would have said it immediately to me. He wouldn't have needed to think. "I think you know exactly how attractive, smart, and fit you are. I think you know how to play all those qualities up to the boys so they're distracted by you. You're smart but you act dumb so that nobody will think of you as a threat. You can easily outrun some of us, but you choose not to because you don't want to show everyone you're best yet. You're saving that. I don't know for what and I don't care for what." I opened my mouth to talk but he held up his hand to stop me. "Don't talk over me." He turned his body toward me and licked his lips as he brought his face closer to mine. "I am confident that I am going to be in that graduating class this year and I can see everybody else's potential too. You are not the only person who watches others. You have so much potential to be an assassin – possibly the best. It is my job to help and protect *my* future assassins."

I just wanted to think about everything he said, but he didn't give me that chance. He commanded that I stand up, and he was so forceful that I listened immediately. He turned around to walk toward the door, and I followed obediently. Not because he told me I was smart or then insulted my intelligence. Not because he told me I was attractive or fit. I followed him because he managed to make me feel comfortable. That last person to do that was Jade.

"Put these on," Colt said as soon as we got in. He handed me safety goggles to put on my face and noise cancelling headphones to put on my ears. Once he had his on correctly, he grabbed my arm and immediately withdrew his hold. I turned around to face him, and he fixed the goggles so they weren't pinching my nose, and he fixed my headphones, so they completely covered both ears. "We're over here."

He led me to where the other assassins were, and I found myself speeding up under Bischoff's gaze. There was a trainer who was actively demonstrating how to dismantle the gun, how to shoot, and then how to reload it. He was loud enough for me to hear even at a distance. I hurried to get to my spot and stood next to Toby. When Colt had caught up, he stood between us despite there not being a window for another spot. He didn't look at me as he bumped me to the corner, and I suddenly felt unsure about this.

However, as soon as everyone's first shots went off, I flinched. I removed my hands from the gun and watched as Colt hit the target's head twice and heart three times and missed only once. When my gaze went further down the line, I could see the instructor telling everyone to stop so that he could bring up one of our targets to look at. With his back to us, I could already see someone grabbing their gun.

Almost in slow motion, Asher's gun went off, and it seemed like the loudest noise I could hear. Justin's gun went off repeatedly after that as he shot people at different ranges. When Colt turned to realize it was happening now, his body slammed into me, and we both fell to the ground. I could hear screams echoing through my ears as people were uncertain of what to do. The screams seemed to lessen and lessen until my head hit the ground, and my headphones flew off. Colt crushed his body on top of mine, and he held my head protectively. With my headphones now off, I could hear exactly what he was whispering. Although, I was sure that I wasn't supposed to hear it.

"We'll survive this. We'll survive this. We'll survive this. We'll survive this. We'll survive this."

#

I hated getting into these vans knowing that every time we were going to come home, I would have to learn about people dying or getting hurt. Soon, I would be one of the people who hurt those around her. I looked at Toby as he started boarding his van and he just nodded at me. That was all the reassurance I needed as I let my breath go and entered the passenger side.

I couldn't sleep again last night. I was tossing and turning so much that when I did wake up, Eddie cursed me out. He claimed he could stand the snoring from Garrett, but my moving was too much for him. I took it upon myself to stare at my TV screen for hours before Toby came over to join me. He stared at his own, and then, in the middle of our silence, we started sprouting ideas for what I could possibly do.

I just had to be better than Nia and Shane as we were all the last three assassins to complete our trial. After this visit, we would not get another one. Bischoff warned us that we were going to go right into our assassinations after our trip.

I kept my eyes on the road as I scanned for different cars. I was looking for one of two that I could possibly use for Toby's idea. After about ten, we came up with a viable one. We came up with one that I was convinced would work but wouldn't hurt too many people. It was realistic if I punched Shane hard enough.

"Punch bug, no punch backs!" I yelled. I put all my strength into the windup and landed squarely on Shane's arm. I made sure that it hit so hard that he turned the wheel and since we were going way over the speed limit, Shane didn't have time to react before our car came too close to the vehicle on our left. I could hear him cursing as he tried to slow down, but he slammed in front of another car, and the cars behind us collided into us.

The world seemed silent for a moment as everyone thought about what had just happened. Shane looked over at me before getting out of the van. I looked behind me to see Eddie and Garrett getting out. When it was Colt's turn, he gave me a half-smile before leaving. I didn't want to get out because I didn't want to see the damage. I didn't want to see how bad it could have gotten. I didn't want to see if I accidentally killed someone.

I did anyway. I got out and looked at the people in front of us and looked at the long string of cars behind us. While smiling when I left the car, I was no longer smiling as I felt pats on the back from Eddie and Garrett. They were congratulating me on a job well done. However, I could hear what people were saying. I could hear the yells of terror and horror. I could hear babies crying in the cars.

"They're assassins!"

"We didn't do anything though!"

"Green!"

"I thought I was a good person!"

I could hear sirens, but there was no way just one ambulance could make it to the root of the problem. One ambulance couldn't possibly get all these people either.

"We'll have to wait for the other van to get us," Shane said. He turned to me and looked me up and down before walking past me. He purposely hit his shoulder off mine and went back inside the van.

I wanted to do the same but knew I should stay here. It was my mess; I would have to live with the consequences anyway.

"Is everyone alright?" a paramedic asked as he screamed down the way. Everyone seemed to answer with a yes, and he had to do a double-take to see our green shirts. He came over and smiled up at us. "Do you guys need a ride back?" I didn't answer but watched as Eddie and Garrett straightened themselves up and acted like body guards. "It's alright."

My eyes got huge as I watched him unbutton his first shirt to reveal a green tank underneath. Eddie and Garrett immediately shook hands with the man while Colt went to grab Shane from the van. I couldn't help but stare at him. Why was an assassin doing the job of a paramedic?

AMY KULP

"Come on," Colt said as he pushed me closer to the ambulance. I looked back at him as he dragged Shane with him. Shane didn't seem to want to go either, and I saw a bit of fear in his eyes. When I looked back at Colt, he was still facing forward and trying to get all of us in the ambulance. "We must get back. We have no way to communicate with the other van."

I hopped in despite every sensor in my body telling me not to. We all sat in the back together and remained quiet as the vehicle started to move. I squished next to Shane on the benches and tried to keep eye contact with any of them. However, everyone was staring at the ground with nothing to start a conversation.

"Is this a thing that inductees don't know?" I whispered softly. All of them looked up at me, but no one answered. "Why is a paramedic, an assassin?" I looked through all of them before they stared at the ground again. It took me a moment of Colt shaking his head minimally to understand that none of them knew what was happening.

Assassins were never allowed to disguise themselves. That was what we were taught in history class. It's what we grew up to know. It's why we all trusted our government because all the people who could kill us were out in the open. We knew for sure whether someone might die. We didn't have to guess if the person passing us on the street was an assassin, and we accidentally messed up in front of them. This messes with everything I know and understand. Were we being lied to this whole time?

"Shut up," Eddie said under his breath. He continued to stare at the floor, but after a moment, he looked at me. He motioned his head toward the driver, and when I looked up, I could see the paramedic staring at us in the mirror.

I stared down at the ground just like everyone else. It felt malicious to know this information. We were not supposed to know about it. It was even scarier to think that the Elitists didn't know about it – they know loads more about these Trials than me and Shane do. I doubt they gave him everything there was to know about it. However, you couldn't fake not knowing about this. This was something huge.

Our government has been lying to us the entire time. About what? I'm not exactly sure. Maybe there were more assassins around than I realized. Maybe everybody was an assassin, and I just didn't know it. It killed me that I couldn't talk about it, though. Was this person an assassin, or was he just posing to be one? Could someone do that?

"Here you go," he said randomly. We all looked up simultaneously, but no one moved until the back doors were opened for us. "After you." He held out his hand to me, and when I just stared at it, Shane shoved me hard on the shoulder. I tried to graciously accept his hand, but I think I was so nervous that I was shaking. He could barely grab onto it to let me down safely before the other guys jumped. "Go straight through the front and you'll wind up before Bischoff."

I nodded my head but waited until the others got in front of me. I followed behind all of them and looked behind me to see the paramedic getting out of his outfit. He fully armored up in his green suit and then followed behind us with his electricity stick. Out of fear, I hurried with the rest of my group and only watched their backs.

What was going on?

"What took you guys so long?" Asher asked as we approached them. He looked between some of the boys, but nobody answered him.

He ended up rolling his eyes and looking back over to Bischoff. He had a smirk on his face and uncrossed his arms. As I looked around, I noticed a bunch of bystanders in the building in green suits. They stayed far away, and when Bischoff stood at attention, I realized that the final standings would be announced out here.

"With more of our Assassins completing their missions, here are the final standings." There weren't any circles but as he called the same names that were the top four previously, they all stood in order with their arms behind their backs. Their shoulders were about touching, and I could see a sense of pride in all of them. I couldn't meet any of their faces as I watched the crowd grow on both sides of us. Some were whispering, and some had smiles on their faces. "In fifth place is Nia Williams with one death and one injury."

She stood up proudly and walked to the front with a smile on her face. I tried to find Toby's gaze, and when I did, he was frowning. I wasn't sure if it was because he was afraid of dying or if he was disgusted with Nia's behavior. She really has changed since talking with Heather. They were inseparable, and she would have to want to win to stay friends with her. It was either that or she would end up dying.

"In sixth place with one death is Asher Johnston."

There were some murmurs in the crowd as people talked around us. It felt weird to be in front of a live audience. Their judgment on how well we did and their intrigue in who was going to die. I could see greens pushing their way to the front. I could see the excitement in some of their eyes while others tried to mask their disgust.

"In seventh place with forty injuries is Justin Frazier."

I still can't believe that Justin ended up shooting all the civilians at the shooting range. It seemed more typical for Asher to do that. However, he only shot the trainer and the lady who ran up to him. Asher had the impulse to stop, while Justin did not. Justin kept pulling the trigger until he ran out of bullets. When I was lying on the ground with Colt on top of me, I was convinced that we were going to be targets, too. That all of us were. If he survived, he didn't care about anyone else.

We haven't spoken since the last trial.

Before Bischoff could make any movements or say what he wanted, there was a sound in the crowd. My head turned toward it, and I could see others staring too. Four green men moved to the front while four more brought up the rear. I could see the masked person again when they turned to the side and wielded their electricity sticks. They were squealing and making unrecognizable noises as they were forced to watch us. They rushed that when they hit the men, they didn't react with electricity. Instead, they just let the person bounce off them. Maybe they were yelling and making weird noises because they were gagged, or something was wrong with their mouth.

"Taking our final spot with fifteen injuries is Bridget Solomon."

I started to take my step first but was instantly pushed to the ground instead. I could hear yelling and growling coming from the person with the mask on. I could hear them getting riled up and listening to the electricity surge through the air. I could hear the noise it was making. It had to be cranked up farther than anything I could listen to.

"What?" Shane yelled from beside me. I looked up to see his red face yelling at Bischoff. Every time he opened his mouth, spit globs fell out and onto the floor. He wasn't even looking at me right now. If I was Bischoff, I would be frightened. "How many injuries and deaths did I get?"

"Zero," Bischoff said softly.

"What do you mean? I just caused that pile-up on the road!" Shane yelled.

"Actually," Bischoff said authoritatively, "Bridget did. She punched you, which made you lose control."

"Maybe I lost control on purpose," Shane said. "I deserve that, not her!" I could hear others whispering around them, and when I tried to look at everyone in line, Shane turned back toward me. "You deserve to be the one that is killed, and I'll make sure of that! You don't even want to be here, you coward!"

He grabbed onto my leg but didn't get much further than dragging me a couple of inches. He landed on the ground with a thud, and I could feel the liquid seeping through my clothes.

"Take your place next to Justin," Bischoff instructed.

Before I could think about the blood hanging from my clothes, I stood up and planted myself near Justin. He tried to move away, but I moved closer each time he did that. I stared at the blood that was pooling around Shane, and I could see the look of horror and hurt on his face. I had to stop looking when he started gasping out in pain. Everybody in the room was silent.

"Last place is Toby Ernst. We originally had Bridget kill Shane, but we are now going to have her kill Toby."

"Wait, what?" I asked. I looked up at Bischoff and could hear the person with the mask making crazy noises as they bounced against the assassins who were guarding them. "I-I can't kill Toby." I shook my head and looked at him. He didn't seem scared, but he did seem sad. "Don't you mean Nia? She's the closest with him." I didn't have to look to know that I was getting a nasty look from her.

"No, Bridget, it is your time to assassinate Toby using the same instrument that killed Shane."

Bischoff held out a gun and walked it to me. He pressed it into my arms, and when he started releasing pressure, I grabbed it. I shook my head again and again and again until I knew I looked like a broken robot. Tears were welling up in my eyes at the realization that I would be killing my second friend. I looked at him as I held out the gun and felt the pressure against my finger.

"I'm so sorry," I whispered. I closed my eyes and could feel my chin beginning to tremble. "I'm so sorry." I opened my eyes and could see Toby walking closer to me. Trying to make it easier for me. "I'm so sorry." I shook my head again and tried to look at my hands as they shook uncontrollably. Toby pressed his forehead against the gun and closed his eyes. "I'm so sorry." I could see the relief starting to spread on his face.

"I forgive you."

With a smile on his face, I instantly pressed the trigger. There was silence for a moment as Toby's body went to the ground, and I threw the gun off to the side. I could hear a second shot and the person with the mask making crazy noises. I could see blood shooting out and all the men taking them back through the corner of my eye, but I was focused on Toby. I dropped to my knees as he bled out faster than Shane. I watched as my hands began to get covered with red as I tried to apply pressure to his wound. As if anyone could survive a bullet to their head.

I kept apologizing and apologizing. My clothes clung to my body as they grew wetter and wetter from the mixture of Shane's, Toby's, and the person with the mask's blood. I could hear scolding as Bischoff yelled at me to never drop a gun, but I was focused trying to restart Toby's heart even though he was shot in the head. I couldn't tell if I was crying blood or tears. There was so much blood. Too much blood.

I looked up at the other assassins who were behind me and could see all their reactions. Nobody was hiding their feelings right now. This scene was too pitiful to watch:

Justin refused to look at me, but I could see a frown on his face. I called out his name to help me, and the frown deepened. He continued to keep his hands behind his back and stared straight at Bischoff. I begged for him to help me as Toby continued to bleed out. He was smart; he knew how to stop the bleed. When he refused to help me, I moved on.

I didn't know Asher, but I yelled for him to help. His eyes were able to meet me and when he shook his head no, that he wouldn't help, I knew at least I could count on him to tell me yes or no. He was a rule follower.

"Nia!" I wailed as I held onto Toby and put him in my lap. She closed her eyes and choked on her tears. "He liked you! You meant so much to him!" As I yelled for them, they were released from their holding position, and Heather instantly came to Nia's rescue. She hugged her and whispered something in her ear before they both scampered off.

I could see Heather's emotions, though. She was sad and she felt sad for me. She didn't feel sad for Toby. She knew this was the game, and would do anything for her family. Nia was now part of her family. Her job was to protect Nia. Just like she tried with Tanya and Audrey. Just like she wanted to with me, but I wouldn't let her.

"If she's reacting like this to Toby, I don't believe she pushed Jade off that wall," Eddie whispered to Garrett as they passed. They both

scampered into the doorway, but not before I heard
Garrett call me pathetic.

"Shane, please," I whispered as I held onto
Toby's head. "You would never put your back to an
Inductee that needs help. You were always so loyal
to that. Please, help me save Toby."

"He's gone, farmgirl," Colt whispered as he
came closer to me. He knelt and grabbed my waist.
He began tugging me from Toby, and while I wanted
to refuse, I was exhausted. "Come on." He pulled me
close, and I grabbed his shirt for comfort. He shushed
me softly when I started crying and carefully wiped
the tears out from my eyes. "Let's get you cleaned
up. Everybody already left." I looked at the crowds
and could see the last remainders walking away.

I heard him huff deeply as he stood up with
me in his arms. I closed my eyes when we walked
through the rooms. I didn't need to see anybody
else's look of approval or disapproval. Getting closer
to the bathroom, I opened them again to see Heather
and Justin standing next to each other. Neither of
them said anything as he slowly wrapped himself
around her. It made me smile.

"Let's get the dirty clothes off of you," Colt
whispered as he put me down in one of the shower
stalls. He looked at me as he grabbed the ends of my
shirt and nodded his head as if he was asking if this
was okay. I barely nodded back before he pulled it
over me. He balled the shirt up and threw it in the
corner of the room. When it was my pants turn, he
was equally as gentle, but I couldn't meet his face.
Another friend was dead. What was the point of

making friends if they were all going to die? First, Jade and now Toby.

"I'm going to press this against your face and any other place that has blood," Colt whispered as he brought out the sponge.

I nodded and watched as the yellow slowly turned into a deep red. Colt had to ring it out once or twice before getting it all off my body. When it was the final time out, he stopped the water and looked down at my body. I wasn't sure if it was curiosity or to make sure he got all the blood off of me.

"You're shivering," he whispered. I nodded my head again, and he got up to leave. "It's really late," he whispered when he came back. I was thankful he wasn't raising his voice. He bit his lip as he showed me the blanket he brought. "I wasn't sure if you wanted me to go through your things, so I just grabbed my blanket from my bed." I nodded my head, and he threw it on top of me. "Do you want to get up?"

"No," I squeaked. I adjusted the blanket and opened my arms for Colt to join me. He looked at my arms before looking at me. He waited patiently until I nodded my head. He wrapped his arms around me, and the blanket and I leaned into his chest. I was so tired.

"Jade was my friend, too," Colt whispered to me. "I was jealous when she started hanging out with you more than with me." I made a noise escape my mouth but wasn't sure if it was to encourage or dissuade him from continuing. "She was very blunt. Sometimes, I think too much for her own good." He started moving his hands up and down my arms to

                          AMY KULP

warm me. I kind of forgot that's why he was here. "You'll get through this, you know." He paused, and I listened as his breathing begin to level out and start a very slow pattern. "Maybe I was wrong. Maybe, it's okay to show your emotions sometimes."

Even though I already felt comfortable in his arms, his voice started getting softer and softer. As I closed my eyes to drift to sleep, he kept babbling on about useless things. He knew how to make people feel better, though. He knew how to make me feel better.

#

I hated waking up. It was the worst thing about falling asleep. Having to wake up was annoying and often at the worst time. I wasn't dreaming about anything splendid or having any fantasies about my crush. Instead, I just passed out and was super comfortable. When I woke up, I grunted because of my annoyance and forced my eyes open. I was sweating like crazy under these heaps of blankets so when I threw them off me and stepped off my bed, it took me a moment to realize where I was.

I wasn't in my own bed. Instead of being to my left, Garrett was now on my right and in front of me. I looked around at the other sleeping bodies. I blinked multiple times before realizing I was sleeping in someone else's bed. I paused momentarily to touch my hair and figure out when I had come here, but I was clueless.

I forced myself to walk to my bed, but when I looked at the TVs, I saw Toby sitting on the couch.

I dropped the blanket from my body and blinked again to make sure I wasn't seeing things. A smile formed on my face, and when I went to greet him, I was disappointed that it wasn't him. That was our thing.

"I'm sorry, I-I thought you were…"

"It's fine," Colt answered, laying his arms out behind the couch. "You can still join me."

I nodded and sat on my usual side of the couch. I looked at the TV screens and noticed that Toby's was turned off. When I looked over at Colt's, his was still snowing. I also grazed over the other ones until I got to mine.

My mom was finally sleeping in her bed with my dad. His back was no longer to her though and he was carefully cradling her. Despite how much I was watching these TVs, my mom hadn't been home for about a week. I could only see snippets, but she never was in her bed, and she never seemed to be where the cameras were. Maybe they were doing this on purpose, but all these cameras changed after ten minutes. They went to a different room. I carefully watched them sleep and hoped they would get up. I liked to see how she interacted with my dad. They were so full of love and passion even in their arguments.

"My dad was proud of me," Colt started. I broke my gaze from my TV to look at Colt. He wasn't looking at me, though; instead, his eyes were filled with the snowy view of his TV. "Always has been but I have never seen him as proud when he found his bid for me won." Colt had a sad smile on his own face. "He went around and told everyone about how his son was going to be an assassin. He was so proud of me." Suddenly, his smile vanished from his face. "He was assassinated right before I left." He tore his view away from the TV and then looked at me. "They killed him, and then I was taken here." He shut his eyes and breathed heavy for a second. He looked back up, but instead of staring at his own, I could see my mom getting up in the reflection of his eyes. "You look just like your mom."

"I'm sorry," I said as he turned back to the TV screens. I couldn't tell which screen he was looking at, but I could assume it was either of ours. I thought it was his, but there wasn't much to watch except the snow falling on his screen. "About your dad."

"I can do him right by graduating with the official class of assassins," Colt whispered. He kept his gaze on the TV screen and nodded his head. His mask crumbled for a second, and I was able to see the scared person he truly was – his chin trembled, he had frown lines, he had three worry lines on his forehead, and his legs were shaking from the stress. Within a second, he returned to his normal self, but I could see some of his true personality.

He didn't want to be an assassin.

"Why are you here then?" I whispered to him. He looked at me with blank eyes, and I scooched closer to him. My knees pressed into his thighs, but I didn't sense that he wanted me to move. It was weird that I felt comfortable enough for my body to touch his.

He didn't need to answer the question out loud. His reason was probably the same reason that Heather had – he wanted to make his dad proud. Maybe it was just something that I would never understand, but why would his dad send Colt off if he didn't want to be part of this? Why would someone do that if their two choices were for him to be killed in the trials or never seeing him again? It didn't seem right. It didn't seem believable.

"Why is the government assassinating people?" I wondered to Colt. My eyes watched Colt's body shake into someone who was trying to be badass. Someone who was ashamed that they showed his emotions. He masked his face the best that he could, but he still showed anger. "Colt?"

"Now is not that time to discuss that." He looked around to see if everyone was still asleep. His body relaxed, and his arms untensed as he kept them crossed. "Go to bed, farmgirl."

As soon as his body started getting up off the cushions, I straightened myself to watch my TV. I listened to him get into his bed and waited longer before turning around to stare at him. His soft moment was over, and I was now met with the Colt that I have known all of these trials. Jade was right, he was a hard nut to crack.

I knew that I should get sleep like everyone else was, but my mind and body wouldn't let me. Mentally, I was drained. Physically, I ached. However, those aches were too sore for me to ignore. I wasn't sure if it was from the car crash or if it was from everything my body had been put through for the past couple of months. Certain parts of me were pounding, and I could feel it every time I breathed in and out. Every time I moved, my body screamed at me to stop. If I just laid there, all I felt were the aches. My eyes were tired and stinging red, but I couldn't go to sleep because my mind was awake. My mind had thoughts. They were pestering thoughts. I didn't want them. I didn't want to think.

I just wanted to sit there and cry. I wanted to cry for the loss of Toby at my hands. I wanted to cry for the loss of Jade and her unfortunate demise. I wanted to cry for the loss of friendship with Justin. We hadn't spoken at all. I wanted to try, but clearly he was smart enough to stay away from me. Maybe that was his ploy the entire time, get close to me because I wanted friends. I needed friends. While Jade was my friend, she had other friends. I did not. Justin was my saving grace. He helped me in these trials. He helped me learn so much about the history and how to train my brain. He showed me how to use certain weapons. I miss our secret bathroom conversations, too. I wanted to cry because I would never see my mom and dad again. I wanted to cry because I would never see my animals again. I wanted to cry because I would never go home to family again.

The best-case scenario is that I would go home to my newly made family.

The only way for assassins to get a family was to date and marry other assassins. I wanted to look around in the room for possible candidates but stopped myself. I didn't want to think about anyone here like that. I saw all their personalities, and knowing my luck, I'll get attached to them and then they will be assassinated.

We only had to survive one more trial.

I removed the blankets from around me and walked toward my bedside table. Getting some clothes out of it, I surveyed the beds to make sure everyone was asleep before going to the bathrooms. Surprisingly, I haven't felt pressured or awkward while here. There have been a few instances when Eddie and Garrett would come in here and peek over the curtain, but I was too quick for them to see me. I was prepared for it. They never fought back anymore. I didn't know why but I appreciated it.

As I turned the cold water on, I stripped my clothes and stepped in. I allowed myself to shiver as I soaked myself. I stared down at the tile floors and watched as some blood that was missed by Colt pooled at my feet and circled down the drain. It was hypnotizing to watch. When the water at my feet became clear again, I lifted my head and sighed. My eyes lifted as I watched my breath fog up and drift toward the ceiling.

I just wanted to freeze.

I closed my eyes, and once again, tilted my head back so that it felt like little icicles were pounding into my head. After a moment, the pain stopped, and I was able to relax. My body temperature decreased until my fingers started getting a blue tinge. At that point, my fingers were so wrinkled that it hurt to touch the knob to turn the water off.

Getting out of the shower was the worst part. No longer relaxed, I knew that I was freezing. I wrapped the towel around me and waited to hear if anyone was up yet. Besides another shower running, it seemed to be clear. I opened the curtain and was surprised to see Nia and Heather sitting on the benches. Heather was braiding Nia's hair. A small smile formed on her face when she looked over at me.

"How long were you in there for?" she wondered. I shrugged and shuffled toward her. I tugged the edge of my towel to make sure that it was secure and let the water on my hair drip off me. "Our next trial is starting today. I think you were sleeping when Bischoff came and announced that to us."

"Sleeping in Colt's bed," Nia commented. She turned her head, and I watched through the mirror as Heather straightened it back up. Before I could say something stupid, I inserted the toothbrush into my mouth and started scrubbing my teeth. "I saw you clinging to him when you were crying about Toby." I scrubbed even harder. "When you were—"

"Shut up," Heather said as she tightened Nia's hair. I could see her wince and them have a conversation through facial expressions afterward. "Nia and Toby grew apart. She shouldn't have to feel bad about it."

I just nodded my head, but I really didn't understand. Toby picked Nia up, and she left him. She abandoned him. She was no longer friends with him. Instead, she was friends with Heather. How could you throw something like that away? I paused as I snuck a peek at Heather and sighed. I did that with Justin though.

"Are you and Colt a thing?" Nia asked giggly. I walked back over to the shower and started undressing with my towel. "That's cute."

"No," I said. I dropped the towel as soon as I had the shirt around my shoulders and turned toward them. "We're not a thing. I'm tired of fighting people," I answered. "I'm tired of everyone hating me. So, if he gives me a little bit, I'm going to run with it."

"He didn't even do that with Jade, though," Nia said. "You should've seen how they hung out. I swear it was always a yelling match."

"I know, sometimes, I could hear it in the training rooms," Heather agreed. They switched roles when she finished Nia's hairstyle. "I know you think we're being stupid."

"And focusing on unimportant things."

"But this is how we are surviving these trials." She looked at me with sad eyes. "Don't forget, we are the only people who know exactly what you are going through. Have a little fun while you're here."

"You're too focused," Nia interrupted. She pulled Heather's hair up high and began twisting it. From Heather's face, I could tell that it was painful. "I would never be able to just stare at my family all day. It would be torture!"

At once, all of us gasped at the realization. Nia immediately stopped smoothing out Heather's hair and looked insulted. She was left with no words as Heather kept whispering obscenities about Bischoff. My mind was reeling, though. How could I have been so stupid?

I thought that they were showing us our families because we were doing good. Instead, it was weeding out the weak. Instead of training or learning about the other people here, I have been staring at that damn TV all month. I guarantee that I couldn't run as fast as I could when I started. That's why I was so sore. I wasn't exercising and I was barely fueling my body with the correct nutrients.

"What are you doing?" Heather asked as she watched me leave her.

"Whatever it is, we can't miss it," Nia whispered.

I stormed out of the room and listened to Heather and Nia scamper off behind me. I put so much force into the pressure of my legs that as I walked away, it radiated throughout my body. I was mad and angry that I was so stupid. I could not forget that these were the same people that had us here in the first place. The same people who wanted us to kill people because they had different thoughts than them.

I lost all my anger as soon as I saw most of the boys sitting on the couch surrounding Bischoff. I stopped and could feel their stares as I looked at them. When I turned back toward Heather and Nia, they tried to usher me forward first.

"We've been waiting," Bischoff said unenthusiastically. I hurried to a free spot on the couch and could feel myself beginning to sweat from the intense stare he was giving me. No one spoke, though, and as I looked through the multiple faces, I realized it was because we were missing one. Whoever was still showering.

I stared up at my TV screen in the meantime. If Nia and Heather caught me, they were going to give me hell for this. I couldn't stop staring, though. Even though it occupied my mind most of the time, I still found comfort in seeing my mom and dad. Seeing that they didn't tell anyone I was in the trials. Although I'm sure that everyone knew.

News travels fast around town, and bad news travels even faster. It would become obvious as people stopped by the house, and I didn't greet them. It would seem straightforward when I stopped showing up for school. The Solomon daughter was going to die in the trials. They would never know the results, either. Even though they've been broadcasted in previous years, nobody in my community could afford to pay for that.

Plus, it was like my community's little act of rebellion. We would never tell anyone that, but it made us feel like we had control of ourselves. Not buying it equated to it not happening in our minds. Almost like we can forget about it. But how were they supposed to forget about it now that someone in our neighborhood was a part of it? Would everyone be watching their backs to make sure they aren't turned in?

"Thank you for finally joining us, Mr. Marlowe," Bischoff said.

I looked behind me as Eddie came from the bathroom in nothing but a snug towel against his hips. If I didn't know he was in the shower, it would have looked like sweat glistening down his body. Eddie smiled at Heather and Nia and smirked when he turned to me. Swagging past all of us, I couldn't help but inhale the strong scent of wintergreen and watched as he sat next to Colt. My body tensed as soon as Heather elbowed my body, and I remembered the conversation we had in the bathroom: all about Colt.

"Our last and final trial is beginning today," Bischoff announced. "This will test your physical strength, academic abilities, natural camouflage, strategic destruction skills, aim, and the ability to work as a team."

Bischoff knew when to pause for dramatic affect and I always fell for it. None of us were good at working as a team. Someone always wanted to take the lead, and nobody wanted to listen to that person either. I've seen it with bathroom living suggestions, and all the boys retaliated by getting pee everywhere. It was gross and childish. We never found out if it was all of them or just a single person. Sometimes it was boys versus girls, inductees versus elitists, brainiacs versus meatheads, and all other combinations you can think of. We have all tiffed at one point, but we have never all gotten along.

"As an assassin, there may be some missions that you will need to team up with another assassin. You would need to know who should take the lead and who needs to listen. Sometimes, those will be assigned to you. Sometimes they won't be." Bischoff looked at all of us, and I couldn't help but follow where his eyes were going. "Team one will be Nia Williams, Garrett Arnold, Asher Johnston, and Colt Kirkman." They all started looking around at each other, and I felt myself crawling down the couch to hide myself. "Team two is Heather Fleck, Eddie Marlowe, Justin Frazier, and Bridget Solomon." I looked across from me to stare at Justin, but even though we were on the same team, and he had looked at everyone else, he would rather stare at the floor than toward me. I hope he was feeling guilty. "Before we send you off to try and strategize with your teammates, let me explain the trial: it starts off as a

                    AMY KULP

race. There are varying sizes of blocks at the start. You and your team will have to run with these to try and build a tower to ring a bell. The tower has been started already, but you do not have enough blocks to continue the tower. You will need to reshape the tower and remove some blocks."

"Doesn't sound too hard," Eddie bragged. I could see his smirk as he looked at Garrett and Colt.

"Glad you said that," Bischoff said. "Your main objective is to finish the course in less time than the other team. However, remember, you are assassins. You can try to kill people in this trial but that is not your focus. Can you multitask?" Some people nodded as he asked the question but most, were looking at the ground. We weren't sure if we could or not. I liked to think I was good at multitasking, but I knew I wasn't going to try and kill anyone here. "Team one, please follow me so that you can strategize. You only have half an hour. Team two, you may start as soon as we leave."

"Okay, so here is what we're going to do," Justin said as he leaned forward. He clasped his hands together and looked at all of us. "We each get one of them and distract them. Don't get yourselves killed."

"No, please, get yourselves killed," Eddie interrupted. "Less competition for me."

"You're not thinking, though," Justin remarked. He looked over as Eddie got up to sit next to me. Heather then sat down near Justin, and I waited patiently for someone to talk. I was open to all discussions at this point because, right now, I wasn't understanding the objective. I needed a clear visual of what the playing field was going to look like. "We need to try and stay alive."

"If there's less of us, then we won't be able to finish the tower faster," I said. Justin looked at me and nodded his head slowly. He didn't want to agree with me, but he did. It was his idea; I was saying it out loud.

"Plus, we would have already seen it when it's our turn to run the course. We have that advantage," Heather added. She looked at Justin to see if he approved of what she was saying.

"We can also see what the other team was doing and either copy it or completely avoid it," Justin responded.

"Can we focus on one thing at a time?" Eddie asked. "They're running the course first. What are we doing when they're running the course?"

"Distracting them," Heather said like it was obvious.

"I think that we should each get somebody," Justin thought.

"I'll agree with that only if Bridget gets Colt," Eddie said. I looked over at him as he leaned back against the couch. He smirked at me and purposely readjusted the towel hanging on his hips. "While I would love to flirt with my boy, I think it would be more impactful coming from you, farmgirl."

"Hey, you don't call me that," I said without thinking. I shut my jaw tightly and watched as Eddie smiled broadly at me. He had a smug look as if that proved his point. When he sat back and looked at

                                   AMY KULP

everyone else, I rolled my eyes and looked at Justin and Heather. "Who are you going to get?"

"For being second smartest, you sure are dumb," Justin remarked. "I would get Asher, and Heather would get Nia."

"That leaves me with Garrett."

"Yeah, I'm aware."

"What's your problem?" Justin asked as I crossed my arms. I felt my eyebrows shoot up my forehead but didn't know what to say. "Nobody here wants to be stuck with you either. We're making the best of what we can do." He got up and moved closer to me. He placed his hands on my knees, and his face grew red from anger. "If you can't handle this, then you should just give up now. We all knew you would make it to the top, but nobody thought you would make it to the graduating class." He paused to look at how I was reacting. "I see you've learned to hide your emotions. Who taught you that? The only reason you are still here is because of me helping you."

"Justin…" Heather warned.

"You are useless and stupid. We have all worked our entire lives to make it to the trials. Why do some random kids get to be part of this, and they get lucky?"

"I am not lucky!" I yelled. I forced his hands off me and stood up. "Why do you even want to kill people?" I looked at all three of them, but Heather and Eddie wouldn't look at me. Justin wouldn't look away. "You're just mad that I'm doing better than you. You taught me, and I learned. For that, I am always thankful. You were there for me when I was crying in the bathroom and wasn't myself. I made one stupid mistake—"

"Multiple mistakes," Justin said. "You are a hazard."

"You're just mad that I am better than you." I crossed my arms, and I could see the redness now creeping down Justin's neck. "You're just mad that I care about people too much for my own good. I know that, Justin. You also knew that. Don't pretend I don't know what you're doing. You were hoping to get rid of me by not talking to me. I wouldn't be surprised if all of you were in on that."

"Bridg—"

"You're right, I also didn't train to be in these trials. I have a lot to learn when I do become an assassin." I stared straight at Justin and watched his face start to break. "Don't be mad at me because of how our government runs these stupid—"

"Shut up!" Eddie bellowed. He was so loud that Justin and I stopped yelling and looked back at him. He stood up and shook his head. "We are a team right now, and we just wasted time arguing with each other. You don't get along with each other; who cares?"

"This is part of the trials," Heather agreed. "They picked our teams on purpose." She grabbed Justin's arm, and I could see the calmness radiate through him. He stared at her, and I could see his body relaxing. "Don't yell at Bridget for what she cannot control." Justin shook his head and wandered over to his bed. When Heather sighed, she looked back at me. "Justin never planned to hurt you. He always thought you would be friends. He's too much

                    AMY KULP

of an asshole to admit it, but he was scared by the choices you started making. He was scared for you. That's the one thing you can't be in here." She smiled softly. "Reckless."

I watched her console him, and I found myself biting my lips. I wanted to scream and get all my emotions out, but I knew that I couldn't. I couldn't do any of that. They would all think I was still the weakest link on the team. Maybe I was. I didn't like to think so, but they were all trained for this. Justin made the fair point that I did not.

Looking over at Heather talking to him and placing her hand on his shoulder, I felt my shoulders loosen. My entire body relaxed as I got my legs moving to the bathroom. Once there, I pulled myself to the sink and ran the water. I just stared at the water coming from the spout and directly into the drain. There was nothing to obstruct its path so when I put my finger in it, I found it soothing that the water splashed everywhere.

"I'm not mad," I said as I stared at the water. I could hear someone's footsteps approaching the bathroom. They were hesitant to come in initially, but once their foot squeaked against the tiles, I knew they had decided to come in. I heard them walk behind me and plop down on the bench. I wanted to look, but I was too enthralled with the water to begin to wonder if it was Justin or Heather in here. If it was Justin, it would have been Heather's push that made him come in. "I'm happy that he finally talked to me. Acknowledged that I was still here." I heard movement behind me but only caught a small peek from the corner of my eye. "I have been—"

"I'm not here to console you on your feelings."

I nodded and stared at the water my finger was running through. It created a mess on the counter, but I would clean it up eventually. I didn't expect the person to come in the bathroom to be Eddie. I wanted to ask what he wanted and maybe I did assume he would come in to check on how I was feeling. If that wasn't the case, as he claims, why was he here?

"Do not make us lose," he said. I could hear him walking up to me, and he placed his fingers on the faucet to turn the water off. His face was close to my ear, but I refused to glance at him. He just wanted my reaction. "You flirt with Colt. You flirt and distract him so that our team can pull ahead. I'll do my best with Garrett." I had to glance up at him at this point. He seemed so serious. Wasn't Colt his friend? "Do you hear me?" I nodded my head as he started walking away from me. I watched as he took the towel that was around his hips and began undressing. "You are free to look. Since you are adamant about not liking Colt, it would have to be me." He paused. "Or Justin."

I focused back on the ground and waited to hear him pulling up the black jeans. I felt it was safe enough to look when the zipper went up. When he returned to me with a smirk, he grabbed the edges of my shirt and took it off me. Protecting my body with my arms and covering up, I watched as he stretched my shirt out by putting it over his toned figure. When he was done, he smiled again before going to the mirror to check his hair.

                    AMY KULP

"Now Colt will be distracted."

"I can distract him without using my body," I said through gritted teeth. Eddie barely acknowledged that statement since he was too focused on fixing his hair. I waited for him to stop and turn around, and when he finally got it perfect, I grappled at the tight shirt on his back. I could hear him wince when my nails struck his back, and he made rapid movements to get away from my nails.

"If you destroy the shirt, I can't give it back," he whined between my hand attacks. Finally, I could grab the bottom of the shirt and rip it off him. He helped by wiggling out of it until it was over his head and inside-out in my hands. I fixed the shirt and threw it over my body. I waited for him to say something, but when he didn't, I let my breath go and my gut out. He spaced it out. It felt roomier, and I didn't feel as constricted by it.

"You know, Justin's not wrong." He continued to glare at me as he looked back at the mirror. He started fixing his hair again, and I became impatient as I stood there with my arms crossed. "All elitists get mad that inductees just waltz in here for free." When he got his hair perfect again, he turned back toward me and stared. "Especially ones like you who have only been lucky and don't want to be here. Why don't you just give up instead of taking someone's spot who wants to be here?"

"You would love that, wouldn't you?" I wondered.

I turned away from him at once and immediately walked out the door without looking back at him. I was done trying to explain myself to people who didn't care. I didn't want to die. Was that a good enough reason? It didn't seem to be for many people around here. I didn't want to die. I was afraid of how much pain I would be in. I was afraid that the person killing me would make it, so I suffered before I died. Who knew what would happen after I was dead?

Marching back into our living space, I could still see Heather and Justin talking to each other. Although now, all of Justin's redness was gone. I wanted to go over there and talk to him, but I knew better. He needed to keep his head clear and straight, and I would distract him. If anything, I needed to be distracted by something.

I walked over to the TV screens and plopped my bottom right where it was used to being, where I could watch my mom and dad, where I had my talks with Toby, and where I found out more about Colt. Looking up at my TV screens, I waited for the camera to turn so that I could see them somewhere in the house, but knowing the time, my mom would be at work, and my dad would be in the fields right now. When it spanned to their bedroom, I was surprised that my mom was still in bed.

She was never in bed at this time. My mom worked five days a week at her job, and sometimes, she would even go in to see how things were on the weekends. She was the definition of a workaholic. I regret that I don't know what she did for a living. I knew she worked in an office and was an important person there, too. I wish I knew what she did. I watched as she was clearly awake and lying on her back. It looked like she was watching TV, but I knew

　　　　　　　　　　　AMY KULP

there was no TV in the house. Maybe she knew the cameras were there. I tried to concentrate harder, but it took too long, and the cameras switched to a different angle.

In the meantime, I would have to distract my mind with something else. Right now, the only thing that I could see as being productive was thinking about Colt. I liked and wanted to think about him, but I knew how dangerous it was. This was our last trial, and everybody would be out for blood. I wouldn't be surprised if people sacrificed their own teammates so that they were ensured a position in the graduating class. Colt seemed friendly toward me right now, but I wasn't sure why he suddenly changed. He went from bullying and harassing me in the beginning to brief conversations, to helpful hints, and finally to just helping me. It had been building up from the start, but how was I supposed to like someone I couldn't trust? I knew everyone here was pushing for it, but I didn't understand why. There were enough couples and breakups as is.

Cassandra and Anthony.

Justin and Heather.

Nia and Toby.

Why do they need a fourth couple? If I felt stronger about him, then maybe I could see myself going for it. Right now, a relationship would be a distraction. I'm still not entirely convinced that people are saying this because it's true. It feels like when the popular kids would convince a nerdy girl that the jock was into them for it to end up being a joke.

"Alright, your thirty minutes are up!" Bischoff announced as he came back in. His voice echoed throughout the room so loudly that it made me jump. My eyes had to refocus, and when they did, I had to force myself to get up. It was like I was in a little trance. "Please, follow me so that we may begin the trial."

I looked behind me to see Justin and Heather walking together and Eddie walking behind me without a shirt. He pushed me to follow Bischoff, and I hated wanting to talk to him about his choice. Instead, he was the one to speak, ensuring that Justin and Heather nodded.

"Everybody set on what we're doing?" When I nodded, he smiled toothily and raised his lip more than usual. "I figured if it distracted you this much, I could distract the others as they ran the course."

I wanted to argue but knew better than to. I silently followed Bischoff into an unmarked room and was met with complete darkness. I saw the light and followed it up ahead until we went through another corridor. There seemed to be walls taller than the building could be. We went through a door to get through, and when it slammed shut behind Heather, there were about five locks that required gears to turn. I glanced toward the others, but Heather and Justin were already sharing the glance with each other, and Eddie was staring straight ahead. I could see the coldness in his eyes.

"Team two, you may get onto the playing field," Bischoff instructed as he rushed closer to the starting line. I followed him, but as soon as I saw

Eddie climb over a block to get onto the track, I followed behind.

It was weird. The floor was like our floors in the living spaces. They were all white and shiny. I could see a small reflection of myself in them. However, they were surrounded by blocks that would be impossible to move. I had to assume it was so nobody went out of bounds. The first team and the starting line were straight ahead of me. I could see that some of them already had blocks and bails with them while others were a bit away. They looked like plushy Jenga blocks, but I couldn't tell how hard or soft they were. Maybe they were made of gym mat material. As I walked closer to the starting line, I could see a bend in the walkway. It was a loop around the track. That would be stupid because you can quickly run straight across and skip that part.

At the sound of a bell, the first team was off. They all carried their bales or blocks, and Nia was the first to get up. She ran fast, and I could see the hesitation as she looked to her right and straight ahead. Ultimately, Nia decided to go straight ahead and instantly seemed paralyzed. She dropped the block she was holding and fell to her knees with it. Garrett and Colt ran past her, but they went around the loop instead of going straight as she had. They hurried past us, and while Garrett got close to me, I didn't move out of his way. I continued to stare at Nia as she was yelling out in pain. Whatever was giving her the pain seemed to be muffling her screams, though.

"Run!" Eddie yelled. I stopped watching Nia and turned to him as he ran after Garrett. When I looked to see where Justin or Heather were, they already disappeared. I was frozen in fear, though. I turned around and saw that Asher was now in the vortex, trying to help Nia. I can see how much pain he was in as he tried to scoot her out. "Bridget!" As soon as I saw them step out, I shook my head and let myself breathe.

I turned back and started running down the track with everyone else. I wasn't a distance runner, so I immediately stopped when I saw how long the track was. So clearly, the runners would have to follow the track, but would I? I scooched closer to the edge, and when I put my foot down, I braced myself to get a bunch of pain sent through me. There wasn't any, though. I planted another foot outside the track and found myself climbing somewhere higher. The higher I was, the more I could see.

My foot flattened on one of the blocks, and I found it slightly squishy but mostly stable. I ran on it and looked toward all of them until I looked at how wide and long this track was. There were ten towers, too. Which one had the bell at the top? I tried looking at the ceiling, but it was too dark up there to tell. I couldn't see. I had to get higher.

I found more blocks and stepped onto them. As I climbed up, they were getting wobblier. I clung my hands around the wall and moved very slowly. As I looked down, I could see my foot beginning to shake from how nervous I was. I had to calm down, though. I breathed in and breathed out and forced myself to step up higher onto the next block. When I finally found a block high enough to see, I moved around the narrow part and felt myself sigh when I got onto the ledge.

My heart was pounding as I put my back to the wall and looked out to where the other assassins were. They looked like ants, but I could only see a few. I tried finding where Colt was but couldn't find that short, curly blonde hair anywhere. I wasn't moving my back away from the wall, though. I was likelier to fall if my back wasn't near the wall. Besides, this ledge was wobbly anyway. I had to force myself to scoot closer to the edge to see what was below.

Instead, I was met with a black hole that I had met in the second trial.

I immediately rushed back to the wall and found myself breathing deeper in. Okay, if there was the black hole underneath me, that had to mean I was at one of the towers. I tried to look up, but one of the stupid blocks was in my way. However, it didn't seem to be sticking out to the point that I couldn't see the top. I put my hands on the wall and slowly moved to the edge. When my toe was over the last block, I looked up and could make out a small rope to get to the bell.

Okay, so all the assassins would end up here at one point.

I should probably get comfortable until someone is here. With my back to the wall, I sat down with my legs wrapped around each other.

It was just a waiting game now.

I wish I had the attention span to watch out for what was happening in the field, but I was too afraid of falling to think about anything else. It was a mantra in my head: do not think about falling, do not think about falling, do not think about falling…

I finally stopped as soon as I heard someone cursing under their breath. They seemed to be running as they jumped onto this tower; the whole thing shook. I pressed my body further into the walls and closed my eyes as I listened to them pound something into the walls. I let my breath out and peeked an eye open when the tower stopped moving as much. I immediately closed them and pressed myself further into the blocks when I saw a shoe coming over.

When I wasn't touched, I opened my eyes to see Colt standing there. While his body was facing me, he was too busy looking above me to do anything. I wanted to turn around to see what he was looking at, but my mouth did the talking instead. After all, I needed to distract him.

"You're not going to kill me?"

"I'm not focused on killing you. I'm focused on finishing this trial."

He didn't even look at me as I said that. He started moving blocks from around me and moving them to a position he was more comfortable with. He was busy, which was alarming because I was supposed to distract him. I stood up to look at him, and while he paused for a couple of seconds, he shook his head and continued to move the blocks. Now that I was no longer sitting down, he seemed even more focused. I had to stop him, though, so as I looked around for ways to distract him, I did the one thing I swore I wasn't going to do.

                              AMY KULP

I took one arm out of the sleeve of my shirt and lifted the shirt off my body. I awkwardly dropped the shirt beside me and stood there waiting for Colt to notice. He was too busy playing with the blocks, but as soon as he turned to see me, he stopped what he was doing, and his mouth dropped open. I knew that my face was getting red as he continued to stare. This was very unlike me, but Eddie planted it into my head. It was working. Colt seemed to be distracted. He even dropped the block that he was holding onto.

He stepped closer to me, but as he put his foot back down, we both felt the vibrations and movements from somewhere else on the tower. Colt broke his gaze away from me to see where it was coming from, but it was too late. Blocks came flying out of the place at once, hitting Colt and me. Nia popped out, and while she plowed into Colt, Colt fell into me. I quickly reached for him, and he reached for me as I lost my balance and rolled off the ledge.

I felt my hands beginning to get slippery with sweat, though. I grasped onto Colt's hand but knew it was slipping out. His hand was sweaty, too, and when I tried to put my other hand on his, I couldn't reach it. I looked across from me, though, and could see Nia fighting to hold onto the ledge. She kicked her legs up but was short of getting it. I tried to look at Colt as I dangled over the edge but only felt him move toward her. I could see his hands grab her wrist as she started to fall, and there was a lurch forward that made me assume that Colt was on his knees now.

We both knew that he couldn't hold on to both of us long. Nia wasn't calm either. As she bucked and tried to get up for fear of falling, I could feel the strength leaving Colt. I was slipping through his fingers, and while I tried to tighten my hand on his, I was too slippery to get a hold of him.

"I'm so sorry," he whispered. "I'm so sorry. I'm so sorry."

I closed my eyes as he continued apologizing. When I felt his other hand slide onto my wrist, I opened them back up and saw nobody where Nia was supposed to be. Colt instantly started crawling backward, and I could feel his strength leaving his body as my upper body was back on the ledge. I rolled myself over with all my might, and when I got a second to catch my breath, I crawled to Colt and wrapped my arms so hard around him.

He hugged back as I stayed on top of him, breathing in and out very rapidly. My body was sweating from what I thought was going to be the end of me. I squeezed Colt tighter when I felt him let go, and he rewrapped his arms around me as I did so.

"You like me?"

"Don't flatter yourself. I see a lot of similarities between us, farmgirl," Colt said. He let go of the hug and pushed me lightly off him, and when he looked back down toward my chest, I felt myself blushing. Without saying anything, Colt bent down to grab my shirt and threw it over the ledge. "Don't flatter yourself."

I nodded my head and instantly sat down. I didn't need to know that he was checking me out after what he just did. He could deny it all he wanted, but I knew he somehow cared about me. I continued staring at the playing field, where I saw maybe two people looking for the tower. Colt was behind me, and while I didn't know what he was doing, I didn't care. He picked me over his teammate.

"You trust too much. I can push you off right now."

"So do it," I challenged. Looking back at him, he seemed flabbergasted that I would suggest that. "If you see so many similarities between us, then you know I wouldn't hurt anyone if I didn't have to." I brushed my knees off as I stood up and forced myself to get closer to the edge. "I'll make it easier for you, though." Before I could bend my knees to jump, I felt his arms around my waist, pulling me back toward the blocks. As soon as my back hit the wall, the tower started wobbling underneath us. I couldn't help but smirk at him. "Just admit you like me."

He rolled his eyes and instantly turned back to the tower. He put it as a stepping block and got on top to reach a higher-up one. He was so focused, and I knew I had stalled him for a bit, but he was active again. He just sacrificed one of his teammates for me, so if his team didn't come in first, he would probably be the one who would be assassinated. As he threw this block up, he watched as it didn't hit the open space, crashing down the black hole Nia went in.

There was no sound as it presumably hit the bottom. I wondered if there was a bottom to it. There had to be, right? I looked over at Colt and could see him looking down at it. When he was done being curious, he looked back through the playing field in frustration. He probably couldn't do this himself with me right here. He was too distracted.

"Why do you want to be an assassin so bad?"

"I already told you. Because of my dad."

"No," I said. Colt turned back toward the tower to try and get another block to the top. I could feel it becoming wobblier as he scaled it upward. "Your dad isn't here. Why do *you* want to be an assassin?" I could see him contemplating the answer before he shrugged his shoulders at me. "You don't want to kill people, do you?"

I followed him as he put one foot on one higher-up block and one on the other. He hoisted his body up to a hole and squeezed himself through. I followed him patiently, and when I popped out at the other end, I was thrilled to see that there was much more space over here. I didn't have to worry about falling off here.

"You've been to the preparatory school. Why does the government want to kill people?" I watched as he continued climbing and building on the tower. I was right behind him, though, and as he continued not answering, I became suspicious. Wouldn't he rather admit that he didn't know than not say anything? "Colt?"

"Stop asking me so many questions. You're annoying when you won't stop talking." He turned to me to see my reaction, but I wasn't mad about it.

"Maybe that's my team's strategy to make your team lose."

Colt opened his mouth to say something but quickly closed it. I saw his eyes betray him briefly, and he looked confused. When he opened his mouth to speak, I expected to hear a smart remark. Instead, I heard the bell being rung.

#

                                        AMY KULP

"Take this time to relax while the playing field is being reset," Bischoff said. He looked tired. This was the first time I've seen him look anything other than robotic. "Look at the scoreboard, take a nap, maybe a shower. I will be back as soon as it is reset."

The room was extremely quiet as everybody milled around it. I could hear Eddie starting the shower as he wanted to get all the sweat off his body. Heather instantly went to sleep while Justin went to the kitchen. My first reaction was to grab myself a shirt, and when I came back to my usual spot at the couches, Colt was already sitting at the side I usually was at.

I could see him staring at the list. He was staring at his last-place finish. Now, nobody from my team could at least tell me that I didn't do my part. However, I knew this also meant that if their team came in second place to my team, Colt would be assassinated.

I couldn't stare at the scoreboard, though. My comfort was staring at my TV screen. Nia's was now shut off, though, and it concerned me for a moment to see the three black screens compared to the others. Compared to mine.

As the camera approached her bedroom, I could see my mom lying in bed. She wasn't staring anymore but massaging her thigh as she lay down in bed. Once my dad entered the room, I averted my eyes for a second and saw that Colt was still staring at the scoreboard.

"What happened to your mom?" Any emotion on his face was now masked behind the emotionless skin. I scooched my body closer to his and made sure that my legs were pressing into his. I carefully put my arm on his shoulder and lowered my voice when I asked again. I looked up to watch my mom as I felt Colt's hand touch mine lightly. It took me a second to realize what my mom was doing to her thigh, but once I saw the bloodied bandages and a hole in her thigh, I found myself freaking out.

"You don't need to worry about that," Colt said as he squeezed my hand. I pulled my eyes from my screen and then to Colt. Within a quick second, I looked back at the cameras, but they were focused on a different room. "Hey." Colt grabbed my chin roughly and looked me in the eyes. "You don't need to worry about that."

"My mom—"

"Will be fine," Colt said. "You don't need to worry about my mom either."

"I'm not worried, just curious. You said your dad was assassinated. What about your mom? There's something you're not saying and—"

"Has anyone told you you're annoying when you don't stop talking?"

I couldn't help but smile as I said, "You like me." I could see his face crumble momentarily, and he brought his face closer to mine.

"She was assassinated."

"Why?" I looked up at him but could only see sadness in his eyes. They were too on par for someone who rarely showed their emotions.

"I have no idea, farm girl, but it's your turn to run the course."

I looked at the door and saw Bischoff standing there. I breathed out and knew that I wasn't ready for this trial. However, that didn't seem to be the case, as I was the one to ring the bell for my team.

Graduation

I had never worn earrings before, but that didn't stop me from pushing the pointed end against my ear until it tore through the skin. After a few minutes of being stunned that I managed to do it with minimal bleeding and only one lip-biting moment of pain, I stretched my other ear lobe and got the other earring piece ready. I heaved a breath in, but my hand failed to press hard into the skin. Trying again, I knew that it was useless for me to attempt. If my mind wasn't focusing on it, my body wouldn't listen. I put the back on the sink and looked at my other ear. It was bright red against the small green stud. I put more cold water against the unpierced ear and then brought the earring back up.

"What are you doing, farmgirl?" I looked over at Colt as he leaned against the bathroom entrance. He seemed better today, but I knew that everyone was nervous. We still didn't know which team had won the last trial. They were planning on announcing it tonight during our graduation ceremony. One of us was going to die tonight, and the others were going to celebrate.

It explained why everyone was getting dressed up, too. Colt had on an astonishing green suit jacket with a black shirt underneath it. His pants were black, too, but he chose to wear the dark green dress shoes that were offered to him. Nobody could wear the same thing, but we all had to wear the official color of the assassins—green.

"You are beautiful," he said as he removed the earring from my ear. He applied pressure to the hole as he removed the earring and tossed it in the room. "Wear the necklace instead." He took the gold chain from the sink and carefully brought it to my neck. I could feel his fingers moving my hair off to the side before connecting the necklace ends together. He seemed jittery and nervous when he moved my hair back.

I did look good. While given several dress options, I knew I would be uncomfortable in them. I had grown up in overalls and hand-me-downs from neighbors. So, when I saw this beautiful green jumpsuit, I had to take the chance. It had lace up and down the arms with a bow that tied the top and bottom together. While you couldn't see my feet, they were dressed in black boots. They were the only shoe that didn't have much of a heel.

"Do you think that our families will be there?" I wondered as I grabbed some bobby pins to pin my hair up. I looked through the mirror at Colt's reflection and saw him frowning. My smile that was there instantly deflated, and I continued to put the bobby pins in until all the hair was off my neck.

"Don't get your hopes up."

Colt brought his hands up to my shoulders and squeezed them before he moved behind me to the benches. I would rather him be down there than right beside me. He was being touchy because he was nervous he would be eliminated today. If his team was the faster one, he would be fine, and I would be fine. After all, I rang the bell, so I was the one who ended my trial. However, if my team won, he would be the one to be eliminated.

"Is there anything you want to tell me before we find out whose team won?" I asked. I turned around and looked at him. He raised his eyebrows, and I shrugged my shoulders. "Just in case..."

"I die?" Colt asked. I nodded and leaned against the counter as he thought about it. I watched his face roll through some emotions before settling on something that had haunted him. I don't know how long it will last, and I didn't care to know for how long. "Your mom was shot in the leg."

I felt like I was buffering in real life. Colt's facial expression turned into a mask as he watched my emotions. Should I be masking right now? What should I be feeling? I looked at Colt for a second to see if he was serious, but when he didn't say he was playing the prank, I felt nauseous and angry with him.

"By you," he added.

I tried to talk and ask coherent questions, but nothing formed. I breathed in a couple of times and let out the breaths that were supposed to be me yelling, but instead, I just let them slip through my lips. I felt the warmness coming from my armpits and the sweat beginning to drench the lace sleeves. My feet became antsy, and when I looked at Colt, I saw he didn't seem to be joking anymore.

"What are you talking about?"

"I'm—"

"How do you even know that?"

"Well—"

"What do you mean I shot her? I would never shoot her!"

"Just think—"

"Don't you dare tell me what to think!" I demanded. He nodded his head and put his hands up to surrender. When he realized I was still thinking, he put his hands down and watched me. "What do you mean I shot my mom? How would you know that? I've been watching my TV screen constantly."

"Explain the limp."

"I, uh—"

"Explain the bandages you saw. Why is your mom suddenly always home? Do you even know what your mom does for a living?" Colt asked. I shut my mouth entirely and watched him. "Didn't your mom disappear from the screen for a few days?" I nodded my head, unsure of where he was going with this. "When did that happen?"

"Uh…" I had to look up at the ceiling to try and remember. "During the sixth trial."

"When did she return?"

"After the sixth trial."

"What happened during that sixth trial?" Colt asked. My pits were so moist that I was sure anyone could see the ever-expanding stain. "Think!" I flinched away from Colt as he yelled it and watched him try to process why I would have reacted that way.

"I killed Toby?"

"Yes. What happened after?"

"You helped me."

"No, before that. What did you do to your weapon?" Colt asked. He desperately tried not to tell me and wanted me to think of it myself. I shook my head because I honestly couldn't remember. "You dropped your gun, and it went off." He started talking to me like I was a preschooler. "Do you remember who it shot?" I crunched my eyebrows down and started denying that I did. However, I could hear the yells in my head. The female yells of the masked person I had shot.

"That could have been anyone."

"It was your mom."

"How do you know that?" I asked. "My mom… my mom would never step foot in a government building if she could avoid it. How would you know anything about my mom?"

"I'm not lying to you," Colt said. "But stop asking me how I know because I don't like lying to you. When I lie, you can always tell. You always call me out on it or look at me funny. Do not ask me to lie to you."

"Colt…"

"Do I look like I'm lying to you right now?" Colt asked. He stood up and stared at me. I shook my head and watched him as he grabbed my arms roughly. "Look at me. Do I look like I'm lying right now?" I answered him honestly this time, and he let go of me. "Do not ask me to lie to you." I shook my head again so that he would let me go. This time, he did, and I felt awkward standing next to him for a second. "Do you want to tell me anything before I die?"

"You're not going to die," I said instantly. I looked up at Colt and saw the entertainment coming from his face.

"That's all you want to say to me?" Colt asked. He crossed his arms and stood there waiting for me to answer. I didn't want that to be what he heard from me. When I opened my mouth, another person's voice radiated throughout the room.

"Colt, Bridget, we're heading to the graduation."

I looked at the door to see Heather in her beautiful floor-length dress. I have never seen someone look so good in a strapless dress, but she made it look nice. The green complimented the piece in her hair and matched the green heels she dragged across the floor. When she disappeared, I looked back at Colt, and he grabbed my wrist. We walked out together.

"Are we all here?" Bischoff asked as he looked around the room. With all the whitened teeth and gelled hair, I was sure Bischoff would make an off-hand comment about all of us. Instead, he looked us all down and smiled. "Let's see who is going to graduate."

We all walked down the long hallway together, and I could hear music being played loud enough for us to hear. While trying to listen, I could also hear murmurs of people talking behind the white closed doors up ahead. I looked over at Colt, but he was staring straight ahead, and I could see him masking his emotions again. He was scared.

I tried to grab his hand to comfort him, but he shook me off as soon as I did. He stared straight ahead, and as we got closer, I could hear more of the piano playing than the other music.

"It's the Assassin's song," Asher noted. "I've never heard it played live."

"Well, yeah, it's only used for the graduations," Justin remarked.

I nodded with everyone as if I knew what they were discussing. As I looked at all of them, I couldn't help but smile at the fact that I had made it so far. I was the last inductee standing. With zero training, I had beat so many other elitists. I knew that I had a lot of thanks to give to Jade and Justin for that.

"You all will stay here until you hear your name," Bischoff instructed. I nodded my head and acted like he was talking to me. Bischoff didn't look to see if we heard him, though. He went through the tall double-white doors, and a monstrous applause was heard from the other side. It took a few for everyone to calm down, but when they did, Bischoff's voice was amplified across the whole building. "Welcome the current graduating class of assassins to the stage." There was an even louder applause this time. "As always, we will have a demonstration of their skills with the bottom two candidates. Here is the weapon of choice." There was a faint sound of cloth being moved and then a thunderous noise of awe in the crowd. After a moment or two, there was wild applause and whistles behind the double white doors. "Okay, thank you, thank you. Settle down, settle down!" The applause immediately started dying down, but Bischoff didn't continue talking until everyone was quiet. "Let's meet your graduating class!"

Once again, there was thunderous applause. This would be the moment of truth – which team came in first place, and what team came in second place? Regardless, I owed Colt everything. He wouldn't admit it but he purposely distracted my teammates during our run. Anytime he came near me, he turned and went the other way. I barely had anyone stopping me from reaching that bell at the top. Was I absolutely terrified? Yes. My knees were buckling, and the entire top of the tower was wobbling as I rang it. I was convinced I would fall off, but I was helped down.

"Asher Johnston!"

The white doors opened, and I could peer in and see green decorations. When I tried to squint to see if the people in the chairs were wearing green, the white doors closed again, and one less person was in the hallway with us. It took a moment of silence from all of us before the other team hugged and congratulated each other. When Colt noticed us not celebrating, he slithered back to me and nudged me in the stomach.

"You rang the bell; you'll be fine."

"Asher carried his team to victory by ringing the bell at the top of the tower. His team had come in ten seconds before the other team."

"Ten seconds?" Eddie whispered angrily under his breath. I looked at him and saw his jaw setting in a hard line. He angrily unraveled the tie around his neck and shoved it to the ground. Stomping on it and messing up his hair, he kicked the wall and held his arms above his head. "Ten seconds…"

"Garrett Arnold." The doors opened again and closed swiftly behind Garrett as he was met with thunderous applause. "Able to ward off his opponent, he helped his team bring most of the blocks over. However, he had trouble getting onto the actual tower."

"You're safe," I whispered as I nudged Colt. He nodded his head, and I could see the smile appear. He quickly vanished, but as he held his smile back, I could see his lips turning upward as he tried to contain his excitement. "Colt, you're safe." He nodded his head again, and this time, when the person was announced, Colt was already leaving me behind.

When the doors closed, Eddie approached me and grabbed me roughly by the arms. I wanted to call out in pain but instead followed him as he led me over to Heather and Justin. They were both whispering angrily at each other but shut up as soon as both of us came over. Eddie's grip loosened as he looked at all of us.

"We know it's not her," Justin grumbled. He looked up at me but quickly looked back down to the floor. "She rang the bell, remember?" Eddie let go of me as he nodded his head. "Get her away."

"What? Why?" I wondered. It was too late, though, because Eddie grew as tall as he could and pushed me roughly back. He kept pushing me further and further away until my name was called.

The doors opened, and while I knew I had to walk out, I was hesitant as I looked at the three to my side. There was hushed noise coming from beyond the doors, and as I watched the three, Heather looked up at me and nodded. Eddie looked back at me, too, and while he was mad that we were in last place, I could see him give me a smile that I did a good job. Wanting to see Justin's face, he couldn't stand to look at me as his knuckles turned white, and he held onto Heather's wrist.

Stepping my foot past the white doors, they slammed hard behind me. I stared at the green carpet ahead of me and kept my foot going one at a time. On the faraway stage, I could see a highlight and lowlight reel of my time in the trials. Some showed me crying, killing, and smothered next to Colt. They showed me getting taken away, and they showed me watching the TV. Nothing was off-topic there. Once the reel started playing repeatedly, I continued to walk down the carpet. I tried to look at the people in the audience.

They were all wearing green.

"Justin Frazier!"

As I walked ahead, I looked behind me and saw Justin slowly coming up from behind me. He smiled and waved to the crowd as he was applauded. He seemed to be a completely different person when he was where he was supposed to be. Turning around, I forced myself to walk up on the stage and stand next to Colt.

He greeted me with a warm smile and then turned his attention back to the assassins applauding us. I tried to look off, too, but I was only met with shadowy figures as the lights were shining directly in my eyes. When Justin got onto the stage, I smiled at him, and despite him not looking at me before, he smiled back.

"Our last member of our graduating class is Eddie Marlowe!"

There were woops going through the crowd and yells of excitement. I could hear inappropriate language ruffling through the crowd as Eddie played with the crowd – flashing his best smile, flexing his muscles, and winking at the various assassins. When he came on stage, he looked at Justin and me and nodded. It was like his last nod of approval.

"Our last victim of these Assassin Trials will be Heather Fleck." I could hear the double doors open, and from the corner of my eye, I could see Heather being escorted by two other people at her side. When I looked at Justin, he was already watching the ground without trying to look at anyone. Heather was brought up onto the stage, and as she was placed there, she didn't try to move. I could see tears starting to fall down her cheeks. "By popular vote, Colt Kirkman will assassinate Heather with our new flamethrower."

Colt scuffled out of line and shuffled his feet toward Bischoff. He grabbed the heavy flamethrower and immediately pointed it to Heather. I looked at Heather as she started making unmistakable sobbing sounds. She wiped her nose and tears with her hand and fell to her knees.

"Please, don't do this, Colt!" she yelled. I could see him hesitate. "We grew up together! We have been in the preparatory school since we were little!" I looked back at Colt and saw him hesitate before moving his finger to the trigger. "Colt, please!"

I closed my eyes as soon as he pressed the trigger. I could hear Heather yelling for him to stop and pleading with him. I could hear her moaning. What got me most was the smell of human hair burning. Her skin was burning, and soon, she was gagging as she couldn't speak. There was no noise coming from the crowd. I opened my eyes to see them, and most were excitedly on the edges of their seats. When I looked back at Justin, it only took us one moment of eye contact before he grabbed my hand for comfort. I squeezed it and could feel his body shaking.

"Colt!" Heather yelled as her body collapsed onto the floor.

When the flames stopped, Colt returned the weapon without looking at Bischoff. As soon as the weight was removed from his hands, he got back in line with me, and I could see the tears in the corners of his eyes. He blinked them away quickly and masked any emotion he had. Looking over at Heather, I could still see her body twitching, but I knew she wasn't there. Her face was completely melted off.

"Wasn't that exciting?" Bischoff asked into the microphone.

"You okay?" I whispered as he started droning on about what it meant to be an assassin. I tried to break my hand away from Justin's, but he held on tightly as I looked at Colt. He nodded yes, but I knew he wasn't okay. I knew him well enough to know that he was lying to me. I laced my fingers between his and squeezed him with my free hand. I could feel him squeeze but immediately tried to let go as the sweat went onto mine. I let go and looked down at his hand to see that some of his flesh had burned off, too. When I looked back up, he gave me eyes that told me to say anything.

The flamethrower had some flaws.

"Let's give our graduating assassins one last round of applause!" Bischoff yelled as he clapped into the microphone. People started standing and applauding. As the lights began to dim, I could see them putting their fingers in their mouth to whistle loudly. Some were amplifying their voices by putting their hands near the sides of their mouths. No one was sitting in their seats and clapping normally. "Assassins."

We all took a step forward and clasped each other's hands as we bowed to the audience. They applauded louder and louder. It was so loud that I didn't hear any commotion or noise that wasn't supposed to be there until I saw Asher with a bag over his head. All the applause, laughter, whistling, and yelling turned into screams of terror and horror as people dragged Asher away.

Colt grabbed onto my hand, and I followed behind. Keeping my hold on Justin, he followed behind us. As we jumped over Heather's burning body, he couldn't help but stop though. His resistance knocked me off my feet, and Colt had to jolt back. He grabbed my hand in desperation and yanked me, but I was still holding onto Justin.

"You have to leave her!" I yelled at him. He looked up at me, and I could see the sadness in his eyes. It wasn't long before someone with a black bag came behind Justin. I yanked him toward me, but he resisted the move. I had to let go when the bag was shoved over his face, and Colt pulled me. "Justin!"

Colt continued dragging me past the huge white doors as I looked behind me. Justin was thrashing with the bag over him. I could see people ganging up on him as the area was getting destroyed. He was throwing useless punches to the wind, and he only stopped when he was injected in the neck with something. It took him a moment before his body went limp, and he was dragged to the back. Eddie and Garrett were fighting people off as they tried to find an exit.

It was a straight shot through the white doors before we got to the exit. No longer able to see the mess, I let go of Colt's hand and ran with him. People ran around us, but I could still see my blondie through the crowd. People were crashing into us from every angle. One person got me so off-balance that I felt my ankle roll. Continuing to run on my hurt ankle, my pace slowed as Colt started getting away from me. As I started catching up, I felt myself beginning to slow down. I wasn't running any faster. I could see Colt crash into the person before him and look around for me quickly. When he spotted me, he tried to pull himself through the crowd to get to me. He yelled. I yelled for him, too. He couldn't hear me above the roar of confusion.

I reached out for his hand, but all I could see was black starting to cover my vision. I elbowed the person behind me roughly and ducked, so I dropped to my knees. Getting kicked in the stomach and the sides, I continued to crawl through people and around the dresses and the fancy shoes. I could feel someone latching their hand on my ankle and dragging me away. The glossy floor tiles made it hard to fight off anyone, and I couldn't get a grip on the floor.

I tried to look for Colt as somebody tripped over me, but when they fell to the ground, and I could see their face, I stopped struggling. Their face paled immediately, and as they tried not to get trampled, they began running away, too.

"Jude?!"

Before I could see him disappear, the bag was over my face, and I, too, started thrashing about. I felt my knuckle connect with skin and heard the grunt come from behind me. I couldn't figure out if it was just that person, so I started aiming toward them. When I felt a sharp pain in my neck, my body stopped fighting at once, and multiple sets of arms and hands were there to catch me when I fell.

#

"Welcome, everybody," Bischoff said with a smile. I tried to move my head and neck to look around the room that I was in, but Bischoff only shook his head. "You all have been given a sedative to calm yourself. You will get full use of your body in a couple of hours." He stood proudly at the front of the room, and his demeanor seemed to change. He no longer had to prove himself to me. "I wanted to say congratulations on surviving the Assassin Trials, but this is where your work begins."

Despite not having control of my entire body, I forced myself to move my neck to look to my side. To my side was a skinny boy that I had never met before. As he sat there unmoving, I could see his eyes trying to focus on me. His black hair was shaved to his head, and a thick, red cut was across his forehead. Despite his thinness, he was taller than me as he sat there. I didn't know him, but he was still wearing green.

"Ladislava Bereznev, Javier Guimaraes, Patrick Howe, and Bridget Solomon, welcome to the Assassin Academy."

Read the first chapter of Missing!

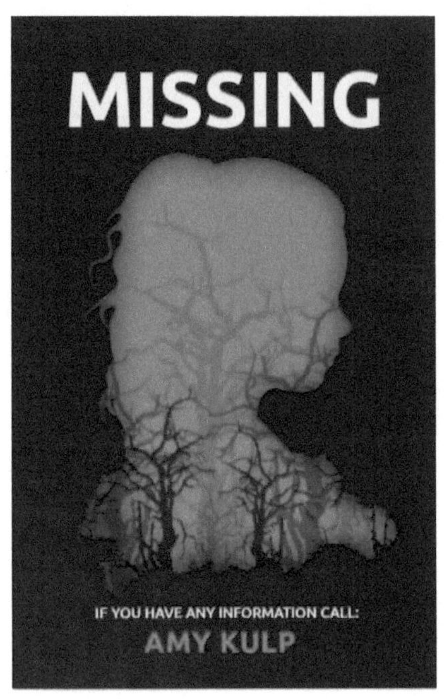

Chapter 1-

I stopped breathing when I saw the new kid walk into my class. I noticed everyone else stopped what they were doing and stared too. An elbow attached to my boyfriend jarred into my side purposely. As he smirked at me, I realized that I was caught red-handed. I was staring. My cheeks blushed a deep red while my neck ducked down like a turtle. Hearing Chad chuckle at my reaction, I ducked my head lower from the embarrassment.

I finally looked back up when the new kid passed my desk and sat in the back corner. I sniffed as he walked by and realized that he also smelt good. It smelt like he just got out of the shower and put deodorant on. I sniffed again and realized that he wasn't wearing that disgusting cologne that Chad wears. I couldn't even sniff in Chad's direction; it was so strong. My nose always burned whenever I nuzzled it into Chad's neck. Maybe I was just allergic to what Chad wore. A coughing attack usually ruined the romantic mood he tried to set for us.

I had to admit that the new kid was amazingly hot. He did not have bulky muscles, but he was tall, which made up for the fact. His eyes were a deep brown that shone in the sunlight. His lips were plump and moisturized; any girl would've died for them.

Most girls from my school probably wouldn't go for him though. He was the type of guy who didn't wear snapbacks, muscle shirts, or anything that the typical boy here wears. He had a button-down shirt and he buttoned them up to his neck. I admit that I always fell for guys who wore those shirts. He had skinny jeans on and contrary to the typical boy in this school, you couldn't see his underwear. That was only speculation though. I was too embarrassed to look.

I let myself pack up slowly as Chad attempted to hold a conversation with me about his football career. He thought it would be a real hit and he's been offered a couple of full scholarships.

I only smiled.

I supported his career options 100% but he didn't support mine. Instead of doing cheerleading as he wanted, I played soccer. He doesn't understand that my dream is to go to the Olympics for soccer. Not be on the sideline cheering for him.

The reason Chad wants me to do cheerleading is because of the status quo. The footballers are supposed to date cheerleaders. He took a major risk even talking to me. Thankfully, everyone knew not to mess with me because my father was very capable of killing each of them.

Seriously, every time I have a boyfriend he shows them his gun and knife collection. He then explains what knife or gun he would use for how bad he broke my heart. Usually, the boy would have police sent to my house but my dad has all of his needed permits.

Chad was the first to stay even though my dad doesn't approve of him. My mom just liked him because he was eye candy. If she had to like him for his personality, she probably wouldn't be seen around me if he was at the house.

I understand though.

Chad is extremely… demanding. He gets what he wants when he wants it. The only thing he hasn't been able to take from me is my V-card and I don't want to lose that yet. Especially not to Chad.

It's just a high school fling.

If you get married to your high school crush, I will gladly sign your divorce papers. I admit sometimes I do believe that Chad and I should be married but other times I'm always on the verge of breaking up with him. I usually think through my anger and realize that I need to let people's flaws go.

Chad grabbed my hand randomly and pulled me down the hall to my next class. I was surprised by his actions since he never held my hand in school and sometimes he wouldn't dare to be caught with me. This was especially true if I was wearing sweatpants or something he deemed embarrassing. He smiled at me and kissed me on the lips before shoving me into the classroom.

Still in shock, I sat down at a random desk and thought about what was going on. Maybe he was jealous of another cute couple. He was a very jealous person and he would go a long way to stalk people and prove that we were a better couple than them.

I always feel bad about it though.

"Can I sit here?" Knocking myself out of my daydream, I looked up and nodded as the new student sat down next to me. "I'm Miguel."

"Miguel?" I questioned. I threw the idea around in my head for a couple of minutes and then nodded my head. "Suits you." He smiled a bit at the comment and then pulled out his schedule. "Need help?" I quickly asked.

He showed me his schedule and I read over it a couple of times. I was surprised to see we had the majority of classes together. Out of nine classes, we had six together and three near each other. I could basically walk to all of his classes, to my locker, and then back to mine and still be on time.

"We're in basically the same classes," I reported. He seemed a little surprised but I saw a smirk playing on his lips. "So I guess I could just show you to most of them. Hold on, let me write down the ones we don't have in the same period." I quickly doodled his schedule down on a piece of paper and smiled. "I'll just meet you at the door of each classroom I don't have with you and I'll show you to your others."

"That'd be great," he replied with a smile.

"You know, it's a bit weird," I whispered. "Usually nobody has the same schedule."

That's when he turned forward and decided to pay attention to class. He had a smile on his lips the whole class period like he knew an inside secret that I wasn't in on. Like it was about me.

"Okay class, you may talk for the last five minutes," the teacher announced.

I instantly turned toward Miguel. "I don't think I mentioned my name before," I said. "I'm Emily."

"Hi, Emily." He smiled at me and I smiled back but I felt a blush creep on my face. He chuckled a bit once he noticed but that only made me blush even more. "You know, you're cute when you blush."

"You know, I have a boyfriend."

"You know, I already know that."

"How?"

"He was acting very jealous when I was going to go up and talk to you during the last period." I felt my lips press together hard and I faced the front of the classroom, interrupting anything he was about to say to me.

I was still going to show him to our next class but almost everybody knows that Chad is very jealous. If he saw me talking to any other boy that he didn't approve of, he would automatically assume I was cheating and then continue to lecture me for hours upon hours. He was like my dad.

When the bell decided to finally ring and wake me from my thoughts, I had already gathered my books and had started out the door. If the new boy wanted to follow me around to our next class, he would just have to catch up to the normal speed of an anxious senior.

"Hey there!" I heard Chad yell. I turned around and continued walking backward as he jogged up to hug me. "Where are you heading off to?"

"You already know my schedule but I'm showing Miguel to all of our classes," I repeated. "He has a lot of classes with me."

"Whose Miguel?" He squeezed my shoulders tighter and I felt his muscles begin to tighten.

"He's the new guy. Don't worry he's chill," I replied. Once those words left my mouth, I instantly cringed at my slang. Chill?

"I don't know about him. He doesn't look right."

"What do you mean? He looks perfectly fine."

"I don't know, he just seems too…" I knew where this was going and I knew Chad was going to say something stereotypical about Miguel.

That was the bad thing about being with Chad. He was stuck in a poor mindset. I disapproved of it completely but Chad was brought up in a first-class very snobby and prude white family. They hated anyone different than them and were huge racists. Nobody would ever call them out on it though. I still have yet to meet them because Chad knows that my mom is Latina.

It just aggravates me when people judge others by their skin color, eye color, sex, deformity, mental progression, or looks. People should be judged by their personalities because nothing else matters.

Having a nice personality and being attractive is a nice combination though.

I will admit that I do tend to judge people before I meet them. Even if they look like a snob to me, I will still give them a fair chance at being nice to me, and half of the time, they exceed my expectations.

"Emily, are you ever going to wait for me?"

I felt everyone turn to stare at me and Chad together. Once Miguel reached us, Chad clamped his hand on my shoulder tightly but Miguel didn't seem to notice it. He walked right beside me with a sly smile on his face.

When we reached the doorway to the classroom, Chad spun me around and kissed me hard on the lips. I backed away from him and squirmed out of his grip and went inside the classroom. I hated shoving my relationship into other people's faces.

I know I'm going to hear a lot about it later though because Chad was going to lecture me about how I'm his girlfriend and not Miguel's. I would just roll my eyes and get a makeup kiss that I never really wanted. It was like a routine with Chad and me.

And I was sick of it.

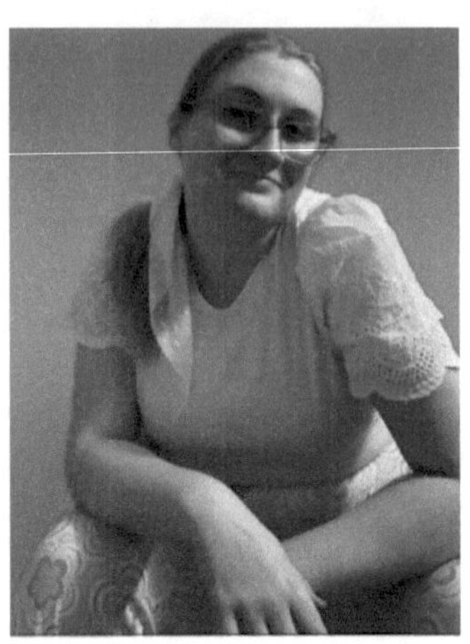

ABOUT THE AUTHOR

Amy Kulp is a middle school STEM teacher and theatre director with a passion for writing novels that break YA genre norms. An avid reader and writer since childhood, Kulp now enjoys creating stories that investigate darker, more challenging topics and help young adult readers feel less alone in their struggles. The Assassin Trials came to her in a dream. Once awoken, she had written it down incoherently before falling back asleep to continue the dream.